Twenty-One

Alice Anne Blackwood

For my partner, my family, my children (though the latter
had better not read this until they're old enough.)

For the iNation, my beloved darkling throng,
in whatever form you take as the years pass.
You will always be my Neverland.

And for all those who are a little dark,
a little twisted, and a little mad.

Chapter 1

"I am Twenty-One. I am a slave. I will obey. I will be used. I will not question. I will please my Master. I am Twenty-One. I am a slave."

Chloe despised the words that tumbled out of her mouth. She could think of nothing else to murmur to herself while she waited, lying on her back in the blacked-out room that had been her prison for God knew how long. Months of meticulous training had embedded the twisted mantra into her brain. Weeks of starvation and torment in this room had beaten out any other prayer she could have hoped to recall.

Chloe took a deep breath through her nose and retched from the stench of the waste-soaked bed sheets in the stifling tropical air. The sliver of light beneath the door blurred. She focused on the light with every ounce of energy she had in her bruised body, whispering her mantra with new fervor. If she passed out again, she was done for. She knew that because Mama knew that. Chloe didn't look for Mama, but she knew she was there, whispering along with her, fingering the scars on her worn and withered cheek. Yes, the man who forced Chloe to call him Master had said he would come for Chloe *"when the other one rots."*

Mama said it was time. Chloe breathed through her mouth, whispering.

"I am Twenty-One. I am a slave…"

Footsteps echoed from a part of the house Chloe had never seen. She knew the ritual well. The door would open and the monster would amble in, lean over to see if she still breathed, and rouse her for whatever deranged games he had planned for her that day. But today, she had a weapon: a splinter of wood the width of her fist, ripped from the dilapidated bedframe. She had picked away at it until the end came to a point. She could only hope it would be sharp enough. Chloe buried her fist in the filthy sheets on which she lay, clutching the wooden shard as if it would slip away from her somehow. She feared her weapon was another hallucination from the heat, that she held nothing to save herself from her captor, but Mama's reassuring voice in her ear gave her strength. She continued to whisper the words that had bound her body and soul for so long, whispered every vow that she was about to break.

"I will be used. I will not question. I will please my Master."

The door opened and closed. Chloe barely opened her eyes, catching sight of a figure coming toward her. The fetid bed sank with his weight as the figure leaned over her, coming close to her face, checking her breathing.

Mama's voice rang in her bones. *Now. Now.*

With a raw, guttural cry, Chloe sprung.

Chapter 2

Mariane's lips brushed Chloe's ear as she spoke, but Chloe still had to strain to hear her above the pounding music.

"I said, if you don't put your phone away, I'm going to throw it on the dance floor and goth stomp it to death."

Chloe dodged Mariane's reaching fingers with a laugh, holding her phone out of reach.

"Just give me two seconds. I'm saying good night to my dad."

Mariane rolled her blue eyes and propped her elbows on the polished black bar, the only thing at the Oryx night club that looked sleek and new. The rest of the décor, from the worn leather couches in the lounge areas to the billiard tables, looked as if they had been plucked out of a junkyard. But that was the theme, Chloe supposed. Mariane had mentioned an apocalyptic vibe when she had been dressing Chloe up to go out. That seemed accurate, but as Chloe stared at the strips of corroded metal and frosted glass mosaics decorating the rust-colored walls, she didn't understand the appeal. Why make a nice place look like a wasteland?

"Come on, sweets," said Mariane, tossing her long white-blonde hair over her shoulder. "Daddy will keep 'til morning. How do you say, *go to bed, dad* in French?"

Chloe stole a glance at her father's text message – *Bon nuit, ma bichette. Miss you!* –before wedging her phone into the long black boots she had borrowed from her friend.

"It's the first time he's been alone in twenty five years," she said. "Cut me some slack."

Mariane shook her head, "Way to make me feel like an asshole." But she broke into a grin when Chloe tried to apologize. "Relax, Chloe. We're out tonight to let loose, right? So no more phone. Time to experience something new."

She turned to flag down the bartender, leaving Chloe to people watch. The more she studied the Oryx crowd, clad in everything from leather to Victorian lace, the more out of place she felt. Mariane had dressed her for the theme, her ever-present cigarette hanging from her heart-shaped lips as she dug through her own closet to find the perfect outfit for Chloe's first time at the mysterious club. She had caked Chloe's hazel eyes in black eye shadow and stuffed her into a too-small black bra and a cropped shirt made entirely out of tight, ripped black fishnet. A black and white petal skirt just barely covered her upper thighs. Chloe had never shown so much skin in public. She had been anxious until they had gotten to the Oryx and found that exposed flesh was commonplace. Even Mariane bared herself in an under-bust corset of blue leather with nothing but two black strips of electrical tape crossed over each nipple in an X-shape. Still, Chloe felt uncomfortable, as if she were in disguise and everybody could sense it. She watched dancers move like hazy apparitions, distorted by the wall of thick tarnished glass separating the bar from the dance floor. She had long been curious about the Oryx and its dark, eccentric crowd, a novelty in an otherwise unexceptional rural college town of Hollington, Ohio. It was bizarre to be within its walls after passing its long black doors every day on her way to campus.

"Snap out of it, Chloe." Mariane put a thick double shot glass in her hand. "No zoning out. Just drinking."

"Sorry," said Chloe. "It's just so weird in here. I'm not used to everybody around me looking like *you*."

Mariane grinned. "Hey, in here, you're the weird one." She reached over and clinked glasses with Chloe. "This is the bar's specialty. Drink up."

Chloe studied her glass. It looked as eerie as the club itself, with a bottom layer of green licking like flames into murky red at the top of the glass.

"What the hell is it?"

"A Wolf Bite," said Mariane with a wink. "Cheers."

Mariane tilted her long white neck and swallowed the shot. Chloe hesitated before following suit. She wasn't a complete stranger to bars, but her mother's long illness had kept her clear of the hard partying so common of the college lifestyle. The shot went down more smoothly than she had anticipated, leaving behind a lingering taste of sweet anise and some sort of fruit. She licked her lips. As strange as the Oryx was, Chloe was glad she had finally given in to Mariane and gone out. It had been over a month since her mother's suffering had ended, and returning to Hollington University so soon afterward had been agony. She couldn't stop worrying about her father, alone in her childhood home, which seemed so empty without her mother's laughter filling every room.

Mariane ran her fingers through Chloe's short brown hair.

"Come on, daydreamer," said Mariane, hopping off her barstool. "Let's dance."

Chloe's remaining trepidations dissolved the moment she stepped onto the dance floor, swallowed by the vivacious energy of the crowd. She lost her heartbeat to the bass that vibrated from the massive speakers. The music was palpable; she let it move her hips, bring her hands to her hair. The floor was in nearly complete darkness, shattered by a multitude of neon lights cutting through the darkness in brief flashes. Chloe became a part of the crowd around her, moving as a collective unit. There was a comfort in losing herself in a mass of dancers, becoming one of many. She cheered mindlessly with the rest at every command emanating from the cavernous DJ booth, which stood elevated on the back wall of the dance floor. Chloe noticed a figure just underneath the booth, a female form wrapped in black gauze, stone still amidst the writhing bodies. Another glance around the dance floor yielded a half dozen of these bandaged mannequins standing on elevated stages along the walls. Dancers on the platform ran their hands along them, caressing their curves, and they did not move.

"Mariane!" Chloe shouted over the music, pointing at one of the figures. "What are those mannequins?"

Mariane's smile seemed to fade, or maybe the lights hit her strangely, Chloe couldn't tell.

"They're not mannequins," she replied. "Those are the dolls. They're people. They don't move, though. They're not allowed."

Chloe frowned, watching person after person caress the dolls, stroking their faces and every inch of their bodies.

"Why?" she asked. "What are they for?"

Mariane tossed her narrow shoulders, grabbed Chloe's hips, and forced them to dance. Chloe laughed.

"They're just a thing here," she said. "The Oryx is a theatrical place, hun. Don't worry about the dolls. Just dance!"

Chloe obeyed, letting her curiosity ebb into the beat of the thrashing music. She knew she would never understand the Oryx, but for tonight, it was the perfect place for her to let go of her troubles. She and Mariane danced until their breath ran shallow. Mariane brought her fingers to her lips, mimicking a cigarette, and led Chloe off the dance floor toward the back patio of the club.

The late September air that had chilled Chloe before now steeped her skin in delicious gooseflesh and cooled the sweat that clung to her from the dance floor. She took a deep breath and found the air misted with the smoke of a dozen cigarettes despite the back patio being open to the night sky. Beside her, Mariane blew a cloud of her own smoke from her pursed pink lips.

"So, what do you think?" she asked. "Is the Oryx the mouth of hell you were so scared of?"

Chloe smiled and shook her head. She looked into the crowd on the patio, a sea of pierced f/lesh and tattoos, of colored hair and combat boots. It was by far the most exotic crowd she'd experienced. A pink-haired woman in a shiny PVC skirt caught her gaze and flashed her a smile.

"Everyone's so friendly. I wasn't expecting that from a goth crowd. It's goth, right?"

Mariane chuckled and plopped down onto a wood patio chair, remarkably plain compared to the décor inside.

"Good to know you thought we were all antisocial twats," she said with a wink. "Goth, industrial, rivet head, cyber, I wouldn't get into semantics. Half the time we don't even know what the fucking differences between us are."

"I didn't understand half of what you said."

"Exactly," Mariane said with a wink. "Just dress up and dance, sweets. We're a great crowd, whatever we call ourselves. Beautiful freaks." She took a long drag of her cigarette. "By the way, something fun happens at midnight around here to club virgins like you, and you're doing it. No arguments."

Chloe frowned. "What?"

"Hey, I'm in charge tonight," said Mariane with a sly smile. "I said no arguments. It'll be fun, trust me."

Chloe sighed, reaching out of habit for a strand of her honey brown hair to twirl between her fingers before remembering she had just cut it short. She fiddled with the choppy layers so close to her ears. Mariane's words tied her stomach in knots. She imagined being thrown onto one of the podiums on the dance floor, forced to do something embarrassing like dance in front of everyone, fingers pointing at her.

"You're not going to single me out, are you?" she asked. "Isn't it enough that I let you put me in this outfit? I thought I was supposed to blend into the crowd."

"Calm down, princess," said Mariane. "It'll be fun. Nothing you'll need to take a Xanax for."

Chloe threw Mariane a theatrical pout. "I like new experiences, not surprises."

Mariane laughed again and patted Chloe's bare knee. The heat from dancing had worn off and the cold invaded her exposed skin. Chloe folded her arms over her barely concealed chest to keep warm and tried to keep herself from obsessing over whatever she would be subjected to at midnight. She looked into the crowd again, at the plumes of fragrant smoke hovering over their heads and curling up to the stars. Everyone was so at ease. She had gone out tonight to feel the same way, to let loose, to have a new experience. She didn't want her silly social anxiety to ruin things for her. The summer had been so draining; months of sitting in her mother's dark bedroom, holding her hand, talking with hospice nurses and keeping her father as happy as he could muster in those final weeks. Her mother's death had been long expected, but grief had still hung like a heavy shroud over the house. Chloe would never admit it aloud that she was relieved to move back to Hollington for fall semester and be free, albeit temporarily, from that empty house.

She people-watched as Mariane finished smoking, catching sight of a small crowd that had accumulated at the back corner of the patio. The group surrounded three people that caught Chloe's attention immediately. Two beautiful women, dark-eyed twins, stood arm in arm, blowing smoke over their naked shoulders. Their pale, willowy forms were identical but for their short pigtailed hair, one dyed bright purple, the other peacock green. The man between them stopped Chloe's breath. He was taller than the twins, dressed in combat boots and faded black jeans with buckling straps, attire not unlike other men in the crowd. He was shirtless despite the young autumn chill. A mask concealed him from the bridge of his nose down, made of worn black leather and studded with a thin row of spikes down its center. Long black hair fell loose over his shoulder, undercut on both sides, as if he had let a mohawk grow all the way down to his chest.

Chloe drank in the stranger, at the contrast of his pallid face and the black mask, at the lean, slender muscle of his bare torso. Something about him raised the hair on her arms. She was so distracted by his appearance that she didn't realize he had noticed her. Her face flushed when she finally saw him staring back at her. She wanted to look away, as was polite when caught gawking at a stranger, but she couldn't. His gaze paralyzed her as it crept down her body and made her feel more naked than she had all night. They locked eyes again, and Chloe's throat went dry. There was something about him, something that beckoned to her, tempted her to come to him, like a magnetic force pulling at her limbs, calling her closer. The thought of meeting new people normally made Chloe anxious. Even Mariane, whose appearance had roused her curiosity in their art history class two years ago, had to be the one to strike up a conversation in order for them to meet. Chloe had never felt the urge to approach a complete stranger in her life.

Mariane tapped Chloe's arm, dragging her back to reality.

"I said, do you want to go in?" she asked. "What the hell are you thinking about so-"

Mariane broke off as her gaze drifted to the man who had so captured Chloe's eye, who had returned to his conversation with the group surrounding him.

"Let's go in," said Mariane, her voice flat. "I'm getting cold now."

She spun on her heel and headed inside so quickly that Chloe struggled to keep up with her as they weaved through the crowd.

"Who was that?" Chloe asked. Mariane did not respond. She repeated her question, but the thumping music of the dance floor swallowed her voice. She grasped Mariane's shoulder. Mariane's bright blue eyes were hard-edged, a cross look on a normally carefree face.

"Hey, are you all right?" Chloe asked. "Do you know that guy with the mask on?"

Mariane nodded, her blonde hair swishing over her shoulders.

"Yeah, I do," she said with a bite in her voice that startled Chloe. "And he's not the kind of guy you should be flashing your tits at, Chloe."

Chloe took a step back. She had seen Mariane lose her temper with people before, seen that nasty glint in her eye, but her anger had never been directed at Chloe herself.

"Mariane," she said carefully, "why are you so upset? Did I do something?"

Mariane sighed, shaking her head. She patted Chloe's hair. "I'm sorry, sweets. I'm being a bitch. I was hoping you'd get some tonight because God knows you need it, but I never thought…look, I know things about everybody in this bar, and Demetrius-" she jerked her thumb at the patio, "-is fucked up. Just trust me on this."

Chloe raised an eyebrow. "What, is he a serial killer? I should have known from all the black clothes."

Mariane did not smile at the joke. She glanced behind Chloe. "He could have been one of your mom's patients."

Chloe's smile died. Her mother had been a therapist for maximum security inmates in a Cleveland prison. The stories she had told Chloe throughout her life had given her nightmares. She was still too frightened to read any of her mother's case studies.

"That's not funny."

Mariane fixed Chloe with a steady stare. "I'm not joking. Look, I'm not saying he's going to kill you in the alley or anything, but he's just…fucked up with women." She sighed, running a hand through her long hair. The sardonic smile Chloe had seen on her lips countless times returned. "There are plenty of hot goths around here who aren't clinically insane, sweets. Just forget about it, okay? I'm still in charge tonight, and I say it's time to dance."

Mariane took Chloe's arm and dragged her back onto the dance floor. Chloe tried to shrug off the one blip in an otherwise fantastic night out, which soon blurred into streams of pounding bass, cheers, and writhing bodies.

Every now and then, Chloe scanned the crowd for Demetrius with a strange combination of dread and anticipation, but she did not see him amongst the eclectic Oryx hoard. Eventually she lost her worries in the excitement of the club. Chloe secretly savored the accidental brushing against strangers on the dance floor. Summer had been solitary, and the first month back at Hollington University had been solitary as she recovered. On top of that, she had been single since spring, when things with her casual boyfriend had come to an anticlimactic fizzle. She hadn't realized how lonely she had been until tonight. She found herself less shy than usual as Mariane introduced her to fellow regulars and she chatted casually with exotic strangers.

Later into the night on the dance floor, the music dissipated and did not immediately start up again. Chloe stopped moving. She glanced at Mariane and found a wicked grin painted on her friend's face. Her heart sank. Shit. It was midnight, wasn't it? She had forgotten about the dreaded surprise Mariane had refused to explain. Mariane took Chloe's hand and pointed toward the elevated DJ booth at the front of the dance floor.

"He's up there, but don't worry about it. He won't come down," she said. "Just go with it, okay?"

Chloe tried to peer into the booth. An ominous beat rumbled through the crowd and everyone on the floor began to stomp. The energy at the Oryx entered her like a contagion and ate away her anxiety.

"It's that time of night," came the now familiar low, growling voice of the DJ. Bright light burst through the booth so suddenly that Chloe jumped, thinking something had shorted out, but the crowd cheered. The masked face in the booth made Chloe's heart jolt. Demetrius, the stranger on the patio, stood in the booth, his long fingers curled around a mic. He raised his fist in the air and the crowd mirrored him, screaming. Chloe stared at Mariane, who shook her head and opened her mouth to speak. Demetrius' voice drowned out her words.

"Bring the virgins to the wall," he said, his voice reverberating through Chloe's body. "It's time to welcome them to the Oryx."

A new song burst over the crowd's cries, pounding steadily like a military march. Mariane slung an arm around Chloe and pulled her toward the long glass wall that separated the bar from the dance floor.

Chloe's nerves spiked. Oryx regulars pressed giggling newcomers against the wall, pinning them playfully. She was being singled out, as she'd feared. Mariane must have been able to read the apprehension in her face. She smiled, ruffled Chloe's hair, and took her shoulders.

"Relax, sweets," she shouted over the din. "Just go with it!"

Chloe tried to comply. She pressed her back to the wall, a cool shock against her hot, sweat-tinged skin. She exchanged glances with the other "virgins" who seemed just as clueless as she was, though they were smiling. Chloe took a deep breath. Mariane was right. She needed to lighten up.

A pale figure appeared behind Mariane as the music swelled to a climax. Chloe's heart stopped. Demetrius took Mariane's shoulders and brushed her away as if he were parting a curtain. Mariane released Chloe, her face pale beneath the veil of her blonde hair. Her eyes darted from Chloe to the masked man, wide and near panic. Chloe stood up from the wall and reached out to her companion, but Mariane had disappeared into the crowd. Only Demetrius stood before her, close enough to touch.

The music grew frantic as if taking its pace from Chloe's heartbeat. The crowd wailed reached toward the ceiling. Chloe could not look away from Demetrius. He seized her shoulders and lifted her off her heels as effortlessly as plucking fruit from a branch. He pinned her against the glass wall with his legs, pressing his thighs to hers. She did not know why she didn't struggle. Her mind went blank the moment he touched her, consumed by the flex of his hands, the heat of her skin quenched by his cool fingers.

The crowd erupted into ecstatic cries, and a deluge of warm liquid flowed from the top of the glass wall and rained down upon Chloe and the other newcomers. Chloe gasped, her hair drenched, her eyes swimming red. For a moment, she thought it was real blood, but when it reached her lips, she tasted a sharp, artificial cherry flavour. It seeped into the crevices of her fishnet top and ran in warm rivulets down her breasts, her stomach. Demetrius' grip stayed firm on her shoulders in spite of the slippery mess. She saw him through a haze of red, leaning toward her, his face looming near. She found herself leaning toward him as much as he would allow, as if they would kiss in spite of his mask. She felt him near, as if the air just around him was palpable, raising the hair on her arms and calling her closer. He leaned into her ear, his voice deep and clear behind the mask, and murmured a simple command.

"Say yes."

A spike from his mask grazed her cheek, the smallest sensation in a storm of sensations, yet it made Chloe's spine bow. Her lips parted, slick with the stage blood pouring down her body. She answered reflexively, as if responding were as natural as breath.

"Yes." Chloe closed her eyes and threw her head back into the rush of blood. Her breasts grazed his chest. The contact ignited her skin with sweet heat as if her bra weren't there. She repeated the word every inch of her body screamed, a plea erupting from some dark, hungry part of her she had never known.

"Yes."

For a moment, Chloe felt the brush of his fingers along her left cheek, and then her feet returned to the floor. Demetrius slipped away and melted into the crowd like a phantom. The wall stopped bleeding. Chloe's awareness of the world around her returned slowly, as if she had just woken from a dream. Sound returned; the throbbing pulse of a new song, the laughter of the other newcomers and their dry companions. Chloe stood, numb and dumbstruck, her short hair dripping with stage blood. She still felt his grip on her shoulders, lifting her so effortlessly, the weight of his thighs against hers. Her skin tingled in a way she didn't understand. Mariane reappeared. Her wide eyes broke Chloe from her spell.

"It's okay," Chloe said quickly. "Nothing happened. He just-"

Mariane grabbed her arms with a startling grip.

"Are you okay?" she demanded.

Chloe frowned. "Yeah, I'm fine. I told you-"

"What did he say to you? Did he invite you anywhere?"

"Mariane, what-"

"Don't go anywhere with him, okay?" Mariane's frantic tone sped Chloe's heart. "What did he say to you?"

"Nothing. He didn't say anything. He just held me against the wall."

Chloe surprised herself with the lie, but Mariane gave her no time to think. She tugged at Chloe and dragged her off the dance floor. Chloe nearly crashed into a bouncer with a mop, ready to clean up the stage blood from the midnight theatrics.

"We have to go," said Mariane, throwing glances over her shoulder. "I'll take you home."

Chloe's stomach flipped. Mariane's panic was infecting her. She tried to slow her down.

"Hold on, hold on, okay?" she held Mariane's arm. "Mariane, just talk to me. Why are we going home? What's wrong? Nothing happened, he's gone."

For a moment it looked like Mariane would burst into tears. Chloe could not wrap her mind around her friend's panic. Even if Demetrius was as bad as she said, he had disappeared, probably back into the DJ booth. He hadn't asked for her number or invited her somewhere. He had just...

"Chloe," Mariane said. "You don't get it. I already told you. You caught the eye of the worst guy in this place." She sighed. "I'm sorry I'm freaking out. I never thought he'd be interested in you. Otherwise I would have…we should call it a night, sweets. He'll move on to the next when you've gone."

Chloe didn't know why those words stung her. She shook her head, calming down now that Mariane was no longer near panic. A night that had begun so well had certainly taken a turn. Mariane gave Chloe a shadow of her usual sly grin.

"It's all right," she said, leading her past the bar. "We'll get you laid at some point. Just…not by a psycho. Okay?"

That made Chloe smile.

"I guess I'm lonelier than I thought," she said. Mariane nodded with a small laugh, tossing her hair over her shoulder. Chloe's anxiety ebbed with the return of Mariane's humor.

"I have to close my tab," said Mariane. She released Chloe's hand. "Hang on."

Chloe waited. Beyond the red streaked glass wall, the dance floor continued to thrive. Was Demetrius back in the booth, leading the mass of skin and sweat to new ecstasy? She fought not to think about the way his gaze held hers, the magnetic pull she felt. Mariane's reaction was so strong, and she seemed to know everyone at the Oryx intimately. Chloe would be a fool if she dismissed Mariane's fears.

"Hey. You in the fishnet."

Chloe turned. A young woman holding a tray of tube shots flashed Chloe a smile dotted with piercings.

"Have a shot," she said. She rotated the tray, revealing a single shot glass among the tubes. "It's on the house. Our DJ said to tell you, *thanks for the fun.*"

Chloe looked down at the glass. It was a layered shot, green mixing into red, the same one Mariane had ordered for her earlier in the night. But this one had come from the man that Mariane was afraid of. She hadn't seen the drink made, and though the young woman was an employee of the bar and Chloe might be able to trust her, she couldn't ignore the dread creeping into her gut.

"Thank you," she said, taking a step away, "but I've had enough to drink tonight, I think."

The young woman smiled again and tossed her shoulders. "Okay. Have a good night."

Chloe nodded as the woman left. She stood alone between the dance floor and the bar. She took a deep breath. For the first time that night, she felt eyes on her; perhaps the judgmental gazes she had feared all night…perhaps something darker. She was relieved when Mariane reappeared from the bar and led her toward the open doors into the night.

X X I

Chloe startled awake with a racing heart. For a moment she thought that her mother had called to her like she used to in the middle of the night toward the end. Lingering sleep faded, and she remembered that she was in her off-campus apartment with no one there to call to her. Her bedroom was thick with the dead stillness that only existed in the first hours of the morning. Nothing looked out of place; her cheap posters of classic art pieces hadn't come off the wall.

The picture of her parents hadn't fallen from her nightstand. What had woken her? She listened for any foreign sound. There was only the distant and familiar hum from the old radiator in the living room. She swallowed back a tense lump in her throat and pulled back her covers. Maybe a picture had fallen in the living room. She knew she wouldn't be able to relax until she made certain she wouldn't be waking up to a mess. Her apartment was old, and as October neared, it grew draftier. She folded her arms over her chest. Soon it would be too chilly to wear her favorite nightgown, a short slip of pale blue satin and lace. Her legs were chilly, as were her feet on the hardwood floor.

No sooner had Chloe reached for her living room lamp than the full force of a stranger's body struck her from behind, grabbing a fistful of her hair and wrenching her head back. Chloe screamed, her legs buckling beneath her. The intruder clamped an arm around her waist, pinning her arms to her sides. Chloe kicked and struggled, but the body against her back was as unyielding as stone. She screamed again.

"Help! Somebody's in-"

A gloved palm smothered her plea. The stench of the leather glove sickened her.

"Your name," a deep voice hissed too close to her ear. "Give me your name."

The intruder slid his hands from her lips for a moment. Chloe jerked against him, fought to free her arms.

"Get off of me!" she screamed. "Get-!"

Wild laughter erupted against her ear. The intruder dropped, wrestling her to the ground. He twisted her in his arms and pinned her legs beneath him. She managed to free one of her arms for a moment, but he caught her wrist before she could do any damage. Her mouth, however, was uncovered. She again tried to cry out, to alert anyone in the old, thin-walled apartment building who could possibly hear her, but a fall of black hair slipped across her face like a descending spider. She twisted to free herself from the web of hair, and her intruder's face loomed above her. The sight paralyzed her. Even in the unlit living room, she recognized the harsh line of a mask cutting across the bridge of his nose. The kohl around his eyes made them cavernous pits in the darkness.

Demetrius tossed his long hair away from Chloe's face. Chloe couldn't stop staring at him. She was too shocked to scream, to move. This had to be a dream, some nightmare brought about from the night's events. There was no way this was happening. Chloe's senses told her otherwise. The smell of him was utterly foreign to her; a sharp, sweet scent tinged with sweat. His grip on her wrist was as powerful as it had been at the Oryx. His weight seemed immense, as if his lean, muscular frame was carved from stone. For a moment, Chloe felt as though she were standing outside of herself, watching the scene before her and wondering why the girl on the floor was just lying there, staring, instead of fighting.

"Your name." Demetrius' low and simmering voice was as startling as the rest of him, hollowed by the mask yet perfectly clear away from the noise of the club. His fingers curled around her neck and flexed, giving a brief squeeze just strong enough to threaten pain.

"Chloe," she whispered, trembling. Her name, so freely shared in any social situation, felt a far more important piece of information than it ever had. But why?

A low, terrible sound came from Demetrius' throat, some sort of growl or moan. The sound shattered Chloe's strange moment of detachment, and now the weight of him on top of her was all too real.

"Chloe." He spoke the word in a slow breath. "Chloe, Chloe. Perfect."

He struck, snapping an arm around her neck before she had time to scream. Chloe fought until she could breathe no more, until her living room darkened and faded into blackness.

Chapter 3

SEPTEMBER 25, 2011

Chloe did not normally have dreams of memories, however the lilac bush in which she lay from her childhood was unmistakable. She was four years old and her father's shouts roused her from her nap. She and the neighbor kids had been playing hide and seek and young Chloe had crept into a hedge of lilac bushes. The sweet, heady fragrance of the blossoms had lulled her into a doze. She didn't want to wake up, but her father's voice, calling to her in his native French, dragged her from her dreams.

"Réville-toi, Chloe."

She opened her eyes, still expecting to see her childhood sanctuary of leaves and white petals. Instead she saw not the dirt-stained digits of a four year old, but her adult hands, bound at the wrist with a zip tie. Chloe's grogginess vanished in an instant. She sat bolt upright. Her head struck metal. She gasped and crouched back down. There were bars around her on all sides. Chloe was in a cage so small that she couldn't extend her legs. She touched the cold bars, unable to comprehend. It was no bigger than a dog's crate. Her mind was sluggish with shock. Thoughts drifted and faded before meeting conclusions. Where was she? What was happening? She looked down at herself. She was completely nude, save for something warm and snug around her neck. Her fingers flew to her throat, tracing what felt like a thick strap of leather with a metal ring in front and some sort of lock at the back of her neck.

"God," she whispered. Her heart sank like a brick in her chest. She was trapped. The moment the thought crossed her mind, she lost herself in a frantic scream. She kicked at the bars with all her strength, tried to force her wrists apart to break the zip tie until they bled. Her legs were weak, her body ached, but she couldn't think, couldn't focus on anything but escaping the cage. She didn't care where she was or how she had gotten there. All that mattered was freeing herself from her tiny prison.

"Help!" she shrieked. "Help me, somebody, please!"

Her pleas dissolved into animal-like cries. She kicked and kicked against the bars.

"That cage is bolted to a concrete wall," came a voice that stopped Chloe dead in her struggle. "I'm afraid all the adrenaline in the world couldn't help you."

Chloe looked beyond the cage for the first time. She was in a bedroom with dark wood floors, grey walls, and sleek black furniture. It was a bedroom that belonged in a designer's portfolio. Demetrius looked out of place leaning against the bed's footboard in his ripped and faded black jeans. He wore a black denim vest, open to reveal a thin strip of bare flesh underneath. His body, from his thick hair to his boots, was speckled with what looked like talcum powder. It gave him an eerie dusty look, as if he had just crawled out of a tomb. At a club or a bar, Chloe might have found the look strange and intriguing. But here, naked and caged, this man she had found so enticing the night before was monstrous and terrifying.

The attack in Chloe's living room sprung from the back of her mind, and her screams returned. She gripped the bars of the cage and tried to use them as an anchor to force her wrists apart. When that failed, she kicked at the cage door. She knew she couldn't open it, but she could not control herself. Every ounce of her screamed *fight!* Her thoughts were frenzied and primal, *"Get me out, get me out, fight, get me out of here!"*

"You struggle beautifully. Fluidly, like a dance," said Demetrius. He crossed the room with slow, casual steps. Chloe shielded her nude body and shoved herself into the furthest corner of the cage against the concrete wall. Her breath came ragged and gasping. She was going to die. She was going to follow her mother to her grave at the hands of a psychopath like the ones her mother worked with in prison.

"Oh, God," she cried, her voice raw from screaming. "God, please..."

"Sh, sh, sh," Demetrius chided, as if soothing a crying child. "Choose your words carefully, *ma chère*, because this will be the last time you're allowed to speak without permission."

He paced back and forth before the cage. Chloe sprang back from its edges and wrapped her arms around herself, but there was no security in such a miniscule space. She twisted and turned to keep her eye on him, to never have him at her back. She thought fast, thought back to those terrible stories her mother had told her about people like him. Her mother used to say that they saw their victims as objects, not people, so they could act out their violent fantasies without guilt.

"My name is Chloe," she said, looking up at him as he circled her. "My name is Chloe. I'm twenty-two. I'm a student at Hollington University." She didn't know what to say, what information would trigger a shred of compassion. Demetrius stopped at the cage door and she panicked, throwing out anything about her that came to mind, no matter how mundane. "I paint watercolors sometimes, and I like to go stargazing in the summer. Please, I'm an only child. My family-"

"I know who you are," Demetrius murmured. He crouched in front of the cage door and met her eyes. "Chloe Madeleine Leroux, senior of Hollington University, an art history major. Your father is a cardiologist in Beachwood and your mother just died of breast cancer." He curled his fingers around the bars of the cage door. "I know exactly who you are, *cheri*. And *I don't care*."

Chloe froze, dumbstruck. Words failed her. She stared at her captor face-to-face in clear light for the first time. She could think of nothing else to do. He wore another mask of simple and unadorned leather that looked dusty and worn like the rest of his clothes. His hidden face made any expression unreadable, and that blankness frightened her. His eyes were the cool, nearly colorless grey of the winter sky. They were light pinpoints surrounded by black kohl, and they were devoid of compassion or shame. She felt she was looking into the eye of a storm, empty but for the promise of destruction. He had no eyebrows, Chloe realized, a detail that made him look almost inhuman. His gaze travelled down her body, as it had at the Oryx, the same consuming stare. Chloe pressed her back hard against the bars bolted to the wall, curling her legs beneath her.

"Please..." she whispered. Any more warnings from her mother's work stories melted into cold, prickling panic. "Please. I want to go home."

Demetrius chuckled under his breath. "This *is* your home, my little Chloe. *Bienvenue à la maison.*"

French. He had been speaking it here and there. It was her father's native language, normally a source of comfort for her. Coming from *him*...tears rolled down her cheeks. Panic infected her, filled her chest until she was certain it would burst, that she would die of fear. Her mouth moved, spilling out words that she knew were useless.

"Please let me go. What do you want? God, please. My dad is all alone, he can't lose...he will pay whatever you want-"

"Ah," Demetrius looked up, nodding. "Yes, he probably would, wouldn't he?"

He was listening. Chloe felt heart would burst. No human heart could beat this fast for this long. Her nudity forgotten, she dropped her arms and crawled to the door of the cage, toward the bizarre and frightening man on the other side of the bars. If it was money he wanted, her father wouldn't hesitate to pay for her return. Her nightmare could be over in a phone call. She gripped the bars close to Demetrius' hand, so dangerously close to him.

"Call him. Call my dad and he'll pay anything. Please, I know his number, we can end this right now." She felt heat emanating from Demetrius, heat that she could feel even through the cage. "Just tell him how much and let me go. Please..."

Demetrius tilted his head to the side. His eyes crinkled at the corners, the only evidence of a smile behind the mask.

"Oh, but I don't want his money," he said. He wrapped his hand over Chloe's and leaned in close to the bars. "I want his baby girl."

The look in his eyes turned Chloe's blood to ice. She jerked back and scrambled to the back of the cage. Demetrius laughed and shook his head. He pulled a key from his pocket and slipped it into the padlock on the cage door.

"No!" Chloe cried. She clutched the cage bars and curled as tightly into herself as possible. "Stay away!"

Demetrius made chiding *tsk* sounds with his tongue. He opened the cage door and reached in. Chloe screamed, kicking at his hands, but he dodged her blows easily and caught her legs. Chloe held fast to the bars, but all it took was a single good pull for her grip to fail her. Demetrius was as strong as she remembered from the struggle in her living room. He dragged her out of the cage with ease and pinned her on her side with his body, trapping her bound wrists with one hand. He bore down on her, his hair cast like a net over her face, until she stopped struggling.

"Sh, sh, sh," he whispered again, his mask brushing Chloe's ear. "It's over, *ma chère*. The life you had is over. You have no father, you have no friends. You are a slave, and you only have your Master. I am your life now."

Chloe began to sob. "I don't understand."

Her strength had failed her. Even in her terror, she couldn't struggle anymore. Demetrius' weight trapped her so completely. She had never felt so helpless. His words echoed in her head like a bell ringing in a tower. More than that, he invaded every one of her senses. The heat of his body seeped from his clothes and penetrated her skin, and she felt the same warm spark she had when he had touched her at the club.

"Don't you?" his voice, so close to her ear, reverberated through her bones. "Listen to your body. Yes, you felt it at the Oryx and you feel it now, don't you? The way our bodies speak to each other."

He ran a hand along her back, an infuriating caress that reminded Chloe of how naked she was, how weak. She thrashed beneath him, yet the brush of his fingers made her spine bow reflexively, as if he had flipped a switch in her body.

"Get off of me," she growled, a flicker of anger spurring her into one last struggle. She threw her head back hoping to strike his face, but he had been ready for it.

"Sh, sh," he purred, stroking her hair, mocking her helplessness. "Don't fight it. You were meant for me, oh, yes, and you know it. The way you looked at me, the way you searched for me as you danced…"

Chloe squeezed his eyes shut, as if that would drown out his voice. "No. No, no, no," she muttered over and over, but Demetrius' voice carried over her own.

"And how you *melted* in my hands," he sneered, "responded to every little touch, well, *well*...I couldn't let *you* go, now, could I? No, no, you were relentless."

Anger bled into Chloe's fear and brought no strength.

"No," she snapped. "No, I didn't ask for this. I didn't fucking ask for this."

Demetrius shushed her again. He brushed a lock of her hair behind her ear and leaned in close.

"No, *ma chère*, you didn't ask for this," he whispered. "But you were meant for this."

He sat up and flipped Chloe onto her back with an ease that stoked her anger, straddling her hips. She was forced to look at him as he reached into his pocket and pulled out a thin black switchblade. The color drained from Chloe's face. She did not dare struggle.

"After this night," said Demetrius, flicking open the switchblade with a sickening *click*, "you are Twenty-One, and you are my slave."

Demetrius traced the tip of the blade up her stomach, too light to cut. Chloe couldn't command her body to move. She couldn't breathe. She couldn't think. One flick of Demetrius' wrist and she would bleed. He caught her gaze and held it, trapped like the rest of her. There was something in his eyes that terrified her, a sinister light that revealed just how much pleasure her fear gave him. That light was like an injection of adrenaline into her heart. Chloe screamed wordlessly and forced her useless limbs to struggle. She clenched her fists and threw them at Demetrius' chest, bucking her hips to throw him off balance. Demetrius' laughter was infuriating. He crushed her own arms against her chest, thrust his weight onto her, and leaked the air from her lungs. Spots flooded her vision. She gasped for air.

"Ah, there's the second wind," he said, shaking his head. "Oh, Chloe, Chloe, you are exquisite. Don't you understand? It's already over." He lifted himself off her chest just enough for her to catch a breath. She gasped in air as he tilted up her chin with his cool, strong fingers. "You were mine the moment our eyes met."

She had to get out from underneath him. She felt every coil of muscle in his torso, the strength of his arms.

"I will break you," he said, bringing his face close to hers. She felt the knife blade slide between her wrists against the zip tie. "And I will shape you into a perfect slave. And in time, I will sell you. But for now, *cheri*, you're mine."

Break. Slave. Sell. Chloe couldn't wrap her mind around his words. The press of his body was too much. She felt him hard against her bare sex as if his clothing weren't even there. Her body grew numb and heavy.

"You have a choice now, Chloe." The way he said her name, as if it was some sweet little secret he had discovered. She couldn't bear it. "We can begin today and you'll be rewarded with food. Or you can continue this little tantrum."

The knife bit through the zip tie around Chloe's wrists. Blood rushed back to her fingertips. Demetrius was still, watching her. Chloe didn't know what to do. Those grey eyes ensnared her, lit with a heat that didn't match his cold words. His fingers softened on her chin, slid down the stiff collar around her neck. Her skin tingled when he traced her collarbone, brushed the mound of her left breast. She rose to meet his touch, to feel that cool hand encase her breast, without thought. Something snapped in her in that moment. What had she just done? Did she just encourage the man who kidnapped her to touch her? No. No, she couldn't crave his touch. She flushed with shame. It was self-loathing that spurred her to strike out at him. She threw her fist at the side of his head.

Demetrius' head snapped to the side, his eyes widening a fraction of an inch. He caught her free hands, digging his nails into the bruises from the zip tie. Chloe cried out, unable to free herself from his grip. Her death was in his eyes when he stared down at her. Tears came, but she met his fierce gaze.

"Have it your way," Demetrius snarled.

He grabbed a fistful of her hair. Chloe cried out, her scalp ablaze with screaming nerve endings. Her captor rolled off her and dragged her back toward the cage. There was no lascivity in his touch now, nothing but calculated violence.

"No!" Chloe shrieked, scratching at the brutal fingers in her hair. "Help! Somebody!"

Demetrius threw open the cage door and clutched Chloe's face.

"This is what you wanted, wasn't it? Wasn't it?" he shouted over her cries. "Oh, Chloe, Chloe, you just made things much harder for yourself."

He hurled Chloe into the cage, slamming the door so fast that it nearly struck her ankles. Chloe sobbed over the sound of keys locking her in. Demetrius lingered for a moment, watching her through the bars. She felt his eyes taking in her nude body like pinpoints of heat traveling down her skin.

"So beautiful." He took in a breath through his teeth, sharp and shivering, and Chloe couldn't tell if the fire in his eyes was rage or desire. His voice came in a seething whisper.

"Bonne nuit, chéri."

He rose and headed for a black door at the other end of the room. It closed with a mechanical beeping sound. Chloe drew her knees into her chest and wept against the cold cage floor.

Chapter 4

SEPTEMBER 25, 2011

9/20/11
Ms. Dia Belaire
2717 Straeleni Street
New Orleans, LA, 70130
My Dear Demetrius,

I know it's about to be your busy time and it might be a few weeks before I hear from you again, but I just have to tell you this. I have amazing news…

Demetrius hovered over Seven, keeping a careful watch for signs that she was close to orgasm. She lay sprawled on her back on the high oak table, bound at the wrists and ankles in leather cuffs, legs dangling off the table. Her attendant, Nick, stood between her legs, pressing a vibrator against her clitoris. Her tattoo-spattered skin was flushed, her face as red as her short neon mohawk. Demetrius stroked her small, high breasts and found her nipples diamond-hard. She was ready.

"You have to wait until the slave has reached a state of *extreme* arousal for this," said Demetrius to the nineteen attendants observing around the table, their nude and collared charges kneeling at their feet. He turned on the stun gun in his hand and approached the table. Seven's small brown eyes snapped open at the electric whine of the stun gun warming up. She looked up at him with a silent plea on her face. Demetrius tugged on the D ring of her steel collar.

"Eyes down, slave," he ordered. Seven's face twisted into a grimace somewhere between fear and need, but she obeyed. Demetrius looked at Nick. "What have I told you about her eye contact?"

Nick flashed him an anxious smile, "Nah, D, she's gotten a lot better, we've been working on it. She just gets nervous sometimes."

Demetrius stared at him until the attendant broke and looked away.

"Don't let it happen again."

Seven flung her head back. Her thighs quivered with every circle of the vibrator around the apex of her sex. It was time. Demetrius leaned down to Seven's ear and gave the command.

"Come for me."

Seven screamed, her back arching off the table. Demetrius struck her in the ribs with the stun gun. The slave's scream intensified, her hips bucking against the vibrator so hard that Nick had to steady her thighs to keep her from sliding into him. The attendants applauded, many of them grinning. This was usually their favorite group training session of the year.

Demetrius switched off the stun gun and handed it to Nick.

"Bring your slave to a high state of arousal, give the command, and incorporate the stimulus. Soon you'll begin using the stimuli and the command simultaneously, and eventually you will use the stimuli alone to induce orgasm." He took a step back, tossing his hair from his face. "Pain eroticism in slaves is tricky. Many of the leather slaves will resist it. Fear of the pain is your biggest hurdle. That's why you need to make sure the state of arousal is just on the brink of orgasm. Obviously, Seven already has strong masochistic tendencies, so Nick has it easy this year."

Demetrius gestured over his shoulder for the twins, who stood behind him with crops and vibrators in their arms.

"Leather slaves get the leather crops," he instructed. "Steel slaves have the studded ones."

The basement buzzed with activity. Attendants strapped their charges to the row of tables and soon the cement walls echoed with mechanical buzzing and soft moans. Demetrius observed, giving direction as it was needed, but the attendants did well enough on their own. Most of them had been working for him since the beginning. With six years of experience they could probably train an adequate slave without his supervision. His thoughts wandered to the frail girl locked in the third floor suite. Chloe. What a perfect name for such a delicate creature. The vision of her nude body loomed in his mind, flushed with terror and shame, her milky skin suffused with pink. Oh, she was exquisite.

For six years, Demetrius had broken young women into the most sought after slaves on the market. He had seen the most beautiful women naked before him, season after season. In June, they fought, begged, struggled, each one of them, and by September, he broke them and shaped them into the docile, obedient creatures he saw before him now, submitting to whatever he wished, desperate to please their attendants and their Master.

But it was September now. He had never had a new slave so late in the season. And her background…oh, his heart had sunk when he discovered just whom he had stolen away. The only child of a celebrated cardiologist was a far cry from his own "low risk" rule. This was the most dangerous risk he had taken in all these years by far. But what could he do? He couldn't have let her slip through his fingers, no, no, not the sweet little newcomer who had stared at him with such awe, his wide-eyed little Capulet locking eyes with him across a crowded room. Chloe…Chloe was a slave by her very nature, he knew that from the moment he thrust her into the theatrical "virgin wall" at the Oryx. A single touch had stripped her of any inhibition and she had surrendered to pure sensation. He, a total stranger, could have fucked her against that blood-drenched wall and she would have submitted, as she had submitted to the vaguest of requests: *Say yes.* The very thought made him swell hard against his pale jeans. Oh, yes, breaking her would be heaven. But at what cost?

The twins returned to him, arm in arm.

"Everything looks good," said Charity, fingering one of her green pigtails.

"Abigail called for you earlier," her sister Faith chimed in. "We couldn't get you on the intercom."

Demetrius tossed his hair over his shoulder. He was not in the mood for Abigail today.

"What did she want?"

"She didn't say," said Charity.

"Of course not," Demetrius handed Charity the stun gun. "I have business to discuss with her, anyway."

He scanned the basement. The attendants were hard at work, watching their charges for signs of high arousal, save for those who had glass slaves. The glass slaves did not participate in this training session. Their category catered to clients who preferred to inflict a more traditional response to pain in their slaves and to do much of the breaking process themselves. The glass slaves were treated far more gently than the steel and leather slaves as a result, especially when it came to pain response. Today the glass slaves were perfecting their oral skills, servicing their attendants on their knees, their hands at their necks. Three caught his eye, one of his most delicate slaves of the season. Her attendant, Rodney, had her white blonde hair balled up in his fist, forcing himself down her throat. She was further along than some of the other glass slaves, and she had never lashed out or broken down. She, like Chloe, seemed to be a natural slave. Demetrius turned to the twins.

"Tell Rodney I have a new task for Three," he said. "The intercom is off in the suite because I have a new slave up there in the isolation stage."

Demetrius studied Faith and Charity's faces. Their biggest physical tells were their eyes, which was rare, despite popular assumption. People learn very quickly to lie with their faces. Normally overlooked parts of the body, like the feet, revealed far more than the face. The twins were quite talented at keeping their porcelain faces blank and doll-like, but their compulsive need to check in with each other always betrayed them. Their black eyes met for a moment before returning to Demetrius' face. He waited for Charity, always the bolder one, to choose her words before daring to question him.

"Are we losing a slave this season?" she asked, finally. Demetrius resisted a sigh. Predictability was a useful quality in those under his employ, but it was dull.

"Her purpose here is business of mine and my partners," he let a cold edge creep into his voice and fixed the twins with a steady gaze. Faith began to fidget first, breaking eye contact to brush an imaginary piece of dust from her sheer blouse. A couple of years ago, he might have smiled at his power over their nerves. But it was an old dance. He let it go. He would have to tell them his plans for little Chloe eventually, but not when they questioned him.

A ragged scream broke through the hum of the training session. Demetrius and the twins snapped to attention.

"Seventeen," said Faith, pointing to the far end of the long room.

Seventeen was a breathtaking specimen, tall and slender with smooth Mediterranean skin and glossy hair the color of ripe black olives. She screamed again, thrashing wildly against her restraints, writhing away from the vibrator between her legs. Gabe, her attendant, struggled with her flailing legs. Gabe was a large man, but Demetrius knew that Seventeen was quite strong during her outbursts.

"Gabe," Demetrius called.

"I don't know what happened," Gabe responded, his voice more exasperated than anxious. He had been with Demetrius for all six years and was one of his best attendants. "She's just having a tough day, I guess."

Demetrius gestured for the twins to stay where they were and headed over to Seventeen's table. She was a unique slave. If not for her behavior problems, she would certainly be the bestseller of the season. When she had arrived, she had fought like an animal and refused to utter a single word. At first, her rebellion and her silence had intrigued him. It had taken him three months to get her to speak. Even now, she only said what was absolutely necessary; *Yes, Master, if it pleases you, Master*, et cetera. Soon, however, even Seventeen's outbursts became routine, a tedious chore. He knew it would only be a matter of time before he found her poison, the one punishment or manner or method that finally broke her.

Gabe had managed to pin her legs down by the time Demetrius reached them. Demetrius retrieved his switchblade and flicked it open. Sometimes that ominous sound was all it took, but Seventeen hadn't heard it over her own screams. Demetrius caught her head and lay the flat of his blade against her cheek. She hesitated, looking him full in the face in defiance. Her almond shaped eyes betrayed her fear.

"You know," said Demetrius, meeting that angry, frightened stare, "in six years, I've never allowed a slave to rebel as long as you have. I see *so much potential* in you, Seventeen, oh, yes, I do. But my patience is wearing thin."

He placed the blade just over the tear duct of her left eye. The slave froze in an instant. Those lovely full lips quivered just a bit. He let the very tip of the knife touch the space between her eye and the bridge of her nose.

"Should I just…run through this delicate bit of flesh here now, cut my losses, burn your corpse like I've had to with other slaves who just wouldn't get with the program?"

Seventeen's terror was palpable. Tears pooled around the tip of the knife. Her body was rigid, as if breathing wrong would cause him to drop the knife. She was lithe and built with well-defined muscle, like a thoroughbred horse. Her curves were perfect, with smooth hips and plump, round breasts that most women would have to pay a fortune to achieve. Demetrius reached down the line of her body and cupped her left breast with his free hand. She quivered like a cornered animal. Demetrius was painfully erect now, looking into those wide, pleading, terrified eyes.

"This is the last time I will indulge your little tantrums," he hissed. He took the knife away from her eye, tracing along the contours of her face, those lips, her high cheekbones. "One more outburst, and I will have no choice but to dispose of you. Don't make me do that, Seventeen."

He surprised himself by dragging the knife along her cheekbone. Seventeen gasped. Her skin gave under the blade, a small wound, and quick to heal, but the blood flowed immediately. Desire burned through Demetrius' veins like a swift poison. He looked away from her face, from the cut. If he didn't, he would do it again, and again, and again, until that tempting body of hers was decorated in sweet red streaks.

Demetrius drew a silent breath to steady himself. He had even grown weary of the sensation of arousal; the ascending pulse, the ragged breath, the need to dominate, to penetrate, to release. The need was there, all-consuming as always, and it would need to be satisfied so he could get back to work. However, the thrill of it had long ago soured.

He looked at Gabe when he felt he had regained control of himself.

"Put her in isolation," he said. "No food. Tie her to one of the crosses outside for a few hours before sunrise. I'll deal with her in the morning."

Gabe nodded and began to unbind his charge from her table. The rest of the attendants scrambled to pretend that they hadn't been watching the incident instead of doing their job.

"Continue until your charge reaches orgasm," he ordered, walking toward the twins, his pulse thick in his chest. "Be sure to strike them just as they begin to climax." He folded the knife and returned it to his pocket. "Faith, go tell Three that she is on isolation duty for the new slave. Then come join your sister in my bedroom."

The twins parted ways immediately. Charity fell into step behind him, her stiletto heels clacking over the sounds of resumed training. His mind returned to Chloe and the heat of arousal intensified. If only he could go to her now, to take out this tedious need on her sweet soft skin, but it was too soon. He held onto the image of her tear-stained face, looking up at him with wide, desperate eyes. He carried that image upstairs to the bedroom, where the twins would quench this fire.

Chapter 5

SEPTEMBER 27, 2011

The low beep of the door made Chloe scramble into as much of a sitting position as she could in her tiny cage, her arms wrapped around her knees.

It had been at least a couple days since Demetrius had thrown her into the cage, though she could only guess. There was no measure of time in the room; no windows or clocks. It was maddening. With no dimming light or chirping birds, time stretched into an indiscernible eternity. She marked the passing hours only by her growing hunger and thirst. Bruises formed on her arms, marks of Demetrius' brutal grip. Eventually a heavy, urgent sensation grew in her bladder despite the fact that she hadn't had water since she had woken in this damned place. She screamed for someone to come, beat her palms against the bars, but her pleas went unheard. Finally she could hold it no longer and she soiled herself like an incontinent animal. Chloe had never felt greater humiliation. She hardly felt human, trapped and nude in a puddle of her own waste. She cried until her ribs ached, screamed until she had no voice. Still no one came.

Now that someone actually was at the door, Chloe panicked. She wasn't ready for another fight. She wasn't ready for Demetrius to finish what he had tried to start. The very thought filled her with dread. She clutched her arms and stared at the opening door.

A small figure stepped into the room, far too small to be Demetrius. Chloe peered through the bars, too afraid to lean forward. A girl no older than sixteen or seventeen came toward the cage with a coil of chain over her shoulder and a large white bucket in her hand. Other than the curtain of long, layered white-blonde hair, she was completely nude. She crouched by the cage door and unlocked it, setting the bucket down beside her. Chloe's heart jolted.

"Who are you?" she demanded, her voice still raw from countless hours of tears. "Get away. Get away from me!"

The girl looked back at Chloe with round blue eyes and said nothing. She opened the cage and held something up. Chloe caught sight of a plastic water bottle in the girl's hand. Thirst cut through her panic like a sharp blade.

The girl held the water bottle out to Chloe and beckoned with the end of a chain. Chloe saw a clip attached to the chain and fought the urge to touch the D-ring on the leather collar locked around her neck. The girl beckoned again, shaking the water bottle. The sound made Chloe's throat ache.

"Who are you?" Chloe repeated cautiously, though she had already begun crawling out of the cage, thirst overtaking fear.

The girl touched a finger to her lips. Her face, heart-shaped and seashell white, looked far too weary for one so young. She handed Chloe the water bottle. Chloe opened it with trembling fingers. Her knees buckled at the sensation of water flooding her mouth and down her throat. She slurped and swallowed without grace and forgot herself entirely. Water. Oh, God, she hadn't known just how thirsty she had been. The bottle was empty so quickly, her thirst slacked but not quenched. Still, her mouth was no longer dry and she was out of the cage. She stretched her legs. Her muscles were stiff and weak from spending so many hours curled up. Chloe felt a small tug on her neck. The girl had hooked the chain to her collar and she hadn't even noticed. Chloe was leashed like a family dog, nude and coated in her own waste. She folded her arms to shield her breasts as tears returned to her eyes. The thoughts that maddened her in her isolation threatened again: How could this have happened? What would become of her?

The young girl crouching beside her seemed to understand. She reached out and patted Chloe's hair. Chloe nearly jerked away, but the touch was tender, the first contact she'd had in days, and it soothed her despite herself. Chloe looked at the girl, naked and collared like Chloe herself. She had to be a slave, just what Demetrius planned for Chloe to be. Had this girl been locked in the cage before Chloe? Had she been starved?

The girl beckoned for Chloe to rise. She complied. Her legs felt a little stronger than they had a few minutes ago.

"Why won't you talk to me?" Chloe demanded.

The girl just shook her head and pressed her fingers to her lips again, her eyes wide. But the sight of her made Chloe's stomach twist. The girl was unbound, armed with a chain and a key to the cage, and Demetrius was nowhere in sight. Why didn't she run? Chloe thought back to her mother's stories, how patients of hers who kidnapped people would receive letters from their victims in prison. Had Demetrius broken this young creature so utterly that she was nothing but a compliant zombie? Chloe clutched the girl's wrist, ignoring her silent and frantic warnings. No. No, this girl had to see reason. She had a mind of her own, just like Chloe, and Chloe couldn't believe that a man could extinguish all that a person was, every shred of self. It couldn't be. It couldn't happen to her.

"We have to get out of here," Chloe hissed. "We don't belong here. You're not a slave. Please, you know the code to the door. We can-"

The girl took Chloe's face in her hands and pressed her lips against Chloe's mouth. Chloe froze, dumbfounded. The girl's lips were soft and insistent before she pulled away and pointed to the walls. Chloe blinked rapidly. Her throat had gone dry again. She followed the girl's pointing. At first, she saw nothing. Then she noticed small holes where the walls met the ceiling, and a small red light here and there. Chloe's heart sank. There were cameras in the walls, many of them. Demetrius had probably heard her cries from them, had probably watched her scream and struggle against the cage and soil herself. Her face burned with shame. When the girl tugged on the chain, Chloe followed her, numb.

The cage key also opened the second door in the bedroom, which Chloe had not yet seen open. She was surprised to step into a full bathroom, as modern and elegant as the bedroom itself. Chloe didn't know what she'd been expecting, but it hadn't been something so mundane. The girl led her to a walk in shower with warm grey stone walls. She removed a handheld shower head and tested the water on her palm before gesturing for Chloe to come closer. Chloe hesitated. She didn't know what to think. The girl's nudity didn't make Chloe any more comfortable with her own. A part of her was relieved by the opportunity to bathe, but her mind raced. Cameras or no cameras, she had to get out. The girl's compliance scared her to death. She beckoned again and Chloe came to her. She held the chain on Chloe's neck, but she was such a tiny thing. Chloe could definitely overpower her if she had to.

A stream of hot water flooded over Chloe's head and dampened her short hair. Her muscles yielded to the warmth instinctively. She sighed. Something as simple as a shower became so significant after her isolation. She began to feel human again. The girl gently unfolded Chloe's arms and washed her body. Chloe found herself staring at the girl's breasts, bare like the rest of her, her small petal pink nipples barely veiled by strands of her bleached white layers. How could she be so comfortable nude? How long had she been trapped in this place? What had Demetrius done to her?

The girl turned her back and picked up a towel from a nearby rack. Chloe caught sight of a mark on the girl's shoulder blade peeping through her hair, something dark and raised. It was a large Roman numeral three. Chloe feared her heart would stop. The girl was branded. Like a cow. Now the thought of overpowering the girl to escape made Chloe's heart ache. She couldn't hurt this girl, a victim, just like Chloe was. "What's your name?" Chloe whispered. She glanced around the bathroom for cameras and found nothing. The girl shook her head, her eyes downcast, and held up three fingers. She patted the spot on her back that was branded, and patted her chest.

"Three...you...oh," Chloe whispered. Her lip quivered, fresh tears pooling in her eyes. She understood. The girl had no name; only a number that had been seared into her back. A wave of nausea rolled over Chloe. Demetrius' words came back to her. *"After this night, you are Twenty-One, and you are my slave."*

How long would it be until Chloe was branded? How long until she was silent and nameless and washing newly kidnapped women like this girl, slave number Three? How many other slaves did Demetrius have locked away? Was she in a house full of bedrooms with cages? No. She had to get out. Now. She looked at Three, so frail, her eyes lowered, her face blank. Was this what it meant to be "broken?"

"I will break you, and I will shape you into the perfect slave."

No. That couldn't happen to her. It wouldn't happen to her.

Three tugged on Chloe's chain and turned around to lead her to the bedroom. Chloe sucked in a breath. She didn't want to hurt the girl, but this could be her only chance.

They stepped into the bedroom and Chloe sprung. She grabbed the chain with both hands and wrenched it from Three's grip. Three jerked back, surprised. Chloe charged her and pulled the chain around Three's tiny throat.

"I'm so sorry!" Chloe said in the girl's ear, pulling the chain back so Three could not free herself. She held Three's back close to her own chest and dragged her to the door. "Open the door."

Three struggled, flailing her arms, clutching at the chain around her throat. A cry escaped her lips, a tiny, pitiful sound that threatened to break Chloe's resolve.

"Please stop," Chloe begged. "Please don't. I don't want to hurt you. Just open the door!"

Chloe was surprised by her own strength after days in a cage, though it was dwindling fast. Her arms already began to ache from the struggle.

"Open the door!" Chloe hadn't meant to shriek, but Three responded, punching in a numbered code. The door beeped and opened. Chloe nearly laughed in relief. The door was open. It was open. She was free from this room, this horrible room.

"I'm so sorry," she said again. "I'll get help for you. I promise!"

Chloe unclipped the chain from her collar and shoved Three to the ground. The girl landed hard on the wood floor. Chloe had no time to make sure she was all right. She slipped through the door and barreled toward freedom.

Chapter 6

9/20/11
Ms. Dia Belaire
2717 Straeleni Street
New Orleans, LA, 70130

…His name is Daniel, and he's everything I ever wanted. Demetrius, I wish you would take some time off and come meet him before the wedding. Even you would love him. I just know it. He's the sweetest, most gentle man I've ever met. And he's biracial, so you know Mama Dede would have approved. Speaking of Mama, I have something to ask you. You and she were the only real family I ever had. You took care of me and protected me when I had nobody else. It's been years since you've come to visit. I love our letters, but I miss you so much. Please come home. Come, and give me away at my wedding. Please say you will…

Demetrius would never say so aloud, but he vastly preferred oral sex with the twins to penetration. He sat with his back against the headboard of his master bed, his legs lost in a tangle of limbs and black satin sheets. The twins' heads blanketed his lap, their firm lips gliding in unison up and down the length of him. He sucked in a breath through his teeth, watching the twins work. Faith and Charity moved with perfect coordination, as if choreographed, their noses and lips touching, trapping him between their mouths. They took turns glancing up at Demetrius' face, an old habit of theirs. They knew they would find no expression in his eyes, but he knew they didn't care. Faith and Charity were creatures of their own pleasure, selfish lovers. But so was he. Faith took just the tip of him between her lips and swirled her tongue around that so-sensitive ridge before sliding him into her mouth. Demetrius resisted the urge to thrust against the back of her throat, closed his eyes, and focused on the various sensations of sex. He shivered when Charity licked the smooth white seam of his scrotum and his back arched when Faith's teeth grazed the tip of him, but he did not revel in the flash of teeth or the sway of their pigtails as they did their task. He sighed and wrapped his fingers around the back of Faith's neck, forcing her to take him down her throat. Faith bore him with little difficulty despite his size and the abrupt change. The twins did not talk about their past. Demetrius suspected that they had been on the streets of California long, long before he had rescued them from an abusive pimp. They had the expert touch of seasoned prostitutes. Still, even their skill, even the sensation of Faith's throat enveloping him, gave him no spark of satisfaction. He surrendered, letting his hands fall into the sheets, and waited for release to take him.

How awful goodness is.

"I still can't believe you wear that mask even during sex. Really, D, it's ridiculous."

Demetrius opened his eyes. The gigantic flat screen on the opposite wall of the bed was on, and the face of a woman loomed large, her lips curled into a smirk. She was nude, and her loose blonde curls doing little to conceal her large breasts. She sat supine on the edge of the bed, white sheets tousled, obviously posing. A muscular young man with light brown hair lay before her, his head resting in her lap. His blue-grey eyes were wide as he took in the sight of Demetrius and the twins.

"Abigail," said Demetrius, pulling the twins away from their task. He slid past them to sit at the edge of the bed. "This must be urgent for you to override the channel lock."

Abigail smiled, her dark blue eyes taking in Demetrius' erection, "I didn't have to override anything. The channel was open. It looks like one of your twins is an exhibitionist."

Demetrius felt the twins tense behind him. He knew one of them had opened the channel in anticipation of his meeting with Abigail. They also knew that he did not like being interrupted during sex. He would deal with their error later.

"I could call back later," said Abigail coolly, her voice husky and low and theatrical, "when you've had a chance to...relieve your tension. Not that I mind the view. I always love watching you work."

Demetrius clenched his jaw and cut his eyes to the slave in Abigail's lap. "So does your new favorite, apparently."

The young man's eyes widened. He lowered his gaze as he should have since the beginning but the error had been made.

"I'd hate to think you've gone so soft, Abigail," said Demetrius. "Spoiling your favorite to the point where he looks a Master in the eye? No, no, no, we can't have that now, can we?"

Abigail's face was all pleasant sweetness, though her smile sharpened around the edges as she ran her fingers through the young man's hair. He tensed. He knew the danger he was in.

"Ash knows his manners," she said. Her nails grazed his scalp, probably a little too sharply, and her slave gasped. "I'll set him straight. But you are quite the spectacle right now, D, naked with your mask on."

She was emphasizing the mask today, Demetrius noted. She had probably hoped to catch him without it. In the years he worked with Abigail, she had learned not to pry into his past but often the mask proved too strong a curiosity for her.

"While you're interrupting, why don't you tell me why you called earlier?" Demetrius leaned back. A dull ache crept low in his groin. He had grown accustomed to delaying release, and though it would have to be satiated, he was able to ignore the discomfort with ease.

Abigail sighed, tilting her head back to expose her neck, her hair falling on either side of her breasts. Her nipples betrayed her portrait of perfect ease, hardened to a dark rose pink. Demetrius noticed this and nearly gave a sigh of his own. There was something making her anxious. He braced himself for bad news.

"Well," she began, "Konri just received another application for purchase from a former client. We spoke about it, and we both think it would be best for business if we allow him to bid this year."

Her nipples were even harder now, and her foot, crossed so demurely over her ankle, began to bounce. Demetrius rolled his eyes. Only one person would make her so nervous to discuss with him.

"No."

Abigail frowned. She sat up straight. "I haven't even given you the name. How can you say-"

"*Dr. Ghede* has been banned from my client list for the past two years," Demetrius snarled. He shoved the twins away from his thighs, their proximity now irritating. "You and Konri shouldn't even have bothered speaking with him."

Abigail pushed her full lips into a pout, "He's a *very* high bidder, D. The last slave we sold him was mid stock at best and he paid more than twice her worth."

Demetrius worked his jaw. He was not in the mood for Abigail's histrionics today. He just wanted to satisfy the ache in his loins and get back to training. He lowered his chin and looked up at Abigail, smirking when she tensed under the threatening gaze. Abigail was a very skilled Mistress, despite her rather amateur habit of keeping favorites. Her flair for the dramatic was a weakness, however. She enjoyed holding meetings scantily clad or completely nude, often surrounded by her slaves of the season, to entrance and distract those with whom she did business. She did not realize that her little goddess act didn't translate from head to toe.

"I don't spend six months training slaves so they can be starved and strangled two weeks after auction," he said. "We won't have this conversation again, Abigail. *We* don't do business with that necrophiliac."

Abigail sighed, tossing her shoulders. "I don't see why you care what happens after they're purchased, but you're the boss, D."

Her face and voice suggested apathy, though her nipples remained stubbornly hard, her chest flushed with red, revealing her anger. He would keep a careful eye on the client list this season for any names affiliated with Dr. Ghede. Abigail would not directly disobey him, but she was not above underhandedness, especially when it came to money.

Abigail's cell rang from somewhere in the bed sheets. Ash scrambled to retrieve it and handed it to his Mistress.

"That's the warehouse," she said, shutting off the ringer. "They need me. We're suspension training this week."

She snapped her fingers and Ash scrambled off the bed, disappearing off camera for a moment. He returned with a stack of clothes. Abigail held out her arms and allowed her slave to slip a lace bra over her bare breasts. Ash was certainly spoiled and his etiquette was nowhere near what it should be at this point in the season. However, he did seem attentive and eager to please. Demetrius never understood how Abigail made slaves fawn over her so. Over the years of working together, her every carefully constructed mannerism grated on him.

"I'd like to stay in the upstairs suite when auction time rolls around," said Abigail as Ash buttoned her cardigan.

Demetrius nodded. He had originally planned to wait a while to tell his partners about Chloe, after she had been broken, but something about Abigail's smugness made him want to rattle her. Chloe would break easily, he could sense that already, so there was really no point in waiting. A weak justification that he indulged.

"The suite is currently occupied for isolation," he said, "but the slave should be fully broken by December."

He watched Abigail process his words. She waved Ash away from her.

"You have a new slave?" she asked, "In *September*?"

"Yes," said Demetrius, keeping his reply short. Abigail was his partner, though not his equal. Like the twins, he needed to remind her that he was in charge. He didn't owe her explanations. Abigail was often under a different impression, as she seemed to be today. She and Konri had spoken about Dr. Ghede amongst themselves. They had not approached him about it until they had planned some course of action, figured out a "best way" to win him over. The attempt at manipulation was a warning sign that Abigail had grown too haughty. This new information rattled her, as he had hoped. He watched her think, probably calculating the best way to proceed with him.

"Did you lose a slave this season?" she finally asked the same perceived safe question that the twins had asked earlier. "I know you've been having trouble with one of them but I didn't think you'd eliminate such good stock."

"Seventeen is alive and improving," he said. "Elimination won't be necessary."

Abigail folded her arms, "Well would you care to clue me in on your plans for this new addition, *boss*?"

Demetrius smiled behind his mask. She had acknowledged his status despite the snide tone.

"I'm revisiting the idea of a Model Slave," he said. "We'll have a meeting about it when I have time."

He motioned to Faith, who handed him the remote for the screen as Abigail protested.

"Wait, wait," she said, holding up a hand as if to prevent him from shutting off the screen. "A Model Slave? *I* thought of that years ago. You said it was pointless."

Demetrius lifted the remote. "We'll discuss it later."

A frantic knock at the door stopped him from turning off the screen. Three scurried into the room without permission or protocol before Faith or Charity could open the door themselves.

"Master-!" she cried out in her soft, high voice.

"Slave," Charity snapped. "On your knees. How dare you come in without-"

"Shut up, Charity." Demetrius rose from the bed and reached for his clothes. Three was not only perfectly trained but timid to a fault. There was only one reason for her to break protocol.

Demetrius raised the remote and switched off the screen, ignoring Abigail's curious face. He turned to the twins.

"Sound the alarm," he said. "We have an escape."

Chapter 7

Chloe only heard the sound of her own breath and her pulse pounding in her ears, though she was sure she was making noise as she sprinted down the metal spiral staircase just outside of the door to her prison. She had to keep calm enough to find a way out of this place. Her best bet was to get outside and flag down a car on the road. She tried to breathe deeply, reciting her plan in her mind.

The staircase emptied into what appeared to be a study with a desk and mountainous bookshelves, all haphazardly stocked with countless books and scattered with loose papers. Marble busts decorated the blank spaces between the shelves. She scrambled across the room toward two large doors, her bare feet sliding on the smooth hardwood floors. She didn't know which door led to an exit, but she had to get out before Three recovered and after her. She grabbed a door handle and a muffled sneer from the other side stopped her from opening it.

"Spoiling your favorite to the point where he looks a Master in the eye? No, no, no, we can't have that now, can we?"

Chloe ripped her hand from the door, her skin prickling with dread. Demetrius' voice was as startling as it was the first night she'd heard it. A mere pane of wood separated her from her captor. She pressed her ear against the other door. Hearing nothing, she slipped through and shut the door as quietly as she possibly could.

Chloe spotted white French doors that led outside and broke into a run. Outside! She hadn't seen the sky in days. Her feet pounded against white marble, and there were marble pillars on either side of her. The suite and the study had given her the impression that she was in a home. By contrast, this room was wide open with high ceilings and almost reminded Chloe of a chapel. She ran past a massive dining room table and stumbled onto a large raised platform that looked like some sort of stage. Chloe nearly paused. What *was* this place? But it didn't matter. She would never see this room again. Get outside, stop a car, get help. That was all that mattered. She made it to the French doors. They opened up to a wide yard bordered by trees. A stone building, too large to be a shed, stood between the yard and the woods. In Chloe's panic she almost didn't notice the doors to the building opening and a crowd of people coming through. The crowd was a blend of women, all nude, collared, and beautiful, and men at their sides, most of them young, all dressed in black jeans and plain black shirts. The women filed into a line, directed by occasional smacks from long black crops in the men's hands. The crowd headed toward the French doors. Toward Chloe.

Chloe's stomach dropped. She looked for somewhere to run. There were a few doors on either side of the marble room and she didn't know what could be behind them. She had to stay as close to the outside doors as possible. They were her only chance. Chloe slid behind the nearest pillar.

It was large enough for her to hide behind, but if Three came out of the study, she would be able to see her. She could think of nothing else to do. Were there more men with crops behind the closed doors? More naked women bound and caged in bedrooms? The thought made her nauseas. How many women had been ripped from their homes and terrorized by the masked man who had taken her? What sort of hell was she in?

The French doors opened and the sound of footsteps and male voices flooded the room. Chloe pressed her back flat against the cool marble pillar, afraid to breathe. If she was caught…no. She couldn't even think about that. Get outside. Find a road. Flag down a car.

Two chatting voices moved too close to her. Chloe made herself as small as possible, her arms flat at her sides, fists clenched tight.

"Looks like we just missed the rain."

"Shit, it's raining? I just tied Seventeen out there."

"You'd better get her before she gets struck by lightning."

"In a minute. I gotta take a piss."

"*Vaya con Dios*, bro."

Footsteps too close to her. Chloe didn't have time to move before a tall, large man walked past her pillar, so close she could see his tan face in profile. If he turned his head even slightly, it was over. Chloe braced herself, every muscle in her body ready to run. The young man barreled ahead without a passing glance and slipped through the door closest to her.

Chloe didn't dare move until the groups' footsteps faded. She glanced around the pillar. They were partway down a corridor on the other side of the room. She wanted to wait until they disappeared but Three could come down the stairs at any moment, and the man who had passed her could return from the bathroom.

Demetrius was only a couple of rooms away.

Chloe pushed off from the pillar and went through the French doors as quickly as she could, too frightened to look at the descending group. She heard no outcry, no one running toward her.

She was outside. The cold autumn air struck her so fiercely that she could not move for a moment. Thunder rolled across a sky swollen with rainclouds. She heard the rain collide with the forest trees like a thousand staccato drum beats just before it hit her, stinging her exposed back. She wrapped her arms around herself and eyed her surroundings. There was no driveway that she could see, no road. She couldn't tell if the trees were a shallow patch or a forest, whether it led to a road or some vast wilderness. She weighed her options. Should she run around the perimeter of the house and search for a driveway? That would risk discovery. Should she brave the woods? She scanned the line of the large yard for a path of some sort. She caught sight of a patch of large wooden X-shaped crosses, Saint Andrew's crosses, as she knew from childhood Sunday school, rooted to the ground beside the stone building before the trees. She froze. There was a woman bound to one of the crosses, her head down, long black hair soaked with cold rain.

"Oh, my God," Chloe whispered. She broke into a run toward the cross. She had already left Three behind in her attempt to escape, left the group of women she saw in the hands of men with crops. This woman was bound, helpless in the rain. How could Chloe simply run past her and leave her there?

Slick grass tickled Chloe's feet. Rain pelted her face, her breasts. She kept her eyes on the woman. No, she couldn't leave her. She had to at least try to help.

"Hey!" Chloe shouted over the thickening rain. "Miss! Can you hear me?"

The woman was spread eagled on the cross, bound by rope at her wrists and ankles. Chloe touched the woman's leg.

"I'll get you down. Can you hear me?" she repeated.

The woman didn't move. She was nude like Chloe, with olive skin and a slender, graceful figure. A thick metal collar glinted through her hair. Her eyes were closed, her lips moving feverishly. Chloe leaned in to hear her over the rising wind.

"I am Seventeen," she heard the woman murmur. "I am a slave. I will obey. I will be used. I will not question. I will please my Master."

Chloe took a step back, dread creeping through her veins. She looked at the woman's ankles. The rope was tied in a series of complicated knots.

"I'm going to get you down," she said again. "We can get out of here. We'll escape."

She dug her fingers into the rope. It was soaked with rain, and the knots held fast. The woman did not give Chloe any sign of understanding. She repeated the same words over and over again, words that froze Chloe's blood.

"I will not question. I will please my Master. I am Seventeen. I am a slave."

A siren shattered the sound of rain and whirling wind, muffled within the house. Chloe panicked. She tore at the woman's restraints, her breath running ragged.

The siren seemed to snap the bound woman from her stupor. She lifted her head. Her eyes snapped open. She looked at Chloe for the first time. Her eyes were large and brown and wide with alarm. She leaned toward Chloe as much as the restraints allowed.

"Run!" she hissed.

Chloe dropped the rope and sprinted toward the tree line. She couldn't look back at the woman. She had to get to the trees. She ran beside the stone building and toward the woods. She could hide there, and then find a road. Find a road and escape. Get help. Escape.

Suddenly the tree line disappeared. For a moment, Chloe thought she was staring at the roiling storm clouds. The color, though grey, was too light, too fierce, blazing with a rage a storm can only depict in lightning.

Steely fingers clutched her arms. Chloe screamed.

Demetrius' face blurred as rain soaked Chloe's eyes. He flung her into the grass like a discarded doll. Her chin struck mud. She rolled, thinking to spring up and make a break for the woods, but the fall had rattled her, and she was too slow. Demetrius dug his fingers into her scalp and wrenched her up from the ground.

"No!" Chloe screamed into the storm. She tore at the hand in her hair, the nerves in her scalp straining, screaming. She kicked out wildly and struck his stomach. He folded with a grunt, his grip loosening. Chloe had no thoughts as she stumbled toward the trees. She was like a rabbit leaping to escape the wolf at her heels. She was not fast enough. Demetrius caught her by the neck and thrust her against the stone building. Her back hit the wall and knocked the air from her lungs. Lightning raked over the trees, which were just feet away, blocked by her captor's body against her.

Demetrius' face was terrifying with his wet hair flung across it like black tentacles. His mask hid most of his expression from her. His eyes glowed, as if his rage was a gas flame that burned just behind them. He pressed his forearm against her throat, forcing her to tilt her face up or be choked. Rain pelted her face. The sound of it striking the building deafened her. A terrible scream caught in her throat, trapped by his arm.

"I never thought you would hurt Three," came a terrible snarl from the mask, hoarse with hollow panting. "I took you for the nurturing type." He deflected Chloe's weak, flailing arms. "But you certainly felt *bad* about it, didn't you, *ma chère*? That's why you tried to help Seventeen, isn't it? *Petite héroïne?*"

His words stirred a fury in Chloe she had never experienced. If she had imagined herself in a similar situation in the past, she'd have guessed she would be too terrified to be angry, terrified for her life. But it was rage and not fear that coursed through her as she stood crushed against the rough brick, her naked feet barely touching grass, wheezing against Demetrius' arm. How could a man who stole her away not a week ago, a stranger, know her so well? She felt more violated than when she had first woken in the cage, stripped and helpless. Chloe strained against his arm to find enough air to speak.

"Fuck you."

Demetrius' eyes widened. He looked completely unhinged. Chloe braced herself for violence.

Demetrius struck her face hard enough to jerk her head to the side. Lightning ignited the sky. Through the blur of her rain-soaked vision, she saw him rip the mask from his face and lunge at her.

Demetrius' mouth sealed against Chloe's, hot and supple and frantic. He kissed her as if he would eat her alive, his teeth barely concealed by his lips. Electricity pulsed through Chloe. She tasted ozone on her tongue as if the storm itself had entered her through his mouth. He kissed her again and again and she matched his fervor with lips and teeth and tongue, overtaken by his insatiable mouth, lost in the way it melded against hers so perfectly. He pried her lips apart with his tongue and explored her, and she opened to him. His brutal grip softened, his hands slid to the sides of her face. She felt the cool graze of metal studs on one side of his lower lip, a surprise that enflamed her. She was lost, lost, and in this moment, she didn't care. The storm howled around them, but there were only his lips, his hands, his body so hot through his drenched clothes. She pressed herself against him, unable to touch enough of his body, and he thrust her harder against the wall with his hips, grinding himself against her sex. Chloe cried out into his mouth. As her hands found their way to his neck, he tensed as if a switch had been flipped. He pulled back from her and twisted her to face the wall. She strained to turn her head, to see his unmasked face. His arm locked around her throat before she could, and in moments, the storm dissolved into blackness.

Chapter 8

JUNE 7, 2002

Demetrius hadn't expected today to be a day he would never forget. After all, he hadn't even woken up until it was half over, coming to on the sticky floor of one of Mama Dede's spare rooms with his worst headache in recent memory. He struggled to his feet, thankful that it was a cooler day. The piles of miscellaneous trash around him had begun to stink as summer grew warmer in New Orleans. Dede kept her parlor, living room, and kitchen in immaculate condition. The other rooms of the house were packed to hoarding levels. The bedroom she let him stay in was just as bad as this room; he had had to clear a path from the door to the bed. He wasn't sure why he had woken up in a different room; whatever he was coming down from had erased his memory of the night before and left him with his throbbing temples and a dry mouth. He supposed he should just be grateful that he had found his way back to the house and had avoided a mugging or worse while stumbling through their neighborhood in the middle of the night.

In the shower, Demetrius noticed dried blood under his fingernails and a few scratch marks on his arms. He sighed. So it had been one of *those* nights. Dread crept into his veins and remained there until he checked his wallet as

"

he dressed, finding it significantly lighter than it had been. Whoever she was, she hadn't been too injured to accept his money. That was the best thing he could hope for on days like these.

He ambled into the kitchen and looked for something to take the edge off his hangover. He didn't like this feeling…he didn't like not remembering. It was too much like the events that had brought him to New Orleans months ago, when he had woken up in a hospital bed in Toledo. But he didn't want to think about that. He shifted his leather mask for a swig of whiskey from the open bottle on the counter. His face still ached. It had been four months since the attack. He wondered if the pain would ever subside.

He heard chatter coming from the parlor at the front of the house. Mama Dede's low, smoky voice was among them. Her shop was open for business. Demetrius took another swig. He'd have to get a good buzz going to move past the idiotic clients of Dede's Haitian Vodou Boutique to get out the door.

Mama Dede was about as Haitian as apple pie. On one of the rare occasions she had mentioned her past, she had told Demetrius that she had been born in Thibodaux, Louisiana. But she never bothered to correct clients who assumed she was Haitian when they came to her for a lave tet. No one ever dared question the old woman. Despite being only four foot eleven and old enough to have a skeletal appearance, Mama Dede commanded more respect than anyone he knew. Since the day he had stumbled into her boutique, horror stricken by a strange vision he had experienced in the Lafayette Cemetery, he had respected her. And she had taken him in, a nomad off the streets who didn't even remember who he was. She had let him stay the night he had come to her, and he hadn't left.

Despite having lived with her for months, Demetrius still wasn't certain if she actually believed in the religion she sold to brave tourists and socialites in her front room. She sold it like an expert, rattling off various names of loa spirits that would assist her client with whatever had brought them to her door, instructing them on building tables for the spirits and gaining their favor. She performed lave tets; ceremonial "head washings"; and other rather theatrical tasks. She even sold mojo and *gris gris* bags even though they were not relics of pure Haitian Vodou. They belonged to the melting pot of cultures and superstitions that had become New Orleans Voodoo, nearly a religion in its own right.

But Dede had no personal shrines to the loa; only the huge over decorated tables in her parlor for public viewings. She performed ceremonies and pushed various Vodou luck charms on those around her (she never let Demetrius leave the house without a liberal application of lemony Van Van oil on his pulse points,) but Demetrius had never seen her use them herself. Though she often used Vodou to explain situations, tell stories, or justify her opinions, Demetrius often wondered if Mama Dede's involvement with the religion had sprung from profit and, over the years, had developed into a weak superstition, like an excommunicated Catholic who still crosses himself when he feels threatened.

For Demetrius, Vodou was a unique religion, but all religion was simple superstition at its core and therefore became trite and dull very quickly. He found it interesting that the loa were represented by symbols and images of Catholic saints, a trait that Dede told him had sprung from Haitian history, when the French colonized the island and attempted to stamp out Vodou in favor of Catholicism. He found most followers of Vodou considered themselves devout Catholics, as Mama Dede did. He also found it interesting that those who practiced Vodou claimed to barter and even argue with their deities, rather than simply pray to them and wait for a sign from the heavens. The loa were far more involved spirits than the detached, omniscient God of Abrahamic mythology. But even its uniqueness came from the same fears and desires from which all religion sprung; the desire for control over the uncontrollable aspects of life, the fear of death and the unknown; and the novelty of Vodou became as dull as garden-variety Christianity. Still, he found himself in the parlor more often than not when Dede opened it for business, listening to the requests of clients ready to empty their wallets for the illusion of control in love or business or what have you. Their desire for that illusion, desire which drove them far past any logical thought, was fascinating to him. Today, however, with his pounding head and scratched arms, their incessant need for control would only be irritating and juvenile. Today, they were nothing but chattering roadblocks who stood between him and a cup of black coffee from the café down the street.

He had expected the parlor to be abuzz with curious tourists. He only saw Mama Dede, however, her thin frame wrapped in a loose cotton dress, chatting with a couple of regular clients beside one of her large shrines, the one with the eerie portrait of the Virgin Mary with scratches running down her face. Demetrius often saw Dede show that particular shrine to prostitutes and pregnant women, selling special oils or showing off the beautifully curved dagger that lay in the center of the table. Demetrius found himself staring at the portrait frequently, with the Virgin Mary's long, weary face staring off into the distance as she cradled baby Jesus, whom in this painting looked more like a miniature man than an infant. There were two long scratch marks on her right cheek, a feature that didn't fit with the serenity of the work of art.

He caught Mama Dede's gaze, her tawny green eyes looking him up and down before continuing with her conversation. Dede's expression spoke just as loudly as her voice; he knew then that he looked as bad as he felt. He nodded at her and headed past the shelves and shrines for the door. Incense burned on one of the shrines and the stench turned his stomach. But no sooner had he quickened his pace than the sight of a girl standing near a white linen shrine stopped him in his tracks.

He knew immediately that she came from a privileged place in life, standing in the front room with her pale arms crossed over a designer sundress. She ran her fingers along the great white snake statue on the table, perusing the shrine as if she were in a boutique in the French Quarter rather than an old woman's house in the lower Ninth Ward. The fact that she was there at all, alone, pointed to a callous curiosity that only children of money are afforded. Something about her stopped his heart in his chest. He couldn't pinpoint it. It was as if the sight of her wavy brown hair curling down her back made the world stop. Her eyes, large and brown and bored, met his. She gave him a nervous little smile as she studied his mask, his dark attire, the long undercut he had just given himself a few weeks before.

"Do you work here?" she asked. She had a voice that was rich but soft with youth, soft like the gentle slopes of her curves beneath her dress. She couldn't have been older than seventeen.

Demetrius could not speak. Some emotion left him dumbstruck, something overwhelming like fear but with a longing ache in his chest. He was not an idiot. He didn't believe in trite notions like love at first sight. His reaction toward seeing this girl had to be something else. Perhaps she looked like someone from the past he couldn't remember, someone he had loved enough for his heart to burst in his chest. The idea didn't slow his racing pulse.

"I live here," he finally managed to say.

A smile from her again, a genuine smile he hadn't earned from their interaction.

"You look like you had a long night," she said. She looked him up and down. "Why do you dress like that?"

Her blunt attitude stunned him, and it shouldn't have. He had deduced that she was a child of wealth, and they were notorious for never having learned manners. Nothing about her tone suggested judgment or distaste. She looked at him with genuine curiosity, like a small child. When people he had known finally got around to asking him why he dressed the way he did, he normally responded with something cryptic or clever, depending on what he wanted from them. He surprised himself this time by responding with the truth.

"I don't know," he said. "I've always dressed like this."

He had no control over this situation. No control over what came out of his mouth. He wasn't used to this. It terrified him.

The girl nodded as if his gibberish had made perfect sense. "It suits you," she said. "I couldn't see you in anything else."

A response he couldn't have predicted, one a stranger shouldn't have said. Demetrius wondered for a moment if he were dreaming, or if this was a bizarre hallucination like the one that had brought him to Dede's doorstep. He felt the world shift, felt like he barely clung to the ledge of sanity. Was this real? How could he tell?

"Can you tell me about this god?" the girl pointed at the snake statue on the table. "Is he evil?"

She folded her arms over her chest, more tightly than people normally do. She was nearly hugging herself. Demetrius would have taken this to be discomfort but nothing else in her manner suggested anything but the casual curiosity of the easily bored. The gesture made her appear even younger, though she spoke with the confidence a woman much older.

"The loa aren't gods, they're more like spirits. None of them are good or evil." He heard Dede's words coming out of his mouth, words he'd never paid attention to but had heard often enough to absorb. He gestured to the snake statue. "Damballah is the most respected."

The girl looked at the shrine. It was decorated with crystal eggs and champagne flutes. A white chicken egg, which Demetrius knew Dede had rubbed in a sweet smelling cologne called Pompeii Lotion, sat on top of a mound of flour on a crystal dish in the center of the shrine. The girl touched the egg gingerly and brought her fingers to her face to smell the cologne.

"What does he do?" she asked, rubbing her fingers together and wiping them on her sundress. Demetrius followed her every gesture. Words failed him.

"I don't know," he said.

She laughed, a musical sound that was loud enough to surprise him. Her brown eyes, almost too large for her oval face, studied him as if he were part of the shrine. He met her gaze and his headache melted away as if it had never been. Again he felt his pulse jump, a burst of adrenaline, as if his body wanted to run. But he remained, staring into those large liquid eyes, and an inexplicable calm followed, a strange…peace. He could think of no more appropriate word. He stared at the girl and he had no questions haunting him, no pain from the wounds on his face. He knew then that she couldn't have been real. She had to be a hallucination, some figure from his past from the annals of his mind that he couldn't access with his severed memory. He wondered if Mama Dede were actually in the room with him, standing there with her regulars, watching him talk to no one in front of the shrine. He wondered if he were even in the parlor at all, or if he was unconscious somewhere, waiting to wake up. He didn't want to. He wanted to remain in this vision with this girl, forever asleep like Endymion, who dreamt for all eternity that he held the moon in his arms.

The hand on his arm was very real, with Mama Dede's unmistakable grip.

"Miss Belaire," she said to the girl in her alto voice. "You're a ways from home. What can I do for you?"

Demetrius had a moment of disorientation. Dede was certainly real, and she had addressed the girl by a name he didn't know. He stood in stunned silence as Mama Dede made small talk with the woman he had thought was a hallucination. Slowly the world filled in again; the stench of the incense, the throbbing pain in his head. The young woman remained, flesh and blood, the swell of her breasts rising and falling with every breath she took.

"Demetrius," Mama Dede put a hand on his arm. "This is Dia Belaire."

The girl extended a smooth white hand to him. Demetrius hesitated to touch her. Just looking at her had caused him to question reality. But when he took her hand, he felt soft, cool skin pressing against his, and the earth did not crumble.

"Demetrius," she said. The name sounded so sweet coming from her. "Like in that Shakespeare play?"

Demetrius saw Dede tense out of the corner of his eye. He was stunned as well.

"*A Midsummer Night's Dream*," he said.

He glanced at Dede. She remained focused on Dia, a slight crease forming between her brows.

Dia grinned. "That's the one. We read it in class last year. I liked it."

Her smile made him smile. The movement hurt his face. He didn't care.

Dia and Mama Dede chatted a bit more and Demetrius faded in and out of the conversation, his chest tightening every time she met his eyes. He stared at her, watching her hair bounce with every movement she made, her arms folded like a shield despite her apparent comfort in the parlor. What was it about her that made him ache and made him feel so tranquil at the same time? She wasn't a vision of his past, but she had to at least resemble someone from it. Nothing else made any sense. He watched her and a slow, sick fear washed over him. He had fled the hospital in Toledo, fled before the pretty nurse he had knocked over could give him his name. He had fled to a bus station so fast that he hadn't even changed out of his hospital gown, all from the same fear he was experiencing now, fear of remembering. Did he want to remember?

All he knew was that when Dia left with an appointment for a lave tet was that he had to see her again.

The rest of the day passed in a blur for Demetrius. He could think of nothing but the girl in the parlor. Nothing else mattered. He saw her face on every passerby, heard her wild laughter in every bar, even the dilapidated strip club he visited later in the night. He ran through their encounter over and over in his mind, pouring over every detail, trying to pinpoint what *exactly* about her had so shaken him. She was a splinter in his brain.

Mama Dede was in the kitchen when he returned home with two glasses of whiskey beside her on the counter. Demetrius studied the woman who had taken him in. He and Dede often drank together, passing the bottle around on the porch. The last time she had poured a glass for him, she had had a frank talk with him about his living without an identity. The next day, she had a birth certificate and a social security card with the name *Demetrius Heart*. She refused to tell him how she had gotten them. He despised the saccharine surname she had given him but hadn't dared question her.

Dede handed him his glass. If she was drunk already, she gave no indication, not that she ever did. Demetrius often found himself nearly passing out while drinking with Dede, and she remained sitting in her rocking chair on the porch, humming softly.

Dede clinked her glass with his and poured a small amount onto the sticky floor before draining her drink. Demetrius turned his back, shifted his mask, and followed suit. He'd never asked her for whom she poured out her liquor, and she'd never asked him what had happened to his face. They respected one another's secrets.

Demetrius savored the slow burn of the whiskey in his throat and waited. He knew why the glasses were out for him tonight. However, he didn't know what she wanted to say. Dede was not a predictable woman. He looked at her, studied her profile, her freckled skin stretched over her bones, her white hair tied back in a bun. Many of her clients thought she was Haitian or African but Dede's ethnicity was so obscure that she could have been African or Mexican or

Italian or Native American, anything that served the trade she chose. Age had dulled her skin color to a nondescript brown. Though her hair was coarse and wiry now, it could have been smooth and glossy in her youth, or wild and untamable. There was no way to tell, and he would never ask. Demetrius enjoyed her obscurity in an era where ethnic labels defined so much of a person's identity.

"Do you know why you got the last name Heart?" she asked without looking at him.

Demetrius poured them another glass, a sinking feeling in his stomach. "No."

Dede's tawny green eyes remained fixed on the door to the parlor. She took a slow sip of her whiskey and the silence stretched.

"Because your heart's what's wrong with you," she said finally, in that cold, matter of fact way she spoke with her clients about their problems. "You're heartsick. Desire controls everything you do. You want what you want and you take it. I'd bet my left tit a woman landed you in that hospital bed."

Demetrius was stunned. Dede's eyes held a foreign ferocity when they met his. She pointed a finger at him like a scolding mother.

"You leave that girl alone, boy," she ordered, swigging her whiskey. "I seen you looking at her like there's nothing else in the world. But I know what's in you, and *you* know what's in you. Ain't a hooker in New Orleans you haven't scared shitless. You'll destroy that poor child."

Demetrius took a step back. He couldn't help it. Her words struck him like a slap in the face. He remembered the blood under his fingernails from earlier that day, the scratches on his arms. He didn't remember what had happened that night but he remembered nights that were probably identical. He was consumed by the insatiable need to see blood on naked flesh; to dominate, overpower, and terrorize. To learn that Mama Dede knew about it was devastating. He should have known. Half of Dede's clients were working girls, buying Follow Me Boy oil and requesting this or that ritual for luck or protection from the law. He should have known that word would get back to her.

Dede was watching him, waiting. He could think of nothing to say. She had shocked him, and he hadn't been able to mask his emotions. She sighed and shook her head.

"She needs you," Dede's words surprised him. "She'll be back here, and I seen her looking at you the same way you was looking at her. Nothing I say is gonna keep you apart. But don't you touch her, boy. She's not for what's in you. You be a brother to her and nothing else. You understand?"

Demetrius' throat was dry. Dede had never spoken to him that way before. Dia's smile loomed large in his mind, and the peace he felt when they had spoken was slipping away.

"Yes," he said finally. He turned his back on Dede to finish off his whiskey. The burn of alcohol felt like nothing now.

He and Mama Dede sat on the porch that night and drank in silence.

Chapter 9

Chloe had no idea how much time had passed since she had woken in the dreaded bedroom. She had come to in the cage, her wrists bound with handcuffs that were attached to a short chain wrapped around a bar on the cage door.

In those first hours Chloe screamed, struggled to sit up in the tiny cage, tried to turn herself so she could kick at the door but her bound arms forbade even twisting into a different position. She thought she would go insane if she didn't stretch her legs, if she didn't sit up. She would die if she had to remain crouched on her stomach or her side, with her knees drawn to her chest, hour after hour.

Three had returned for the first time just as Chloe's hunger pangs had become impossible to ignore. She had come in with a bottle of water and a bowl of warm soup broth, the first food Chloe had seen since she had been taken. The little slave had thrust the food through the bars, silent and wide-eyed, and she jumped at every movement Chloe made. Her fear stung Chloe. She had threatened the girl and abandoned her, this helpless teen who was as trapped as Chloe was.

"I'm so sorry," Chloe had whispered. Three had just skittered away once she had set the food down. The broth itself had been a new torment as Chloe struggled to feed herself with her arms bound. She spilled the broth all over the cage floor the first day, an accident that reduced her to a pitiful screaming animal. Three didn't return until the next day, leaving again without a word. Each time she left, the silence grew thicker, the isolation more maddening.

After a while, Chloe was hollow. Her thoughts were a dull hum, her growing hunger nothing but a gnat buzzing by her ear. Her escape attempt seemed a distant memory, despite the bruises on her skin and the scab under her chin from her fall. She didn't remember having soiled herself again. She did not cry in shame when she realized she had. She was a shell, a forgotten trinket on a shelf, gathering dust. When she slept, she dreamt of whirling rain, of firm lips against hers, of lilac bushes and branches of ripe fruit dangling just out of reach.

The bedroom door beeped open, just as Chloe's hunger swelled, as if Demetrius could sense when Chloe began to starve every day and knew just when to send Three to her.

Today, however, Chloe didn't hear Three's bare footsteps. She heard voices. Two beautiful young women and a tall blonde man with a dark smirk came through the doorway with Three scurrying behind them, attached to a leash in the man's hand.

The women approached the cage, and Chloe froze like a cornered animal, unsure of what to do. She looked at the women, whose presence made her skin crawl. Their identical black eyes seemed huge as they studied Chloe through purple and green bangs, their bright red lips curled into smirks. She recognized them as the twins she had seen with Demetrius at the Oryx. She couldn't fathom what they were doing here. Right then she realized what made them so strange to her; they were the first women she had seen in this place who weren't naked and collared. They wore jeans and skin tight blouses, casual clothing Chloe could have seen anyone wear on the streets of the outside world. Their smiles frightened her more than anything else. She whimpered and curled her knees into her chest.

"So this is going to be the new Model Slave?" the man behind them said with a short laugh. "Doesn't look like much."

The twin with the green hair nodded as her sister pulled a key from her pocket.

"She's a mess right now," she purred. "Aren't you, little girl?"

Chloe felt a tug at the cage door. She jerked her wrists back, the handcuffs digging into her skin. She couldn't get her mouth to work.

No! She cried in her head, *Don't touch me. Get away from me!*

"Oh, hush," the purple-haired sister chided, unlocking the chain from the cage and tugging at Chloe's cuffs, urging her toward the open door. "Don't you want to get out of that cage?"

Chloe pulled weakly at the chain and tried to scoot farther back. She wanted out, but the twins were terrifying. The man leading Three around on a leash was terrifying. Whatever their purpose for being here, it couldn't end well for her. The green-haired twin shook her head with a smile.

"You'd better learn to cooperate, slave," she said with a stern tone that didn't match her smile, "or pretty soon you'll have more than a little scratch on your chin." She stood and turned to the man behind her. "Rodney?"

The man, Rodney, handed over Three's leash and ambled up to the cage with a theatrical crack of his knuckles. Chloe shook her head wildly, her pulse sprinting in her veins.

"No," she said, her first word in days, raw and rough. "No!"

The man grinned, crouching in front of the cage door.

"Oh, yeah, you're coming out of there, baby," he sneered. One of the twins handed him the chain attached to Chloe's cuffs and rose to stand beside her sister. Rodney jerked the chain forward and Chloe bucked toward him.

"No!" Chloe screamed again. "No, no, no, no!"

She was too weak to put up a fight; every inch of her body protested the moment she resisted. Rodney pulled her across the filthy cage floor with little trouble. The closer she came to him, the more she panicked. Compared to Demetrius, Rodney looked perfectly normal. He had no exotic adornments, a square jaw, and a blonde crew cut. He grinned at Chloe like a jack-o-lantern in November, worn and comical. His dark blue eyes were framed with the beginnings of crow's feet. If Chloe had seen him walking down the street, she wouldn't have given him a second glance. But here, as he hauled her starved body from the cage, plucking her out by the hair like a puppy by the scruff, he was as frightening as the Devil himself.

"Come on, baby," he said, pulling her onto her feet. "Time for you to learn the ropes."

The twins approached her. Rodney's grip on Chloe's hair kept her knees from buckling in panic. The sound of the twins' high heels clicking across the floor deafened her.

"At Attention, slave," the purple-haired twin ordered. Her cold tone made Chloe flinch. She didn't know what to do, what the woman meant. She couldn't think. All she knew was her racing heart, her weak limbs, the hunger that chewed holes in her stomach. The green-haired twin reached out and stroked Chloe's cheek with her fingertips. Chloe trembled, even her breath shaking.

"She's not even broken yet, Faith," said the green-haired twin. "She doesn't know anything." She smiled again. Chloe stared at her smooth red lips, their perfect cupid's bow almost childlike. She couldn't understand how something could look so innocent and so cruel at once. "I'm Charity, and that's Faith. Demetrius is your Master, and while you're here, we are your Mistresses. Demetrius is very upset with you."

A strange combination of emotions jabbed at Chloe's chest. Her first reaction was defiance. Why would she care if she had upset the man who stole her away, starved her, and planned to enslave her? The thought of Demetrius' anger sparked fear, yet there was an edge of shame that she could not deny or understand. She had no time to process her feelings, not with these strangers studying her as if she were in a zoo exhibit.

"We're here to clean you up," said Charity.

"And to teach you a lesson," her sister, Faith, chimed in. "You might be Demetrius' favorite right now, but even favorites have to get with the program."

Favorite? Chloe felt like laughing and bursting into tears all at once. The insanity of her situation threatened to consume her. Why couldn't she bring herself to speak? To fight? Had she been locked in the cage for so long that she had truly become an animal?

Rodney jerked the chain on the cuffs around her wrists. Chloe stumbled. Her legs quivered like a baby calf standing up for the first time. Her limbs were awkward and weak from disuse, her muscles aching even as she stood still.

"Move," Rodney ordered with a sneer. "You wanna try to yank the chain out of *my* hands?"

The words struck her like a blow. She looked at Three, so dutifully trotting behind Faith and Charity as the group moved to the suite bathroom. Chloe had failed in her escape attempt, and it had cost her dearly. Had it also cost Three?

Rodney led Chloe to the shower, "Get on your knees, baby," he said. "We're gonna hose you down while Three draws you a nice bath."

He took the base of Chloe's neck and pushed, forcing her onto her knees. Chloe despised her own weak limbs. Three went to work filling the bath with water. The tub was immense, large enough for three or four people. Three worked frantically. The twins prodded her with a slap or a pinch at their leisure, as if it were a game.

Rodney turned on the showerhead and ice cold water struck Chloe's bare skin. She yelped and retreated from the stream. Rodney yanked her chain so hard that the cuffs bit into her wrists.

"Stop whining," he said. "It'll warm up soon."

Chloe gritted her teeth as Rodney shot cold water over her back and chest. He stared at her with the brashness of a teenaged boy, his gaze creeping down her body. She shielded her chest from his stare and he forced her to lower her arms just as quickly with a pull of the chain. Exposed, the only escape was to turn her face away. The water warmed up and became more bearable. Grime slipped away from her skin in dull, strained rivulets. Chloe remained taut and tense. She could not give into the water's comfort with Rodney's leering presence or the twins hovering around Three, chatting casually with one another as the frail girl filled the bath with sweet-smelling foam. Chloe couldn't understand the twins. Charity called them her Mistresses, like Demetrius was her Master. What did that mean for her?

Charity strolled over to the open shower. Chloe followed the line of her long legs. She and Faith were young, maybe even Chloe's age. When she saw them at the Oryx, they looked like any other club goer in that scene; exotic faces in a sea of exotic people. She could never have imagined they were involved in something like this.

"Demetrius wants us to punish you," said Charity.

Chloe swallowed hard. She thought about the slave she had seen tied to the wooden Saint Andrew's cross, dripping with rain. Was keeping her locked in a cage for days not punishment enough?

"I can't take any more," she whispered.

Rodney's hand cut across her cheek. Pain burst like fireworks behind her eyes. Chloe cried out and recoiled as far as the chain would allow.

"What did I tell you about talking?" he snapped.

"Talk again and we'll have to gag you," Charity warned.

Chloe bowed her head, her cheek stinging. She couldn't take this. She couldn't. She felt Charity's eyes on her, studying her. Faith came to stand beside her sister and slid an arm around Charity's waist.

"She's beautiful," she muttered, "but not as beautiful as some of the others we have downstairs."

Chloe felt tears swell. Faith spoke as if Chloe were a dog incapable of understanding her. Rodney shut off the shower. Chloe remained on her knees, her short hair dripping. She was clean but what did that matter? She was still starving, still frail, still captive.

Charity took the chain from Rodney, who joined Three at the bath tub. She knelt in front of Chloe, tilting her chin up with her fingertips. Again, a voice screamed in Chloe's head: *Fight! Hit her! Run!* But what was the point? She was too weak to fight off three captors, too weak to run. She was certain they had changed the code on the door. She met Charity's eyes, black and empty, a doll's gaze.

"She's so spoiled. The usual punishment for slaves who try to escape is total isolation and starvation."

"And a few hours alone with Demetrius for *reconditioning*," said Faith, with a glint in her eye that made Chloe's stomach turn. The twins' words nauseated her.

"He has a special punishment designed for you, little girl," said Charity. She and Faith stood beside her, facing Rodney and Three.

"Don't move," Faith warned, "or we'll make it worse for her."

Chloe frowned. For her?

"Look at Three," said Charity. "Demetrius told us about your little rescue attempt in the backyard."

"You're a little hero," said Faith. She drummed her fingers along Chloe's scalp. Chloe flinched, too afraid to jerk back. "Demetrius said that this would be the most effective punishment for you."

Charity shook her head, "I still say a beating would do her better."

"The boss is allowed to have a soft spot for a slave every once in a while," said Faith.

"Demetrius doesn't *have* soft spots." Rodney's voice brought Chloe's attention back to Three. She stood beside the bath, her hands behind her back, head lowered. Her chest shivered with staggered breath. She was frightened, and Chloe didn't understand.

Charity motioned to Rodney, "Go ahead."

Rodney tossed his shoulders, grabbed Three by the hair, and thrust her head into the bath water.

Chloe gasped. She jolted into motion, struggling to stand. Faith and Charity held her down by the shoulders.

"Don't move, slave," Faith snapped. "Every move you make, we'll add a minute to her punishment."

Rodney lifted Three's head from the water. The girl gasped, retching. She barely took a breath before Rodney plunged her back into the bath. Chloe felt as if her heart would explode. Three's arms twitched but her hands remained clasped behind her back. Rodney held her under until Chloe was certain she would drown. He lifted her up again, drowned her again, lifted her up, until her frail cries faded, and only Chloe's remained. Tears coursed down her face, and she screamed, screamed because she could do nothing, because this was her fault.

"Look at her!" Charity sneered over the sound of gasping and splashing water. "Look what you did to her."

Chloe felt the twins' hands on her, impossibly smooth and soft, stroking her shoulders, her neck, as they watched Three struggle. Chloe fought the urge to recoil, yet her skin awoke under their touch after so much time without contact. Why did they caress her? She couldn't bear it.

Three's torture stretched for an eternity, almost hypnotic in how methodical it was; submerge, struggle, lift for a single breath, submerge, struggle…Chloe witnessed every agonizing minute. Only when Three's knees buckled did Rodney stop. He scooped her limp form into his arms as if she were a sleeping child and planted a kiss on her cheek.

"Good girl!" he said over her ragged breath.

Chloe felt as if she had been drowned herself. Her limbs were heavy, as if filled with sand, her chest heaving with sobs. She couldn't stop staring at Three's fluttering eyelids, her pink face. Charity was right. This was her fault. She despised Demetrius for punishing someone else for her escape. If he had only punished Chloe herself…but that was the point, wasn't it? He had known what she could take and what would break her from the moment they met eyes, it seemed. How could she fight someone who knew her weaknesses before she did?

"Why?" Chloe whispered. "Why?"

Charity shushed her gently, stroking her hair, "Because your Master desires it, little girl."

Her words broke something in Chloe, something deep inside that she had been clinging to. Now she was adrift, and there was nothing to anchor her to the world outside of this room, this house. She stared at Three again, cradled in Rodney's arms as he stroked her with the hands that had held her underwater only moments ago. Chloe's mind was quiet when the twins urged her to her feet and eased her into the bath. They washed her with swift gliding hands, exploring every inch of her body. She flinched when they pinched her nipples, and her tears returned when Faith's fingers found their way to her sex, spreading it wide, penetrating, searching. Chloe floated outside of herself, watching Faith and Charity assault her body like she had watched Three's punishment; her horror tempered by a thick fog of distance.

Faith and Charity toweled her off and led her back into the bedroom. She knelt by the cage as instructed. Though she didn't understand the numbness that had taken over her body, she found it strangely comforting. At the very least, it was a reprieve from the fear and pain.

Three and Rodney filed in behind the twins. Three set down a bucket of hot, soapy water and a sponge. She was pale, shaking, still unsteady.

"Like I said," Charity began, "Demetrius is very disappointed in you. He's spoiled you so far, but he's very fickle. Soon he might not think you're worth the effort."

A sharper sting in Chloe's chest. Shame crept along the edge of blissful numbness.

"If he loses interest," said Faith, "We'll have to get rid of you."

Chloe's stomach lurched through the haze. Faith knelt in front of her, stroking her hair with a gentleness Chloe didn't trust. Her black eyes were so empty, so blank.

"If you don't want to be a pile of ashes in the back woods," she said, "clean your cage, lock yourself in, and hope he comes for you."

Faith rose and the group filed out, the twins' heels clicking. The door closed with a beep.

Chloe sat on her knees, alone. She was unchained save for the handcuffs, yet somehow she felt more trapped than she had in the cage. She stared at the wall where the cameras had to be. Demetrius had been infuriated in the storm, but...she felt the ghost of his lips against hers, his tongue penetrating her mouth. Was he truly ready to give up on her, to kill her as Faith had insinuated? Her words had cut through Chloe's numbness. Maybe it had just been a threat. But was that how she wanted to die? The thought of being broken and brutalized like Three and the bound slave in the yard was unbearable. But she would be alive. Her father's face floated in her mind's eye. As long as she was alive, she had hope. Another opportunity for escape would have to come eventually. She would have to be ready for it. And next time she could not hurt anyone. Seeing Three punished for her escape…that couldn't happen again.

Chloe took the sponge on the floor beside her and soaked it in soapy water. Hunger swelled in her stomach. To be ready for escape, she had to eat. She had to make Demetrius trust her, as he trusted Three, to give her the freedom to open doors and go about unsupervised. Outwardly, she had to comply. She opened the cage and began to hum *La Vie en Rose*, the lullaby her mother had sung to her until the day she died. It would be her anchor to sanity, her reminder that she had a life outside of this place.

Chloe scrubbed the cage floor clean, locked herself in the cage, and waited.

Chapter 10

Demetrius trudged up the stairs, balancing a water bottle and a bowl of fruit in each hand. His legs were stiff from hours on his feet at the Oryx. It was a successful night as always this time of year, though he had been off his game, unable to keep his mind off what awaited him in the suite.

He hesitated at the top of the staircase, his finger hovering over the keypad on the suite door. His heart was pounding. Why? How many years had he been doing this? How many women had he broken? His method was canon at this point. He could train a slave in his sleep. Demetrius mulled this over. Perhaps that was exactly what he had been doing for the past few seasons; sleepwalking through the all-too-predictable patterns: resistance, struggle, breaking, training, success. He fingered the gunmetal studs on his mask. Was he ready to wake up? What would that mean for him, to care again? Was it even a possibility, or was he beyond his old passion, as he hoped?

She was on the other side of this door, and he stood dumbstruck like some anxious novice. He steeled himself and punched in the new code: 6463. It was the first time he had had to change the code mid-year.

The door opened, and there she was. Chloe Madeleine Leroux, the trembling girl for whom he had taken the biggest risk of his career. The girl he had kissed, bare-faced and exposed in the backyard. The beeping lock must have woken her; she was groggy, her eyes a little puffy. She was in the cage, though the door had not been locked. He knew the twins had left her to clean the cage. It looked spotless, and the bucket was a few feet away. Demetrius glanced at the room. She had slept in the cage despite having access to the bed. Nothing had been moved or destroyed in an attempt to escape again. It looked like his punishment for her had worked, and she had moved on to the next stage of her captivity. Many slaves broke immediately under starvation and isolation alone, though most--including Chloe, he suspected--moved to a state of false compliance, where they "played the game" physically, but still entertained plans for escape or resistance.

"Slave," said Demetrius, "on your knees before me."

Hesitation and fear in those wide doe eyes, also a hunger that wasn't for the fruit she hadn't yet noticed. She drank in his image as if the sight of him could quench the thirst she suffered. He still wore his clothes from the Oryx, tight black pants tucked into studded boots and a form-fitting snap vest, all coated in talcum powder for his popular dusty look. She looked as awestruck as she had the night he had first seen her before she remembered herself and crawled out of the cage. He smiled. He would have to teach her not to look at him without permission eventually. For now he enjoyed how his skin warmed under her candid stare.

She sat on her knees a safe distance away from him, still relatively close to the cage, as if she felt it was a place of safety. She hugged her arms to her chest and her knees were locked together. She peeked at him through the fall of her short hair. Oh, yes, she was still frightened. His breath quickened.

"Bring your hands to the base of your neck," he said. She hesitated again.

"Do it," he ordered, "or I'll cuff them behind your back."

She crumbled under the authority in his voice, raising her arms into the proper position. She would break easily, yet her predictability didn't bore him. Yet.

"Spread your knees wide. Wider."

He drank her in, finally able to study her nude body without distraction. Her pale skin flushed in shame from being exposed. She was trembling, her rose-pink nipples hard, legs tense. The briefest glimpse of her sex stopped his breath, just a hint of delicate pink folds between her spread knees.

"Good girl," his voice was softer than he wanted it to be.

He came toward her and she tensed immediately, her back ramrod straight. He smiled to himself and walked past her, setting the bowl of fruit on top of the cage. He took his time, savoring the tension in her limbs. He pulled a small flogger out of his pocket, a nasty little device with a braided leather handle and a handful of thin rubber tubing around twelve inches long. It was designed for maximum sting, the perfect jolt with which to begin training. He did a slow circle around Chloe, resisting the urge to run his fingers through her hair. She was tense as a piano string with her toes curled beneath her feet as if she was prepared to spring up at any moment. He had to touch her, he couldn't help it. He ran his finger along the back of her shoulders. Gooseflesh sprung up along her skin despite her flinch. Touching her shocked his senses like a bolt of electricity. Oh, he wanted to rip her from her knees and fold that sweet flesh against his, to crush her against him and bury his face in her short hair. But why? What was it about her that did this to him? He thought back to her escape in the storm, how quickly his rage had become pure lust at the sight of her soaked with rain, the flash of defiance as she cursed him. He had taken off his mask, barely able to control himself enough to distract her from seeing his face before that kiss. Oh, that kiss…

"I can't…" Chloe's frail whisper brought him back to himself. "I'm so scared."

An infantile plea. She was terrified. Demetrius stepped away from her, back to the cage, and took a mental breath.

"You will not speak again without permission," he said. "Your little moment on the run has made me wonder if you're worth the trouble, *ma chère*. I don't recommend you disappoint me again."

His words had her openly trembling. He forced himself to look at her with a cold eye. She was thinner than she had been when she had first come, a shade paler. Her fear was obvious and yet she remained in position, ready to comply, or at least pretend to. Despite the escape attempt, she was in right on schedule in the breaking process. She was starving, teetering on the edge of dehydration. She was ready.

Demetrius took the flogger in one hand and the bottle of water in the other. He stood before her, letting the silence stretch a moment further. She looked at the floor, quivering softly. The silence bothered her.

"Look at me," he ordered.

She hesitated before complying, pausing at the strip of his torso curtained by the open vest. Those wide hazel eyes met his, her body radiating fear and awe and, savor the thought, desire. Desire, that was it. The majority of slaves he broke over the years were street-hardened women, who had deadened their desire for others out of necessity. He normally had to condition their arousal, eroticize the need to please and obey. But Chloe wore her desire like a neon sign, bright and burning even through her terror. Desire for *him*.

"Answer my questions correctly, obey me, and this is your reward," he said, holding up the water bottle. Chloe caught sight of it and a different sort of desire filled her face.

Demetrius flicked the flogger, just enough to show off the rubber strands, "If you answer incorrectly or you lash out, I will punish you. Do you understand?"

Her pink lips trembled. Her face had paled. Oh, she was so frightened. She could not keep her eyes off that little flogger. But the water, too, held her attention.

"Slave," he brought her attention back to him. "Do you understand?"

Chloe looked at him. Her mental struggle between fear and thirst was naked on her face. She hid absolutely nothing. She finally spoke, her voice so frail, so uncertain.

"I do...yes," she whispered.

Demetrius grinned, the desperation in her voice inflaming him.

"Lesson one, *ma chère*," he said, coming to stand just in front of her. "I am your Master. When I talk to you, you will respond with *Yes, Master* or *No, Master. Comprenez-vous?*"

A film of tears made her eyes glisten.

"Yes, Master."

His heart gave an unexpected jolt.

"Say it again," he said, his voice laced with something dangerously close to supplication.

Chloe's gaze dropped to the floor. Her chest quivered with a shaky breath.

"Yes, Master," she murmured.

Demetrius closed his eyes, tilting his head back. Those sweet words washed over him like a burst of sunlight.

"Oh, that," he purred. "That is perfect."

He had to get ahold of himself. He felt like the undisciplined hedonist he had been a decade ago on the streets of New Orleans. He tilted her chin up with the edge of the flogger, just a shade roughly.

"Good girl," he said. He nudged the bottle between her lips and gave her a small sip. She slurped without modesty, nearly lurching forward to retrieve the water when he pulled away. He tried not to focus on the desperate little sigh that escaped her slick mouth.

"Now," he said. "Who are you?"

Chloe frowned. She didn't understand, but she wasn't supposed to.

"Answer, slave," he ordered. Oh, that got her trembling. She was already so receptive to the change in his voice. A slave so accommodating to a Master's moods so soon in training was a rare find indeed.

"Who are you?" he repeated.

"I..." her voice was barely a whisper. "I'm...Chloe Leroux."

So predictable, even a novelty like Chloe.

"Incorrect."

He struck her left breast with the flogger, a solid hit, though not full strength. Chloe shrieked, breaking form immediately and curling into herself. Her breast bloomed pink. Each rubber cord left a bright red streak on her white, white skin. Demetrius was hard so quickly it hurt. He clenched his jaw against the rush of heat.

"Stay in position, slave," his voice was rougher than he wanted it to be. He assessed her response. She obeyed his command. Tears, trembling, one nervous glance toward the door. Had she the strength, she would run before she would fight. That was good to know. Her chest heaved, jolting those ripe round breasts. Demetrius sucked in a breath through gritted teeth, uncomfortably firm against his zipper. Oh, her skin was a dream. He would have to be careful; she would bleed with very little work. The thought of that skin breaking, of thin streams of blood cutting through all that paleness...

"Chloe is gone, *cheri*. You're in my world now. My *twenty-first* slave of the season. Now, who are you?"

He could see the wheels turning behind those misty eyes. He had given her the answer outright the night he had brought her to the Manor; *"After this night, you are Twenty-One, and you are my slave"*; but she may not have remembered that moment during such a chaotic period. Still, he knew from the security cameras that she has spoken with Three and learned her name, and the slave on her knees before him was a clever one.

"I'm…" she finally murmured, "I'm Twenty-One?"

The slightest lift at the end, questioning. He lingered for a hair too long, relishing in her tension as she waited for reward or punishment.

"Good girl," he said, bringing the water to her lips. He let her drink deeply this time. He was spoiling her already, all because he couldn't stop watching her delicate little throat undulate with every swallow. He pulled the bottle away abruptly and rose back to his full height. There was so little distance between them. She was close enough to grab the back of her head and force her to take him into her mouth.

He shivered.

"And *what* are you, Twenty-One?" his voice was a bit breathless. It didn't seem to matter. Teasing her thirst had engaged her. She knew the answer, she had figured out the game quickly, but there was caution in her. Oh, yes, she held on so tightly to her hope of escape that she was afraid to even say it.

"I'm a slave."

The last word was barely a whisper but he would allow it. She was definitely deep into false compliance, or so she believed. He had been in the business long enough to understand that false compliance was more sincere than a slave realized.

"What is your purpose?"

A harder question, one he knew she couldn't deduce. She quivered, her wide eyes pleading. He stared back at her, a steady gaze, assuring her that he would give her no help. He squeezed the flogger until the leather creaked beneath his fingers. The miniscule sound turned her a shade paler. Ah, the old dance, so predictable, yet the sight of Chloe's fear set him ablaze, and it was all he could do not to drop the game and drag her to the bed that was so close by. Not yet. Not yet.

She had not answered. He was about to turn his wrist for her second punishment when she babbled a panicked reply.

""You!" her word was more of a plea than a statement. "You are my purpose…Master."

You are my purpose. Why did that reply echo through his bones? Why did he feel it like a chord struck on his spine?

He had been silent for too long.

"No," he said. "Close, *ma chère*, so close. But wrong."

He struck her right breast with the flogger. She yelped, jerking back, then sealed her lips and stayed in position. Demetrius looked at Chloe's pink and shuddering form, and something had changed. He could not specify what, but he felt it. He looked at Chloe, who made him behave so irrationally, who made his body come to life as it hadn't in years, and he knew…she was a piece in a puzzle that he couldn't see.

The thought brought Demetrius back to himself. He felt the ground beneath him again. A thought like that was Mama Dede's voice in his head, the voice of religious falsehood and the delusional concept of fate. He watched the welts form on Chloe's breast. A slave needed training. He could not ruminate on this right now. Perhaps he would later, when his mind was clear, when desire and old superstition weren't fusing and roiling under his skin.

"Your purpose," he said to the whimpering girl, "is to please your Master."

Chloe uttered a sweet little sob, choking on tears, and nodded. Demetrius swept the bowl of water beneath her face.

"What is your purpose, slave?"

Chloe swallowed hard, "To please my Master."

He allowed her to drink.

Demetrius coaxed her through the rest of the mantra that would become her life's meaning, the prayer on the lips of every slave to come into his house. Oh, she was a natural. He only had to punish her once more, though she trembled as if he had beaten her mercilessly. Her breasts bore a bouquet of raised red marks. A hint of sweat played on her features, just enough to give her a natural glow that was beyond intoxicating. She didn't realize how much humiliation became her, or how she would thrive in his care. Perhaps she did feel it, though, how natural it seemed, and that was why he saw such a great struggle in her, the battle between her will and her body. He imagined she had been fighting her own nature all her life, fighting the need to submit, the need to please. A woman willing to relinquish control was not tolerated in today's society, no, no. Chloe's nature wasn't *feminist*, and she would have learned quickly to bury it beneath an independent exterior. But he would break the shell and watch her bloom in his hands, finally given what she needed to blossom.

The water was gone. He had been far too liberal with it. He still had the advantage of hunger; it was written on her face as he reached for the bowl of grapes. He let her focus on the fruit, allowed her need to grow.

"Twenty-One."

She met his eyes immediately, focused on him despite her hunger. He took a moment to drink in her gaze, those hazel eyes so wide, so genuine. To see that stare from beneath him, forcing her to keep his gaze as he rode her…

Not yet. Not yet.

"Who are you?"

"I am Twenty-One," she replied.

"What is your purpose?"

"To please my Master."

No hesitation, no uncertainty in her voice. Her eyes were trained on the grapes. He would easily be able to turn her desire to him in a few sessions. Desire was what ultimately drove little Chloe, he could tell already. Oh, she would be perfect. She was perfect.

"Why are you here?" he continued.

Chloe looked down, her lips quivering.

"To become a perfect slave," she whispered.

Ah, there was a pause there, a glimpse of the defiant flame that he hadn't yet extinguished.

"Oh, come on," he teased, grinning. "Answer me like *that* and I'll be convinced that you're *faking.*"

That got her attention. She looked at him with fresh fear draining the color from her cheeks. His grin sharpened. He took a few grapes in his hand and knelt eye-to-eye with the nude girl. She fought to keep his gaze, but her face lost that defiant edge, swallowed by fear and need. Demetrius brushed her hair behind her ear. Her skin was so soft, so incredibly soft. The urge to fold her into himself returned, to press as much of that soft, soft skin against his. It was unbearable.

"Ah, but *this* is real, isn't it?" he held the fruit just beneath her mouth. "You can play pretend all you want, *ma chère*, but you can't fight the hunger."

Demetrius crushed a grape between his fingers and traced her lips with it, coating her mouth in its juices. She crumbled in front of him. Her eyes closed, her wet lips parted in an ecstasy he had seen when he'd held her against the wall at the Oryx that very first night. Oh, those lips…he remembered the way they tasted, slick with rain.

"Convince me," he murmured, pulling the grape away. "Why are you here?"

Chloe made a small sound somewhere between a moan and a sob, a desperate sound. Tears corroded her glowing cheeks.

"To become a perfect slave."

Demetrius opened his palm to her, offering the grapes. "Good."

Chloe did not hesitate a moment before taking the fruit from his hand with her mouth, as if she knew she would be punished if she used her fingers, clever one. Her lips and tongue brushed across his palm. He made a sound low in his throat. He couldn't wait any longer. She had learned her new name, the mantra, and how she was to speak. It was time for exploration, and he could no longer hold himself back from the heat between them. If he didn't take her now, he didn't know what he would do.

X X I

Chloe had just swallowed the last of the grapes when Demetrius clamped a hand on the back of her neck and slid two bare fingers into her mouth.

"Suck."

It happened so fast that Chloe could only react instinctively and close her mouth around them. She sucked, sliding his fingers back and forth between her lips. His skin was cool and had a soft iron taste to them that she hadn't expected. Demetrius tilted his head back.

"Mmm…" he growled. "Oh, yes."

The hair on her arms stood at the sound of his voice, the promise it held. She knew what was going to happen, what he was going to do. She should have been terrified. She had been that first night, when she felt him hard and eager against her. But right now, she found herself running her tongue along the underside of his fingers, rougher than the smooth skin on top, tasting him. She dissolved under his touch, dissolved like she had when he had kissed her. Even now she couldn't think of anything but the heat of his body, so close to her. Again she felt an inexplicable pull toward him, like a magnet, drawing her closer.

Demetrius pulled his fingers out of her mouth. He tilted her chin up toward him, and those grey eyes froze the blood in her veins. They seemed distant, or maybe not. Were it not for the mask, she might have been better able to understand his expression. He had seemed so cold and meticulous to her so far today, yet she sensed tension in him, as if he would burst from his skin. His gaze on her made her tremble. She didn't know what to expect. The fruit and water were gone. Only the two of them remained.

Demetrius slid his fingers down her neck, still wet from her mouth. He drew a hot, wet trail down her collarbone, between her breasts, down the smooth plane of her stomach. Chloe moaned through sealed lips despite herself. He brushed the mound of her sex and the world narrowed to the pinpoint of his long fingers on tender flesh. He paused a moment, lingering just over the edge of her crease before sliding a finger over the folds of her sex. A shockwave rippled through Chloe, a burst of sensation that she didn't want, didn't know how to handle. His touch severed the connection of her mind and body. Her legs opened wider as if his finger were a key opening a lock, and he slid up and down her sex.

"Perfect," he said. "Already so wet."

Chloe bloomed beneath Demetrius' expert hand. He seemed to know exactly how to touch her, as if her body were a code easily cracked. Every slow circle around her apex, every pressured stroke buried her fear in primal longing. He pulled away from her sex and she made a small sound in protest before she could stop herself. Demetrius chuckled.

"Selfish, aren't we?" he said, making her flush in shame. "But eager. Eagerness is very good, *ma chère*. It is much harder to train a slave to want than to teach them to control their desires."

Chloe was ashamed of her body, ashamed of her tears. Demetrius had stripped her of every defense, shown her how weak her resolve had been. Food be damned, her "desires" be damned. She was pathetic. Was there no fight left in her? Did a handful of grapes and experienced fingers buy her soul?

Demetrius took her nipples between his fingers and all thought ceased.

"Ah, these are *very* sensitive, aren't they, to stop your breath like that?"

"Yes, Master." The words came like a breath. Oh, she hated herself in that moment, hated the red hot ache that grew as Demetrius worked her nipples, rolling them with his thumbs in agonizing circles. He stroked her breasts in an almost clinical way, gauging the reactions she just couldn't hide. He slapped her left breast, still raw and throbbing from that nasty rubber tool with which he had punished her. Chloe clenched her jaw to keep from crying out in pain. She felt his gaze on her face. She wouldn't meet it.

Demetrius raked his nails hard across the raised welts on her breast. She screamed for him now. She ripped her arms out of position to shield her chest. Demetrius snatched her throat, his grip firm but not squeezing. Chloe froze nonetheless, too stunned to move.

"Look at me."

The ferocity in his voice made Chloe fear for her life. His eyes were wide, not with the rage she had witnessed during her escape, but something darker, something that frightened her to her core.

"Don't you hold back," he snarled. "When I hurt you, *slave*, I want to hear you scream."

He had switched moods in an instant. He seemed almost as wild as he had been in the storm. He leaned close to her ear and she flinched, expecting violence.

"And when I allow you to come, I want to hear you scream."

He took her left nipple between his fingers and leaned in even closer. He smelled like sweat and talcum powder, and a distant odor of sweet smoke lingered in his clothes.

"Now, what do you say?" he demanded.

Chloe opened her mouth to reply and he pinched her nipple so hard that she could only scream again.

"Yes, Master!" she wailed, writhing from his grip.

"Ah, ah, ah," he chided, squeezing harder. Chloe cried out again. Her breast was ablaze, as if each nerve ending in her had burst, "Don't move away. Don't *ever* move away."

He released her nipple. The hand on her throat was tense, his fingers trembling. Chloe looked at him and found his eyes locked on her aching breast. The sight made her pulse jump. She remembered her mother's stories about her patients in prison; men for whom pleasure and violence were only a blink away from one another, interconnected in their brains. This thought should have terrified her. However, it gave her a strange rush. She had discovered a weak spot in him. Demetrius had stripped her of every ounce of control, of her fate, her body, her food and water. Everything. This was an opportunity to regain some fraction of control, and though it meant violence for her, maybe even death, Chloe could not stop herself. She had to feel a moment of control.

Demetrius reached for her and she flinched, leaning away from his hands. She wouldn't try to be brave now. Her fear was her only power.

"No, no, Twenty-One," Demetrius said, grabbing her wrists. "You were doing so well."

He forced Chloe's arms back in position, hands at her neck. Chloe made a small pain sound even though he hadn't harmed her. Demetrius hesitated, and again Chloe felt tension in his body, saw his wild eyes. Chloe's breath hitched in her chest. The power her reactions held over her self-proclaimed "Master" inflamed her. She gave him wide, fearful eyes and he froze, looming over her, his chest nearly bumping into her chin. He gave her wrist a fast squeeze and she cried out, but he had barely put pressure on her. She had expected him to squeeze her hard, and her cry had been too loud, too much. His eyes crinkled at the corners and Chloe's heart sank.

"Oh, my little thespian," he sneered. "You've just made a *big* mistake."

He grabbed the back of her head and wrenched it back so hard that spots flooded Chloe's vision. She screamed in earnest. His grip was so brutal that she felt as though her neck were bent at an impossible angle. Her throat was stretched taut and she could barely breathe.

Demetrius crushed her against him. His free arm constricted around her waist. She couldn't move, couldn't breathe.

"Do you think this is a game?" Demetrius shouted into her upturned face, his mask doing nothing to muffle the venom in his voice. "Do you?"

Her head shook with the force of his grip, emphasizing every word.

"No, Master!" she cried.

"Are you in control here?"

"No, Master!"

"*Who* is in control here?"

Chloe broke down into sobs. "Oh, God, I'm sorry, please, God-"

"I said, who is in control here?" he bellowed over Chloe's tears. His grip set her scalp in white hot pain.

"You are, Master!" she screamed without dignity. "You are, Demetrius!"

Demetrius stopped, his grip loosening for a moment. In an instant, the rage in his face had softened to something less urgent but no less dangerous. He moaned, a low purr in his throat, and threw his head back. The movement thrust his hips against her, and she felt him hard against her stomach. The sensation cut through Chloe's terror like a blade. Every inch of him shivered like a piano string about to snap.

"Ohhh..." he purred. "Ohhh, no, no. Don't you say my name, *cheri*, no, not you. Oh, *mon Dieu*."

Suddenly Chloe was off the floor, her feet barely dragging along the hardwood. She twisted and struggled and she knew it was no use. Demetrius threw her onto the bed she had never touched and pinned her face-down against the grey bedding with his own weight. He traced a hand down her spine and, to Chloe's horror, spread her buttocks wide. She felt his fingers creep close to her anus. She clutched the blanket, choking down panic.

"Untouched," Demetrius' voice had taken on a cruel edge. "What a *treat*. I usually save this for later on, but you've been *very* bad, *ma chère*. I should give you true pain for *faking* before, shouldn't I?"

Chloe couldn't speak. She couldn't think. Her legs trembled and Demetrius chuckled under his breath.

"Well, you're not faking now, are you?" he teased.

"No, Master," she whispered into the sheets.

Demetrius seized her arms with a bruising grip and flipped her onto her back. The sight of him looming over her snapped something in her mind. With a cry, she sprung up and struck his chin with the heel of her palm, snapping his head back. Demetrius grunted and caught himself on the bed, and Chloe took the chance to slide out from beneath him. She tumbled out of the bed, her limbs weak despite the adrenaline coursing through them.

Laughter cut through the sound of her heart sprinting in her ears. It burst from Demetrius like lightning from the sky, a wild, chaotic laugh such as Chloe had never heard. It wasn't the low chuckle she had heard from him before. He laughed as if he couldn't stop, as if his ribcage would crack. Chloe flung herself into motion. It was too late. Demetrius caught her ankle with the grip of a steel trap and yanked her across the floor as if she weighed nothing. He hauled her onto the bed, pinning her beneath his body, and held her wrists over her head with one hand. Chloe sobbed, and again her mind raced with the same useless thoughts. This can't be happening. Get away. Run!

"Just when I thought you had no more fight left in you," he said, the wild laugh still echoing in his voice. "It's time, *ma chère*, oh, yes, it's time."

He reached down and brushed away the hair that had flung over her eyes. The tender stroke along her face broke a dam in Chloe, and she broke down. Even in this moment, his touch maddened her. She craved it, damn her, but she did.

"Why?" she sobbed, shaking her head.

Demetrius shushed her, stroking her cheek. He brushed her tears away with the pad of his thumb. Oh, she would go mad herself. She was mad already.

"Because you are mine, little one," he said softly. "You have always been mine."

Chloe's chest tightened. She felt a burst of rage, sorrow, and then she felt nothing but his hand on her cheek, his hard body on top of her. He raised himself up and removed his vest. She did not move. She couldn't move. His words bound her to the bed like ropes.

"Who are you?" asked Demetrius. He was shirtless, pale muscle marred by smooth scars; broad horizontal slashes on his pectorals and down along his abdominals. Chloe stared at the scars in horror and awe. At first she thought someone had attacked him with a very sharp knife.

Looking as close as she dared, she noticed the scars were straight and symmetrical, horrifying decorations on his arms and torso. They had to have been deliberate. Chloe could not understand. But her mind faded as Demetrius unbuttoned his pants and lingered, waiting. Chloe's throat went dry. She no longer knew what she felt. She no longer cared.

"Who are you?" Demetrius murmured.

"I am Twenty-One," she barely heard her own voice.

"And what are you?"

His pants slid away and he was naked before her, coming toward her. He held himself up with one arm, pressing the length of him against her bare sex, flesh against flesh. The feeling stole Chloe's breath.

"I am a slave."

Demetrius slid himself against her sex. Chloe's back arched. The feeling of him sliding so effortlessly against her, pressed against the apex of her sex, was too much to bear. She had lost. She was lost.

"Look at me."

She obeyed.

Demetrius slid himself inside of her.

The bedroom prison blurred. The walls crumbled. Demetrius filled her so completely that the mere feeling of him working his way in, opening her to accommodate him, nearly brought her over the edge. She felt every muscle in his torso tremble, the smooth strength of him. The powdery scent gave way to the soft, strange fragrance of his skin, simultaneously sweet and sharp, almost like gasoline, copper, or blood. She moaned without control as he slid nearly out of her, a low growl rumbling in his throat.

"Oh, yes," his voice was hoarse. His low moan vibrated in his chest, against Chloe's body. He curled his fingers around her hips and thrust as deeply as he could. Chloe gasped.

"You must ask permission to come," he murmured. "Do you understand?"

"Yes, Master."

He slid out and back in, inch by agonizing inch, until he filled her again, and began a slow, careful rhythm. A steady pressure swelled inside of her in response, building with each thrust. Chloe's hands were free, and somewhere in the recesses of her mind, she understood that she could strike out, but she could not escape the sweet pressure, cresting and waning as he moved inside of her. She lost herself in the ebb and flow, each wave promising to break before pulling back just enough to keep her from tumbling over the edge. She moved her hips, rising up to meet his thrusts, begging for a release from the slow, teasing waves.

"Ah, ah, ah," came Demetrius' scold, a sound that threatened to bring Chloe back to herself, remind her that this man on top of her, inside of her, was her tormentor. But Demetrius seemed to sense her feelings. He hauled himself onto his knees, lifted her hips from the bed, and plunged into her. He thrust as if he meant to break her, slamming against her core again and again. Chloe gasped, arching off the bed, throwing out her hands blindly to either side of her, searching for something, anything to hold onto. She clutched the satin sheets beneath the rumpled blanket so hard her nails dug into her palms through the fabric. Demetrius altered his angle and found a spot deep within her, a spot that opened her to him completely. He ran himself over it again and again, his fingers digging into her hips, his low growl rumbling in her ears.

The pressure swelled with each brutal stroke, blurring into one swift movement, harder and faster, until she could take it no more. Her cries grew louder. Demetrius seemed to know that she was close to the edge. He balled a fist into her hair and locked eyes with her. His skin shone with sweat, his hair thrown over his shoulder, grey eyes blazing through smudged kohl. Lust became him. In that moment he seemed almost supernatural, an elemental creature carved from the moon.

"Oh, God," Chloe whispered.

Demetrius leaned into her, his mask brushing her ear.

"Come for me," he said.

He thrust over that sweet spot one final time and Chloe screamed. Her body dissolved into heat and light and electricity, wave after wave breaking inside of her. Distantly she felt him withdraw, felt hot, hot fluid splatter her stomach, as the rest of her sparked and tingled like the tendrils of a bursting firework. Demetrius cried out above her, his voice vibrating in her bones. She sank into the sheets and drifted back to her body like autumn leaves drifting down to the ground. Demetrius had half collapsed on top of her, his breath ragged against her neck.

"Oh, Chloe, Chloe...what are you doing to me?"

Chapter 11

Ms. Dia Belaire
2717 Straeleni Street
New Orleans, LA, 70130
Demetrius,

I know it's your busy time, but I usually hear from you by now. I'm getting wedding jitters and I need you to keep me calm. You're the only one who ever could. Don't make me break our 'holidays only' pact and call you...

The sky was spattered with faint stars by the time Demetrius pulled the truck onto the loading dock at the Oryx. He was late, and he had no one else to blame for it. It was mid-October, the Oryx's busiest time, and he couldn't tear himself away from that first session with Chloe. Oh, she had been a dream. She learned quickly, obeyed instinctively, yet had just enough fight in her to keep it interesting. She had even tried to manipulate him, and it had very nearly worked. He had never imagined she would pick up on his sadism and know it for the Achilles heel that it once was. Four years ago, three, even, her little show would have worked. He would have torn her apart, tormented her until she was a quivering mass of broken skin. He hadn't been expecting such a seamless jump from false compliance to self-destruction. She had to be experiencing intense inner turmoil to leap from survival to a *better dead than here* mentality in the same session. Ah, but she had given herself over to pleasure so easily. In the end, the ineffable chemistry between their bodies would break her. But Demetrius wondered if it would break him, too. The way he reacted to her, the way she seemed to strip him of nearly all control…it was all very, very dangerous.

Demetrius pulled open the back of the truck. His seven slaves were as he had left them, mummified in stiff black gauze and strapped to individual dollies. Tonight was the Oryx's infamous Sin Night, and the slaves would be posed representing each of the seven deadly sins. The mummification was an integral part of the slaves' training: literal objectification. The moment they were wrapped, they were regarded as lifeless dolls to be used.

Demetrius studied the slaves as he waited for the bouncers to come to unload them. They were his best behaved slaves of the season, as they had to be to participate in public viewing. He could identify them by their figures, see their too-familiar faces through the wrappings. He passed a tall figure that could only be Two, standing on her dolly at nearly six feet tall, only a few inches shorter than Demetrius himself. She was German born, blonde beneath the wrappings with wide set blue eyes and full lips. She had just gotten her feet wet as an escort when Demetrius had taken her. She'd been stubborn at first, a substantial fighter. She had broken easily under the whip. She was a marvelous leather slave, resilient and quick to obey, though also quick to tears. The tears were a bit of a problem in a leather slave; most buyers preferred to work the tears from them, rather than the girls giving them up so freely. But he was confident that Two's obedience skills and her full figure would bring in a decent profit.

Twelve, standing beside Two, had been even more dull and predictable. A tiny glass slave with Bettie Page bangs and pursed lips, she had been too easy to break. Twelve had been eager to comply from the moment he had slipped the collar on her. He always dug into slaves' backgrounds, and Twelve's life had been a constant string of relationships from a young age. All it took was a male authority to break her.

Demetrius paused beside the smallest wrapped form at the back of the line. One. The slave who had begun this unsettling season. Before Chloe, Demetrius had considered his taking One to be his biggest risk of the year. It was not due to her background; she had been a prostitute with no familial ties to speak of; but because he had taken her a full month before he normally began recruiting for the season. Demetrius had been a guest DJ at a Chicago night club when he had spotted her. Her face held doll-like exaggerations of a woman's features, with very large green eyes, full pouting lips, and high cheekbones. Small, firm breasts, a delicious apple bottom, and mocha skin made her an all-around impressive specimen.

Despite her beauty, Demetrius probably would have passed her by had he not noticed the two faint vertical scars near her mouth. The moment he saw them, he had been transported to Mama Dede's parlor from years ago, where that bizarre portrait of the marred Virgin Mary hung over a shrine. The scratches on One's face bore an eerie resemblance to the scratches on that portrait. He had felt that strange sense of foreboding then, too, just as he'd recently experienced in the suite with Chloe. He felt like the presence of the little prostitute was something purposeful, something…he despised the phrase *"meant to be"* and the powerlessness it insinuated. However, he could think of no more appropriate term.

In the truck, Demetrius extended an arm and brushed the edge of One's shoulder. He felt nothing but the scratch of bandages; no spiritual heat, no sense of foreboding. He patted the slave like a good horse. He had taken her in a moment of weakness, a momentary desire to recapture the past. Simple nostalgia, perhaps a brief longing for the passivity encouraged by the concept of fate. There was release in the belief that one's choices are not one's own, a sense of relief that leads to relinquishing control, which is why he used such a concept in breaking some more spiritually-inclined slaves. *You were meant to be a slave. Destiny crossed our paths.*

Ah, but with Chloe, he felt it himself, didn't he?

The truck echoed with heavy thuds that could only be Rafe's footsteps. Demetrius kept his hand on One's shoulder in a casual fashion, glancing over his shoulder.

"Rafe."

"Hey, Boss," came Rafe's baritone greeting. Demetrius turned, letting his hand drop. Rafe was a solid wall of bulk, his muscled arms crossed over his chest, nearly bursting through an Oryx staff shirt that looked at least one size too small. Four bouncers filed in line behind him, awaiting command.

"Wheel them out," said Demetrius. He exited the truck as the men unloaded the slaves on their dollies and followed them through the back to the dance floor. The platforms were already lit up with their special colors, ready to illuminate five sins on display. Lust and Envy, the remaining two, he would suspend by rope on either side of his booth just before the doors opened. He scanned the two suspension bars hanging above the booth. Both were up to his standards, and Lust and Envy would be portrayed by One and Ten, two of the season's most delicate glass slaves. It wouldn't take long to tie them but he needed to take special care with the knots to keep them both safely suspended and avoid cutting off circulation to any of their limbs.

Demetrius set to work tying rope around Ten's tiny waist. A tight sensation in his right shoulder made him curse under his breath. He rolled his shoulder out of habit knowing it would do no good. A gunshot wound always left some sort of permanent damage. Demetrius was lucky he only had occasional muscle tension; the bullet could have shattered his collarbone.

"Boss," Rafe appeared beside him, his footsteps lost in the chatter of bouncers and bartenders preparing for the night. "Little blonde piece is askin' for you at the front."

"She'll wait 'til we open," said Demetrius. "We're working."

Rafe tossed his massive shoulders, "Ain't a customer, Boss. Says it's important. Says she wants to talk to you about someone named Chloe."

Demetrius successfully fought an expression of shock from crossing his face. He met Rafe's gaze with dead eyes.

"That name means nothing to me."

Rafe shrugged again. "She's being a pain in Bobby's ass. Won't leave 'til she talks to you." His mouth splintered into a smirk. "She's a firecracker. Said she'd split Bobby's dick if he put a hand on her."

Demetrius licked his lips behind his mask. That had to be Mariane, the Oryx regular with whom he had first seen Chloe. He could tell Rafe to let Bobby handle it, but Mariane would only return when they opened.

"I'll handle it," he said, locking eyes with the larger man for a moment, "but if your bouncers can't handle a pissy *piece*, you should look into replacing them with someone who knows how to do their job."

Demetrius passed Rafe, letting his last words distract the veteran bouncer from the bigger picture. Mariane stood just outside the main doors of the Oryx, smoking as always. Demetrius weighed his options as he approached her. He could have her banned from the club, but she was a well-known face in the underground, useless though she was, and her absence from the Oryx would not go unnoticed. Her ban would have his fingerprints on it, and people would start to ask questions. But as he came to her, he saw that there was little need for such drastic action. Her head turned too quickly at the sound of his approach, her body tensing despite her attempt to look casual as she leaned against the wall. If she had truly been relaxed, her feet would've been crossed, or her knees bent. Those lovely long legs of hers were rail-straight, her arms folded over her chest like a shield. So easy. The girl had the potential to be a threat, being the only one able to link him to Chloe. But fear had always been her poison, and more than anything, he knew she feared him.

Demetrius advanced on her just a shade too quickly for her comfort. She flinched as he snatched her cigarette from between those heart-shaped lips and flicked it away. She was standing upright now. Her knuckles were white around her arms. He stepped into her space, his face a breath away from hers. To the Mariane's credit, she stood her ground despite the flush of panic so easily seen in her dull blue yes. He smirked. Mariane was a pretty girl. Pretty face, pretty lips, pretty legs, pretty all over. But she wore the gothic style like a costume, an illusion to bring her run-of-the-mill attractiveness to an exotic pique. Strip her of her of her fishnet and her heavy eyeliner and she was just another skinny blonde with *pretty* features. Nothing exceptional. That, and her firm placement in the local subculture, saved her from Demetrius' collar.

"Give me one reason not to ban you for making a scene," he growled, seeping agitation into his voice.

A spark of resolve in her face. Oh, yes, she thought she had the upper hand, she thought she had him. She feared him, yes, but there was a certainty there, a confidence of some secret knowledge.

"My friend Chloe went missing," she finally forced out.

Demetrius kept his eyes trained on her, stone still. He said nothing. Let her dig her own grave, let her reveal her little epiphany. She let a long moment go by before she summoned her nerve.

"She went missing the night I brought her here."

A weak insinuation of his involvement. He could toy with her further, drag out the moment and savor her little internal struggles. Unfortunately, he had work to do. Bobby was keeping the growing group of clubgoers a safe distance away, a group growing fast. Soon there would soon be a line to get in, and the sins had to be safely up and ready before the doors opened.

Demetrius leaned closer to her, invading her space. "Of all the scraps of pretty f/lesh you've paraded in front of me in hopes of getting my attention, how many have I actually been interested in?"

Mariane opened her mouth wordlessly for a moment, as if his proximity sucked the breath from her.

"But…Chloe wasn't for-"

"And if I ever *did* take an interest in one of your offerings, what did I say?"

Mariane's lip trembled. "That they're gone." She took a small shuddering breath. "But I didn't bring Chloe for you. I stopped doing that back-"

Demetrius laughed, cutting her off. "You might have a little inside knowledge, Mariane, but do you *really* think I'm responsible for every terrible thing that happens in this town?" He wanted to let his words sink in but he didn't have time. He had to use quick intimidation to put her in her place. He brushed her cheek with his fingers and leaned down to bring his eyes closer to hers, as if he were scolding a child. "I don't remember any of the faces of your little *friends*, and your little *friend* last time was just as useless to me as any other you've tried to throw into my lap."

He slid his hand down her neck, barely a graze of fingertip, and the color in her face drained away.

"Oh, you look nervous," he said with a low chuckle. "You've never been worth one night's fuck to me. And you'd be dead for what you know if I were a man who forgot old favors."

He squeezed her neck for a moment, enough to startle her into stillness.

"Don't make me forget the favor you did me by asking stupid questions."

He released her with enough force to put her off balance and went back into the Oryx without another glance. He tried to shake off the incident and lose himself in the series of intricate knots he stretched along bandaged bodies. His blank face hid a cloud forming in his mind.

Oh, Chloe. What did you make me do?

Chapter 12

OCTOBER 14, 2011

"Wake up, little girl, come open, now. I've got two of you to take care of today."

The sound of a stranger's voice woke her like a boom of thunder. A round face peered through the bars and jerked back from the cage door.

"Whoa, easy, it's all right," he said, holding up a water bottle. "My name's Gabe, and I'm your attendant. The boss wants you processed. I'm going to take you to the baths, okay?"

Gabe unlocked the cage door and stepped back. Chloe hesitated.

"Processed?" she dared to ask.

Gabe nodded, folding his arms over his chest. He was large, at least a head taller than Chloe with a stocky frame, rich brown skin, and black hair. Something about him struck her as familiar immediately. Chloe was too startled to figure out what.

"Don't talk out of turn, sweetie," he said. "Now come out of there and have a drink."

Chloe bit her lip and complied. He hadn't answered her question, but what else could she do? Rodney had dragged her out of the cage and he was nowhere near Gabe's size. She crawled out onto her knees. She wasn't sure how to behave. A new face made her aware of her nudity, a detail to which she had grown accustomed. She wanted to cover herself but remembered Demetrius punishing her whenever she tried to in the past. She looked down at her body. Her breasts were still painted with tiny red streaks from her encounter the night before. But Gabe, like everyone she'd encountered in this place but Demetrius, didn't bat an eye at her nudity.

"On your feet," said Gabe, opening the water bottle. "Come get your drink and let's get going."

The sight of the water bottle made Chloe's throat go dry, as if her body had only just remembered how thirsty she was. She rose to her feet and Gabe took her by the shoulders to feed her the bottle. The sudden contact startled her. She jumped. Gabe's firm grip kept her in place.

"Easy, easy," Gabe coaxed her lips open with the bottle. "A little wound up, aren't you? That's okay, sweetie. All of you are in the beginning."

Chloe only gulped down a few sips before Gabe pulled away. Chloe moaned before she could stop herself.

"I know, I know. I'm sorry, but we've got to get going. I've got someone watching Seventeen for me."

He pulled a leather leash from his pocket and hooked it onto Chloe's collar. The feeling made Chloe's stomach knot. Gabe's words stunned her. *I'm sorry.* It was the kindest thing anyone had said to her in weeks.

"We're going downstairs now," said Gabe. He patted her hair softly. "You gonna behave for me? Your little escape attempt has made you infamous."

Chloe's face flushed. Infamous. Was it wrong to feel shame for having tried to escape her prison? In this moment, she was too exhausted to condemn herself for it.

"Are you going to behave?" he repeated.

Chloe nodded. "Yes, Master."

Gabe's face split into a smile.

"I'm your attendant, sweetie, not your Master," he said with a laugh. "Demetrius is your Master until someone buys you. Call everyone else here Sir."

Chloe's cheeks burned, "Yes, Sir."

Gabe grinned and tugged on her leash, "There you go. Let's get a move on."

Chloe followed Gabe out of the room, trying to temper her growing anxiety. The spiral staircase clanked under his heavy boots. Chloe kept her eyes down through the strange office and pillared room, taking deep breaths. She didn't want to see these rooms again, to remember her bungled escape attempt, or hurting Three. It seemed like it had happened so long ago. How long had it been? A week? Two weeks? Time was lost to her in that windowless bedroom, where the lights never shut off.

Gabe pulled open the French doors and led her outside. The autumn air was colder without the adrenaline that had aided her the last time she was out there. In the bitter grey morning, she walked down the same dewy path she had run before. The Saint Andrew's crosses in the yard were empty, but Chloe could still see the dark-haired slave she had tried to free, her head down, muttering the mantra that Chloe had found so eerie then. It was the same mantra Demetrius had coaxed her through the night before. The thought made her shiver more than the bitter breeze tickling her skin.

She and Gabe approached the mysterious stone building. Her heart thudded her in her throat as Gabe punched in a code and swung the door open.

Steamy heat coaxed Chloe out of the cold. She stood in a huge room with over a dozen shower stalls lined along its edges and three inground pools that resembled hot tubs in the center. Six or seven women stood in the shower stalls or sat in the pools, getting washed, kneaded, and stroked by men in uniform black, like Gabe. The women were slaves, like Chloe, most wearing leather collars around their necks. Chloe caught sight of glass and metal as well. The slaves were nearly limp in their attendant's arms, listless and apathetic. Chloe stared at a sea of blank faces and dull eyes, as if the steam were an opiate seeping into naked skin and lulling the women into a warm, soft stupor.

Gabe shuffled her past the pools and into a shower stall with a little cart beside it. It was doorless with shallow walls and a small drain between her feet. The walls gave no feeling of privacy. Chloe need only tilt her head to see other slaves in their stalls. The slave in the stall next to her was on her knees. Her attendant unzipped his fly. Chloe began to tremble immediately. No. No, no. She wasn't ready for that. Demetrius had just taken her and she still reeled from the aftermath. She had to comply to survive, but the way her body came alive under his touch, the way he seemed to draw her to him, the way she ached when he was near…that wasn't simply compliance. Chloe tried to quiet her mind. If she thought too long on that, she would go insane. Right now, she had a new danger to address. She looked at Gabe as he busied himself with the little cart of soap and toiletries behind her, and she finally realized why he was so familiar to her. He had been the man who had nearly discovered her on the way to the bathroom the day she tried to run away. He had been the man who had tied the beautiful black-haired slave outside in the yard.

"Alrighty," he said, taking a step toward her. "Do you know any poses yet? Can you stand in Display for me?"

Chloe trembled. She had to comply to survive, she repeated to herself. *Comply to survive.* But fear left her frozen.

Gabe raised his dark eyebrows. "Come on, I still have another slave to take care of."

Chloe's lips quivered. She found herself staring at Gabe's hands, large and limp and hanging at his sides. So far he had been gentle handling her, but she knew he had tied up that slave in the backyard. He was just as capable of violence as anyone else in this place. She felt weak suddenly, as if her malnourishment had only just caught up with her.

"Display..." Chloe didn't understand. "I-I'm sorry, Sir…I d-don't..."

Gabe reached up and patted her head. Chloe flinched, her limbs too heavy to move. What was happening? Had she reached a point where her body could no longer handle fear? Did such a point even exist?

"All right, all right, hush, calm down. You don't know anything yet, do you?"

Chloe lowered her chin and shook her head. Gabe flashed her a surprisingly warm smile. He seemed to sense her distress and moved slowly and deliberately around her as he turned on the shower and rolled up his sleeves. Warm water ran down Chloe's face. She lowered her head.

"Don't worry, sweetie," said Gabe, coating his hands in soap. "You've got the easiest attendant here. I'm the teddy bear." He placed his hands on her shoulders and waited until she had relaxed a little to start massaging. "And I've been told not to touch you except to process you, so don't worry about what's going on in the other stall for now, okay?"

Chloe was so relieved that she uttered a small sob. Once she began, she couldn't stop; tears burst over her cheeks and she cried as if it were her first night all over again. She could not pinpoint an exact reason for her tears. The memory of Demetrius' body pressed against her invaded her brain, so vivid that she could almost smell his sharp, smoky skin, could almost feel him move inside of her. Her heart jolted but she could not identify how she felt. Fear, horror, shame, desire, all were meaningless words to describe some depth of feeling that was beyond her, somewhere beyond the dark, hollow pit into which she had been thrown.

Chloe barely registered Gabe's touch as he kneaded her back in small, hard circles. She allowed it. She had learned her lesson about resisting. Demetrius had even known when she resisted in mind only. There was no escaping, even within herself. Slowly her sobs faded into the sound of running water and the soft moans of the attendant in the other stall. Chloe squeezed her eyes shut but there was no escaping the sound. Chloe's only comfort was that she would not be subjected to the same treatment…for now.

But was this the daily life of the poor girl on her knees next door? Why did Chloe deserve special treatment, even "for now," when twenty other women suffered around her?

Chloe couldn't continue the thought. She was tired. So tired. She let her mind drift away into the strokes and circles Gabe kneaded into her back. He rubbed her scalp with sweet-smelling shampoo, the same as the shampoo in the suite bathroom. She remembered the day the twins had taken her into that bathroom, when Rodney had hosed her down like a horse. Here in the baths, the water was warm, and Gabe's touch was gentle. She was in an open stall in view of strangers, yet she felt safer. Gabe shut off the water and toweled her off. It was the first time she had been allowed a towel since her arrival.

"Good girl," said Gabe, patting her buttocks and holding up his water bottle. Chloe's throat dried despite her damp skin. She took the bottle between her lips and suckled like a baby calf, swallowing gulp after gulp as quickly as she could before Gabe could pull it away and slip it back into his pocket.

"I know, sweetie, I know," he smoothed her wet hair. "It almost makes things worse, doesn't it? But you look good. I've seen worse for sure. I'm just going to examine you now and you'll be done for the day, all right?"

Chloe swallowed. Her throat was drier than it had been before the water. "Yes, Sir."

Gabe laid a hand on the back of her neck. His grip was gentle but firm, "I'm going to put you in the Inspection position now. You're new so it might be uncomfortable."

He pushed Chloe's neck down until she bent at the hip at nearly a ninety degree angle. Immediately her frail sense of security evaporated. Her legs were spread, her sex and buttocks utterly exposed. She moved to cover her breasts.

"No," said Gabe, as if correcting a dog. "Hands at your neck and arch your back."

Chloe struggled to obey, her face flushed. The pose was both humiliating and uncomfortable. Her back protested and her legs strained to keep balance with her weight thrust out in front of them. Gabe slid a hand just above her breasts to steady her.

"Don't worry," he said. "In a month, you'll be able to stand in this position for hours." His free hand slid to the base of her neck. "Now, don't spook on me or I'll have to punish you. You won't make me do that, will you?"

Chloe's skin prickled with fear. "No, Sir."

"Keep balanced," said Gabe, removing his hand from her chest. "This'll be quick and painless. I promise."

Gabe stepped out of sight and she felt his presence behind her. She forced herself to breathe deeply. Gabe cupped her sex and she jumped as if he had struck her.

"Easy, easy," he muttered. "It's okay, sweetie. You're okay."

Chloe gritted her teeth against her shuddering jaw. *I'm okay*, she mentally chanted. *I'm okay, I'm okay, I'm okay.* She clamped down on the shameful tears that threatened to swell. There was no point in shame, no point in bemoaning the great injustice of what was happening to her. It wouldn't stop anything. Gabe slipped a finger inside of her and she dug her nails into her neck, continuing her mental chant.

Her sex ached with the unwanted intrusion. She squeezed her eyes more tightly shut and, remembering her promise to herself, sang her family's song in her mind.

"Quand il me prend dans ses bras, il me parle tout bas, je vois la vie en rose."

"Everything looks good," said Gabe. "The boss was gentle with you." He stroked her buttocks absently. "I don't even see any marks, other than on your chest."

Chloe tried to keep her mind blank. She didn't want to worry about what Gabe meant, or what marks he might have expected to find on her body. She had no idea what the future would bring. The present was all she had to get through, one moment at a time.

"You can relax now," said Gabe, taking a step back.

Chloe released her arms and stood upright. Her back ached. Gabe reached into his pocket and pulled out a plastic bag of ripe green grapes. The sight of the fruit weakened Chloe's knees. More than water, she craved food in this place. The daily broth was so bland that the fruit became the most delicious thing she could ever hope to taste.

"I know I'm not supposed to feed you," said Gabe, "but you've been very good for a new girl." He pressed a grape to her lips. "You won't tell on me, will you?"

The grape slid along her mouth as she spoke. "No, Sir."

Gabe slid the grape into her mouth and Chloe moaned as firm ripe fruit burst between her teeth. She devoured two more. Nothing in the world tasted so sweet.

Gabe wiped her tears from her face and smoothed her hair with the flat of his palm. His touch was detached, as if she weren't a thinking, feeling person, but some sort of domesticated animal he was in charge of. Chloe was surprised to find his detachment soothing. He was quite the opposite of Demetrius, who ripped from her soul every thought, every idea, every secret.

"Thank you, Sir," she whispered, the taste of the grapes lingering on her tongue. There was a warmth in his brown eyes, a simple, kind warmth devoid of any entitlement or obligation.

"Keep your eyes down," he said with a smile. "If you want to thank me, you can kneel and kiss my boot."

Chloe hesitated a moment before dropping to her knees, fearing that once she got there she would be too weak to stand again. She pressed her lips to the rough black leather of Gabe's studded boots. He chuckled softly.

"All right, sweetie, get up. Let's get you dolled up and back upstairs."

Chloe had just climbed to her feet when a sharp cry broke through the casual chatter echoing through the baths, a cry immediately followed by men shouting. Gabe took Chloe by the back of the neck.

"Back on your knees," he ordered, the cheer gone from his voice. "Put your forehead to the floor. Hands behind your back. Good."

Chloe fell back to her shaking knees and pressed her forehead against the tile floor. Her head stuck out from the stall. She heard movement around her and didn't dare turn her head to look around.

"Gabe."

Chloe's stomach twisted. She recognized Rodney like a voice from her nightmares. She saw his black boots out of the corner of her eye.

"It's Seventeen."

"Shit." Gabe shuffled into motion. "Keep an eye on this one for me."

Gabe's footsteps faded. Rodney approached her, reached down, and patted her buttocks. Chloe gritted her teeth. Rodney's touch wasn't like Gabe's. It lingered in a way that made her skin crawl.

"Let's go, baby," he ordered. "Get up."

Chloe rose again, feeling Rodney's gaze on her body. He led her with the D ring of her collar, his elbow bent, forcing her to keep so close to him that her bare breasts brushed his arm.

Chloe looked up as much as she dared. Every slave was on their knees with their foreheads to the floor, their attendants standing behind them. All eyes were on Gabe, who had emerged from a shower stall, bear-hugging a thrashing slave, the very slave Chloe had seen tied to the X in the yard. An attendant was on his knees near them, cursing and clutching the side of his face. Chloe caught a glimpse of blood seeping from between the attendant's fingers just before Rodney startled her with a hand in her hair. He turned to face her, a sly smile on his lips, so close that Chloe's nipples brushed his black shirt.

"On your knees," he said. Chloe sank down immediately, trying not to brush into him further. He stopped her, pulling back on her hair, when her face was in line with his groin. Chloe stumbled, anger swelling in her chest like a flash fire. He tugged on her hair again, forcing her to tilt her head up. She caught his gaze before remembering to lower her eyes. His smile had become a wicked grin. He released her hair, satisfied with his game, and allowed her to fall into position.

Chloe felt her face turning pink, tingling with anger she struggled to suppress. In a moment, Rodney had humiliated her more than Gabe's entire examination had. She turned her head, tilting it just barely to the side, and saw Three lying beside her, close enough to touch. Chloe hadn't seen her since her punishment, and her chest stung at the sight of the girl. Three's head was tilted the other way, watching Gabe struggle with the slave in his arms in front of the pools. Chloe followed suit. Gabe had taken the flailing slave by the hair, his other arm around her slender waist, pinning her arms to her sides. She screamed, kicking and trying to scratch at Gabe's arm. Her brown eyes were wild and slivers of her long hair clung to her face. Her mouth was smeared with blood.

"Fucking cunt!" the attendant on the floor screamed. "Rip those teeth outta her fucking head!"

Gabe hauled the woman over his hip like a well-trained bouncer dragging a drunk from a bar. He jumped into one of the pools and Chloe's heart nearly stopped. The slave kicked her legs and howled with abandon. She was beautiful, even with Gabe's thick arms wrapped around her lithe body. Chloe remembered her tied to the X, almost in a trance, muttering her mantra over and over again. It felt like Chloe was staring at a completely different woman now.

She mesmerized Chloe; her chaotic eyes, the violent grace in her struggle.

"Why?" Gabe barked at the slave. "Do you want to die? Is that what you want?"

Gabe yanked the slave's head back and dunked her into the water, holding her under as the woman bucked and flailed. Three flinched beside her. The scene was identical to what Chloe had to watch the young girl go through. This time, Chloe could not tear herself away from the sight. Gabe jerked the slave's face out of the water, giving her just enough time to breathe before plunging her beneath the surface again. The crowd of attendants and slaves watched Gabe repeat the process three, four, five times, bringing the slave up for air and holding her under again, until like Three, her arms and legs began to weaken. Gabe brought her up for air one last time. She gasped, coughing and sputtering, and to Chloe's surprise, the wild slave raised her arms to encircle Gabe's neck and pulled her body close to his. Gabe scooped her up and crawled out of the pool. The slave, so fierce only moments ago, clung to Gabe's neck, her head limp against his shoulder, wet and shivering.

The sound of whimpering brought Chloe back from the spectacle. Three trembled beside her, crying so softly that Chloe could hardly hear it. If Rodney heard her as well, he gave no indication. Chloe felt tears in her own eyes. Without thinking she reached for the girl, squeezing her small hand, before sneaking back into position. Three's whimpers softened.

Gabe pushed his slave into the arms of another attendant.

"Cuff her and take her to the basement for punishment," he said. "And for Chrissakes, nobody fuck with her this time." He looked down at the wounded attendant. "When you call Demetrius about her biting you, tell him I figured out that water punishment can break her."

The attendants began to pick up their slaves and continue with their grooming. Rodney tapped Chloe's buttocks with his foot, which she took to mean that she should rise. She and Three crawled to their feet. Chloe resisted the urge to glance at the girl beside her. She was sure it was forbidden.

Gabe approached them, dripping wet. He took Chloe by the collar.

"Thanks, man," he said to Rodney.

"My pleasure," Rodney replied. Chloe did not have to look at him to know that that infuriating grin was on his face again. "You think D will give you a bonus for figuring out Seventeen's poison?"

Gabe laughed and tugged Chloe's collar to lead her away. "We'll see what happens."

Chloe followed Gabe. She could not resist looking behind her and stealing one last glance at the rebellious slave, now limp and panting, curled up in the arms of an attendant like a child.

Chapter 13

"Ah, ah, I see those legs quivering, *cheri*. If you fall, you won't get your little treat."

Demetrius watched Twenty-One's face contort with frustration, her little nose scrunched, her brow furrowed. She breathed deeply and he noticed her relax on the exhale. That told him she had some knowledge of breath and body; perhaps she had been in yoga. Good. She was already a few steps ahead of some of this season's slaves in that regard. Some of them couldn't hold a position for more than ten seconds in the beginning.

He sat on the corner of the bed, a safe distance from Twenty-One, though not so far that he could not reach her with the end of the short single-tail whip in his hand. She hovered over the floor in a half-crouch position, her fingers interlaced behind her neck, her legs wide apart. She had been rising from a kneeling pose back to Display when he had stopped her and ordered her to hold the position. He smirked at the flash of anger on her face when he had stopped her. She had found a flow from position to position, and the interruption of something she had just begun to accomplish smoothly seemed to agitate her. Excellent. She needed to be kept on her toes.

Today he had bent her body into the first slave positions she would learn. He taught them like a yoga series, which seemed to register well with new slaves. She began in Display, which he knew Gabe had shown her in the baths. She had strengthened considerably with food and water and handled the wide-legged stance very well, standing on her toes with her arms behind her head and her breasts lifted. Inspection was difficult but she knew that one as well. He had thought she would break down when he bent her toward her feet to grasp her ankles. The positions where the slave's sex was completely exposed for the world to see were always the most difficult. She had been relieved when he brought her down to all fours, through Abasement, and up to a kneeling position, ending the series. He led her through the series, over and over again, drilling it into her brain. Now he had stopped the flow to keep her focused. Twenty-One had a habit of dissociating from the moment. He had to break her out of her mental escapes.

"Slave," his voice cut through her silent struggle.

"Yes, Master," came the strained reply.

He tried to ignore the swelling sensation in his chest. Hearing *Master* on her lips still felt far, far, too good.

"Would you like to kneel and have your treat?"

He heard her swallow from the short distance between them.

"Yes, please."

"Ah, ah," he chided, snaking the end of the whip along the floor. He had yet to use it, but he knew the sight frightened her. No, no, her virgin skin had never tasted a whip. "You know how to answer me. I ask you again, would you like your treat?"

He watched her jaw clench and unclench.

"If it pleases you, Master," she said through clenched teeth.

Demetrius smiled, making his mask shift up the bridge of his nose.

"Good girl," he said, rising from the bed. "Now kneel."

Twenty-One's knees struck the floor a shade too hard to be a controlled movement. Her luscious chest quivered as she perfected her pose, tucking her feet beneath her buttocks and spreading her knees to a perfect 'v.' She clasped her hands behind her and arched back just enough to display her breasts, a habit she had already begun to get more comfortable with.

Demetrius approached her, letting the whip slither behind him. He parted her lips with a fresh cut of peach and she ate greedily, the fruit juices dribbling down her chin. He was overwhelmed with the thought of ripping off his mask and catching those juices with his tongue, prying open her plump lips and lapping at the sticky sweetness inside her mouth. He shivered, his erection in direct eye line of the slave. She obediently kept her gaze on the floor in perfect form.

Twenty-One was in exceptionally good form today, as if their first few sessions had cracked some wall in her. Tears flowed, humiliation flushed her cheeks, yet there had been no flash of defiance, no refusal to comply that didn't dissolve with a slap on the ass or threat of the whip. Oh, she still had fight in her, little Chloe, he knew that, yet she was fast becoming the ideal slave he had seen in her from the beginning.

Chloe. He had to stop referring to her as anything but Twenty-One or slave, even in his own mind, but her name stuck like a thorn in his finger. Normally his knowledge of his slaves' identities before they came to him held power over them. In Twenty-One's case, it seemed to hold just as much power over *him*. It unnerved him.

He backed away as soon as the slave at his feet had taken the last bits of peach from his hand. He wiped his palm against his tight grey pants, smearing peach juice against the steel studs running down his thigh. The entire training process with Twenty-One was unnerving. He had no time to explore those reservations, however. He only had a couple of months before Abigail and Konri came to his doorstep, and she had to be a true Model Slave by then. The Dinner party held to kick off the auction was an overwhelming experience for even the most seasoned slave. He was certain that Abigail would want her to participate in some of the games. He had to be certain she would be obedient and have the stamina for humiliation and pain. He had to prepare himself to see her in those games as well. If she were selected to fuck one of Abigail's slaves...he refused to entertain the thought further. The very idea of Twenty-One in the throes of another man's passion sent venom into his veins. It was ridiculous; he had taken her to turn her into an instrument of pleasure for whomever desired her, after all. Yet the thought of her writhing beneath someone else, those sweet agonized screams escaping her throat as she came under another man's touch…

He shook the thought away. There was no reason for him to feel this way, and there was no reason for him to focus on it right now.

"Slave," he said a little too roughly. "Toe Touch."

Color rose to her cheeks immediately. Oh, yes, this was her most despised position of the series. But she complied, curling her toes beneath her and coming up to stand. Her splayed legs quivered; she was tired; but she was stronger than she had been just out of the cage. He worried for a moment that he had fed her too much, that she was no longer in a state of hunger so crucial for obedience at this early stage in a slave's development. Her good behavior today was testament that she was hungry enough to obey.

His breath hitched as she bent to clasp her ankles. Her back was still a bit rounded but would flatten with increased practice and flexibility. It was her sex that made him pause, those delicate pink folds open and exposed to him, glistening with a hint of moisture. The fresh memory of rubbing himself against the slickness of those folds, of forcing himself into her, so tight, so wet, threatened to overtake him. He took a breath to steady himself, slipped a hand into his pocket, and pulled out his digital recorder. He approached the bent-over slave and ran his fingertips over the bend of her back. She shivered, her knees shaking ever so slightly.

"You must not break form," he said, "or you will be punished. Do you understand?"

"Yes, Master," came her soft voice laced with a mixture of fear and anticipation. Oh, he loved how each note in her voice betrayed her every little emotion.

"You must answer my questions or you will be punished."

"Yes, Master."

"You must ask permission to come," he said.

Orgasm control would be a challenge for a slave with such a sense of entitlement to her own pleasure. He always found that trait in slaves who had not been prostitutes before coming to him. Having them ask permission to come forced them to focus more on their own arousal and begin to learn to delay it, to await his approval. It would be difficult for Chloe, but with the way she was progressing, he had every confidence that she would take to it in time. She was silent, a troubled crease between her brows. She had not answered him.

"Slave," he injected irritation in his voice to move her. "You must have my permission to come. Do you understand?"

"Yes, Master," she said quickly. The slightest tremor ran through her limbs.

"Good." Demetrius turned on the digital recorder and bent to show it to Twenty-One. "Now...who are you?"

The slave gave him a pleading frown, staring at the recorder as if it were some sort of torture device. She responded nonetheless.

"I am Twenty-One."

He gave her a gentle pat and approached that imploring little sex of hers. "Good. Now chant your mantra."

The slave shivered. She could feel his presence somehow, and he felt her, too; a sultry heat pressing into the fabric of his clothes, coaxing him to tear them off and close the distance between them.

Twenty-One recited the slave mantra. "I am Twenty-One. I am a slave. I will obey. I will be used. I will not question. I will please my Master. I am Twenty-One. I am a slave."

Even though she had only recently learned the mantra, there was a distance in her voice, as if she weren't really hearing her own words. She had already begun to drift somewhere else, somewhere safe and far away from him. Demetrius flipped the whip up so it landed limply on her back with no strike. The slave jumped, expecting a blow. She had come back.

"Again," he ordered. "Stay focused."

"Twenty-One's voice quivered. "I am Twenty-One..."

He let the end of the whip slide down her back and onto the floor. He roamed her body with his free hand, dragging his fingers along her spine, up the back of her thigh, along her buttocks, stopping short of her most tender parts.

"Again," he murmured.

Twenty-One began again, her voice taking on a breathless quality. Her sex glistened from his touch. It was tantalizing. It was as if she had been starved of physical contact and his hands were the first that touched her in years. Gabe had not mentioned her reacting this way to his examination of her in the baths. Demetrius nearly laughed at himself for such a juvenile thought. There was a strange connection between them that he couldn't yet explain, but hoping that her charms were open to him and him alone was comical if not dangerous. Again the thought of her with one of Abigail's slaves came to him, making his blood simmer. He had to keep calm. It would happen eventually, if not at the Dinner party, then when she was inevitably sold. But for now…for now she was his and his alone. Not even the attendants could touch her without his permission, and as damaging to her training as that may be, he would keep it that way until he had overcome his childish attachment to her. And he would overcome it. But not right now.

Twenty-One had fallen silent, and his fingers had trailed dangerously close to her wet little sex.

"Again." His voice was a bit hoarse, but she obeyed.

Demetrius brought the thick, braided handle of the whip to her sex and slid it from opening to apex. She gasped, faltering immediately.

"Continue," he ordered. "Stay focused."

"I am Twenty-One. I am a slave. I will obey…"

Demetrius moved the whip handle in slow circles around her opening as she struggled to continue her mantra. He longed to use himself in this exercise rather than a tool, but Chloe…*Twenty-One*…had no hope of controlling herself with how entranced she was by him. *He* had very little help of controlling himself either, and he had to move slowly through this, draw out her arousal, make her more aware of her body. He had begun this with her daily required masturbatory sessions, but in reviewing them, he had noticed that Twenty-One treated them like a chore, finishing her task as quickly as possible. She seemed to take little pleasure in it. He suspected she dissociated during them, as she seemed to with any action once it became repetitive enough.

"Again, until I tell you to stop," he said when she had finished her mantra again. He tested her opening with his fingers and she tensed immediately. She was wet, but she was not ready for penetration. She was a tight little thing, too. He remembered how he had to fight for every inch when he entered her, how snugly she had enveloped him. The whip handle was a little thinner than his own sex, but she needed to be warmed up a little more to comfortably accommodate it. He found the most sensitive part of her clitoris with his middle finger and began rubbing in tiny circles. The movement stole her breath for a moment. Her legs trembled.

"Don't break stance," he reminded her, stroking her apex until his finger grew slick. She recited the mantra, her grip tightening around her ankles. He continued to work her with his fingers and reveled in the sound of her voice growing weaker and more distracted as she grew hotter and wetter in his hand. Finally he pushed the base of the whip against her opening and felt it yield. He slid it a small way inside her.

Twenty-One uttered something between a whimper and a moan; a sad, longing sound that made him hard in an instant. He worked the whip into her, bit by bit, opening her. He continued to torment her apex, which by now felt like a hard ember as he stroked it and rolled it between his fingers. He slid the whip in and out of her, gently at first, until she began to rock her hips to meet it. He smiled to himself. There it was, her entitlement to her own pleasure.

She had tried to control his pace the night he had fucked her, too, and he had nearly let her, enchanted by the way she undulated beneath him. But she had to learn that her place was not to fuck, but to *be* fucked.

"Ah, ah, ah," he said. "Hold still, *cheri*, or you'll get a taste of the other end of this whip."

That stopped her, though she wasn't able to suppress a sigh. He teased her with slower, gentler strides, her soft moans stoking his own growing need. He gave her apex a hard tap, making her gasp.

"I'm not hearing your mantra, slave."

She whimpered and repeated her mantra, though her voice was little more than a series of moans and sighs. Her breathlessness was too much for him. He pushed the whip hard into her, forcing a cry from her throat, and quickened the pace of his thrusts, his fingers working furiously on her apex. Twenty-One's mantra became broken and disjointed.

"I am…oh, God…I am a slave…I will…I will…!"

"Focus," he growled. The whip was slick with her wetness, sliding in and out of her with ease. He tilted the angle up slightly and focused on her g-spot, and from the way her knees shook, he could tell she had never been touched there. He pounded the whip into her and she tried to continue her mantra, tried as hard as she could to remain still in her pose. He saw every muscle in her tense with the effort. His strokes along her apex became swift and frantic, betraying his own longing to discard the whip and replace it with himself, to feel her slick and tight and hot around him. He wanted to fill her with his seed, a desire he had never had trouble ignoring before in a slave. The urge gave him a moment of pause, but Twenty-One's ragged voice cut through his concern.

"Oh, Master, please…please…" she cried.

Demetrius couldn't suppress a low moan himself. Her begging was too much. He forced himself to slow down, to give her a chance to control herself. "Please, what?"

"Please…please, may I-" her voice dissolved into a hoarse cry. He saw her nails dig into her ankles, her face flush red, her eyes close. He nearly came himself from the sight of her in the throes of orgasm. His sex throbbed, aching, needing, so sensitive that the feeling of the zipper of his pants pressing against him was erotic. He could have thrown her onto the floor and taken her now, done everything he'd wanted to do the moment he stepped in the door, but she had come without permission, and the session was over. With great effort, he removed the whip and came to stand in front of her. He reached into his pocket and shut off the recorder.

"On your knees," he ordered, masking his need with a cold voice. Twenty-One, her sweet hazel eyes filling with tears, obeyed. She was pink all over, glistening with sweat, lips parted. He had a mental flash of yanking her hair back and forcing himself between those lips. He gripped the whip until it hurt. He would not let his desires make him a failure of a Master. This girl would not make him fall so far.

"Oh, *ma chère*. You were so close, so close, but you failed. You must put your Master's pleasure above your own, always. And your Master didn't give you permission to come, now, did he?"

He wanted to lick the tears from her cheeks as she whispered, "No, Master."

Demetrius went into the bathroom and returned to find Twenty-One in the same position in which he'd left her, her head down, tears flowing freely down her ruddy cheeks. He called her attention with a snap of his fingers and held up a toothbrush and a small bucket of soapy water.

"Your punishment is to clean the floor using this." He held up the toothbrush. "And to do so while chanting your mantra and listening to your failure." He took the recorder from his pocket and pressed a button. The room filled with Twenty-One's voice from a short time ago, reciting her mantra. Twenty-One's head snapped up, startled. He knew she was aware of the cameras, but she hadn't known that he could inject sound into the room. He smirked, but his amusement was short lived. A dull ache low in his body reminded him that he had business to attend to. He had to punish a slave, or find the twins, or find some other way to extinguish his lust. He could not quench the heat between him and Twenty-One today.

"Oh, and remember the cameras, *cheri*. If you don't do what I tell you, I'll know, and you won't like what I'll do to you."

Twenty-One looked at him with wide and frantic eyes, defying slave etiquette to keep eyes down. The last time he had seen an expression like that on her face, it had been when she had struck him that very first night. This time, she crawled toward him as quickly as her hands and knees could carry her, bent her head down, and laid a hard, tear-soaked kiss on his studded boot.

Demetrius' pulse jumpstarted. Twenty-One sobbed, hysterically kissing his boots again and again, resting her forehead against them, crying as if her heart were breaking. And it was. He had seen this time and time again, though not normally this early on in training. Demetrius was not sure if it would last, but at this moment, she had broken down not because of her punishment, but because she had failed her Master.

The next moment was a blur that Demetrius could not remember when he reflected on it later. Suddenly Twenty-One was on her feet and in his arms, one of his hands cradling her face, the other hand on his mask. He had ripped her from the floor, and her honey-brown hair clung to her face, her eyes wide with terror. He stood frozen, fighting as hard as he could not to rip his mask away, to reveal himself and crush his lips against hers and melt into her and become nothing but the searing flame that consumed him every single fucking time she was near him. He fought against a need so strong that it had become its own entity, a demon possessing his body, controlling it. His fingers curled around the edges of the mask.

Reveal himself.

No.

No, no, no.

He squeezed his eyes shut. He released his grip on the mask. Released her face. She crumpled to her knees, shocked, sobbing. He turned on his heel and walked toward the door in a haze.

"Get it done." He heard his own voice, felt the words leave his mouth, but his mind had retreated into a dark calm, and he was no longer truly there.

The door locked behind him.

Chapter 14

Dia shook her head with a laugh, holding heavy wet strands of Demetrius' hair above his head.

"It's so long!" she said. "I still can't believe it takes two bottles to get through your hair."

"Just don't stain my scalp," Demetrius said, trying to look up at her without moving his head.

"Oh, it's too late for that," Dia replied. "Your head's as spotted as my hands."

Dia slid off the bathroom counter, coiling strands of the long part of Demetrius' hair and pinning them into tight knots until he could wash out the dye. He caught a flash of her thigh as her cotton sundress settled along her legs. Both her dress and her legs were smudged with dye. Demetrius reached out and grabbed her knee playfully. She gave an adorable little cry and shied away.

"How did you get dye all over your legs?" he asked.

Dia shrugged, "I'm a messy girl." She looked at Demetrius' head and grinned. "You look hilarious."

"You say that every time." Demetrius rose from the side of the bathtub and stretched. "Forty minutes."

"You're higher maintenance than a drag queen." came Mama Dede's unmistakable voice from the bathroom doorway. She stood with a hand on her hip, so slender that she couldn't even fill the door frame. Demetrius had noticed that she had been getting thinner the past few months. Even now her dress gaped in places it shouldn't have.

"Mama!" Dia squealed, her cry echoing in the tiny bathroom. She threw her arms around Dede, who struggled to hold her at arm's length.

"Don't hug me girl, you're covered in dye." She looked past Dia to Demetrius, looking at his knotted hair, his eyeliner, his ripped and faded black jeans, "I don't know why you insist on dressing like the devil. You ought to dress like a man."

Demetrius smiled and shook his head. He had lost count of how many times Dede had chided him for wearing makeup and dying his hair. Dia took Demetrius' hand and swung it as if they were skipping down a flower path together.

"Stop it, Mama," she said with a grin. "He just wouldn't be Demetrius if he looked like everybody else."

Mama Dede raised an eyebrow at the girl. Demetrius knew exactly what she was about to say. They had heard it from her lips countless times since the first day Dia had shown up in her parlor.

"What are you doing spending so much time here? You should be spending your mama's money in the French Quarter-"

"*-flirting with rich boys*," Dia chimed in. "I know, I know. I'd rather be here any day, listening to your crazy voodoo stories."

Mama Dede waved an arm to shush her and headed for the side porch, "Put a shirt on, boy," she said over her shoulder. "You look like a shark chewed you up."

Demetrius' smile withered when Dede's harsh cough echoed behind her. Dia looked at his arm. She ran her fingers along one of the broad horizontal scars, one of the newer ones that hadn't faded to white.

"I wish you'd stop doing that to yourself," she said, her own smile fading at the corners. Demetrius rolled his eyes, put his arm around her delicate shoulders, and hugged her close.

"Don't you start," he teased. "I don't need another Mama. Now come on, I think she's dipping into the bourbon tonight."

The house creaked and moaned beneath their feet. Today had been hot and sticky, and the night would be no different. The humid air hung heavy in the old house, seeping into the neglected floors and walls, swelling the worn wood. Hot days like this made it hard for Demetrius to breathe with his normal leather mask on, so he had fashioned a few out of cotton and muslin. Dia had teased him, saying he looked like a surgeon about to operate. She had pestered him about his mask for months when her visits to Dede's parlor had become daily. A heartfelt discussion and a peek at the left side of his face had sated her curiosity, though she would still tease him from time to time.

Dia looked up at him. Even after a year of constant contact, her large brown eyes still quickened his breath.

"I had that dream again," she said, circling her arm around his waist as they walked. "Where I'm sleeping with the big white snake curled around me."

"Oh?" Demetrius reached out and grabbed a bottle of dark rum as they passed the kitchen counter. "Was anything different this time?"

Dia leaned into him, rising on her toes to whisper into his ear. "Well, this time I was naked." His expression broke her into peals of laughter. "You can't frown at me when you have no eyebrows!"

Demetrius grinned. "You were not naked."

"I wasn't," said Dia. "But wouldn't it be funny if I told Mama I was?"

Demetrius pushed open the screen door. "Oh, you won't, *cheri*. Because you actually believe her *crazy voodoo stories*."

"*Oui, Monsieur!*" said Dia. "*Bien sûr.* Seeing is believing."

Demetrius shook his head. "They're dreams, Dia."

Dia shook her head, her long hair tickling Demetrius' arm. "They feel like more than just dreams. I can *feel* the snake around me." She bumped her hip against his. "You're too cynical."

A choir of cicadas greeted them as they stepped out onto the porch, singing from the mossy cypress tree in the backyard. Dede was already in her rocker, looking out into the darkness, a bottle of bourbon on the floor beside her. Demetrius settled into the second chair and Dia settled in his lap, leaning against his left side. No matter how hot it was, they always ended up on the porch like this.

"You had another dream then?" asked Dede.

Dia told Dede the same dream she had told Demetrius she'd been having here and there for a couple of years. Dede had heard it many times, and every time she asked the same questions.

"Did you see any railroad tracks?"

Dia shook her head. "No intersecting roads or anything. It was pretty much the same as every other time. I was sleeping in bed with the big white snake around me."

Dede nodded. Her face looked more severe to Demetrius than it had in the past, her cheekbones sharper.

"What color were the bed sheets? White? Blue?"

Dia shrugged. "I never remember, Mama." A mischievous smile crept onto her face. "But I'm pretty sure I was naked."

Demetrius chuckled and Dede shook her head, rocking in her chair a little more vigorously.

"Shut your mouth," she said. "The loa don't like nudity. It's disrespectful. Damballah would never come to you naked."

Dia laughed and nodded, "It was just a joke, Mama."

Dede took a gulp of bourbon and passed it over to Dia. "This isn't for joking. Demetrius can say what he wants, but you're loved by Damballah, girl, and you have to treat him with respect. How did you feel with him wrapped around you?"

Dia quieted, softening in Demetrius' lap. "Peaceful." she said. "Like everything was going to be okay."

Dia took a sip of bourbon and handed it to Demetrius. He set it aside. He rarely drank around Dia because he had to shift his mask to do so. He stroked her hair as they sat listening to the night.

"You should thank him for the dream on Thursday," said Dede after a moment. "Burn a white candle on your altar."

Dia slumped almost unnoticeably. She studied the hem of her dress. "Nancy made me take my altar down. She said she didn't want any crazy satanic shit in her house."

Demetrius circled his arms around Dia and she rested against him. Dia's biological mother was rarely sober enough to exercise any parental skills, but when she put her foot down, Dia usually buckled.

Dede waved her hand dismissively. "So build it in the closet. Your mama hardly sees you coming and going, she won't even remember you had a conversation. You need to thank him. Damballah don't keep his favor without gratitude."

Demetrius fought a sigh as the trio settled into a comfortable silence. He held Dia. Dede and Dia's religious discussions never failed to frustrate him. He brushed it off and the three drank and talked late into the night. Dia never moved from his lap, idly stroking the buzzed sides of his hair as they listened to Dede's stories of Damballah, the great white snake, father of the loa, who rewarded those he favored with peace of mind and good fortune. Dia grew quiet and finally drifted to sleep as the night softened into early morning, as she so often did, her breath soft and warm against the curve of his neck. Demetrius shifted, careful not to disturb her, and snuck the mouth of the rum bottle under his mask for a quick sip. The shift let in the sticky floral heat of New Orleans and the sweet fragrance of Dia's jasmine perfume, a scent that always lingered on his clothes long after she left.

"The two of you act like lovers," Dede's voice was less than kind. Demetrius met her gaze with an even stare. He didn't want to have this conversation again.

"You know we're not."

Dede rolled her hazel eyes. Her chair creaked with each sway. "Lovers don't have to fuck, boy. You read people like billboards. You see the way she looks at you. You *know*. And you let her sit in your lap anyway. You let her stroke you like a housecat. You let her hang around here and dye your hair and teach you French like you some kind of born and raised Creole." She leaned against the arm of her chair. "Will you see her face when you feed your demons tonight?"

Demetrius looked away. In the past few months, Dede had been more and more frank with him, bordering on harsh, about how he and Dia interacted. She was right that he could read people. Her change in behavior, paired with her thinning frame and the cough that rattled her very bones told him what she had, for some reason or another, refused to mention.

"How long do you have, Mama?"

The question hung in the air like the moss on the cypress tree that Dede stubbornly stared at, refusing to meet his gaze.

"Dr. Boukman said I've got about six months," she said finally. Her low voice was fainter than Demetrius had ever heard it. But her resolute attitude returned as quickly as it had gone. "I know I've got longer than that. You won't be rid of me that fast."

They sat for a long time, sipping liquor as the cicadas filled the silence. Demetrius became very aware of his heartbeat, hard and quick. A stupid fear that it would wake up Dia came and went. He had been living with Dede for the past two years without question or discussion. He'd given no thought to a future of any sort. He had done so little with the identity that Dede had given him. Demetrius Heart was a thief and a nomad. There was no address in his name, no pay stubs, no rap sheet. Despite having a name and a social security number, he was still a ghost. He was nothing. Nothing but those brutal, insatiable urges that consumed him in cheap motel rooms and whore houses. Nothing but a trail of bruisedskin, tears, and threats to keep silent. Dede and Dia were the only proof that he even existed outside of that darkness at all.

He felt it now, that terrible need, growing as he thought on it. He would have to leave soon, to tuck Dia in on the parlor couch and *feed his demons*, as Dede had said. He despised the accuracy of the phrase. Dia's face was placid as she slept, her eyelids fluttering. Would he see her face on the woman he found tonight? It had happened a few times. Every time it did, it was unbearable. Every time it did, he drank himself into oblivion, or punished himself with a fresh cut, though he hardly felt them anymore. No, no, he would never hurt his sweet girl. He would destroy himself first.

Dede's voice cut through his growing unease. "I seen some old faces around recently, Demetrius," she said. "Faces from before you showed up at my door."

Demetrius stared at Dede, dread growing in his stomach. Dede gestured for him to hand her the bourbon. She took a long drink before continuing, her eyes closed.

"Those boys still come to town sometimes, looking for you."

"Those boys?" Demetrius repeated. Dede shot him a look that made his insides cold.

"Don't play stupid," she said. "Vision or no vision, you think I would let a stranger into my house knowing nothing about him?" she gestured to his mask. "You dress like the devil, but you're smart. You don't look nothing like you did when they knew you, whatever they knew you for. They come down here sometimes, once or twice a year, looking for you. But they don't recognize you anymore with that hair and those clothes. So they go back to Toledo."

Demetrius felt the world tilt. He'd had no idea that Dede had known about what had happened to him before he had shown up on her doorstep. He'd thought she had taken him in because of his hallucination in the cemetery, that she had believed it had had some deep meaning, some religious significance. Dede did not react to his shock. She rose slowly out of her rocking chair. Though she had always been a petite woman, as she stood with her dress hanging off her bones, this was the first time she seemed small.

"When I do go," she said, "you'll get this house. But you need to go somewhere else. One of these years, they'll come down and they'll recognize you."

Demetrius shook his head. His pulse thundered in his ears. He still remembered their faces, the four of them, distorted in the darkness, deaf to his pleas.

"Stop! Please! I don't know who you are! I don't know you…"

"Where did you see them?" he asked, his voice rougher than he meant it to be. "Are they still in town?"

Dede shook her head. "I know that look in your eye, boy. Don't do anything stupid." She pointed at the sleeping girl in Demetrius' arms. "You got family now. You keep her safe from them." She pulled open the screen door. "And from you."

Demetrius sat on the porch, cradling Dia in his arms. His mind raced faster than he could keep up with, wracked with conflicting thoughts that threatened to tear him apart. Soon enough, though, the terrible hunger returned, the need that gnawed away everything else. He stroked Dia's cheek to gently rouse her from her sleep. She opened her bleary eyes and raised a hand to his hair.

"You didn't wash it out," she mumbled.

"I have to take you home now, little one," he said softly. She frowned up at him, perplexed.

"But I can sleep on-"

"No, not the couch," he whispered. He lifted her into his arms and rose, putting her on her feet. "You need to go home, *ma chère*. To your own bed."

Dia stared up at him, studying his face. "What's wrong?" she demanded.

Demetrius shook his head and stroked her hair. She leaned into his touch, as she always did, which he always tried to ignore. Dede was right. She was always right. He needed to pull back from her…as much as he could bear.

"Are you angry with me?" she asked.

The hurt in her eyes wounded him, but something else stirred at the sight of her pain, that sickening fire within him, the urge to dig deeper, to open a wound, to fan the flame. Oh, yes. Dede was right. He pulled her into him, folding his arms around her, kissing the top of her head through his mask. He wished he could smell her hair.

"Of course not," he held her tightly as she returned his embrace. "I have some things to do. I'll be back in a few days. All right?"

He met her eyes, and again he felt he was looking at a girl who was both older and younger than her body's age, wise and childlike. A calm washed over him, exactly like the peace he had felt when he had first seen her. He would pull back as best he could, to keep her safe. But he couldn't live without this girl.

"Let's get you home, *ma chère*," he said. "I'll tuck you into bed and everything."

Chapter 15

"I am Twenty-One. I am a slave."

Once again Chloe found herself in the dreaded suite with no idea how much time had passed. Her fingers around the toothbrush were numb, like she had gone out into the snow without gloves. Her back burned from hunching over the floor, her knees bruised by the hardwood. She had long ago stopped focusing on the pain, but she could not tune out the recording, the desperate animal cries in her own voice. She couldn't stand it. At first she listened as some sort of self-punishment. *Listen. Listen to your failure. You're weak, pathetic. You failed him.*

You failed him. That was the most maddening thought of all. Failed him? The man who kidnapped and starved her? Failed a monster? The fact that she even had these thoughts disgusted her. She had to get out of here. She had to get out before she went insane.

But thoughts of escape faded as pain and thirst swelled. When would he come back? He had left her alone for days after her escape. This hadn't been such a harsh transgression. When she had escaped, he had been enraged. This time he had seemed more disappointed than angry. Sickening dread made her empty stomach lurch. Should she fear his disappointment more than his anger?

The sound of her forbidden orgasm bounced off the walls and once more the thought came: *I have failed him.*

That was when Chloe started screaming. She cursed, she howled, she mocked her own recorded voice, mocked the hot, aching tone, her pleas, her cries. She clamped her hands over her ears and screamed, but her failure still bled into her.

"Please…please, may I-"

Did she hear him sigh through her cries, or was it in her head? Why did it hurt her so much?

Finally she had no more voice with which to scream. She scrubbed the floor inch by inch with the toothbrush, whispering the mantra. She hoped the cameras would show her lips moving so she wouldn't be punished for her loss of voice. She drifted between blissful numbness and emotional turmoil. All the time she scrubbed. She began to see patterns in the grains of the wooden floor, ghastly faces with their mouths twisted in silent howls. For a heart-stopping moment, she thought that her own recorded screams were coming from those horrible frozen mouths.

The sound of the door beeping stopped the haunting recording in an instant. Chloe's first urge was to scamper into her cage. She remained where she was, too startled to move. She was surprised to see Seventeen walk through the door, her eyes downcast, her dark hair partially veiling her face. Gabe walked in after her with a bowl of broth in his hands. Chloe was so relieved she nearly cried.

"Good morning, sweetie. Come over here and stand At Attention."

Chloe scrambled to obey. She stood in as perfect form as she could muster, her legs wide, her back arched, hands at the back of her neck. She could smell the broth, hearty and steaming. She tried to keep her eyes down, but Seventeen proved too much a curiosity to ignore. The other slave stood At Attention beside Gabe, her steel collar glinting in the low light. If she had any thoughts, they did not show in her face, as still and impenetrable as a mannequin's. Gabe praised Chloe for her posture, but Chloe couldn't help but feel inferior to Seventeen's perfect form.

"I was told you're having problems with orgasm control," said Gabe, dipping a spoon into the broth. "We're here to help you."

Chloe's face flushed. Once again her sense of shame threatened to consume her. But Gabe put the spoon to her lips and her torment gave way to satiating her terrible hunger.

"Everybody has trouble with it at first," Gabe assured, feeding her carefully, "You'll get there. The boss said that's all we're going to focus on this week. Have you been tied down before, sweetie?"

Chloe looked up at Gabe before she could stop herself. His easy smile met her, but he shook his head and pointed his finger downward. She lowered her gaze, her stomach knotting.

"No, Sir," she murmured.

Gabe slipped the last of the broth between her lips. "Well, don't be scared about it, it's not that bad. In fact, it usually helps you relax more, if you can believe it."

Chloe didn't believe it. The idea of being bound nauseated her. She had adjusted to the collar around her neck and the cage, but to be physically bound reminded her of her first night here, when she had woken up with zip ties around her wrists.

"This is actually one of the easy training sessions," Gabe continued. He set the empty bowl of broth down on the cage, reached into his pocket, and pulled out a thick black vibrator. "All you have to do is lay back and try not to come."

Chloe's skin grew cold. Gabe pointed at the bed.

"All right, sweetie, lie down."

Chloe hesitated, but she knew she had to comply. She lay down on the bed. The sensation of the bedspread on her bare skin sent her back to the night Demetrius had dragged her onto the bed. She pushed the memory away. Gabe opened the top drawer of the dresser beside the bed and pulled out four leather cuffs.

"Spread your arms and legs," he said. "Seventeen, give me a hand."

Seventeen took a pair of cuffs and slid one around Chloe's ankle. Chloe's heart skittered in her chest. She didn't like this. This was going to be mortifying. She remembered the slave beside her in the shower stall when Gabe had taken her out into the stone building.

"Sir…" she whispered, though she didn't know what she wanted to say other than, *please don't.*

Gabe shushed her and patted her head. "I know, sweetie. You're still new, and this is all scary. Just take deep breaths and try to relax. I'm not going to hurt you. I promise."

Chloe nodded. There was nothing else she could do. Seventeen spread her legs further open and she was exposed to the world, to these strangers. She believed Gabe wouldn't hurt her, but if he wanted to, she couldn't stop him. If he struck her, she couldn't even curl up to protect herself.

Gabe switched on the vibrator. It roared to life with a dull, mechanical hum and Chloe balked at the sound. She tugged at her restraints and panicked when they wouldn't give way. Gabe shook his head.

"Hush, hush," he said. "You know that's not going to do you any good."

"I can't, please Sir, I can't..." Chloe whimpered. She was trapped. The cuffs were too tight. The bedspread clung to her skin. Gabe's attempts to calm her only inflamed her sense of helplessness. "Please untie me," she pleaded. "Please, Sir, I can't..."

Seventeen's cool hand stroked Chloe's thigh. Chloe looked up at the slave beside Gabe. Her dark eyes were not empty now, but warm and kind. She patted Chloe's thigh, and a shadow of a smile appeared on her pillowy lips. The heart-wrenching panic that had threatened to overtake Chloe began to abate in the presence of such warmth. It occurred to Chloe that Seventeen had to have gone through all of this. Worse, she knew from having seen Seventeen tied to the Saint Andrew's cross outside. Chloe's panic began to give way to a familiar sense of shame. Seventeen, and all of the other slaves, had experienced so many horrible things, and Chloe lay there panicking over a vibrator. She clenched her jaw and forced herself to relax against the bed. She would not be weak in front of such a strong, beautiful slave.

Gabe's gaze bounced from Chloe to Seventeen, his brow furrowed.

"I think things might go a bit easier if you handle this," he said, handing Seventeen the vibrator. "All right, get between her legs." He smoothed Chloe's hair back. "I promise this won't be bad, sweetie. This is easy compared to everything else you're going to go through in training. Hell, a beautiful girl's going to try to make you come. I'd enjoy myself."

Chloe bit her lip and nodded. "Yes, Sir."

Gabe gave a nod to Seventeen, who crouched onto the bed between Chloe's legs. Again Chloe burned with the shame of knowing her sex was exposed to a stranger. The vibrator appeared just above her crease, and tingling warmth spread through her from hip to toe. She shivered and closed her eyes, but that only made her focus more on the sensation. Seventeen moved the vibrator just over the apex of Chloe's sex and the warmth became a flame. Chloe gasped, her legs ramrod straight. She fought her restraints. She wanted to close her legs. The vibrator pressed to her clitoris was far too much.

"Ease off," Gabe ordered Seventeen. "Try lower."

Tears leaked between Chloe's eyelids. This was too humiliating for her to comprehend and she couldn't escape it. Any attempt to think of anything else disintegrated when Seventeen slid the vibrator down her sex, testing her opening with little circles. Chloe's fear ebbed, pushed into obscurity by a growing pressure, the pressure that had gotten her into trouble with her Master. She pressed her lips together to suppress a moan. Seventeen slipped the vibrator inside of her and Chloe's hips rocked of their own accord.

"Good, good," said Gabe. "Just stay there a bit longer."

Seventeen rocked the vibrator gently, gliding it along Chloe's inner walls. Chloe gasped. Her back arched from the bed sheets. Images flashed in her mind, images of Demetrius hovering over her, his scarred and muscular torso pressing against her.

"Okay, okay, pull back."

Chloe didn't understand Gabe's words, but the vibrator retreated from her, just barely touching her sex now. Chloe moaned and tried to slide her hips forward.

"Ah, hey, now," Gabe chided. "That's what's getting you into trouble. Don't be greedy."

Chloe opened her eyes, coming to herself. No, she would not fail again. She stared at the ceiling, breathing long through her nose and out of her mouth. She saw Gabe out of her corner of her eye and avoided looking at him.

"That's it. Good girl. Think about baseball," Gabe laughed. "Seventeen, go ahead."

The vibrator returned and with it the delicious pressure that was almost too much to resist. She wanted to rock her hips again, wanted to press vibrator deeper inside of her, to feel it touch her very core. Demetrius was kissing her in the rain, kissing her as if he would rip her apart. She shook her head, pushed the image away. She wouldn't fail again. She wouldn't.

Chloe didn't fail the entire week. Gabe and Seventeen appeared at what seemed like the same time every day, binding her to the bed and pushing her to the very brink of ecstasy, only to pull back. Chloe focused on her breathing or on the ceiling, keeping her mind as blank as she possibly could. It grew easier to fight the tide of desire, even when Seventeen ran the vibrator over her apex. At the end of each session, Gabe and Seventeen would bathe her and reward her with fruit and water, then lock her into her cage again, where Chloe would sleep and dream of rain and fire.

A week may have passed. Chloe couldn't be sure. Seventeen had been particularly aggressive today, focusing almost entirely on her apex, and Gabe had ordered her to caress Chloe as well. The unrelenting vibration paired with Seventeen's soft hands running along her breasts, her hips, was difficult to ignore. Chloe found herself at the brink, fighting to stay on the edge, when the beeping of the door lock cut through the incessant hum and Gabe's encouraging words.

Chloe didn't have to look up to know who had entered the room. Seventeen's hand had tensed on her breast and Gabe had fallen silent.

"Move," came Demetrius' unmistakable voice.

The vibrator disappeared. Chloe looked up, but Demetrius' fingertips brushed her eyelids down immediately. Chloe closed her eyes, her pulse in her throat. The vibrator returned, wielded by a far more aggressive hand. The flame came back, blazing bright, as the vibrator circled her apex.

"Master…" she whispered. She wanted to warn him, to tell him to be more careful, or she would fail him again. Heat and pressure stole her breath away. She knew there was no turning back.

The bed shifted and she knew Demetrius was hovering over her. She felt his hair brush her breasts. The vibrator remained between her legs, coaxing her too close to the edge. She threw her head back and moaned. She was lost. She was going to lose.

Demetrius' voice appeared beside her ear, low and even, just as Chloe went tumbling over the edge.

"Come for me."

Chloe cried out as one of the most powerful orgasms she'd ever had coursed through her limbs with electric light.

Chapter 16

Rafe took one last long drag of his Marlboro and flicked it toward the retreating truck in the Oryx's loading dock. Off they went, the silent bandaged women in the back of the truck. Off to wherever the fuck Demetrius kept them the rest of the week. *She* hadn't been among them tonight, his lady with the light hazel eyes that haunted him day and night.

He ran a hand over his shaved head. *His* lady. He was fucking crazy or suicidal to think like that. She, and all of them, belonged to the boss. Wherever he got them or whatever he did with them, they were his. That was the way it had always been, and for six years, from summer to Christmas, Rafe had never questioned anything. Now he just wished the fucking bandages hadn't slipped three weeks ago and he hadn't seen those eyes, wide and weary and gilded with tears.

Rafe turned and went back into the Oryx for the closing cleanup. He tried not to think of her. He didn't know why he couldn't get her out of his mind. It wasn't like he had ever spoken to her, or even seen that tiny, curvaceous frame beneath the bandages. Hell, he hadn't even seen her mouth. He didn't know her name. Demetrius only called them by numbers. She was number One, whatever that meant. He didn't know. Maybe it meant she was Demetrius' favorite piece, a thought that knotted Rafe's stomach.

"They're objects, Rafe," Demetrius said when he first started bringing them years ago. "Toys. They have no names. They won't move. They won't talk to you, and if any of them do, let me know immediately."

Rafe did know that she squeezed his hand every time he handled her, a fierce squeeze when patrons got too rough with her, and soft, gentle squeezes when he helped suspend her or took her down at the end of the night. His heart skipped every time her fingers pressed against his, warm through the bandages.

Rafe rubbed his eyes and tried to clear his head.

Inside the Oryx, the bouncers and bartenders were busy cleaning up after Halloween, their busiest night of the year. The lingering odor of sweat mingled with the sweetness of spilled alcohol. Rafe grabbed a mop from the back closet.

"You never been to D's place either?" Rafe heard Bobby's gruff voice by the bar. "Don't he throw any parties?"

"D's not like that," said James, the bartender, as he washed glasses. "He's private."

"Privacy? Don't he keep all those dolls at his place? What, he lock them in the basement or something?"

Rafe cut his eyes to Bobby. The door man's round face was coated in sweat. Rafe had seen Bobby's face like that in the summer, when the nights were sticky and humid, but not in the dead of autumn.

"You're an idiot," came Heather's voice, the little shot girl with pink hair. "I think they're hookers or something. He probably just takes them back to the streets at the end of the night."

"I always thought they were art models from campus," said James.

Bobby shrugged and cleared his throat. He fiddled with a cheap watch peeking out from his hoodie sleeve before grabbing a rag and rubbing the polished bar counter in rough circles.

"Look, I don't give a shit about the dolls," he said, abandoning the counter and crossing his arms. Rafe had never seen him so wired. It made him wonder if he hadn't taken something tonight. He'd had drug problems with Bobby in the past. "I was just wondering where the guy lives."

"Boss don't like to be talked about, Bobby," Rafe warned. "If you're so curious, ask him yourself tomorrow."

Bobby clammed up after that, yet the sweaty fidgeting continued. Rafe shook his head and continued mopping. He didn't want to have to fire Bobby. The guy was dumb as a fucking brick, but he was a good bouncer, and he'd been with the Oryx for a few years. It'd be a pain in the dick to have to train another person during the busiest time of the year. Unfortunately, he'd given Bobby his last warning about being high at work months ago and there was definitely something wrong with the twitchy asshole.

The early morning wore on and the smell of stale booze gave way to the stench of chemical cleaner. The crew headed out one by one until Rafe found himself alone. He uttered a deep sigh and headed to the office to lock up, his mind drifting back to the conversation about Demetrius. He didn't know much more than his staff about the dolls Demetrius brought with him, but he'd bet they weren't models from some art program on the campus. He did all the books for the Oryx, so he knew the club sure as hell didn't pay them to be there.

"They can be touched," he remembered Demetrius saying, "but treat them like art, Rafe. If anyone gets rough or tries to move them or take off their bindings, kick them out."

It was pretty much November, and by Christmas the girls would vanish, replaced by a fresh crop of them next year. His lady, whoever she was, would be gone in a couple months. His stomach turned. He had seen the tears in her eyes, felt the message in every urgent squeeze of her bound hand: *Help me. Help me.* Something in him knew there was no way the dolls were there voluntarily. But then why didn't they run in the crowded chaos of the club while the boss was in the DJ booth or outside smoking? Why didn't they scream for help? What did Demetrius do to them to keep them quiet? It didn't make sense.

Rafe pressed his palms against his face until his eyes ached. Six years. For six years he had never questioned, never cared. Who gave a fuck where the boss got some wrapped-up bitches for some stupid ploy to make the club stand out? Who cared what he did to them outside these walls? It wasn't Rafe's problem.

Until One.

Rafe opened the door to his office and there was Bobby, still caked in flop sweat, elbow deep in the file cabinet in the corner of the room.

Bobby made a sound somewhere between a grunt and a shout, springing back as if a snake had bitten one of his grubby fingers. "H-hey, Rafe."

"What the fuck?" Rafe demanded, but even as the words left his mouth, a switch flipped in his head. Bobby spent the night sputtering questions about Demetrius' home, and now Rafe caught him digging through the file cabinet where the employee information was kept.

"Do you have a death wish?" Rafe asked over the stuttering door man. "What the fuck are you doing?"

Bobby's sweat had become streaming rivulets. He spoke as if his tongue were too big for his mouth.

"They got me up on drug charges, man. If I don't do this I'm back in prison!"

Rafe frowned as Bobby backed away from him, perhaps expecting some kind of blow.

"Cops? What do the cops want with D?" he demanded.

Bobby shook his head wildly. "I don't know, man, something about a missing girl. They told me if I wore a wire and got him to talk about her…but he don't talk to me much. So they told me to find out where he lives so they-"

Rafe's mind raced as Bobby talked. Missing girl. He remembered Mariane coming to speak to Demetrius about some girl a little while ago. Everyone in town had heard of a student gone missing, some bitch last seen around the Oryx. He remembered the tears in One's eyes, the way she squeezed his hand.

"Give me the wire," Rafe ordered, cutting off Bobby's rambling. "And get out."

Bobby ripped the watch out from beneath his hoodie sleeve, dropped it onto the desk, and scrambled out of the office. Rafe locked the door behind him and sat down at the desk, taking a moment to let everything sink in. Bobby's cheap accessory lay on the desk, its face smeared with greasy fingerprints. A watch. Didn't know why Rafe hadn't thought that was weird before. Nobody wore watches nowadays, not with everyone carrying a cell phone. He couldn't see a tiny camera eye or a microphone. He glanced at the door in case Bobby was lingering, but the door man had fled like a frightened rodent.

"Hey," Rafe muttered into the watch. He took a deep breath. "I don't know if Demetrius was involved with that girl, but if he was, you aren't gonna get anything from Bobby. He's a fucking moron."

He hesitated. What the fuck was he doing? Demetrius had an ominous reputation, and Rafe had been him around long enough to believe at least some of the rumors surrounding the DJ. But he had no proof to claim that Demetrius was some sort of kidnapper. No proof but the tears of a silent woman.

In his memory, One squeezed his hand. Help me. *Help me.*

Rafe swallowed.

"Demetrius trusts me. He'll talk to me. Give me a call."

Chapter 17

Demetrius fought to control himself. The crop lay discarded on the bed. He was supposed to introduce a little pain to Twenty-One in this session, but he had thought better of it. One look at her on her knees in front of the cage, waiting for him, and he knew that if he struck her today, he would not be able to stop. This week had proven to him that *he* was the danger here, not the quick-witted little slave in the suite. She had already mastered the basic slave poses and had even shown progress in some of the more advanced ones. She spoke perfectly. She barely hesitated when he gave a command. There was still quite a bit of psychological resistance, and her tendency to dissociate was still strong, but all in all, Twenty-One was fast becoming the ideal Model Slave he had proclaimed she would be to his partners. But for *him*…for him, every session was a battle for self-control, eerily similar to the days in New Orleans when every single encounter was a struggle, when he had to give the prostitutes he picked up extra cash for a trip to Urgent Care. He had far more command over himself than he had in those days, but the strength of his urges still concerned him. Even now, as he held her against the cement wall, he knew that his grip on her hair was too tight, that he was pressing against her too hard. Her muted whimpers stoked the flames. He struggled to keep them at bay.

Still, the strangest moments in his encounters with Twenty-One were the tender impulses, the gentler urges he had never really had toward a slave before. He suspected it was because of the kiss he had stolen in the rain, but he wanted nothing more than to rip off the mask and kiss her again. Her punishment for her failing to ask permission to come had been so long because he very nearly *had* ripped off his mask in front of her. He wanted to hold her in his arms, a feeling he hadn't experienced since he had left Dia behind in New Orleans. This, more than anything else, gave him pause.

Thoughts, whither have ye led me?

But Demetrius slid himself inside of Twenty-One, and his reservations faded. She gasped, and he had to cover her mouth with his hand or he would go mad. She was wet but far too tight; not ready for him, but that was the point. He had given her no warm up. Not only did it reinforce that she was a vessel to be used for her Master's pleasure, a lesson with which she struggled, but it also served the sole purpose of this brief training session.

But only if he could control himself.

He forced himself all the way inside of her, steeling himself against her muffled cries, and threw his head back. Oh, this was so difficult. He wanted to thrust into her over and over again, but he had to be brief. Unlike most slaves, Twenty-One became very aroused by simple penetration. He did not think it was the act itself—most women are not aroused by penetration alone—but rather the *meaning* she placed on the act. He felt something break within her every time he was inside of her, her defenses cracking like a door under a battering ram. He suspected that for Twenty-One, him taking her in this way was the truest demonstration of his domination of her, of owning her. It was a very traditional belief, an outdated one for most, but this little slave held fast to it like the good little Catholic she had probably been. Either way, it worked wonders for her. Despite herself, she enjoyed the domination, the ownership, the loss of control. She was a born slave.

His second thrust was easier. She had already opened up to him. He had to move quickly or she would become too aroused and defeat the purpose of the exercise. He looked down at her quivering breasts he forbade himself to touch, at the sight of him sliding out of her. Fierce need threatened to overtake his senses. Oh, that was a mistake. He shouldn't have looked. He tightened his grip on her hair and buried his face in her neck. The urge to lift his mask and take in the scent of her skin was so strong it hurt.

Twenty-One's elbows twitched; he had ordered her to keep her hands at the base of her neck. Maybe she was struggling with balance, or maybe she had just resisted the desire to put her arms around him. Demetrius banished the thought before he could imagine what it would feel like for her arms to encircle him. He thrust into her, hard and swift. She moaned into his hand, a sound that sounded pained as much as inflamed. Demetrius steeled himself. It was now or he would fail this session completely and lose himself, fuck her into the wall with abandon.

"Come for me," he ordered.

The response was immediate, as he had hoped. She clenched around him, a sensation that ripped a moan from his lips, threw her head back, and screamed as her first involuntary orgasm rolled over her. The sounds she made were so intoxicating that he had to think of something, anything else, or he would fuck her, finish her, and destroy the lesson. For no reason he could identify, a snippet of a Keats poem sprung to mind, and he clung to it like a life raft through the storm of her orgasm, mouthing the words to keep in control.

"Now more than ever seems it rich to die…to cease upon the midnight with no pain, while thou art pouring forth thy soul abroad in such ecstasy."

The storm passed. Twenty-One quieted, her body soft and pliable against his, doused in sweat. He allowed himself to look at her. Her eyes were wide with shock. She looked at him, and his order to keep her gaze down died on his tongue. He cupped her cheek, stroking her with the pad of his thumb. He smiled. Her face, with that bewildered expression, was so innocent.

"Congratulations, Twenty-One," he said, brushing the hair from her eyes. "You've done it."

X X I

"Well, I just don't understand why you even decided to take up a Model Slave when you *yourself* told me it was pointless years ago," Abigail's voice had taken on an annoying whine. "Not to mention you don't even talk to us about it, you just snatch some girl off the streets halfway through the season. It just doesn't sound like you, D."

On the TV screen, Abigail sat at the corner of her bed, her arms and legs crossed, her top foot bouncing up and down rapidly, a perfect portrait of irritation. She did not bother with theatrics this time. Her faithful slave, Ash, was nowhere to be seen, and she was fully clothed in a dress that did not flatter her figure, though Demetrius would bet that it boasted a designer label.

Demetrius cut his eyes to Dr. Konri Boukman, his second business partner, who had remained characteristically silent through the entire meeting. He wore his usual slacks with a button up shirt, his lab coat slung over the back of his office chair. His unreadable face often reminded Demetrius of Mama Dede. Their complexions were similar, though where Dede's light brown skin and freckles were ambiguous, Konri's pointed to his part-African heritage. His expression was far sterner than any that had ever crossed Dede's face; he wore it like Demetrius wore his mask.

"Konri?"

Konri's light eyes bounced from side to side, probably looking at both Demetrius and Abigail on his screen. He sighed and scratched absently at his greying temple.

"A Model Slave," he said, as if tasting the phrase in his mouth, "serves as an example for the following season's slaves?"

"Yes," Demetrius replied.

Konri's eyebrows raised almost imperceptibly. "That means you'll be keeping her for the entire year."

Demetrius nodded.

"Which is *exactly* why you told me a Model Slave wouldn't be *profitable*," Abigail countered, throwing up her hands. "You said that it was risky and pointless to keep a slave in the off season, and they'd never-"

"Has she been examined?" asked Konri.

Abigail's face rouged at the interruption, but she quieted down. Konri rarely spoke unless directly addressed, which was part of what Demetrius liked about him. His question was brilliant; it revealed to Demetrius that Konri also questioned his impulsivity in kidnapping Twenty-One, but there was no way Demetrius could deflect the question with a threat or promise of pain, as he frequently did with Abigail and the twins to keep them in line.

"She has been examined," said Demetrius, choosing his words carefully, "but she has not had a physical, so I will need you to see her the moment you come to town in December. I assume you can't make a trip before then."

Konri nodded, his face blank, but Demetrius could guess what was going on behind those pale eyes. Demetrius himself was only just realizing how foolish he had been in taking and using Twenty-One with such abandon. Konri normally visited for the month of June and all slaves were questioned and checked out before use. Demetrius could make the excuse that she wasn't a prostitute and therefore less likely to be a concern, but he knew that that was a fallacy, and so did Konri. He also did not want to reveal Twenty-One's identity. Konri worked in Cleveland and it was highly likely that he interacted with Twenty-One's cardiologist father. He knew how his partners would react if they knew who Twenty-One had been before she had come into this house. He already knew how stupid a risk he had taken. But to use her without an exam…he hadn't given that a single thought, and that was quite possibly the biggest blunder he had made in his career.

And Konri knew that much, at least.

"I don't get it," said Abigail, chewing on the inside of her lip. "You make us consult you on every little thing, and you didn't even broach the subject with us before running out and snatching a girl for the job."

Demetrius took a breath. To reply to her or explain himself would only reinforce her belief that they were equals in business. He was not in the mood for power play. He fixed Abigail with a cold stare and let the silence stretch. It only took moments for her to fidget. She gave a dramatic sigh and rolled her eyes, tossing her loose curls over her shoulder.

"Well, I wish you would have informed me," she said, avoiding his gaze. "I could have found one myself and we could have run this little experiment together."

Demetrius turned his attention back to Konri.

"Twenty-One is progressing very well. She'll be branded tonight. If there are any issues, I'll call you."

Konri nodded. Whatever he thought, he was wise enough to keep it to himself.

"At least tell us what a Model Slave *means*," Abigail demanded. "Are you going to sell her in the next season, or keep her forever like some little housewife?"

Demetrius fought a grin behind the mask. He had expected Abigail to react harshly to his picking up an old idea of hers, but she was outdoing herself by pouting like a punished child in a corner. He wondered what her adoring slaves would have thought of her after seeing her in such an infantile state, so far removed from the golden goddess persona she emulated in their presence.

"This year is unorthodox," he said, "but should I choose to continue this, a Model Slave will be taken at the beginning of the season like any other and trained along with the rest of the stock. After the auction, she will remain with me for extensive training; advanced positions and pain eroticism, domestic training, everything will be expanded upon. She will serve as an aid in breaking the new slaves in June, and will be a model for them as they learn, the ideal they should strive to reach, always by my side. She will be sold with the crop of slaves she helped teach for double the price due to her extended training."

He studied his partners. Konri gave him nothing. Abigail tried to do the same, but couldn't keep her mouth shut.

"It sounds like an awful lot of work," she said. "Can we at least see the girl that inspired this brilliant idea? She's moving through training pretty fast if she's ready to be branded already."

Demetrius didn't like the way her question made him tense.

"You'll see her when you get here in December," he said, leaning back against his headboard. "Now, unless anyone has any other idiotic questions, I think we can conclude for the day."

Konri shut off his screen immediately. Abigail held up her remote and gave Demetrius a smile that threatened to stir his temper.

"Enjoy her, D," she said, slowly spiraling a lock of hair between her fingers. "You work so hard. You should let yourself have a *favorite* every once in a while."

The TV went blank, leaving Demetrius' own face glaring back at him.

Demetrius sighed and let his head fall back against the headboard. The meeting left him with a cold feeling in his chest, the same feeling he had when he had first figured out who Twenty-One was, after she already lay naked in a cage in the upstairs suite. Once more the thought invaded; *What have I done?* Dread prickled along his spine, and he had the same sensation as he had when he touched One in the truck, and when Twenty-One had first uttered the word *Master.* He brushed it aside. Fate was a superstition. His own impulsivity had gotten him into this, and there was no need to search for a deeper meaning. He had made sure his tracks were covered. Mariane was too frightened to say anything, and no one else knew of any connection between him and the missing Chloe Leroux. All that was left to do was the same thing he had done for six years; break, train, own.

A neglected pile of mail sat on the nightstand beside the bed. He knew that at least one envelope would hold a New Orleans address. He dug through the pile until he found it. He traced the sender's name with his fingers. *Dia Belaire.* His sweet girl still wrote to him religiously, even though he had stopped replying a couple months ago. To stop writing to her was like tearing out a piece of himself, but he had to. She was getting married. And no matter how badly he wanted to deny it, the subtext of her letters spoke loud and clear. She wanted him to rescue her.

Demetrius adjusted his mask and pressed the sealed envelope to his nose. Did he actually catch a hint of her jasmine perfume, or did he just imagine it? The same Keats poem that had sprung to mind earlier with Twenty-One crept into his consciousness.

Was it a vision, or a waking dream? Fled is that music:--do I wake or sleep?

Demetrius set the letter aside.

Chapter 18

NOVEMBER 6, 2011

It was dark, too dark to see for a moment. Her eyes adjusted and she could make out the blank walls of her suite prison. She lay tangled in the bed's satin sheets. Demetrius had rewarded her by feeding her a bowl of strawberries dipped in honey, so overwhelmingly sweet, and by allowing her to sleep in the bed tonight rather than her cage. He had shut off the lights for the first time since she had come to this place. The darkness terrified her at first. However, the comfort of a bed in the dark gave her the deepest sleep she had experienced in a very long time. Now she was wide awake without knowing what had stirred her. The room was silent, yet something in the air was strange, as it had been the night Demetrius had taken her from her apartment, a night that seemed so long ago.

"Time to wake up, *cheri*."

Chloe tensed, frozen in mid breath. She felt him now, standing at her back on the other side of the bed. She sprung to her hands and knees, scrambling to sit At Attention.

"No," his command stopped her. "Stay there, on your stomach."

Chloe sank back onto the bed, her breath shallow. Silence stretched and Chloe felt exposed with the sheets having fallen away from her bare body. Demetrius' fingertips appeared on her back, trailing down the length of her spine. His touch was delicate, and she shivered beneath it, but her heart would not slow. He never visited her twice in such a short span of time. She did not know what to expect. She had orgasmed at his command, orgasmed long before she was primed to do so. She would never forget the feeling, how his voice simply summoned the flame with no spark at all, bringing her body from calm to ecstasy in an instant. It had been terrifying and...wonderful. She did not know if she was ready for it again.

"Look at me."

Chloe turned her head to face Demetrius. He was shirtless, wearing a white mask and pale pants that in the darkness seemed to blend with his skin. He held a black toolkit in his hand. Chloe opened her mouth to ask what was going on, but she stopped herself. She was a slave. She would not question. Instead, she stared at her Master while he allowed it. His hair and makeup were a stark contrast to the rest of him. He looked like an elemental thing in the dark, the same cold white as the stars, with hair as black as the night sky. He stood still a moment longer, letting her drink him in, then he reached into his pocket and the lights in the room rose to a dim glow. Chloe wondered if he always carried a remote with him, if he always had control of every room in the house. He set the toolkit down on the nightstand and opened it. Chloe dared to steal a glance. She spotted a metal clamp, a thin, flat wedge of steel not an inch long, and something cylindrical she couldn't identify. She had no idea how the pieces fit together, or what it meant for her.

"I'm going to brand you tonight," said Demetrius.

Brand you. Chloe stared at him, feeling the color drain from her face, her skin prickling with sickening panic. Thought escaped her. Demetrius laughed softly. He reached over and stroked her cheek with his knuckle.

"Oh, sh, sh, sh," he murmured, "It's time, slave. It's time."

She didn't fight tears now. They misted her vision as she nodded. She had known on some level that she would be branded like the other slaves. She had known she would join their ranks as a number. She swallowed hard. Yes. It was time.

"It's going to hurt, *ma chère*," said Demetrius. "Yes, it's going to hurt more than anything you've felt before. But I'll be here with you."

The words sounded strange coming from the man before her. His gentle tone, too, sounded strange. Chloe did not allow herself to question it. Instead she clung to it, as she clung to his soft fingers on her cheek.

"I am going to tie you down," said Demetrius. "You've been very good lately, you have, but even the most obedient slave struggles with this stage." He knelt and retrieved a coil of black rope from the floor that he had to have carried in while she slept. "Give me your wrist."

Chloe extended her arm, trembling. Demetrius caught her hand in his, stroking it with his fingertips. He studied her face and she felt the same helplessness she had every time he looked at her. She fought the urge to look away when he had not ordered her eyes down. Her suffering was his to study.

"You've never been tied down before," he murmured.

Chloe had to clear her throat to speak. "Just when Gabe and Seventeen…trained me, Master."

Demetrius shook his head. "Ah, well, I'm sorry these are your first experiences with it, *cheri*."

She stared at him, fighting to keep her face blank. Again, gentle words. An apology, even. There was no sign of the cold wall she had begun to expect to see him behind during her training. But this tenderness was new to her as well, and she did not know what to make of it.

She lay still as Demetrius tied her wrists to the nylon straps under the mattress, her arms outstretched on either side of her. He bound her ankles as well, similar to how Seventeen had done it, though she was on her stomach this time, less exposed. She tested the restraints at his order. They were tight around her limbs, but not painfully so. She knew she would not lose circulation in her hands or feet. But she also knew she was trapped by the expert knots and the inability to pull her arms into her chest was no easier than it had been the first time.

Once Demetrius was satisfied that she was secured, he returned to the toolkit, ripping open a small packet and tossing the wrapper on the table. Chloe whimpered when she saw what he had opened: medical gloves. Latex gloves.

One of the benefits of having a doctor for a father was that Chloe had learned of her allergies in childhood, and her allergy to latex topped the charts. She remembered her first visit to the dentist, remembered feeling feverish as the dentist poked around in her mouth with gloved fingers. She remembered her throat closing. She couldn't recall the paramedics coming in, or the epinephrine they had given her, but she would never forget the terror of being absolutely unable to take a breath, as if her lungs had swelled into something solid and incapable of expanding. Chloe tugged at her restraints without meaning to.

"Master-"

"Ah, ah, ah," Demetrius shushed her. "You're doing so well, Twenty-One, don't go backwards."

"But I'm-"

Demetrius put a gloved finger to her lips to silence her. Chloe cried out and jerked as far back as the bindings would allow.

"*Slave,*" Demetrius snarled, grabbing her chin roughly. "Be still."

His fingers promised pain if she didn't comply. The feeling of the gloves on her skin stopped her struggle. It was too late.

"I don't want to have to punish you," Demetrius' voice had become soft again. "This is going to be punishment enough. Do you understand?"

Chloe's heart had reached a breakneck pace against her ribs. Her body was cold, clammy.

"Yes, Master," she whispered.

Demetrius released her face and turned back to the toolkit. He fit the small steel wedge into the clamp. Chloe fought to take deep, slow breaths, waiting for her throat to close, but nothing happened; no itchy skin, no heat, no wheezing. She swallowed and took a breath. No heaviness in her chest. She squinted in the dim light and tried to read the wrapper from the latex gloves. It was nearly out of her line of vision, but she still made out the word that flooded her with relief: *Nitrile.* Her father had made her memorize it. Demetrius wore latex-free gloves. Tears of relief swelled.

"Hush, now," said Demetrius, almost to himself, as he fitted the steel plate onto the clamp.

Chloe's relief gave way to new fear as Demetrius leaned over and swabbed her right shoulder blade with an alcohol wipe. She watched him flick a switch on the cylindrical object. A small burst of blue flame made her jump. She should have guessed it was a torch from the look of it.

Demetrius held the edge of the metal wedge into the flame until it began to glow, and a wave of nausea rolled over Chloe, spotting her vision.

"I don't brand my slaves with a single strike, like a cow," he said over the roar of the small flame. "I will brand you with this single piece, reheat it again, and make my mark inch by inch. It's going to take a few hours. You may scream, you may cry, but remember who is Master, *ma chère*, and keep your manners."

Chloe forced herself to nod. She stared at the glowing piece of metal that would touch her skin. The bindings had been wise; staring into that glow, Chloe knew that she would have run if she could have.

Demetrius looked at her, the flame's reflection in his pale eyes.

"Are you ready?"

Chloe laid her head on the pillow and wrapped her hands around the ropes binding her wrists, clinging to anything she could.

"Yes, Master."

Demetrius sat beside her on the bed, curled his fingers around Chloe's neck, and pressed the thousand degree steel into herskin.

Chloe's fingers convulsed against the rope. What escaped her lips was less of a scream than a strange, throaty outcry like an animal caught in a hunter's trap. She had never experienced pain like this before, an instantaneous searing agony. Even when Demetrius removed the steel wedge to reheat it, her skin continued to burn.

She heard the hum of the torch again.

"Please, Master, don't. Stop. Please, not again. Not again, Master." Words tumbled out of her mouth with no regard for obedience, no fear of punishment. But Demetrius continued as if he didn't hear her, and the dreaded steel wedge glowed fiercely once more. Chloe thrashed against the ropes with all her strength, but they held fast; she could not even bend her knees or elbows to shrink away.

"No, please, Master!" she begged, ragged with panic. "Oh, God, please, no, no, no-!"

Demetrius was silent as he pressed the wedge into her again, just below his first strike. Her skin hissed and Chloe screamed without restraint. She lost herself completely after those first two strikes, her world fractured into the stench of burnt flesh and the sound of her own skin sizzling like meat in a hot pan. She screamed until her throat could no longer sustain a human voice, and then what came out of her were hoarse moans and pitiful, hollow sobs. Her shoulder blade felt as if it were molten and melting away like rocks becoming magma. Each strike was agony, each pause to reheat the steel was pure dread. Chloe did not fade into an empty dream world as she had so often during her periods of isolation. Rather, everything was utterly clear in the worst of ways. She felt every strike as if it were the first until she was certain Demetrius had to have burned her to the bone. There had to be noskin left to scorch.

When Chloe grew quiet, unable to scream any more as the metal hissed against her, Demetrius lifted her chin, studied her eyes. Chloe barely felt his hand on her, barely saw his eyebrowless face leaning so close to hers.

"Twenty-One," his voice was distant, as if she were underwater. "What are you?"

Chloe could not comprehend the question. What was she? She was the aching throb in her shoulder. She was the flash of heart-stopping pain with each strike. There was nothing else to be. Demetrius' face blurred for a moment. She saw rather than felt him lift her bound hand and place it against his bare chest.

"You're starting to go into shock," Demetrius explained. He pressed his fingers against hers and held her hand just beneath his collarbone. Chloe felt the barest whisper of the gloves he wore. "Listen to my voice, Twenty-One. Can you feel the scar?"

Chloe swallowed, her mouth dry. Her hand seemed detached from her body when she tried to move them. Her fingers finally responded, sluggishly dragging down

Demetrius' skin. For a moment, there was nothing, and then she felt something raised and rough, not like the smooth, firm scars along the rest of his body.

"Yes," her voice was hardly a whisper. "I feel it."

Demetrius nodded. He let her hand go. She didn't see the water bottle before he put it to her lips, but she swallowed reflexively, and with each sip of water, the world grew clearer. She saw the scar he had put her hand against. It was round rather than horizontal like the rest of his scars, with rough tendrils of knottedskin stretching from it like a sunburst. Chloe had seen enough news stories to recognize a bullet wound, though she had never seen an old one. She wondered how she hadn't noticed it before, but what was one scar in a multitude of scars?

"Who are you?" Demetrius asked. He pulled away the water bottle.

Chloe swallowed again, "I...I am Twenty-One," she whispered, "I am a slave."

"Good girl," Demetrius whispered. Chloe wondered if she imagined the relief in his voice. "Good girl. Let's continue."

The metal wedge returned, the pain returned, but Chloe had no more screams left in her. As the brand stung herskin, she laughed. She laughed with the same wild abandon that Demetrius had when she had struck him during her first training session. She laughed madly as her Master continued his work, laughed as her sex throbbed with heat in time with each molten strike. Agony blended into ecstasy and back again, until she no longer knew whether she cried out from pleasure or pain. The words to

La Vie En Rose disintegrated in her head. By the end of things, the tune, too, burned away.

Chloe lay in sweat-soaked sheets, her hair clinging to her face, breathless and silent by the end of it all. She did not have the strength to move her arms and legs when Demetrius untied them. She did not see any evidence of rope burn on her writs or ankles, which she had expected to have after struggling so hard against her restraints in those first hours.

"Good girl," Demetrius said. "You did well, *cheri.*"

Chloe turned her head to watch him remove his gloves and pack up the toolkit. She could see his erection pressing against his zipper, a sight that quickened her pulse despite her exhaustion. He had enjoyed her pain. She had known he would. She was relieved that she had done well, that her slipping into shock had not ruined his pleasure. The thought was a strange one, but it felt appropriate.

Demetrius sat down beside her and rubbed a dollop of ointment onto her fresh wound. Chloe sucked in a breath. The ointment stung on contact, but soon began to soothe. She savored the feeling of Demetrius' hand moving in slow circles along her burntskin. He reached forward and brushed the hair from her face. Chloe leaned into his hand, into the cool press of his bare skin. Demetrius laughed softly and stroked her cheek.

"You are mine now," he murmured, leaning in and running his fingertip along her bottom lip. "The person you were before I found you is dead. You belong to me."

Tears misted Chloe's eyes, tears she thought she had run out of by now. She thought of his hand on her face, stroking her, how she craved his touch, and she knew his words were true. There was no place for her but here, no one who mattered but him. She waited for some inner protest, but there was only silence, only his hands and his mask and his eyes.

"Yes, Master."

The world seemed to hold its breath. Demetrius rose.

"Do you want to see it?" he asked.

Chloe hesitated. She had seen Three's and Seventeen's marks, and the marks on every slave in the showers. Did she want to see the number etched into her ownskin? She did. She had to.

"If it pleases you, Master," she whispered.

"Oh, yes, I think you should, *cheri*." The low purr in his voice had returned, the chaotic rumble that vibrated in Chloe's bones.

Demetruis took her into his arms as if she were made of porcelain and carried her to the bathroom. Chloe rested her head against his chest, breathing in his sharp, sweet scent. She wanted to run her hand along the smooth scars decorating his body, wanted to feel the roughness of the bullet scar once more, but she kept control of herself. She was a slave, she only touched her Master when he allowed it. His hair fell around her, tickling her face and her chest. He set her down but held her arms for support, which was just as well, as Chloe felt shaky the moment her feet hit the tile.

"Look." He twisted Chloe gently so she could look over her right shoulder. "You have my mark now, *ma bichette*. You will for the rest of your life."

Ma bichette. Chloe's heart stung, but no tears came. The significance of that pet name seemed trivial and pointless. What mattered now was the mark on her right shoulder blade. It was large, about six inches across and three inches wide. Chloe had expected it to be bright red, like a fresh cut, but the actual marks were dull and yellow, instant scabs in a sea of raised redskin. It was a Roman numeral, as she knew it would be: XXI. The letters were thicker than she had expected them to be, given the narrowness of the steel wedge.

Chloe felt her Master's eyes on her. He stood in the mirror behind her pink and sweaty form, fingers curled around her arms, staring at her through his reflection. Chloe leaned into his chest and he brought his arm around her waist. She could not stop looking at herself in the mirror, wrapped in the arms of her otherworldly captor, framed by his pale form. Tears swelled again, though they did not fall.

"You need to sleep," said Demetrius after a long moment. "You're going downstairs to join the others in the morning. You're ready to be one of them."

Chloe barely registered his words. She stared at the branded, collared stranger in the mirror.

"Yes, Master."

Chapter 19

Mariane thought she was going to be sick. She didn't know what she'd been thinking cutting through campus to get to the bars. She had planned to head through the Student Union, the quickest way to Hollington's tiny downtown strip, and there they were, half of the student body, holding a candlelight vigil for their fellow student, Chloe Leroux, now two months missing. Mariane cut through the crowd, burying her face in her blue scarf, her pulse in her throat, watching her own feet scramble to escape the tearful voices and messages of hope.

The flickering *Downstairs* bar sign couldn't have shown up sooner on Mariane's path. She needed a drink. Now. The blast of warm air and the stench of grease from the kitchen made her stomach lurch. She settled onto a barstool a safe distance away from the few other patrons at the bar at 8:00 at night.

"The usual, sweetheart?"

Mariane jumped, looking up from her scarf. She hadn't noticed Gavin, the senior bartender at Downstairs, standing right in front of her. She cleared her throat.

"Double it."

Gavin gave a short nod and pulled a double shot glass from the bar. Mariane busied herself with peeling off her coat. A couple of guys down cheered at the TVs over the bar, making her heart leap. Fucking frat boys screaming at a screen like their enthusiasm actually mattered. This was why she didn't go to sports bars on weekends. She watched Gavin pour a generous amount of Jameson into the glass in front of her, topping it off with a bit of lime juice.

"Your Irish Pecker," he said with a wink.

That was normally Mariane's cue to say, "*You're* my Irish pecker, Gavin," but she wasn't in the mood to flirt tonight. She swallowed the double and sucked in through her teeth. The bite of whiskey bringing her out of her own head.

"I'm going to need another," she said. "Rough night."

Gavin raised a sandy blonde eyebrow. "Am I gonna have to make sure you get home safe again?"

That made Mariane smirk. "Maybe if you were still single."

Gavin flashed her a grin and made his way down the bar to help the cheering frat boys. The candlelight vigil crept back into Mariane's head. She took a deep breath and tried to focus on something else until the alcohol kicked in, yet the tear-streaked faces of the crowd haunted her. Chloe was a shy girl; most of the people at that vigil didn't even know who she was before she disappeared. They weren't her friends, they weren't her family. They wouldn't have given a fuck about her if she hadn't made the news. Mariane had to smile at the thought. She didn't deserve to look down on them when she was the reason Chloe was missing.

"Gavin!" she waved the empty shot glass. "Need booze!"

She'd never forget the way she felt when Demetrius had threatened her outside of the Oryx. It was the same fear she'd felt when he'd pulled her aside years ago and warned her never to speak of what she had witnessed that night. His hand on her arm had been so strong, even while he bled from a bullet wound in his chest. Mariane buried her head in her hands. She wished she had never seen anything. She wished she didn't *know* that he'd taken Chloe. He denied it, but she *knew*. She should never have brought Chloe to the Oryx. She hadn't thought about it. She hadn't thought Demetrius would give a girl like Chloe a second glance.

Gavin couldn't fill her glass fast enough. She swallowed the drink and stared at the ceiling, welcoming the first hazy wave of inebriation. But the faces of the candlelight vigil didn't fade. Chloe's face didn't fade.

"Fuck," Mariane whispered to no one in particular. Her chest ached. She couldn't stop herself from seeing the young man at the bar four years ago, asking her weird questions and claiming that the DJ had stolen his sister. She had seen him climb into Demetrius' truck. She still heard the gunshot, heard the guy shout. He never came out of the truck.

Mariane had kept herself safe with the knowledge of what Demetrius did by keeping quiet all these years and even bringing girls into the club for him to consider. He never had, and Mariane was glad of it now. Maybe she would have actually been all right if she had offered him a stranger even though she only did it to eliminate any concern he might have about her squealing. But he had taken one of her best friends.

An hour passed. Mariane lost track of how many shots she'd taken. Her limbs were pleasantly numb. People had begun to fill the barstools around her, chattering and drinking and shouting. They were obnoxious. The TVs over the bar got louder along with the crowd and blared various announcements about various sports Mariane couldn't have cared less about. She was stifled by the noise, the pointlessness of it all.

"Gavin!" Mariane shouted louder than she had meant to. "Close me out, baby. I'm going home."

She had just gotten her coat back on when a few members of the crowd beside her shouted, "Turn this one up! Turn it up!"

The flat screen just above Mariane's spot at the bar got louder, unbearably loud. The reporter's voice was so loud that she seemed to be in the bar itself.

"Tonight students at Hollington University held a candlelight vigil for Chloe Leroux, a student missing since September."

Mariane's heart stopped. The screen flooded with footage of the vigil. Dr. Leroux was there, bearded and bespectacled as Chloe had always described him to Mariane, his eyes red but dry of tears. Mariane suspected he had run out of tears weeks ago. She stumbled back and hurried out of the bar as his voice followed her.

"The police are doing all they can, but if anyone has any information…please…help me bring my baby girl home."

Mariane burst into tears. She rarely cried, and never this hard. It was like a geyser had exploded. Her sobs were so violent that she had to kneel in a closed store entrance. God dammit. God *dammit*. She took out her phone. Damn Chloe. Damn Demetrius. Damn everything. She couldn't handle this anymore. She had to do *something*. She brought up the internet and typed in Dr. Leroux's name. He was wrong. The police weren't doing what they could. She had been around the Oryx long enough to have seen money change hands between Demetrius and the local cops after bar fights. She didn't see any reason for that not to extend to his activity outside of the club.

Mariane's finger hovered over the number to Dr. Leroux's Cleveland office. She took a breath and hit send. Chloe loomed in her mind, pressed against the glass wall at the Oryx as Demetrius pushed Mariane aside to get to her.

The receptionist's recorded voice irritated Mariane's ears. "If you would like to make an appointment, please leave your name and number after the tone, and we will get back to you during regular business hours. Have a wonderful day."

The beep of the recording stole Mariane's breath for a moment. She cleared her throat and made her voice as low as possible.

"Demetrius Heart. He has Chloe."

Chapter 20

NOVEMBER 10, 2011

Twenty-One awoke just before the wail of the alarm sounded. She heard the shiver of chains as the slaves around her jolted awake, stirring the links attached to medical cuffs that bound them to their beds. The attendants filed into the room as the alarm faded, keys in hand. Twenty-One waited patiently for Gabe to unlock her wrists and ankles. It had taken her a few days to adjust to sleeping on her back, her arms and legs spread as wide as the single mattress would allow. Now she couldn't imagine sleeping without the firm grip of her restraints.

Gabe flashed her a smile before she brought her gaze down.

"Good morning, sweetie," he unlocked her cuffs. Twenty-One curled her legs beneath her and sat At Attention as Gabe released Seventeen beside her. She waited, listening to the familiar sounds of her morning. The attendants' chatter bounced off the cement walls of the slave sleeping quarters. The rows of beds creaked with the slaves' every movements. She filed behind Seventeen and moved with the line of slaves out of the sleeping quarters.

Twenty-One watched her feet make the same path they tread the past few days; through the open training room with its rows of tables and through the banquet hall, the room where she had first seen her fellow slaves being herded as they were now. The outside air held a pure, cold chill against her naked skin as the group moved across the backyard to the baths. Frost crunched beneath her bare feet. Twenty-One had long ago lost track of how much time had passed in this place, but the air smelled like snow. In Ohio, the threat of snow did not narrow down a date for her. It could have been the end of October or mid-December. She no longer cared. Life had become a rigid and unchanging routine; the baths, serving breakfast and lunch for the attendants, the group training sessions, a private training session with Demetrius, sleep. Though the group training sessions were frightening, having to interact with a multitude of slaves after so long in isolation, she found the routine comforting. She especially looked forward to her time with her Master, of being alone with him. She had a very difficult time when he participated in the group training sessions. When she saw his hands on another slave, her heart quickened in a sickening way.

Breakfast was slower than usual this morning, as the glass slaves who cooked were exhausted from their training for the dinner party. Twenty-One smiled at Three, who stood behind the counter of the restaurant-style kitchen. The little slave piled seven eggs and eight sausage links onto Twenty-One's plate. Twenty-One trotted out in a line of slaves to the banquet hall, where the attendants sat waiting for their slaves to deliver their meals.

"Good girl," said Gabe, ruffling Twenty-One's hair as she delivered his plate to him. She accepted the few grapes from his palm with her mouth and knelt beside him on the floor, savoring the sweet fruit bursting on her tongue. Gabe kept a hand near her head, sometimes petting her like a dog, which she now knew to be a nervous habit. She didn't look up at him, so far above her at the table, but she couldn't stop herself from listening in on his conversation with Rodney, who sat beside him, shoveling his breakfast into his face.

"How far along is she?" Rodney asked.

Gabe sighed, "About three months. I mean, I'm happy, but I don't know, we weren't expecting it."

"Shit, dude. You gonna marry her now?"

"I was planning to before this," said Gabe. "I'm gonna get the ring after the auction."

Twenty-One smiled as she finished the last of her grapes. Gabe was going to be a father. He seemed the family type. He took such good care of her, she could only imagine he would make an amazing parent.

Breakfast continued as normal, until every attendant had finished his meal. They had their crisis drill, where an alarm sounded and every slave dropped to her stomach until her attendant ordered her to rise, and filed into the group training room for their first session of the day.

The slaves knelt in a line, waiting for the Mistresses to come down the stairs from the secret door in the study. It didn't take long for them to hear the clicking of heels coming down the stone steps. Twenty-One's heart sped up a bit, as it always did when the twins entered the room. They wore black head to toe today, which made their green and purple hair all the bolder. They held stacks of long tapered candles and lighters in their arms. Twenty-One swallowed a lump of tension in her throat. In her weeks living with the other slaves, she had been gently cropped, she had been spared much of the humiliation her fellow slaves experienced. Demetrius forbade anyone to touch her without his permission, forbade attendants from using her at their whim as they did with the other slaves in the baths or during their meals. Only the other slaves touched her, and only during group training sessions, under her Master's eye.

"Today, leather and steel slaves will be learning the wax game. It's one of Abigail's favorites," said Charity.

Twenty-One didn't know who Abigail was, but the twins mentioned her often when speaking to the attendants about their training. Twenty-One guessed that she was a Mistress, but did not allow herself to ponder any further. She was a slave. She would not question.

Faith held up a candle. "Two slaves will have their arms bound behind their backs, and will hold lit candles in their mouths."

"They will use a third slave as a canvas to draw a shape on her stomach with the melting wax," Charity chimed in. "Whoever makes the best picture gets rewarded by their canvas."

Twenty-One bit her lip, willing herself invisible. She did not like the idea of this game. How would she be able to draw a shape with a taper candle in her mouth? She was relieved when Six and Eleven were called to participate as the "artists." But her relief was short-lived.

"Let's give our Model Slave a little treat," Charity's voice was edged with something that knocked Twenty-

One's heart against her ribs. "Twenty-One will be our canvas."

Gabe's warm hand on her back did little to soothe her.

"Come on, sweetie," he said, giving her a reassuring pat. "You can do it."

Twenty-One rose on trembling knees. Her breath quickened as she filed in line with Six and Eleven. She had had minimal pain training; a crack of the crop here and there as she and the slaves went about there day, but nothing like hot wax. She tried to keep as calm as possible when Six and Eleven's attendants brought a training table over to them, and Gabe ordered her onto it.

"Keep your legs still, sweetie," he warned as he snapped the cold metal shackles around her wrists. "No wriggling around."

"Yes, Sir," Twenty-One murmured, trying to hide the shiver in her breath. Attendants bound Six and Eleven's hands behind their backs with simple rope and led them to stand beside the table. They tied Six's long red hair back. Eleven's black hair was cropped short and wouldn't be an issue with the wax.

Twenty-One's limbs tingled, agitated. The shackles on her wrists had never felt more confining. For the first time in an eternity, thoughts of escape flittered about the edges of her mind, etched in fear. She beat them back, whispering her mantra to drown out the pulse in her ears.

"I am Twenty-One. I am a slave. I will obey. I will be used. I will not question. I will please my Master. I am Twenty-One. I am a slave."

The attendants slipped the tapered candles into each slave's mouth.

"All right, boys," came Charity's voice from somewhere nearby, out of Twenty-One's eyeline. "The prize for this one is a two hundred dollar bonus for the week. Place your bets now."

The cellar erupted into shouts. Twenty-One focused harder on her mantra, forcing herself to breathe slowly and deeply. There was no escaping this. She would behave as best she could. But when the attendants lit the candles and Six and Eleven leaned over her exposed body, she feared she would lose what little bravery she had.

"Begin," said one of the twins.

Twenty-One braced herself as best she could, but she couldn't have prepared for the searing sensation that ignited her skin. Wax dripped onto her bare stomach like molten raindrops. Twenty-One's back spasmed into an arch. Every droplet of wax was a shadow of the pain she'd experienced when she had been branded. Her mind flooded with the memory of her Master striking her skin with glowing steel again and again. She clenched her fists until her nails bit into her palms. She fought to keep her lips sealed, but cries escaped her nonetheless.

"Stop," she heard Gabe's voice above shouts and cheers. "She isn't doing well."

"It's almost over," came Faith's cold tone. "It's just wax. Where is she in her pain training?"

The uncertainty in Gabe's voice stung Twenty-One nearly as much as the dribbling wax. "Demetrius has only done private pain training, so I'm not sure."

"What?"

Twenty-One didn't hear the order but Eleven and Six retreated, leaving a trail of cooling hard caps on her aching skin. She took a shaky breath. The pain that had seemed so intense had gone so quickly. Her cheeks flushed. She had panicked over nothing.

Gabe appeared beside her, a hand on her shoulder.

"Stay on your back, sweetie. Let's see who won."

Twenty-One lifted her chin up to look at the decorations on her stomach. She saw no pattern whatsoever, only swirls of white and blue wax. She hadn't heard the twins announce the shape they were to draw on her.

"It looks like Eleven's was best," said Gabe after a quick study of the wax.

Attendants cheered and booed simultaneously.

"Twenty-One, stand up," Charity ordered. "It's time to reward the winner."

Twenty-One rose with an ache in her limbs that surprised her. Wax clung to her stomach, sealed to her skin. Herskin was pink and tender where the hot wax had struck her. Eleven's attendant rewarded her with a couple of grapes and led her to Twenty-One. Twenty-One kept her eyes down, waiting for an order. She wanted nothing more than for Gabe to take her to the baths and clean her up for her private session of the day. She buried the thought, lest Faith or Charity sensed her reluctance and punished her for it.

Faith's voice came with an irritation that prickled along Twenty-One's skin.

"What are you waiting for?" she snapped. "Fuck her already."

Twenty-One tensed. She looked up at Eleven, tall and elegant with smooth ebony skin and the sculpted face of a runway model. Other than Seventeen's assistance in her orgasm control training, Twenty-One had never had sexual contact with another woman. She didn't know where to begin. Her gaze caught Eleven's mouth, full and plump and glistening with juice from the grapes. After a moment of hesitation, Twenty-One rose on tiptoe and kissed those lips. She felt Eleven immediately return the kiss, but the slave's hands remained limp at her sides, passive. Twenty-One reached up and cupped Eleven's face. A swarm of low chuckles swept through the crowd of attendants around them.

"How romantic," Eleven's attendant sneered, shaking his head.

"Just get to it," Faith's voice snapped Twenty-One into motion. She didn't want to fail this exercise. She had only been used in this house; a submissive bedfellow eager to obey. For the first time, she had to make decisions on how to proceed. She dropped her hands to the small, pointed breasts of the slave in front of her. Eleven's nipples hardened against Twenty-One's palms immediately. She heard her fellow slave's breath quicken. The sound raised gooseflesh on Twenty-One's arms. She felt an all-too-familiar heat bloom between her legs. She kissed the hollow of Eleven's throat, her collarbone, tasting a hint of salt on her skin, and found her way to one of the firm little breasts. She flicked the nipple with her tongue and Eleven shivered, a soft moan escaping her lips. Her long hand curled into Twenty-One's hair, urging her on. Twenty-One closed her mouth around Eleven's breast and she sucked gently, tracing the nipple with her tongue. Eleven gasped, making Twenty-One moan against her breast.

"Cut the foreplay," one of the twins ordered, Twenty-One could not tell which. "We don't have all day."

Twenty-One almost whispered, *"Yes, Mistress"* into the soft skin against her face. She pulled back and looked up at Eleven. She didn't know what to do next. Eleven's brown eyes met hers. The hand on Twenty-One's hair tugged her lightly downward. Twenty-One responded by sinking to her knees. Eleven gave her the slightest of nods. Twenty-One knelt in front of the slave. She tried to remember what Seventeen had done to her during her training sessions. She even struggled to recall lovers from her life before this place, but nothing came to mind. Eleven's sex was close enough to kiss, hidden but for a small slit between the slave's legs. Twenty-One took a breath, pressing her hands into Eleven's thighs for support. She leaned forward and kissed Eleven's sex, flicking her tongue along the slit. Eleven threw her head back, widening her stance, her hand tense in Twenty-One's hair. Her sex opened and Twenty-One could see a hint of dark plum-colored folds, just barely glistening. Twenty-One delved into the slit and tasted the other slave. Roars erupted from the attendants, growling laughter. Twenty-One lapped at Eleven's sex, hot and faintly musky, encouraged by their cheers. She could only hope she was doing well enough to avoid punishment.

"Twenty-One."

Her Master's voice stopped her heart as well as her tongue. She looked in the direction of the voice before she could stop herself. Demetrius stood beside the twins behind her, his arms folded over his chest, face unreadable. The twins looked tense, but no tenser than they usually were around Demetrius.

"Eyes down, slave," said Faith.

Twenty-One obeyed, her cheeks burning. How could she have looked her superiors in the face? She knew better than that. She peeled away from Eleven and pressed her forehead to the floor in a perfect Supplication pose.

"What is she doing?" Demetrius' voice was a little strange, but Twenty-One could not figure out how.

"Rewarding a slave," Charity responded. "We taught them Abigail's favorite game today. Eleven won."

Silence. Not even the attendants spoke. Twenty-One wished she could peek out and see her Master's face.

"How did Twenty-One do with the wax?" he asked finally, his tone flat and even.

Faith's voice was noticeably relaxed. "Not well. I know you've been eroticizing pain, but I don't think she was ready for the wax."

"That's why you're supposed to consult me when you're going to use my Model Slave," Demetrius snapped.

Twenty-One held her breath, too nervous to breathe. Her Master was irritated, possibly even angry, and it had to do with her. She had done what she was ordered, but that did not matter. If Demetrius wished to take out his anger on her, she would endure it. She would be used.

"Have Six finish with Eleven," said Demetrius. "Gabe, bring Twenty-One up to the suite. It's time for her individual training." Twenty-One felt her Master's eyes on her like pinpoints of heat. "She has catching up to do."

Chapter 21

The interrogation room of the Oak County Police Department wasn't the bare, dismally lit hole in the wall that Mariane had seen in so many movies. The walls were a warm wood color, bare save for a plaque of the Miranda Rights on the wall opposite to her. The chair she had been sitting in for two hours was cushioned and comfortable, the desk on which she leaned smelled like disinfectant despite the pile of cigarette butts crumpled in the ash tray. Mariane had chain-smoked her way through a half a pack while two detectives dragged her through a string of monotonous and repetitive questions. She had come into the department terrified and ready for a battle with combative cops, but the past two hours had crawled by with about as much excitement as standing in line at the DMV. The detectives sitting across from her in drab street clothes had taken her through series after series of dull questions regarding the message she had left on Dr. Leroux's office voicemail. Her fear had quickly dissolved into boredom.

"How much alcohol had you consumed at the time you left the voicemail?"

"Why did you leave a name and not more information?"

"Who is Demetrius Heart?"

She had answered and re-answered the same questions, including her name, job, years attending the Oryx, and she was finally at the breaking point.

"Look, I was drunk, I was confused, and I was missing my friend, okay?" she snapped, tossing down her cigarette. "I've already answered the same fucking questions a million times. Can I fucking go now?"

Detective Gatz, a mousey woman with an unremarkable round face and wire-rimmed glasses, fixed Mariane with a stare that somehow seemed both blank and invasive.

"We're just about finished, Miss McCandal," she said.

"You said that a fucking hour ago!" Mariane shouted. She rose halfway out of her chair and stopped. There was nowhere to go. She sat back down with a sigh.

"Look," Mariane said again. "Chloe's my friend. I *want* you to find her, and you're wasting your time on a stupid drunk dial I made."

Detective Gatz adjusted her glasses but said nothing. Her partner, an equally dull middle-aged black man named Billman, made a sound like a frog clearing his throat.

"What we don't understand," he said, folding his arms over his chest, "is why you would give Dr. Leroux the name of a local DJ in reference to his missing daughter."

Mariane groaned. "I *told* you, I took Chloe to the Oryx the last night I saw her."

"Where she met the DJ?" Detective Gatz asked.

Mariane shook her head. "No. They never met."

Gatz steepled her fingers and rested her elbows on the desk.

"Let's walk through the events of that night one more time."

Mariane cursed loudly.

"I've fucking had it!" she said, throwing up her hands. "You two are fucking idiots! I took Chloe to the Oryx, we danced, we drank, we went home. That's it. Demetrius DJs there every night and I don't know why I said his fucking name. All he did was push her into the wall of blood, okay? That's it."

Gatz and Billman exchanged a glance.

"So Demetrius *did* have contact with Chloe Leroux that night," said Gatz.

Mariane's heart dropped into her stomach.

"No," said Mariane. "Well, I mean, kind of." She took a couple of steps back and pressed her back against the wall, which felt unbearably solid and confining.

Billman stood up. "What sort of conversation did Chloe and Demetrius have at the Oryx on the night of September 23rd?"

Mariane felt the color drain from her face. Billman was speaking as if to a hidden camera, and Mariane had watched enough cop shows to know that there probably was a camera somewhere.

"No," she sputtered, her fingers tightening around her forgotten cigarette. "Stop, no, I didn't say that, they didn't have a conversation. You're putting words in my mouth."

Gatz slipped off her glasses. "Ms. McCandal, you called Dr. Leroux's office and left the name Demetrius Heart on a message. We traced it back to you and now you're lying to us about the relationship between Demetrius Heart and your missing friend."

"No, I'm not," Mariane insisted, panic thick in her throat. "There was no relationship-"

She felt Billman move closer to her, too close for comfort. "Were they seeing each other in secret? Did Dr. Leroux disapprove of his daughter seeing a man like Mr. Heart?"

Mariane sprung back from the wall, her skin cold with panic. "Oh my God, are you serious? There *was no relationship*. She was a stranger. They're always strangers."

The words spewed out of her mouth before she could clamp her lips shut. A sickening dizziness washed through her. The little room spun with such velocity that she nearly missed the chair as she went to sit down. Billman and Gatz moved around her. She saw their lips move, but she couldn't hear their voices. Mariane buried her face in her hands. Slowly, her hearing returned.

"...indict you for withholding information if you don't tell us what you mean," Gatz was saying.

Mariane's head swam. She had just fucked up her entire life with a single slip of the tongue. Gatz and Billman may be FBI detectives, but the facility was still Oak County, and she knew Demetrius had his hands in the department on some level. Word would get back to him. Even if she shut up now, she was dead.

She stared at Gatz and Billman, who had enough sense to shut up and let her think. They had backed her into a corner with skill, but that didn't mean they could find Chloe, or protect Mariane. But what else could she do?

"I want you to get me out of here," she said, trying to regain her composure. She smashed her cigarette into the ash tray.

"What do you mean?" asked Billman.

Mariane hugged herself and took a deep breath. "Get me into witness protection or whatever, and I'll tell you everything I know."

Chapter 22

NOVEMBER 11, 2011

11/8/11
Ms. Dia Belaire
2717 Straeleni Street
New Orleans, LA, 70130
Demetrius,

Where are you? I've never gone this long without hearing from you. I even tried calling you. I know you hate talking on the phone, but I didn't think you would ignore me. Have you forgotten about me? Please, Demetrius, I understand if you don't want to give me away, but please don't ignore me. I'm terrified and I need you now more than ever. I need you to tell me everything's going to be all right. The wedding's in two weeks. If I don't hear from you, I don't know what I'm going to do…

Demetrius was on fire.

He clutched his black jeans so hard that the open fly bit into his hand. The other hand he kept buried in Twenty-One's short honey brown hair, straining to let her control the rhythm as he slid in and out of her mouth. He was supposed to be evaluating her skills. The moment those wet pink lips slid over him, however, he'd wanted to snatch the back of her head and fuck her until he bruised the back of her throat. She stroked him with lips and tongue, grazing his most sensitive spots with just an edge of teeth, as per his instruction. He had grown used to the slaves he had taken from the streets, prostitutes who sucked hard and fast to get the job done quickly and move on. Oh, but he could tell it was a much more novel act for Twenty-One; she explored every ridge and crevice, savored every little sensation. She did not even neglect the testicles, though many women did at first; carefully taking one at a time into her mouth, rolling her tongue around them, sucking gently. Demetrius had no control over the low sounds that came out of him. He curled his fingers into her hair, squeezing until she moaned, her lips humming along his shaft.

Demetrius looked down at his slave. Her eyes were closed, her nipples hard, her hands straining to remain clasped behind her back. Slaves were not allowed to use their hands until they mastered using their mouths alone. It would not take Twenty-One long to reach that level.

He stroked the side of her cheek and she opened those sweet hazel eyes and looked at him. He smiled at her, letting it spread to his eyes so she could see it. Tears in her eyes, again, tears. She had broken marvelously. The branding and her time with the other slaves had shattered her last shreds of resistance, yet the tears still came, especially when he showed her tenderness. The tears were no longer a sign of inner struggle, no, no, he could tell that she no longer fought against the chemistry between them. They were signs of her guilt at having embraced her fate. Soon that, too, would pass, and she would finally accept what she was, and to whom she belonged. He caught a hot little tear with the pad of his thumb.

"When I come," he said, "I want you to swallow."

He pulled himself out of her mouth just long enough for her to utter a breathless *"Yes, Master"* before he plunged back between her lips and began a rough rhythm. Twenty-One tensed at first, her elbows twitching as if she would release her hands and try to regain control. Demetrius nearly squeezed her hair to remind her of her place, but she did not break form. Rather, she took a deep breath through her nose and closed her eyes. He felt her throat open when it had been resisting his thrusts before. She gagged a little when he reached the very back of her throat.

"Relax your throat, slave," his voice was strained. "Open up to me."

Twenty-One obeyed, taking another breath, and he felt himself slide into the sweet pressure of her throat. He threw his head back. Oh, it was so delicious, it was too much.

"Ohhh, good girl," he purred.

He pulled out of her throat, delighting in the rush of cool air hitting him when she took an involuntary gasp of breath. He let her recover a moment before returning to a steady rhythm. By her reactions, it was clear she had never deep-throated before. The thought of having penetrated her virgin throat lent a ragged urgency to his thrusting. It felt so good it hurt; the seal of her lips, the delicate tongue running along the underside of him, her silken throat. With one last buck, he came, hard, pumping the back of her throat and giving her no choice but to swallow. He came until his legs shook, and his vision blurred when he opened his eyes.

Twenty-One sat on her knees before him, panting, her skin gleaming with sweat. Her hair was tousled, her lips slick, those beautiful breasts of hers heaving. Seeing her like that gave him the dangerous urge to gather her in his arms and kiss her lips, her pink cheeks, her eyelids. He clenched his fist and turned his back on the sight of her, refusing to give it another thought. He had assessed her oral skills. His own regiment dictated he leave her unsatisfied, emphasizing that his pleasure is more important than hers, but the pink marks that still decorated her stomach from the candle wax reminded him that he had much more work to do with her in eroticizing pain. He had been far too gentle with her for far too long, and his weakness had been exposed to his entire staff during that insipid little game downstairs. He could procrastinate no longer. She was ready and he had to trust himself to control his urges, no matter how strong they were around this particular slave. Was he a Master or not?

"Are you ready to be bound again, *chérie?*"

He turned back to the slave, whose eyes had grown just a bit wider at his words.

"If it pleases you, Master," she whispered.

She was already trembling as she lay down on the bed by his orders, shifting so her brand didn't hold any of her weight. It would take weeks to heal. Demetrius went to the bathroom and unlocked the storage chest, selecting a sturdy set of four leather cuffs. He loved the timeless feel of binding a slave with ropes, but after the branding he sensed he would have to gradually return to ropes with Twenty-One, lest she link ropes with the trauma of the branding process. He also chose a wide-tongued crop and a blindfold that matched the satin sheets on which she lay. The leather crop squeaked when he gripped it. The thought of striking Twenty-One's soft, sweet skin still sent a dangerous jolt into his chest. It would be a trying day for both of them.

He kept her unblindfolded while he fitted her wrists and ankles with the cuffs, had her watch him strip her of the power over her limbs. He let her see the crop. Tears again, most likely from fear this time. She whimpered.

"Sh, sh, sh," he whispered, stroking the warm slope of her cheek. "Those tears are charming, but keep them quiet. The only sounds I want out of your mouth are the ones I force you to make. Understand?"

Twenty-One swallowed back a sob. "Yes, Master."

He couldn't stop himself from stroking her cheek one last time before slipping the blindfold over her eyes. She looked exquisite, her arms and legs spread wide, her glistening sex betraying her desire, her short, shivering breath betraying her fear. The combination summoned a lust that almost hurt because he had just spent himself.

Demetrius ran his fingertips from the hollow of Twenty-One's throat down to her stomach, the barest of touches. The slave gave a shivering breath, her nipples growing hard immediately. He traced the curve of her hips, her collarbone, her exposed lips and cheeks, savoring the softness of her skin and the little sounds she made through closed lips. It was so easy; the simple sensation of their skin touching brought her to the state in which he needed her, without having to touch her sex or those tempting little nipples. He took them between his fingers and gave them a hard, fast pinch. Twenty-One gasped and released a little cry, her arms jerking against her bonds, but he had gone back to stroking her skin, and she lapsed back into pleasure almost immediately. Excellent. She had grown wetter, as he figured she would. It was much easier to eroticize pain in a slave who already had masochistic tendencies, no matter how subconscious they were. He continued the pattern, caressing her to the perfect point of arousal and pinching her or raking his nails across her skin without warning. Oh, she liked that pain outright, arching her back as he slowly scratched streaks across her ribs, up her thighs, down her chest. The red marks marring that pale skin made him hard again, painfully hard. He stopped before the temptation to draw blood became too great, reaching instead for the crop.

Twenty-One froze the moment he brushed her skin with the crop's tongue. So here was her wall. She feared the crop as she had feared the flogger he had used on her first training day, and the whip he had threatened her with. It was a common wall he met in training. Most slaves he had dealt with feared a tool that did far less damage than what they endured by bare hands. It was an amusing psychological quirk. Demetrius ran the crop softly along her skin as he had done with his fingers, but her limbs were tense, her fists clenched, her jaw locked, waiting for a blow.

"*Détends-toi*, Twenty-One," he murmured. "Relax."

But he knew his command alone would not do it. He brushed his free hand up her thigh and gently parted her sex with his fingers. Her entire body seemed to hesitate. He stroked up her midline with the crop and stroked the length of her sex with a finger.

That did it. Her mouth opened in a silent cry, her knees struggling but unable to bend. She grew hotter beneath his touch, and as he stroked, she ground her sex into his fingers, the crop all but forgotten. He chuckled under his breath, brushing the crop tongue over her nipple as he worked her over. When she had gotten to the point of writhing against her bonds, he raised the crop and slapped it against the swell of her right breast.

Twenty-One gasped, her head flinging back so violently he feared she had shaken the blindfold loose. His fingers were slick with her wetness, so very wet. He struck her again with the crop, sooner and harder than he should have at this stage in her training, but though her cry was more of pain, her hips twitched to meet his touch. He took a breath to control himself, circled her apex with the pad of his thumb and struck her again, more gently, over the nipple.

"Master!" she gasped. "It hurts!"

Demetrius grinned outright at the ache in her voice. "But you're enjoying it."

Twenty-One pressed her lips together, her cheeks flushed, her pulse pounding so hard he could feel it along her thigh.

"Yes, Master," she admitted finally.

Demetrius' grin widened. He slid a finger into her sex, open and ready.

"Yes, *what?*" he growled. His own desire had reached a slow burn, but he would not take her again, not yet.

"Yes, Master," she murmured again, breathless.

Demetrius looked down at the pink folds of her sex, and the image of Twenty-One's face buried between Eleven's legs. A strange combination of lust and anger flared. He shoved it aside.

"Can you see?"

"No, Master."

He cupped his mask, anxiously fingering the smooth copper rivets.

"Lying to your Master merits terrible punishment, Twenty-One," he warned. Twenty-One writhed a little away from the direction of his voice.

"I can't see, Master," her voice laced with an edge of fear. "I promise."

Demetrius let his silence agitate her a bit more, drawing strength from her fear of him. He took a long breath to calm himself, and slid the mask off his face to hang around his neck.

The air that stuck his bare skin seemed so cold. He licked his lips, unable to set himself into motion for a moment. What was he doing? In six years, he had never taken off his mask in front of *anyone*. Mama Dede was the last person to see him without it. Her expression had bound the mask to him more than anything else; pity in the eyes of a woman who pitied no one. Yet twice he stood bare-faced before this slave. He recalled his savage impulse on the stormy day she had tried to escape him, a need so sudden and uncontrollable that he could scarcely remember ripping off the mask. But the kiss, oh, that sweet stolen kiss, he would never forget.

He studied her, the trembling girl who caused him to take such foolish risks. She was tense as a piano string. His silence was a powerful tool for her fear, he noted. The crop had yielded half a dozen beautiful welts across her skin, red and raised. Her sex glistened like a dewy fruit, exposed and vulnerable. The blindfold made slaves less self-conscious, or she would probably have the urge to cover herself as she lay so prone.

Demetrius leaned over her, bringing his face close to hers. She tensed again. She could feel him nearby, feel his body hovering close to her. He was dangerously close to her lips, so close he could smell her sweat.

"You're learning so quickly, slave," he said.

The clarity of his voice, clear of the hollow din of the mask, shocked him nearly as much as it shocked her. Her lips parted in a silent gasp, and in a moment the pink blush had drained from her face. Demetrius shivered. Oh, her fear was thick enough to taste. He slid his lower lip against hers, barely a touch, letting the two metal studs beneath it brush along her lips. She gasped again, her breasts shivering despite her struggle to stay still. She uttered the sweetest, most piteous little moan, her breath hot on his mouth. Demetrius moaned himself, his low growl a crisp alien sound outside of the mask. His body thrummed with the thrill of it all, his heart a thick meaty throb in his ears. He tore himself away from her lips before he lost control. He could not kiss her again. He would not let her make him fall that far. She had been the first person he had kissed since that wonderful and terrible moment with Dia so many years ago. Both had been dangerous. He didn't know why he had done it; only that she was irresistible soaked with rain, eyes wild with rage and defiance.

But if he thought about that again, he wouldn't be able to stop himself. Even now he was planning to do something he had not done since he started wearing masks, a task left exclusively to the twins or some talented attendants.

Demetrius moved down the length of Twenty-One's body, the crop discarded. He grazed the raised welts with his nails. She jumped, twitching against her bonds. Her reactions, always so strong, seemed amplified with the blindfold. He knelt between her legs, stroking her thighs to keep himself grounded in reality. She lay before him, waiting. After one final hesitation, Demetrius licked a long line down the length of her sex.

All it took was Twenty-One's breathless *"Oh,"* to throw Demetrius into a frantic fever. He explored her with his tongue and lips in a way he hadn't explored a woman in years, caressing the silken folds and circling the tiny kernel of her apex until she writhed and made helpless and imploring little noises. He kissed and lapped and nibbled lightly, though he wanted to sink his teeth into the sweet, tenderskin. The taste of her was intoxicating, sweet and hot and heady, like the air of New Orleans. Her rocking hips became more urgent, her moans louder. He backed away from her sex, licking his lips. Twenty-One uttered an animal-like groan, straining against her bonds to get closer to him. Demetrius laughed outright. She was well on her way to being a perfect slave, but her protests had the edge of anger to them. Despite his teachings to the contrary, she still felt that her pleasure was owed to her. He continued to laugh, running his fingers over the curve of her hipbones, her inner thighs, anywhere but that greedy little sex of hers.

"I have no one to blame but myself for spoiling you," he said. "But never forget this."

He dug his nails into her thighs with brutal strength, and growled over her screams.

"This is *not* a relationship, *ma bichette*. I am not your *boyfriend*. Any pleasure of yours is a privilege from me. I am not obligated to give you release."

Her cries inflamed him. He squeezed her thighs so hard that he felt her skin give beneath his nails.

"Now, what is your purpose, slave?" he hissed.

Twenty-One's response was half a scream. "To please my Master!"

"Is it my purpose to please you?"

"No, Master! Please, please-"

"Ah, ah, ah," he said, but he relinquished his grip a little. "Don't beg, little one, not when you've been doing so well. I'll do what I want to you."

He released her thighs, leaving little half-moon nail marks welling with blood. His breath caught at the sight. He licked his fingers and tasted the blood under his nails. Oh, yes. Almost as delicious as her sex. The hot coppery bouquet sent jolts through his veins. Twenty-One whimpered softly, almost as if she didn't want him to hear. He smiled down at the blindfolded slave.

"Good girl," he whispered. "You look so sweet in those cuffs, *ma chère*. You were born for this."

He gathered a trembling droplet of her blood on his fingertip from the front of the wound and painted a thin red line from her belly button to the mound of her sex. He leaned over her, his breath warming her navel, and took in the sweet, salty scent of her.

"You were born to belong to me," he whispered.

He traced the red line with his tongue, taking her blood into him, and tasted her sex once more. He felt Twenty-One tense, fighting to keep still, but her hips seemed to have a will of their own. He loved her writhing, even her lingering sense of entitlement, but he needed to reinforce the lesson. He held her hips and gave her a warning squeeze. She took a deep breath and fought harder to be still. As he worked her, his hands slid down her thighs, exploring the marks he had made. He pressed into them, a light pressure, and the sound she made was not of pain. He circled her apex with the tip of his tongue, flicking and teasing the hard little nodule, and pressed his fingers hard into her wounds. Twenty-One moaned, her breath coming in rough gasps. Demetrius groaned against herskin. Oh, he would fuck her again tonight. Protocol be damned. Everything be damned. All that mattered was her writhing under his touch, the marks he made in herskin, the taste of her and the sensation of being inside of her.

"Master," Twenty-One's voice was distant, urgent.

Demetrius pulled back a moment, licking her sweetness from his lips. "You may speak."

"Please...please, Master, may I-"

Demetrius just barely heard the beeping of someone punching in the code for the door. Panic struck him like a blow to the chest. He stood bolt upright as the door opened, snatching his mask from his neck and scrambling to cover his face as the twins walked in. Charity's mouth was open as if frozen in mid-word when he was able to turn to face them. Faith's black eyes were wide, and she inched a little closer to her sister.

"What?" he snapped, his panic sparked to rage. "What is it?"

He ripped deductions from their faces and bodies. Shock, yes, fear, but not enough for them to have actually seen his face. They had seen that he had pulled the mask to his face, however, and they had probably guessed what he had been doing.

Faith recovered first. "We're sorry but we had to interrupt-"

She flinched when he took a few threatening steps toward her. He forced himself to calm. If he behaved like nothing unusual had happened, they would follow suit. He tossed his shoulders, folding her arms across his chest.

"You will make up for it later," he said. "Now, what is it?"

The twins exchanged a look, but Charity answered him. "Konri's here."

Demetrius' pulse jumped. He fought not to look back at Twenty-One.

"He's early," he muttered. "I'll be down in a moment."

The twins headed for the door a little too quickly. Twenty-One's breath grew shaky. He finally allowed himself to look at her. She lay as he'd left her, glistening with sweat, her knees twitching slightly, as if she wanted to close her legs. He sighed softly.

"Tonight, you will remain unsatisfied," he said, summoning a commanding tone. "Konri will examine you. Answer all of his questions, *ma chère*, and do not lie to him. Do you understand me?"

Twenty-One's voice was thick and rough and near tears. "Yes, Master."

He took one last look at his slave, bound and vulnerable, her white skin raked with nail marks. He stared until her image had burned into his eyelids when he closed them. It took a great deal of effort to leave the room.

Chapter 23

The bar was packed tighter than Demetrius would have thought possible, heavy with the chatter of a thousand pointless conversations. Demetrius did not want to be out tonight. Tonight the alcohol on his lips was true poison; no matter what he drank, the warm haze of intoxication would not take him. Rather, he seemed to skip right to the hangover; a relentless aching beat behind his eyes.

Dia flourished in this sticky hole on Bourbon Street, unashamedly drunk and grinning at the harried bartenders who always managed to keep her glass full. Demetrius smiled to himself. Whomever believed that the old Creole elitism was dead in New Orleans must have had their eyes sewn shut. He looked at his glass, empty of whiskey for nearly thirty minutes now. It was for the best. One more sip of the stuff and he'd start looking for a fight. A little blood always eased headaches like this.

As if on cue, Dia reached over and clasped his hands, her touch cool and luscious. Her cheeks and the bridge of her nose were bright pink.

"Come on, Demetrius, talk to me!" she said with an exaggerated pout. "Don't be the brooding big brother right now. Be *fun!*"

Demetrius smiled at her beneath his muslin mask, but it was strained, and she knew it. She shook his shoulders playfully.

"Be fun, be fun, be *fun!*" she chanted, swaying a little too violently and knocking into a man behind her. She tilted her head back, still clinging to Demetrius. "Sorry about that!"

The man, rough cut and unremarkable, flashed Dia a smile that Demetrius had seen on a thousand men in a thousand seedy bars.

"Oh, don't you worry about it, darlin'," he crooned.

Demetrius' blood began to simmer. He pulled Dia's stool a little closer to him. Dia slumped into his chest with a giggle. His heart jumpstarted. He hesitated a moment, then gently urged her to sit up straight.

"I think you're done for the night, *ma chère*," he said, brushing a brown wave of hair from her eyes. "I'll bet you're seeing double by now."

Dia grinned, "Two Demetriuses. *Moi, je suis chanceux!*"

She slumped into his chest again and caught him in her arms. Demetrius relented, pulling her close to him. He caught a faint hint of her jasmine perfume through the muslin over his nose. A flame bloomed in his chest, a flame that had crept into his interactions with Dia too often lately. He had spent the past year keeping as much distance between them as he dared, with Mama Dede's warnings cutting into him nearly every night they spoke. He had stopped touching her as much as he had, stopped pulling her into embraces when she stood alone in the kitchen or on the porch, stopped stroking her hair whenever she was within reach. He returned her affection when she wrapped her arms around him or held his hand or sat in his lap, but he restrained himself as much as he could. Though even these small steps were excruciating for him, it was vital for him to step back. In the past year, as Dede's strength and frame faded with every bone-rattling cough, his "demons," as Dede liked to call them, had grown worse. He indulged in his urges often twice a night now, leaving a far bloodier scene behind him, yet the flame grew. It burned brightest after Dia's eighteenth birthday, as if that had been some sort of barrier holding it back. Though touching her still soothed him, now the sickening desire came with it, unbidden and unwanted. He found himself fixating on her soft, delicate skin, wondering if it broke easily, wondering if her cries of pain were as loud and sporadic as her laughter. Those thoughts threatened to drive him mad, they threatened Dia's safety, yet he couldn't cut himself out of her life completely. He wasn't strong enough to live without the sweet girl.

He let himself hold her for one more moment before pulling back.

"We should get out of here," he said. "It's too crowded."

Dia laughed, tossing her hair back and catching the eye of more than a handful of male patrons. "Too crowded? You sound so old. You'd never leave Mama's house if I didn't drag you out, old man."

Demetrius wanted to smile, but he couldn't. He felt eyes on Dia, lecherous and longing. A dark voice inside of him whispered, *"she'd be safer with any of them than with you."* He clenched his jaw.

His new cell phone's vibrations thrummed along his thigh, startling him out of his anger. He flipped it open with a little struggle. Dede had just gotten it for him a couple of months ago and he rarely got a call. The damndable thing answered the call the moment he flipped the phone open.

"Shit," he muttered, bringing the phone to his ear. "Hello?"

The voice on the other end was barely audible in the din of the bar, "Mr. Heart?...nurse…Hospital."

Demetrius' stomach dropped.

"Hold on, I need to step outside," he said into the phone. He looked at Dia, half-slumped over the bar, a delicious little smile on her lips. "I'll be right back," he said, tilting her chin up with the tips of his fingers. "Don't move from this spot, all right?"

Dia nodded and turned back to the bar. Demetrius' chest felt tight. He didn't want to leave her alone, but if this call was about what he thought, he didn't want her hearing it, either. He signaled to the bartender.

"Watch her," he shouted over the din of the bar. The bartender gave him a nod and went back to his job. Demetrius hurried out of the bar, pressing the phone to his ear the moment the sticky summer air touched his skin.

"What happened?" he demanded.

"We have you as an emergency contact for Ms. Suzanne Glapion?" The voice on the phone, undoubtedly a nurse, sounded a little uncertain.

It was the first time he had heard Mama Dede's first name, but he knew the name Glapion from bits of mail scattered around the house.

"Yes," he said. "What happened?"

"Ms. Glapion's neighbor brought her to the hospital after seeing her collapse on her porch. She's stable, but she hasn't yet regained consciousness."

Demetrius' blood went cold. He wasn't ready for this.

"I'll be right there."

He flipped the phone shut before the nurse could reply, his mind reeling. He took a deep breath. The air smelled like rain. He had to get Dia out before the rain started or he'd be competing for a cab with a thousand wandering drunks. He shoved his way back into the bar, trying to bury the image of Dede unconscious in a hospital bed from his mind. No, no, he wasn't ready for this.

Dia still sat at the bar, grinning and laughing, but something was wrong. A tall young man had taken Demetrius' stool beside her, leaning close to his sweet girl. Demetrius stared at the man's hand, at his fingers curled around her bare knee, just below the hem of her dress.

Demetrius got to the two so quickly he might have flown there. He didn't know and he didn't care. He saw Dede, a skeleton, surrounded by nurses, her cotton dress pooled over her bones. Demetrius grabbed the stranger by the back of the head, dug his fingers into his hair, and smashed his face against the bar counter.

Dia screamed. The bar erupted into movement as people scrambled out of the way. Demetrius heard only the man's cries, felt him struggle against his hand as he slammed his face into the counter again. Blood spattered the bar, a sleek and soothing red stain. Demetrius let the man fall to the floor, crumpled like a crushed flower. Demetrius looked at Dia. Her eyes were wide, her arms tight around herself. He saw true fear in her eyes. The look seared him like scalding water, but the bouncers were making their way through the dumbfounded crowd, and they had to leave or he would be arrested.

Dia flinched when Demetrius reached for her hand. Her fear made him feel sick. He pulled her in close to him.

"Mama's in the hospital," he said into her ear. "She's not waking up."

In an instant, Dia's fear of him became urgency. She gripped his hand so hard it hurt as he led her out of the bar, dodging the approaching bouncers, and slipped into the night.

Chapter 24

Twenty-One struggled to keep her breath steady, her heart in her throat, as the twins led her down the spiral staircase into Demetrius' study. They had said nothing to her when they untied her, talking amongst themselves as if she didn't exist. Twenty-One preferred it that way. The twins were always frightening to her, with their strange blend of cruelty and sensuality. She followed them dutifully, her arms at the base of her neck, elbows out, stealing glances at the study while she could. She had only seen the space when she had tried to escape and when the attendants took them to the baths, so she had never been able to get a good look at it. The oak bookshelves were filled from wall to ceiling, the sort of shelves you expect to hold dusty old tomes years untouched. But the books all looked modern, with glossy paperbacks and sleeved hardcovers mashed together in no obvious order. Folders full of papers and random loose leaf pages were stuffed between the books. The shelves seemed so chaotic and disorganized, yet the gigantic corner desk at the end of the room was immaculate. Statues stood between the bookshelves, all replicas of Greek or Roman pieces, she noted. They were spotless, as if someone wiped them down daily. Order and chaos in the same space. This could be no one's room but her Master's.

The twins stopped in front of one of the statues that stood between the bookshelves. At first glance the armless woman looked like a reproduction of the Venus de Milo, but Twenty-One quickly realized she was different. She still had the soft, rounded figure of the Ancient Roman ideal, her arms gone just below the shoulders, the long nose and tiny bow lips. But this Venus did not have the same curved pose. She stood rigid, her chest high, her chin tilted slightly upward, her legs a little over hip width apart. Twenty-One suspected that if the statue had arms, they would be at her neck, At Attention.

Faith reached over and caressed the statue as if brushing a lock of hair behind her ear, and the bookcase beside it twitched with a heavy *click*, some hidden hinge activated. The twins pulled the bookcase to reveal a staircase behind it. So far as Twenty-One knew, this was the only way to the basement where the slaves were kept. Faith gave her a soft pinch in the arm to prod her forward. They went down the staircase, dark and gaping like the mouth of an underground cave.

The stairwell opened up to the training room where the group training sessions always took place. Twenty-One looked down. She had been in this room plenty of times. She didn't need to see it again. She kept her eyes on the concrete floor, stained gray as a thundercloud, and tried to move gracefully past the dreaded wooden tables with leather restraints chained onto them, the standing crosses that resembled the ones outside in the yard. She had not been bound to one of those crosses yet, but she remembered Seventeen in the yard and could easily imagine herself tied to one, her arms and legs splayed, her body fully exposed. She shivered, though a tingling sensation pulsed between her legs.

The twins herded her into the sleeping chambers. Twenty-One was surprised to find every slave and attendant in a flurry of activity.

The slaves sat unbound on the beds while their attendants oiled them and fussed with their hair and smudged their eyes with kohl. She caught sight of Three sitting on a bed near the front of the room, but if she saw Twenty-One, she gave no indication. Her gaze was on the floor as Rodney teased her choppy blonde layers like a demented hairdresser. Her blue glass collar shuddered against her throat with every breath. Twenty-One stared at the frail girl for as long as she dared. She expected her heart to ache, but there was nothing.

Charity called out to Gabe, who stood behind the third bed on the left, deftly brushing Seventeen's dark hair. She was as still as the rest of the slaves were, her vacant black eyes staring at the bed ahead of her, Twenty-One's bed. Her face was blank, her hands limp in her lap. Gabe met Twenty-One's eyes and broke into a smile. She looked down, but she felt her lips curve a little.

"Hey, there she is," said Gabe, patting the bed where Seventeen sat. "Come sit, sweetie. I'm almost finished."

Twenty-One obeyed. The other slave did not react as Twenty-One sat beside her. She had seen Seventeen at the height of rage in the baths, screaming and struggling in Gabe's arms, her lips bloodied from biting the attendant who had crossed her. She had seen Seventeen alert and obedient, silently maneuvering the vibrator during Twenty-One's orgasm control training. Now she was as blank-faced as she had been when Twenty-One had first come across her bound in the yard; silent, awaiting command. Her outburst in the baths seemed almost an illusion looking at her now. If she had come back from that, perhaps Twenty-One had a chance. Perhaps she could be as good a slave as Seventeen one day. Seventeen's collar caught her eye, a wide steel shackle that a few slaves also wore. Twenty-One thought of Three's glass collar and her own, made of thick black leather. She did not quite understand the slave categories, though she knew that each group was trained differently. She stole glances at the other slaves as Gabe chatted with the twins. About half of the women wore leather collars like her own, and the other ten were glass or steel. Each slave was unique, some exotic like Seventeen or the heavily-tattooed Seven, while still others had a clean and wholesome look. They were diverse in figure and ethnicity, but each one was beautiful.

Twenty-One relaxed the minute Gabe began to rub her shoulders, his hands slick with gleaming oil. The muscles he worked seemed to melt, and Twenty-One no longer cared about the other slaves or what their collars meant. It was not her business unless her Master chose to tell her. Thought dissipated into the rolling and kneading ofskin. Even the lingering ache around her brand felt soothing. Gabe moved along her breasts, down her stomach, along her thighs, and Twenty-One remembered how she had cried during her attendant's pampering not too long ago. She did not flinch now. When he smudged eyeliner along her lids and dabbed rouge on her lips and cheeks, he behaved as if she were a blank canvas, or a mannequin, or some other uncomprehending thing he was altering.

"Finished," he said after running a dollop of mousse through her short hair. He wiped the oil from his hands onto his ripped black jeans and popped a grape into her mouth. The fruit burst on her tongue and Twenty-One closed her eyes. She was regularly fed now that she was an obedient slave, but compared to her daily bland vegetable soup, the fruit treats were ambrosial.

"I've got a present for you, sweetie," said Gabe, reaching again into one of the many pockets of his jeans. He pulled out a flat circlet, similar to the steel collars but a delicate antique gold. Copper rivets ran along it in vertical rows, and three small blood-red jewels hung from the copper D ring on a long gold strand.

Twenty-One stared at the collar in awe. The other collars, though beautifully crafted, were very plain, even the glass ones. None were studded or bejeweled. She couldn't help but look at Gabe, burning with questions she knew she shouldn't have. *I will not question.* Gabe met her gaze. He shrugged off her curiosity with a smile. There was a weary crease at the corner of his dark eyes. He reached over and unbuckled the leather collar around her neck. Cold air hit her throat for the first time in months. For a moment, she was too startled to breathe.

"The boss always has a reason," he said, an edge of fatigue in his voice. The decorated collar slid into its place and locked, the perfect circumference of Twenty-One's neck. Twenty-One tilted her head from side to side, testing the feel of the new collar. It was lighter and less snug than the leather, but it was cold, unyielding, a constant presence against her throat. The jewels, garnets, she guessed by the look of them, tickled when they brushed against her skin. For a moment she wondered how she looked oiled and made up with a new collar, but she let the thought die before it became a genuine curiosity. It didn't matter how she looked. All that mattered was that Demetrius approved, or rather, Konri, whomever that was. The thought brought a fresh wave of anxiety. Twenty-One drummed her fingers along the thin mattress.

"All right, stand up, girls. Let me look at you," said Gabe, taking a step back from the bed.

Twenty-One and Seventeen rose in unison. Twenty-One had nearly forgotten the other slave was there. Gabe studied them. He ruffled Twenty-One's hair a bit and evened out Seventeen's eyeliner. Finally he nodded.

"Now look at each other. Everything look good?"

A sudden timidity brought color to Twenty-One's cheeks as she turned to the other slave. Seventeen was nearly the same height as Twenty-One. From a distance, Seventeen was beautiful, but now so close and so still, Twenty-One realized that the slave was one of the most beautiful women she had ever seen. Gabe had brushed her black hair so it hung in glossy waves over her shoulders. She had the figure of a woman who worked on her body, with curves of muscle etched into her smooth skin. Her face was fine-boned and perfect as any runway model's, with full sensual lips and dark almond eyes made larger with eyeliner. Twenty-One felt caught by those dark eyes, not like

Demetrius' predatory gaze so often trapped her, but more like she had stepped into a pool of something thick and black, sucking at her, pulling her down into some terrible depth she would never escape. Before Twenty-One realized what she was doing, she reached over and stroked the other woman's cheek with the edge of her knuckle. Seventeen blinked in surprise, looking at Twenty-One as if seeing her for the first time.

Gabe laughed. "Easy, sweetie. Save it for the photos."

Twenty-One's cheeks burned with embarrassment. Seventeen took her hand before she could draw it back. She pulled the hand away from her cheek and gave it a gentle squeeze before she let it drop. Twenty-One bowed her head and turned back to Gabe, knowing her face was pink. Gabe laughed again and patted her shoulder.

"Should've let them kiss," came a voice that made Twenty-One cringe inside. Rodney approached them with Three in tow. Twenty-One took a breath to steady her nerves. Rodney's black boots appeared in her eye line and she tensed when he tapped her chin to raise her head. His leer hovered less than an inch from her face.

"Pretty, pretty," he said, grabbing Seventeen's face in a similar fashion. He let go and fingered Twenty-One's new collar, flicking the strand of gems.

"What is this, the favorite's collar or something?" he turned to look at Gabe, who tossed his shoulders.

"She's the Model Slave," he said, giving Three a quick once-over.

Rodney's laughter was sharp to the ears, like a dog's unexpected bark. "Whatever he wants to call it, but we all know what she's really doing here."

A beeping sound from the intercom system interrupted Gabe's response. Twenty-One jumped at the sound, her muscles tight as if Gabe had never massaged her.

"Report to the training room," came the voice of one of the twins.

"All right, girls, move out," said Gabe, taking Seventeen by the D-ring and filing in behind Rodney and his slave. Twenty-One followed, trying to ignore her fluttering pulse. She lined up in the training room with the other slaves, standing At Attention like a line of statues, their attendants behind them. Silence crept over the normally chatty attendants. It was so quiet that Twenty-One could hear the creak of the bookcase in the office upstairs swing open, hear the heavy steps on the stairs. Demetrius emerged from the shadows, looking as otherworldly as ever. He was shirtless, but his arms, neck, and chest were covered in a solid layer of some sort of body paint, a messy blend of black and rust red, ending across his upper stomach. Twenty-One was struck by the way it adhered to his pectorals, the slender grooves of muscle in his arms. Even his clavicle was etched in stark relief. She was so struck by his appearance that it took her a moment to notice the other man standing beside him, a man she had never seen before.

The man was a few inches shorter than her Master, with mocha skin and short greying black hair. His skin was smooth, save for a few lines around his eyes and the corners of his mouth. Something about the way he held himself, exuding an air of knowledge and experience, stirred memories of a father that Twenty-One no longer had and did not want to think of. It struck her that he was the oldest man she had seen since her arrival at the house. She had no idea how old her Master was; older than her, she suspected; but he was closer to her age than this man's. Though the new man was blessed with smooth, dark freckled skin, he still appeared to be somewhere in his fifties. His light dun-colored eyes swept over the line of slaves with a stoicism that made Twenty-One's insides cold. He stopped at her. She lowered her gaze immediately.

"The Model Slave," Demetrius said softly. She felt both of their eyes on her, boring into her skin. "Boyd will be here soon, so start with her and we'll ready the other slaves for the photo shoot."

Gabe's hand appeared at the small of her back. "Go over to Konri, sweetie."

Twenty-One forced her feet into motion. The man, Konri, led her to an unused training table.

"Sit."

Twenty-One obeyed. She put her hands to her neck, arching her back up, At Attention.

"Arms down. I'm examining you," said Konri.

He opened a bag beside the table and pulled out a stethoscope. Twenty-One took a deep breath. This man was a doctor. Again the face of a bearded man with a warm smile threatened her mind. She shoved the image aside, focusing on the cold bite of the stethoscope on her skin as she breathed deeply.

Konri did not speak to her, other than to order her to change position. His hands were as cold as the stethoscope as they roamed her ribs, the various little marks on her body from training and sessions with her Master, her mouth and her sex. Twenty-One clutched the table when he examined her sex. Something about him made her want to cover her breasts and squeeze her legs closed.

"Medical conditions? STIs?" Konri asked as he packed up his bag.

Twenty-One shook her head, "No, Sir."

"Allergies?"

"Latex, Sir."

Konri met her gaze for the first time.

"Severity?" he asked, raising his brows over his glasses.

"Severe, Sir," she said. "I almost died when I was-"

"You're finished."

Konri closed up the bag and walked away from her, leaving Twenty-One on the table, alone. After a moment, she rose and walked back to Gabe, who was in the process of posing Seventeen for a short man with a camera. Gabe flashed her a smile when he saw her approach.

"All healthy?" he asked.

"Yes, Sir," said Twenty-One.

"Good news. Was Konri the same old robot he always is?"

Twenty-One blinked rapidly, afraid to speak. Gabe chuckled.

"Don't worry, you don't have to answer. I'm just poking fun at the old man. He's about as friendly as the Terminator."

Twenty-One lowered her eyes, but couldn't help nodding. Gabe laughed again.

"All right, get in there and pose pretty for Boyd. We've got to get the catalogues out to the buyers."

Twenty-One obeyed. The photographer led her through a series of poses, most of them slave positions she already knew. Her mind, however, was far from the camera. Her gaze drifted toward Demetrius more than once. He paced around the basement, talking to Konri, the twins, and the attendants. He plucked slaves from the line and examined their makeup. Twenty-One saw him grab One by the collar and pull her close to him, leaning into her ear, his hand travelling to her buttocks. Something burned in her as her Master handled a slave the way he so often handled her.

"Don't scowl," the photographer said. "We're all sexy pouts and bedroom eyes here."

Twenty-One bowed her head to compose herself, burning with shame. She pushed everything from her mind; her Master, Konri, the man from her past who still hovered in the corners of her consciousness; and posed for the buyers' catalogues. She was a slave. She would obey.

Chapter 25

"Fuck you and this fucking shithole!"

Rafe didn't even bother going after Bobby as the door man stormed out of the office, throwing his meaty fists into the door as he departed. It was 4 am and Rafe was fucking done with this whole night. There had been an incident at the Oryx involving a couple of frat guys coming in to provoke patrons. Though the thirty dollar door charge for customers not dressed to theme had almost eliminated such incidents, it still happened with enough frequency for the Oryx bouncers to have specific protocol for handling the situation. They were to escort the trouble-makers out with as little force or fuss as possible, so as not to provoke them or the crowd. Such situations had become full blown attacks in the past, complete with police, lawsuits, and threats to shut the club down.

Tonight, Bobby came to work strung out on meth and punched a frat guy in the face before he had even caused any trouble.

The police had come and gone, Demetrius having "spoken" with them and contained the situation as usual. Rafe ran a hand over his shaved head. It was ironic that he had been trying so desperately to gather evidence against a guy whose crooked relationship with local cops had saved Rafe's workplace from trouble more than once.

It had been a week since the feds responded to the message he'd left on Bobby's idiotic watch bug and outfitted him with a recorder in the shape of a button. They had called at least four times since then, desperate for him to glean any sort of information about the missing girl. They didn't quite understand how masterful Demetrius was about keeping silent, if he even was guilty of the crime. But even as the thought crossed his mind, Rafe knew that Demetrius had had a hand in the girl's disappearance, and worse. He had no evidence, but he knew like you know when it's going to rain. If he weren't absolutely certain, he would never have agreed to wear a wire, right?

"Rafe!" Marcus, another bouncer, ran up to the office door, his face tense and wide-eyed. "Bobby's going fucking crazy outside. He's slashing tires."

Rafe sprang up. "Fuck."

He followed the other man out into the chilly parking lot, where sure enough, Bobby sat crouched on the pavement, his face contorted in inebriated rage, stabbing tires of the staff's cars.

"Fuck you!" he screamed over the hiss of escaping air. "Fuck all of you!"

Rafe got to the man in a few strides, grabbing him and twisting him into a Nelson hold. Bobby struggled, slamming Rafe against Demetrius' white truck, but he was too fucked up to put up much of a fight. Rafe wrestled the man to the ground and knocked the knife out of his hand.

"Call the cops," Rafe ordered Marcus. He pinned Bobby with a knee on the back, but he doubted the ex-bouncer would try to get up again.

"Fuck you, man," Bobby slurred against the pavement. "This job was all I had."

Rafe shook his head, looking at the row of damaged cars. Bobby had only gotten to four of them, stopping just short of Demetrius' truck. If he had slashed the tires on the truck...

Demetrius maintained a rigorous schedule regarding the coming and going of his dolls. If something were to interrupt that, maybe something would happen that could help the police. But what?

Rafe took the knife in his hand and hesitated. The parking lot was empty, save for the incoherent lump ofskin under his knee. Rafe gripped the knife, took a steadying breath, and thrust the blade into the truck's back tire. The tire bucked and hissed, and the truck sank lower to the ground. It was totally flat by the time the police arrived and lifted Bobby off the pavement. Rafe got to his feet and answered the officer's questions in the same rote tone he always did. His heart thundering in his chest was the only evidence of his discretion. If anyone had seen him, or if Bobby were able to comprehend more than Rafe guessed, word would get back to Demetrius.

The police had just finished up when the DJ himself appeared, casting a long shadow in the back doorway, his arms folded across his chest.

"Rafe."

Rafe walked over to him. He briefed Demetrius, praying that he could behave no differently than he usually did during an incident at the club.

"Sorry, Boss," he said. "He got your truck, too."

Demetrius didn't move, only cutting his eyes to the retreating police car, then to his truck. There was no change in his face, or what Rafe could see above the mask, anyway, and yet the air around him felt tense and dangerous. Rafe had witnessed this before in the years he'd worked with Demetrius. This was the only time he had ever wanted to take a step back. His mind raced. He had no plan past slashing the tire.

"I can call a tow truck for you, Boss," he said, unable to think of anything else.

Silence stretched. Rafe had the same feeling he'd gotten when he and his brothers were kids and played chicken by seeing who could bring their fingers close enough to a red hot stove burner.

"Was your pickup damaged?" Demetrius said finally, his eyes still on his truck tires.

Rafe looked over at his F-150. It was tucked away in its usual spot at the far corner of the parking lot, far from Bobby's vengeance.

"No, truck's fine."

He felt like an idiot waiting for Demetrius to respond. A smart guy would have had a plan.

"Is there anything in the bed?"

"Just a tarp," said Rafe.

Demetrius gave a small nod. He looked at Rafe. The anger had dissipated, but there was still a strange tension in the air.

"I need you to help me now, Rafe."

Rafe's throat went dry. He cleared it.

"Sure thing, Boss."

"Tell Marcus to call the tow truck, then help me load the dolls into the truck bed."

X X I

Rafe wound down what had to be the longest driveway he'd ever encountered, hoping Demetrius couldn't see his white-knuckle grip on the steering wheel in the dark. Demetrius had ordered him to shut off the headlights when they had turned onto a private residential street. Rafe didn't have any bearings; he knew they were somewhere in Sylvania, near Toledo, but Demetrius had directed him down many back roads. The few homes he had seen in between large patches of woods were mansions. He knew Sylvania was a wealthier area, but he'd never seen a neighborhood like this, if it could be called a neighborhood with so much distance between each residence.

He and Demetrius had carefully loaded five girls into the truck bed, laying the tarp over them as if they were a pile of lumber. The two smaller ones sat with them, one in between them and one in Demetrius' lap like a child. Rafe's heart was racing; not only because he had driven forty minutes with five human beings in his truck bed, but also because the girl in Demetrius' lap was *her*. His lady with the sorrowful eyes. One.

Other than Demetrius' directions, they had not spoken a word. Demetrius did not even say the street names as he directed Rafe, saying only, "Left here, right here." The feds probably would have gotten more information from him if they had bugged him with a GPS rather than a mic.

Demetrius put the cell to his ear, casting a jarring light in the complete darkness of the wooded driveway. Rafe caught the glint of Demetrius' black nails absently drumming against the curve of One's waist. The sight sent a dangerous anger through Rafe, chased by a terrifying thought: Did Demetrius *know* about his affinity for One? Is that why he had selected *her* to be the one in his lap, why he petted her in that possessive way? Was he toying with Rafe?

Rafe prayed Demetrius couldn't see him clench his jaw. He had to keep it together. Demetrius was known for reading people so well that it made some of the new staff uncomfortable around him, but he wasn't supernatural. Demetrius hadn't been there the moment the bandage slipped and he saw One's eyes. Rafe hadn't acted like Bobby and asked stupid questions when the feds bugged him. And would Demetrius have him help with transporting the girls if he didn't trust him? Rafe looked at the blanket of endless trees along the obscure, winding driveway. Wherever they were going, it was isolated, far enough from anything else that even a gunshot might not be heard. He wished he hadn't had that thought.

"We're here," Demetrius murmured into his phone. "Rafe, bring up the lights."

Rafe turned on the headlights. He had come to an elegant mansion with four tall white pillars in front of the door. A line of men stood in front of the home, dressed in black.

"Hey, it's Rafe!"

"How you doin', man?"

"Rafe's here!"

Rafe squinted into the lights and realized that he knew all of the men. They were from the Oryx, either regulars or former employees or affiliates. The men pulled the tarp from the truck bed and hoisted the women out, sorting each doll to a specific man. Zach, a former bartender at the Oryx, took One from Demetrius and clamped a hand on Rafe's shoulder.

"Good to see you, bro," he said. "It's about time you were an attendant."

Rafe raised an eyebrow. "A what?"

"You'll fucking love it, dude," Zach flashed him a tobacco-stained grin. "The pay's great, and you don't have to just fuck your one charge, because all the girls need experience with different dicks, right? So-"

"Zach," Demetrius appeared beside Rafe so quietly he nearly jumped. "Rafe's just doing me a favor tonight."

Zach's lips spread thin over his teeth. "Oh. Sorry, D. I didn't mean to…I mean, Rafe's cool, right?"

"Just take One inside," Demetrius ordered, his voice as cold as the autumn air.

Zach scrambled away, taking Rafe's lady by the back of the neck and leading her blindly toward the huge house.

Rafe expected Demetrius to explain away whatever Zach had said, but he remained silent, his grey eyes on the house, browless ridges knitted in a pensive frown. Rafe didn't break the silence. He glanced past the pillars in front of the front door to catch a glimpse of the address, but he found nothing. Still, he could identify Zach and every other man in black that had unloaded the girls from the truck. He hoped that would be something for the feds to go on.

Rafe looked at Demetrius, the man he had followed so blindly for so long. He'd seemed different this past month, distracted. Even during October, the busiest time of year for the Oryx, his mind had seemed to be elsewhere. Maybe he was as crazy as the Oryx crowd claimed in their endless gossip. Maybe it had to do with the missing girl. Or maybe Rafe was looking for reasons to justify selling the guy out, he didn't know. But something was different.

As if he had heard his thoughts, Demetrius turned to Rafe, and even though Rafe was the bigger man of the two, he felt smaller somehow, as if he stood before a giant. Silence stretched and Rafe stood his ground like he always did. Many of the other bouncers were unsettled by Demetrius' long, probing stares, but they had never bothered Rafe. He'd never had anything to hide from the man. Some of the more spiritually inclined Oryx regulars whispered about Demetrius' ability to read minds, but that was nothing but New Age bullshit. Demetrius was just a man who knew how to read people. And Rafe was a man who knew how to hide emotions. Rafe's mother once told him that someone only had as much power over you as you give them. Demetrius was good at getting others to give him power. His very presence demanded it. Rafe met the man's stare with the same blank face he always had, trying not to think of the button mic, the feds, or his lady. He had willingly been bugged by feds and slashed a tire to find the truth about the man he called *Boss*. He wouldn't back down now.

Finally, Demetrius spoke.

"Let's go back to the Oryx," he said. "The tow truck should be there by now."

Rafe almost smiled. He hadn't expected a thank you; perhaps a threat or an entreaty for his silence. It was almost endearing that Demetrius knew Rafe wouldn't have spoken of this to anyone had the circumstances been different. A strange feeling gnawed at his conscience for a moment, somewhere between guilt and regret. He thought of One's eyes, of her hand squeezing his. He gave Demetrius a small nod.

"Sure thing, Boss."

Chapter 26

NOVEMBER 26, 2011

"My name is Mariane McCandal."

"Your age?"

"Twenty-eight."

"Where were you born?"

"Findlay, Ohio," she pursed her lips. "Look, can we skip all the bullshit and just get to saying what you actually want to hear?"

Detective Gatz's dark brows met over the bridge of her glasses.

"Fine," she muttered. "How do you know Demetrius Heart?"

Mariane tensed at the sound of his name, and again she asked herself what the fuck she was doing. Here she was, sitting in a hotel room somewhere outside of Cleveland, about to spew the secrets she had kept for years to a video camera pointed at her face. She'd hoped that Billman and Gatz would take her to Florida or Washington or somewhere else far away, like she'd seen in movies. They weren't able to enroll her in Witness Protection until a case was made against Demetrius, so they carted her off to bumfuck Northeast Ohio to "put her at ease." All Mariane could do now was cross her fingers and hope that Demetrius' reach didn't stretch this far.

"He's the manager and resident DJ at a club I go to all the time," she answered.

"And what club is that?" asked Gatz.

Mariane rolled her eyes. "The Oryx in Hollington, Ohio. Can we hurry this up?"

Billman, seated on the shitty double bed, smirked. "You have somewhere to go?"

Mariane glared at him. Gatz held up her hand to halt a potential argument. "We know you're nervous, Mariane, but the sooner you cooperate, the sooner we can build a case."

Mariane snorted and leaned back in her chair. "Yeah, right. You guys don't have shit. The only reason you even knew about me is because *I* left the fucking message."

Gatz shook her head. "We have more than you think."

Something in Gatz's expression made Mariane believe her. She wondered who else they had gotten to talk, but she knew they wouldn't tell her anything.

"Now," Gatz continued. "On the night of November fifth, you left a message at Dr. Leroux's office regarding his missing daughter and you left Demetrius Heart's name in that message. Why did you implicate this man?"

Implicate. The word made Mariane want to call everything off. She imagined hitching a ride from the hotel and getting as far as she possibly could. She steadied herself. It was too late now. The least she could do is give up as much information as possible in hopes that Demetrius would end up in prison. She rested her forehead on the heels of her palms.

"Because Demetrius sells women."

Gatz reached over and patted Mariane on the arm. "Can you say that louder, please?"

Mariane swallowed. "He sells women."

The silence was agony.

"When you say he sells women," Billman said slowly, as if he thought Mariane would spook, "what do you mean?"

Mariane sighed. Her hands were shaking again. "Like for sex. Sex slaves. Human trafficking, or whatever."

"How do you know that Demetrius Heart is involved in human trafficking?" Billman asked, rising from the bed.

"Well, everybody thinks so," Mariane said, trying not to watch Billman pace back and forth. He reminded her of a lion at the zoo, pacing endlessly in a glass enclosure, maddened by the scent of unattainable prey. "Like, he brings in these girls wrapped in black bandages to the club every year. They don't move or talk to anyone. The bouncers say he brings them from his house, and they're different girls every year."

"And you think these women are prisoners?" asked Gatz.

"That's what some people say. A lot of girls have asked Demetrius if they could be one of the dolls next year, but he says he finds them himself."

"How do you know these aren't just rumors and he hires these women to be *dolls* every year?"

Mariane looked at the detectives. "You told me I won't be implicated for withholding information," she said. "But if some of my information is about…another crime, can I get in trouble for that?"

Gatz and Billman exchanged glances. Mariane told herself to breathe. She was already in so deep. She couldn't panic now.

"Was this a crime you committed?" asked Gatz.

"No, I kind of…witnessed one, I guess. I'm not even sure if it was a crime, it was more self-defense. I just…don't know what happened after."

She was babbling and she knew it, but Billman seemed to make enough sense of what she said to reply.

"All right," he said, flexing his fingers. "Tell us what you saw. How does it pertain to Heart's involvement in human trafficking?"

Mariane felt a little sick. She swallowed a lump of tension in her throat. "It confirms them. In a way."

Gatz nodded for her to continue.

Mariane's hands trembled uncontrollably now. The room began to wobble.

"Can I please have a smoke?" she gasped, suddenly struggling for breath. "I'll tell you, I promise, I just…I need to calm my nerves."

Another glance between Gatz and Billman. Billman gave his partner a nod.

"Out on the balcony, please," said Gatz.

Mariane didn't even remember getting up and putting on her coat. She was just outside, a light but brutally cold wind nipping at her shaking fingers as she struggled to light a cigarette. She couldn't believe she was doing this. She'd never breathed a word of what she had witnessed to anyone, and now she was about to spill her guts to two detectives and a camera. Christ, what was she *doing* here?

Why had she left that fucking message? She'd kept her mouth shut about Demetrius for years. Why hadn't she done the same now?

Chloe's face hovered in her mind, and she felt a shadow of the guilt that had driven her to leave the message for Dr. Leroux. She didn't need another face haunting her. She already had one; the face of a dark-haired man, young and wild-eyed with anger and fear. Ramirez. That was the only name she'd known him by, and that was only because it was tattooed across his forearms in big bold lettering. He'd been wearing every day street clothes at the Oryx, which made him stick out in the worst way at the themed club. Normally men who wore street clothes into the Oryx came in there to start trouble, so her fellow patrons had done their best to leave him isolated. Mariane would have avoided him as well but the space next to him was the only spot available at the bar, and she'd needed a drink.

He'd been quiet when she'd first sat down to order a drink, and she'd tried to give him his space. He looked wired, his body tense like a coil ready to spring. It was only after she'd taken her first sip of whiskey that he'd spoken.

"Do you know where the dolls are?" he'd asked in a shaky voice she could hardly hear over the blare of the dance floor.

Mariane had relaxed a bit then. He must have been here before if he knew about the dolls.

"They're on the dance floor where they always are," she'd answered.

Ramirez, a boy no older than eighteen, if that, lapsed back into silence. The rest of the night had been routine for

Mariane; she drank, she danced, she socialized. She was a regular queen of her hive, and she didn't give Ramirez a second thought until he'd appeared at her side out on the smoking deck, his dark eyes flitting about as he babbled about Demetrius. She was used to newcomers asking about the DJ, but the boy's questions weren't typical.

"Is he always in the DJ booth? Does he take breaks? Does he ever come out here?"

"Dude, I don't know," Mariane had said finally. She'd been about to walk away when the boy grabbed her arm.

"He has my sister," the desperation in his eyes had made her nervous. "She was in Detroit, and he…took her."

Mariane had heard the rumors about Demetrius having sex slaves by that point, like everybody had, but she'd always thought those rumors had been about kinky BDSM-type shit, if they were true at all. She didn't link the rumors with what the boy was trying to say. She just thought he was crazy.

"Get off," she'd said, wrenching herself from his grip and heading back inside. She made a mental note to tell the bouncer she'd been dating at the time about Ramirez, but as the night wore on, it slipped her mind.

Mariane had lingered after the bar had closed, waiting for her bouncer in the parking lot. She smoked and watched Rafe and Demetrius load the dolls into Demetrius' truck. A few minutes after they'd headed back inside, Ramirez appeared in the parking lot. Mariane watched him circle Demetrius' truck a couple of times.

"Amanda?" she'd heard him call. "Amanda, are you in there?"

Then, to her shock, he pulled a handgun out of his pants and climbed into the passenger's side.

The sight of the gun had made Mariane's stomach lurch. She'd run back inside and practically barreled into Demetrius himself.

"You can't be in here after hours," Rafe called to her from the bar. But Demetrius saw the lit cigarette in her hand and pulled her back into the doorway.

"What is it?" he demanded.

"There's a guy with a gun outside! He's in your truck!"

What she could see of Demetrius' face didn't change at all. His eyes were as expressionless as the mask below them. He went outside without a word to anyone.

Even now, she couldn't explain why she followed him out there, why she stood in the doorway like a peeping child, but she had. She'd watched Demetrius take his ever-present knife from his pocket and storm right up to the truck. It all happened so fast. He ripped open the passenger door. Mariane heard a sound like a firecracker that didn't immediately process in her brain, because her bouncer had opened the door and dragged her inside. He'd refused to listen to her about what she'd witnessed.

"It's D's business," he'd said. "Don't say anything about it."

Mariane smashed out her cigarette on the hotel balcony rail. Her hands were no longer shaking, yet she didn't feel any more at ease. Demetrius never mentioned that night again, and Mariane didn't, either. She didn't dare ask him what had happened to the Ramirez boy, or about the bandage that concealed a bullet wound. She hadn't breathed a word. But she was about to.

Mariane walked back into the hotel room, bypassing Gatz and Billman without a glance. She sat back down and faced the glaring red light of the video camera. The faces of Chloe and Ramirez loomed in her mind. Maybe this would make them go away once and for all.

"Okay," she said. "I'm ready."

Chapter 27

Abigail's half-nude body filled Demetrius' flat screen as she stood in a Detroit hotel room. Her favorite, much improved from the last time Demetrius had seen him, stood behind her, lacing her into a leather corset. She stood in front of a long mirror, fussing with her patent leather boots and her blonde hair as if her conversation with Demetrius was the last thing on her mind. He knew better, of course; all of this was a show for him, as if he were some fantasy-ridden buyer dazzled by her body and her command over her slave. It was pure vanity and he was in no mood to indulge her.

"When will you be down?" he asked, leaning against his bed. "Everything here is set."

Abigail gave him a sideways glance. "My boys will need rest after the show tonight."

"I don't know why you insist on going there every year," Demetrius snarled, not caring if his tone betrayed his mood. "You have no clients in Detroit."

Abigail brushed her hair over her shoulder and gave Demetrius her full attention, putting a hand on her hip. "Temper, temper. You have your little nightclub incorporated in your training regimen, and I have the Fetish Ball in mine. I've already taken Ash to a few back home, and look how much he's improved." She reached up behind her and stroked her slave's muscled torso as he finished lacing her corset. His task complete, he knelt on the floor, head bowed, waiting for his Mistress's next command.

"Oh, yes," Demetrius growled. "Now he's where he was supposed to be a month ago."

Abigail's eyes hardened, but she pursed her lips into a theatrical pout. "You always get this way before the dinner party. Everything's going to be fine, D. It always is. The boys already have their satyr horns. All we need to do when we get there is to dress them up in that latex paint of yours."

"We're just using body paint this year," he muttered needlessly.

The attendants complained about the metallic latex being too hard to scrub off last year. He didn't care. He didn't want to talk about this right now. Demetrius rose. He was restless. Konri was settled in his usual room at the Manor, the slaves' pictures had been taken for the buyers' catalogues, and the dining room had been decorated for the ridiculous Roman theme Abigail had insisted upon. Yet something still felt unfinished about it, imperfect, and he couldn't shake that feeling.

"Body paint's going to make a mess when the games start," Abigail muttered. "But you're the boss, D."

She stepped around her kneeling slave and sat on the bed, opening her legs just enough to show Demetrius that she wore no panties beneath her leather mini skirt before demurely crossing one ankle over the other.

"I am," Demetrius said, letting his voice drop to a low hum. "And you've become very rich by following my lead,

Abigail. Don't let yourself slip so far into self-indulgence that you become a useless caricature of a true Mistress."

Ash flinched ever so slightly on the floor, telling Demetrius that the slave knew of her short fuse all too well.

"Now, when will you be here tomorrow?" Demetrius said slowly. He smirked at the sight of Abigail's mouth tightening.

"No later than nine, my dear boss man."

The venom in her voice made him grin outright.

"Eight thirty," he said before cutting off the feed to the flat screen.

Demetrius rose from the bed, his mood lifted just a bit. He knew the source of his unease; the sweet little deviation from his usual pattern. But Twenty-One had broken marvelously, and Konri seemed to have accepted the idea of a Model Slave. He made a point not to mention Twenty-One to Abigail. She had grown too comfortable with their successful business. She needed to be kept in line. Still, he would need Abigail to accept the Model Slave as well, and though she was going through training in record time, Twenty-One was not ready for the dinner party. Her uncertainty during the wax game proved that. He had been too selfish with her, and he needed to get her comfortable performing for others.

Demetrius reached over and pushed the intercom button on the wall beside his bed.

"Yes?" came the voice of one of the twins on the other end. He could never tell which was speaking on the intercom.

"Bring Twenty-One to the upstairs suite," he said. "It's time to play a game."

Chapter 28

Twenty-One cried out. She couldn't help it. The strain was too much. The champagne flutes shivered on the silver trays balanced on her palms. If one flute fell, she knew she would be punished. The thick, dull sting of the large leather floggers on her back and buttocks was already punishment enough.

"Slave," came Demetrius' warning. "Keep quiet."

Twenty-One gritted her teeth and fought to keep a proper position. Her legs were spread wide, her back arched, as if she were At Attention, but she held two silver platters with five or six crystal champagne flutes in her hands with her arms stretched out to either side. Demetrius had praised her for being able to hold the position so well…but then he ordered the twins to use the floggers. They felt different from the sharp sting of the rubber flogger Demetrius had used on her so long ago. Their strikes were heavier, the sting more of an afterthought. At first the impact was almost soothing in a strange way, like a rough massage. But soon her skin grew tender and ached more with each strike. Her arms began to grow heavy, the champagne flutes trembled, the trays felt like weights on her open palms. And the smooth, methodical strikes of the floggers took their toll. Twenty-One took deep breaths through her nose to remain calm and steady, her eyes on the floor.

"Good girl." Twenty-One's heart swelled despite the cold edge in Demetrius' voice. She longed to look up at her Master, sitting on the suite bed only a few feet away, to take him in and let him fill her attention. She knew that his command to look at him would not come. How many times had he scolded her to remain in the moment instead of distract herself from the task at hand? She knew he would sense her drifting, so she tried to focus on the pain in her shaking arms, to feel the welts rising on her buttocks as the twins struck her.

"Faith," said Demetrius. "Go to the next step."

One flogger disappeared from Twenty-One's back. She tried not to tense when the sound of stilettos clicked on the hardwood floor. Faith sidestepped one of the trays and stood in front of Twenty-One, so close that each blow from Charity's flogger caused the slave's breasts to brush against the young Mistress. Twenty-One fought to keep her breath steady, her eyes on Faith's pleated skirt and the thin strip of bareskin below her cropped blouse. Faith ran her nails up Twenty-One's thighs, a delicate touch that sent shivers through the slave. Twenty-One trembled. Faith's fingers traveled along Twenty-One's hips, her belly, and finally over the mounds of her breasts. She pinched Twenty-One's nipples, teased them until they hardened. The slave's breath caught in her throat. Charity's blows persisted, but their sting had given way to the hot tingling sensation of Faith rolling her nipples between her fingers. Her sex throbbed with each tug, the flogger strikes urging her breasts into

Faith's hot hands. Twenty-One moaned through closed lips and struggled to keep her gaze lowered.

"Twenty-One," Demetrius' voice cut through the storm of sensations. "Keep your position."

Tears pooled in Twenty-One's eyes. Her arms had begun to sink. She lifted them higher, but she felt like weights were tied to her wrists, urging them lower and lower. All the while, Faith played with her, her hands traveling from her breasts back along her stomach, sliding lower.

'*Oh, please, don't,*' Twenty-One begged silently, but she knew what was coming. Faith's fingers glided along the slick folds of her sex, filling her and leaving her and filling her again, as slow and methodical as the delicious blows from her sister. Twenty-One's eyes closed against her will. Her arms dipped. The champagne flutes shook.

"*Raviens-moi, ma chère,*" said her Master. "Come back to me."

Twenty-One forced her eyes open. She looked up before she could help it, stealing a glance of Demetrius over Faith's purple hair. Meeting his gaze jolted her heart. She knew she should look down, but she drank him in, regaining strength from the heat in his eyes. She raised her arms, though every inch was agony.

"Eyes down," Demetrius ordered.

She obeyed, clinging to the image of him reclining on the bed, shirtless as he so often was, his hair and his mask seeming to melt into the shiny blackness of the satin sheets. The twins continued to work her, but she held fast, until finally he spoke once more.

"Good, good girl," he purred. "Set the trays down and come to me."

Faith and Charity stepped back. Twenty-One brought the trays to the floor as carefully and gracefully as her shuddering limbs would allow. The moment she bent her knees, she knew she would not be able to stand again without great effort, so she fell to all fours and crawled to the bed, kneeling beside Demetrius' studded boots. Her chest heaved with each breath, but her exhaustion was met with a burst of satisfaction. She had succeeded. She had pleased him.

His hand was cool as he smoothed back her sweat-drenched hair, a quenching chill against the sticky heat of her skin. She savored it, the first time he had touched her since that strange day when she had heard his voice without the mask on, the day he had tasted her. Her sex ached with the memory of lips and tongue and the bite of his nails on her skin. How long ago had that been? Two days? And then she'd been taken down to the basement and he hadn't touched her at all. She'd watched him interact with the other slaves during the shoot, but he hadn't touched her. She had become smaller that day, and realized how insignificant she was to this dark man that had become her world. She may be a Model Slave, something new and important to her Master's business, but he touched the others the same way he touched her. They coaxed out of him the same lascivious growls she did when he used her. His words echoed in her head: *This is not a relationship, ma bichette. I am not your boyfriend. Any pleasure of yours is a privilege from me.* The word *boyfriend* had never crossed her mind. It was laughable, in fact. But it wasn't until she had seen his hands on another slave that she realized her own feeling of possessiveness for her Master. Twenty-One felt her cheeks flush with shame. She had come so far, but she was still so selfish. The mantra returned to her. *I will obey. I will be used. I will not question. I will please my Master.* She formed the words silently with her lips in prayer. Some day she would truly embody the mantra. Someday she would embody the title of Model Slave. The perfect Model Slave.

Demetrius lifted her chin and parted her lips with a metal basin full of water. Twenty-One drank greedily, her eyes down. For a moment she thought she could catch Demetrius' reflection in the water if she sipped more slowly, steal another glimpse of him. But this, too, would be selfish. She would look at him when he wished her to look.

"She's wonderful," came Charity's voice, closer than Twenty-One had thought she was. "I can't believe she's the same girl we first saw up here."

Twenty-One felt a small hand in her hair, stroking her like a cat.

"She still hasn't played with the other slaves," said Faith. "Will she be ready for the games at the dinner party?"

Demetrius pulled the basin away from Twenty-One. His boots slid a few inches away from her.

"She's not for sale this season," he said, "so she won't be participating at the party. Abigail may use the games as entertainment, but they're also training tools. No, no, you mustn't forget that. They're tests for our slaves. Twenty-One doesn't need to play with other slaves until next year.

But she does need to learn to obey other superiors. Have you hidden everything, Charity?"

"Of course."

Twenty-One tried to ignore her heart thudding in her throat. Charity curled a finger into the D-ring of Twenty-One's collar and pulled her up. The slave rose, her legs still trembling slightly.

"Look at me, pretty one," said Charity.

Twenty-One obeyed, meeting the liquid black eyes beneath green bangs. Charity's small plump lips curved into a smile.

"Faith is going to tie your hands behind your back," she said, "and when I say go, you're going to search this room for a rose to bring to me. But when you find anything else, you have to bring that to me, too. You can only use your mouth to carry them. Understand?"

"Yes, Mistress," Twenty-One whispered. She felt Faith slipping tight leather bindings over her arms, pressing her elbows close behind her back. She fought not to look at Demetrius, who had risen from the bed and stood at the edge of her peripheral vision.

"Good girl." Charity sat down on the bed where Demetrius had been, crossing her slender legs. "Lay what you find at my feet."

Faith stepped back. Twenty-One's arms were bound together from the elbow in stiff leather, her hands clasped, her spine forced into an arch. Her gaze flicked to Demetrius. She couldn't help herself. He stood near the bathroom door, his arms folded over his bare chest, staring at her.

The thick *thud* of a leather flogger cut across her buttocks. She cried out.

"Don't look to Demetrius." Venom had seeped into Charity's voice, as quick and angry as Faith's blow had been. "*We're* in charge of you now. You're playing this game for *us.*"

"Yes, Mistress," Twenty-One whimpered, dropping her gaze to the floor, her cheeks flaming with shame.

"What was that?" Faith sounded as angry as her sister. Another blow came. Twenty-One yelped.

"Yes, Mistress!" she cried.

"Good," said Charity. "Now go find me a toy."

"Twenty-One turned and scampered off in a random direction, her buttocks burning, her breath shallow. She stared at the room she knew so well. There were few hiding places. The dresser, the nightstand near the bed, the dreaded cage. She headed toward the cage when a glint of metal caught her eye in the far corner of the room, where the walls met the sleek hardwood floor. She changed direction, stumbling, her balance off from the strange location of her arms. She went to her knees and peered closer. There was a thin chain of some sort tucked in the wall's crease. She paused. Was this something they'd hidden? She heard Faith walking up behind her and braced herself for the flogger's strike across her shoulder blades.

"Pick it up!" Faith ordered. "Move!"

Twenty-One leaned forward, catching the chains with her tongue and clenching her lips around them. They came up with a gentle tug; three long, slender strips. Faith struck her across the back of her thigh to get her up and moving.

Twenty-One trotted toward Charity, knelt in front of the bed, and dropped the chains at the young Mistress's feet. She stayed there for a moment as Charity picked up the chains, catching her breath. Her heart already raced, yet her mind was blank. She stayed, waiting for a command.

Charity held up the chains. They were light and delicate like jewelry, linked in a Y shape. Twenty-One caught sight of two clamps attached to the chain's ends. She couldn't imagine what the strange chains were for.

"At Attention, slave," said Charity in low tones.

Twenty-One rose, spreading her feet into a wide stance, her chin up, her eyes lowered. She wasn't able to clasp her hands at her neck with her arms bound, so she hoped her stance was satisfactory. If Charity was not pleased with her posture, she gave no indication. She approached Twenty-One, opened those little metal clamps, and captured her nipples between their teeth.

The pinching was an odd sensation, pressure with an edge of pain. Her nipples stiffened and she felt the clamps press harder against the erect tissue. Twenty-One shivered but remained still as Charity handed the final end of the chain to her sister. Charity reached up and stroked the side of Twenty-One's face. Her hand was soft and small, so unlike Demetrius' firm strength, but the slave's skin burned where she touched. She leaned into her Mistress's hand.

"Such a sweet one," Charity murmured.

She pressed her lips against Twenty-One's, and the feeling of a hot mouth on her made Twenty-One shiver. Kissing. Whatever the reason for her Master's mask, its presence had prevented such contact, save for that one time in the storm. The absence of kissing had somehow elevated the simple act to exotic heights. Twenty-One moaned against Charity's mouth, her sex instantly wet. She nearly followed Charity's lips as she pulled away, not ready for the kiss to end.

"Now, find me that rose," Charity ordered.

Before Twenty-One could take a step, Faith tugged on her end of the chain attached to the slave. It was a gentle movement, but the chain went taught and the clamps twitched and that strange tickling in Twenty-One's nipples burst into full blown pain. Twenty-One gasped, nearly tripping over her own feet to follow Faith and create slack in the chain. Faith and Charity's laughter was dark and breathy, like their voices. The slave searched with Faith at her side, standing just far enough away for the clamps to twitch with every movement. Twenty-One had never been so aware of her breasts. She felt every sway in the chain, every small movement of Faith's hand that wielded the bizarre leash. She headed to her cage this time, searching the well-known space for anything new and strange. She dropped to her knees and tried to ignore the maddening tug of the clamps. It felt odd to be back in the cage, though she had only been gone from it for a week. She did not miss having to curl up in order to fit inside of it, unable to stretch her legs. Her new bed in the basement was equally confining, but straps around her wrists were far more comfortable than the steel bars of this dreaded box.

Finally, she spotted something just inside of the cage, a small vial of frosted blue glass. Twenty-One scooted over to the cage door. It was closed. Her hands twitched behind her back. The tug of leather reminded her that she was bound.

"What are you waiting for?" asked Faith, giving the chains another tug. Twenty-One's nipples stung, such a cruel sensation for such a small movement. "Open the latch."

Twenty-One leaned forward. The latch on the cage needed to be flipped up and slid over, like that of a dog's cage. She mentally thanked her Mistresses for leaving the padlock off the door and took the latch between her teeth. It took a little more force than she would have guessed, but after a moment, she was able to lift the latch. A sudden self-consciousness turned her skin pink. She must have looked ridiculous, opening a cage door with her mouth.

"Excellent!" said Charity, applauding from the bed. "Good girl!"

Twenty-One's heart swelled. She pulled the cage door open, the tug of the chain little more than an inconvenience, and retrieved the little glass vial with her lips. She nearly sprinted over to her Mistress, who extended her hand to receive the gift.

"I was hoping she'd find that," Faith purred, coming up beside Twenty-One and trailing her fingers idly down her spine. "It's my favorite."

Charity nodded. She opened the vial and tipped some of its contents into her hand, a slick, glistening oil. She looked up at Twenty-One, who glanced down immediately, reproaching herself for the accidental eye contact. But this only solicited a laugh from her Mistress.

"Spread your legs, slave," she said. "And come closer."

Twenty-One swallowed hard, but obeyed. Charity poured more oil into her hand, coating her fingers, and gently spread the folds of Twenty-One's sex. The slave sucked in a breath. The oil was warm on contact, and grew warmer immediately. Charity circled her apex, coating it in oil. It felt as though her Mistress's fingers were embers, growing hot and hotter, until her sex became sweet, aching fire. It tore a moan from Twenty-One's throat, threw her head back. Hot, tingling, it was as if her sex had swelled, longing for her Mistress's fingers, for any contact at all.

Charity withdrew. "Go."

Twenty-One forced herself to move. The heat in her sex did not relent, and now the smallest movements of the chain held a new delicious torment. Tears stung her eyes. She walked in a circle, unable to focus enough to choose a direction. She could think of nothing but the seething sensations in her breasts and her sex. She looked at Faith, at the curve of her mouth. She wanted to open those lips with her tongue, crush her breasts against the tight black blouse, feel the pleats of Faith's skirt against her thighs. Faith's smile told her that her Mistress knew exactly what was on her slave's mind. She jerked the chain and Twenty-One cried out, pain and pleasure merging for a terrible moment.

"Eyes down," said Faith, laughing. "And focus."

"Yes, Mistress," Twenty-One was unable to bring her voice above a murmur.

She trotted over to the dresser. Nothing on top of it. She felt her own wetness mixed with the oil begin to run down her inner thigh. She barreled ahead, increasing her pace, crossing the room and passing the stone still Demetrius to get to the nightstand. Yes, the drawer was ajar. She went to her knees and wrenched the drawer open with her lips without a moment's hesitation. She uttered small frustrated sounds when she discovered that it was not a rose in the drawer, but a small golden ball, only a few inches in diameter. She dipped her head into the drawer and struggled to get the ball between her lips, not caring about how silly she may have looked as she carried the ball in her mouth over to her Mistress. She did not even care to guess what the ball meant for her. She thought only of the maddening heat on the most delicate part of her body, of any release at any cost.

"Oh, Charity, I think she's ready for our little game to be over," Faith giggled as Twenty-One dropped the ball into Charity's palm.

Charity ordered the slave's legs apart. "Too bad she hasn't found the rose yet."

Twenty-One came to herself at the touch of Charity's hand on her sex. She balanced the ball on her fingertips, brushing it against the wetness between Twenty-One's legs.

"Oh, Mistress," Twenty-One whispered. "Please, I can't-"

"Quiet," Charity ordered. The golden ball nudged Twenty-One's opening, colder than it had felt in her mouth. "Let me in, slave. And you may not come."

Tears spilled over Twenty-One's cheeks. She had come far in her training, able to come on command even when her sex was not touched. She had not come without permission since the one time for which she had been punished. She would not fail when she had come so far. She took a deep breath and forced herself to relax. The ball slid into her slowly, and the sensation of her sex receiving it, tightening around it, made her gasp. She felt pressure build with the feeling of the ball inside of her, cold and hard and strange, a pressure which promised forbidden release. She sobbed, digging her nails into her palms behind her back. She would not come without permission. Not again. Never again.

I will obey.

"Good girl," Charity whispered. "Excellent control. Now, find me the rose. You were there already, you just missed it."

Twenty-One clenched her jaw, *"You just missed it."* She looked at the dresser. Nothing had been on top of it, but the golden ball had been in the nightstand drawer. She had to find a way into the dresser without her hands.

Moving had become agony. The oil continued to torment her. She felt the ball inside of her with every step. It seemed so much bigger than she knew it was, solid and heavy. She feared it would drop out of her if she took a wrong step, and she would undoubtedly be punished for that. It was strange to have an inanimate thing within her, unyielding and unresponsive to her sex enveloping it. Faith had tightened the slack on the chain; even Twenty-One's breath caused the clamps to pull.

She stepped in front of the dresser. The drawers were lacquered black, smooth and shining. It would be difficult to grip with her teeth, but she had no choice. Twenty-One bent at the waist, squeezing her legs together to keep the ball from slipping, and struggled with the round knobs. She barely found a grip with her teeth. Faith tugged impatiently at the chains, sending small shockwaves of pleasure from Twenty-One's nipples to her groin. The flogger came when she still couldn't get a grip, and Twenty-One squealed against the heavy blows, but not from pain.

"Use your teeth," said Faith. "Bite harder."

Twenty-One whimpered and big the dresser knob, gnawing at it with her molars. She almost laughed in relief when the drawer slid open. A long-stemmed rose, blushing pink and fully bloomed, sat in the drawer.

"Lucky girl," laughed Charity. "I don't think she'd be able to handle opening another drawer."

Twenty-One lapped at the rose with her tongue, catching it on a thorn before trapping the stem between her teeth. It didn't matter. Her Mistresses' laughter didn't wound her. She didn't care how ridiculous she looked as she scampered over to Charity, lay the rose in her lap, and knelt on the floor with her legs clenched to keep the ball within her. She was beyond shame, beyond tears. She was one relentless, pulsing need for touch.

The twins descended on her, cooing their praises through whispers. Their sweet mouths left searing kisses on Twenty-One's skin, their hands roamed her hair, her neck, her back. The sensation of the clamps releasing her nipples nearly pushed her over the edge. She opened her mouth to Charity, tasted her, gently sucked her tongue. She leaned into Faith's teeth as they grazed her neck, leaned into the endless caresses. Such soft, sweet ecstasy.

"Oh," Twenty-One whispered, her mouth forming words of its own volition. "Oh, yes, please, yes, I love you. I love you."

"Enough."

The world stopped. Faith and Charity melted away. Twenty-One moaned, longing to retrieve their embrace, but she knew they would not spite him. They would not disobey. They were slaves themselves to that voice.

She felt the heavy thud of Demetrius' boots against the floor, saw the twins rise out of the corner of her eye. Her limbs trembled. Her skin had begged to be touched, and now that she was abandoned again, it was unbearable. The tears returned, and her sex felt impossibly hot, impossibly wet. She would go mad if she was given no release. She prayed that that was not her Master's will.

Demetrius set his boot on the back of her neck. Twenty-One sank down immediately, her forehead against the floor. He kept his foot on her neck, pressing just hard enough to dig her forehead into the hardwood. Twenty-One remained as still as possible, her pulse in her ears. Silence hung in the air, holding a familiar, dangerous charge. Finally Faith spoke, her voice soft and uncertain.

"You've trained her well."

"She's as obedient as any of the others," Charity dared to add. "Don't you think?"

Twenty-One kept her breath as quiet as possible.

"Oh, *yes*," Demetrius replied, his voice louder than Twenty-One had expected. "She played this game *very* well, didn't she, our *eager* little slave."

Twenty-One swallowed hard, her throat tight, skin prickling with dread. She had not heard that tone in his voice in a very long time; that tone that didn't match his words. She had played the game, she had succeeded, or so she'd thought. Had she done something wrong?

"Go see that the attendants have their charges in bed," he said to the twins. "We have a big day tomorrow, after all."

Faith and Charity left without a word. The door clicked shut, and Demetrius fell into silence once more. Twenty-One felt his eyes on her, felt them digging into her as his boot dug into her neck. She remained still, her breath shallow. Her tormented sex throbbed in time with her heartbeat, stirring desire even as fear crept along her spine.

Demetrius lifted his boot and stepped back.

"On your knees," he ordered.

Twenty-One lifted herself up. The twins had not removed her bindings before they had gone, leaving her arms tight behind her back, her hands resting against her buttocks. She straightened her spine in the best posture she could muster, spreading her knees apart in typical form. The golden ball, still inside of her, sank toward her opening. She snapped her legs closed immediately.

Demetrius' low chuckle cut through the quiet like a razor through silk.

"Ah, yes," he said. "The twins do enjoy their little torments, don't they?" He took a step toward her and ran a finger across the back of her shoulders. "Do you like the feeling of that ball inside of you, Twenty-One?"

Twenty-One swallowed again. "Only if it pleases you, Master." she whispered.

Demetrius' languid fingers caressed her neck. "Oh, it pleases me, *ma chère*, yes, it certainly does."

He crouched down behind her, his knees on either side of her waist. The heat of his bare chest felt almost solid on Twenty-One's back. She fought the urge to lean back into him. To touch her Master without permission…but Demetrius' arm roped across her waist, and he cupped her sex, and all thought dissolved into the same terrible need she had been tortured with from the moment Charity had coated her with oil.

"Master…" she whispered.

"Sh, sh, sh," he chided. "Give me the ball, *chérie*. Open your legs."

Twenty-One's cheeks flushed. Holding the ball inside of her had been a natural inclination, almost involuntary. She had to focus to release the muscles she was not even certain she could control. The ball dropped slowly. She breathed deeply to relax her opening enough to allow it to pass into Demetrius' hand.

"Such a good girl," Demetrius' voice held a low hiss that did not feel like praise.

He brushed the ball across Twenty-One's collarbone. It was warm and wet, leaving a streak of heat from the oil on her skin. She drank in his touch, the ball and his free hand stroking up and down her arm, but her Master's tone gave her pause. She did not understand, but she would not question. Demetrius' leather mask brushed her left ear and she heard the rush of his breath inside of it. She shuddered, her sex throbbing.

"Such a *good girl*," he hissed again, dragging the ball back and forth along her clavicle and down over the tops of her breasts. "You behaved so well for the twins, didn't you? The way you *scrambled* to find those little toys for them, prancing for Faith's flogger like a prized pony. And you were *so eager* to please your *Mistresses*, weren't you? Oh, yes, you drank up their attention, didn't you?"

His words had descended into a rumbling growl, his left hand squeezing her arm past the point of pleasure, harder still. His fingers dug throughskin to bone. Twenty-One yelped and Demetrius burst into movement. He heaved the golden ball across the room. It collided with the dresser with a deafening *crack* and came racing back toward them on the floor. Demetrius seized Twenty-One by her hair and wrenched her up from her knees. She screamed for him, terror turning her legs to liquid. Demetrius hurled her onto the bed and pinned her with his hand on her hair. He unlaced her arm bindings with his free hand with feverish dexterity. Twenty-One panted against the sheets, trapped between fear and need. She did not understand what her Master was thinking, whether or not he was pleased or infuriated with her. Questions bloomed and died on her tongue. Had she played the game correctly? What had she done wrong?

But the bindings were gone and he was hard against her buttocks. His hand came and went from her sex before she had time to enjoy it, coating himself in her oiled wetness. He spread her cheeks and pressed against her anus, an opening yet untouched. Fear seized her, but it did not matter. He was inside of her, in an entirely new way, filling her with an alien pressure. She screamed into the pillow, pain overtaking her senses as he forced his way deeper inside, but the pain had gone as quickly as it had come. Thought gave way to his slow, brutal rhythm, and the strange and frightening pressure became sensuous, warm, sweet waves of heat cresting and breaking with the rocking of his hips. She ached for him to enter her tormented sex, and she would have begged had she not buried her face in the bed sheets. Demetrius moaned, striking a chord in her bones, and slid the length of him in and out of her slowly and deliberately. Twenty-One fought to stop her hips from rocking to meet his thrusts, fought to keep herself still. She was not allowed to move. Her mercurial Master teetered on the edge of rage, she felt it; the coiled restraint in his grip and in his thrusts. She did not know why he was angry, but she would not question, and she would do her best not to tip the scale. But soon even her desire to obey ebbed, weathering away with each slow thrust. Demetrius' fingers appeared between her legs, circling the hard ember of her apex, and all the torment of her game with the twins culminated in that single little nodule.

"Oh, God," Twenty-One breathed into the sheets.

"What is your purpose, slave?" Demetrius' voice was rough and steady. He pulled himself out of her completely, waiting.

"To serve my Master," Twenty-One answered, pleading.

Demetrius dipped low, pressing his body into her, bringing his face to hers. "And who is your Master?"

Twenty-One dared to look at him. He met her gaze, close enough to kiss, his inky black hair streaked over his white skin.

"Demetrius," She barely mouthed the word.

He leaned harder into her back.

"Who is your Master?" he repeated.

Twenty-One tumbled into the icy grey storm in his eyes, and somehow she knew she would never find her way out again.

"Demetrius," she breathed.

Demetrius thrust into her with a final stroke of her apex, hitting her very core, and the world became light and ecstasy.

Chapter 29

Dublin was surprisingly green for a city so close to Columbus. Gatz had expected a much more urban landscape. She and Billman had passed patches of woods and even a nature preserve along the Scioto River while they made their way to Old Dublin, where Ms. Renata Ramirez resided. Billman insisted on driving despite his insatiable need to look at every single building, tree, and parking structure they happened to pass. Luckily, he braked like a Hollywood stuntman, or they would have plowed into the car in front of them at every stoplight from Beachwood to Columbus. He also chain smoked, sucking down each cigarette like a teenager about to be caught by his parents. Gatz spent most of the two and a half hour drive with her nose pressed to her cracked window, sucking in the clean oxygen she could glean in this ashtray on wheels.

Her nerves were raw at this point, having spent two months on what had started out as a simple missing persons case. What a clusterfuck it had become, with druggie moles and otherwise non-credible witnesses, a tight-lipped subculture leaking unsubstantiated rumors about human trafficking, and little evidence that a crime had even occurred in the disappearance of Chloe Leroux. Had her father not hired a private eye who had stumbled across evidence of bribery between the Wood County Police Department and Demetrius Heart, Gatz and Billman wouldn't even be here. But the bug they had given Oryx bouncer Raphael "Rafe" Raynal had proven fruitful. Billman was eager to run the names of the individuals Rafe had seen that night at Heart's home and coax one of them into questioning. Gatz, however, had had a gut feeling about the story Mariane McCandal had told her about the assault on Heart and his alleged assailant. She had run the name Amanda Ramirez and found a missing person's report for both her and her brother, Anthony Ramirez, filed only months apart in 2008. A brief but bitter phone conversation with their mother was all it took to convince Billman to drive down with Gatz for an interview. This could be the door to the warrant they needed to search Heart's home.

Renata Ramirez lived in a gated community in the affluent area of Old Dublin. The homes were large and identical. Gatz supposed the residents did not have to lift a finger to keep their manicured lawns immaculate.

Ms. Ramirez answered the door well-dressed and far too drunk for 3:30 in the afternoon, though Gatz could only tell by her breath. She smiled like a suburban socialite should, offering the detectives seats and refreshments in her designer living room. Gatz couldn't help but notice the harsh lines around her tired eyes. She had the air of a woman trapped under the weight of tragedy. But maybe Gatz just interpreted her that way because she knew of the woman's missing children.

"So, what brings the FBI to my doorstep after three years of nothing?" she said, her smile doing little to mask the bite in her words. "I assume you're not just here to open old wounds?"

Unfortunately, Billman beat Gatz to the punch for a reply.

"Ms. Ramirez, we're sorry for your loss, but we-"

"Sorry for my loss?" Ms. Ramirez snapped, her lips growing thinner before Gatz's eyes. "As if my children died in some sudden accident? No, Detective Whomever, they disappeared one after the other, and all I got from the police was a shrug and the same hold music ringing in my ears every time I called them."

Billman opened his mouth again, but Gatz clamped a hand on his shoulder to silence him.

"Ms. Ramirez, I'll get right to the point. We have reason to believe that your son disappeared searching for your daughter, and that their disappearances are tied to a case we're currently trying to solve."

Ms. Ramirez looked away and studied the stitching in her sleek leather armchair. She was a thin woman, fine-boned, but her moment of fierceness had shown a strong personality within her meticulously slender frame. Her green pantsuit held a designer label, but it hadn't been ironed. A large crease broke the line of her waist, as if Ms. Ramirez spent much of her time doubled over. Gatz pictured the woman with her knees on her elbows, her face buried in her hands, sobbing tearlessly, her eyes dry from years of crying.

"I see," Ms. Ramirez muttered.

The three slipped into an uncomfortable silence. Gatz could feel her partner's restlessness, coiled to spring, but he'd learned that Gatz's sensitivity was more appropriate for the situation than his blunt manner.

"Anthony always went out to find Amanda," Ms. Ramirez said finally. "She was our little…problem child." She rolled her eyes at the detectives. "Drugs, boys, theft, what have you."

Billman shifted beside Gatz, antsy. Gatz tried with all her might to will him to remain silent.

"We hadn't heard from Amanda in months, but that was hardly unusual," Ms. Ramirez continued. "Honestly, I was happy to wash my hands of her. But Anthony always went out and brought her back."

Gatz fought to find the right words to say. "He's a good son."

Ms. Ramirez shook her head, tears staining her red-rimmed eyes. She wiped at them before they had even spilled, as if the act of crying had become little more than an annoyance.

"*Was* a good son, detective. *Was*," she said with a sigh. "A mother knows when her child is dead." She stood up, wobbling for just a moment before regaining her stiff poise. "I'm assuming you're here about that Demetrius Heart person."

Gatz couldn't mask her surprise. "How-"

"How do you know that name?" Billman's self-restraint had reached its end. "Was your daughter affiliated with him?"

Gatz tensed at her partner's tone. This was not an interrogation. But Ms. Ramirez just waved her hand dismissively and gestured for them to follow her into the adjoining dining room. She strolled over to a lavish glass bar with rows of high end liquor and poured herself a glass from an open bottle of high-end gin.

"That's the man Anthony went to find," she said. "Demetrius Heart. Amanda had been living in Detroit, apparently, and her friends told Anthony that she'd left a bar with him one night and never came back." She sipped the gin like ice water. "She was always good at finding men to shack up with."

"Is that what Anthony said she was doing?" Gatz asked carefully. "Shacking up with Mr. Heart?"

Ms. Ramirez rolled her eyes. "No. He said Demetrius Heart *took* her, that he had to go and save her. He did like playing the hero, I guess. Saving his innocent baby sister." She spat the words into her glass. Her hand was shaking as she set it on the table and turned to the detectives. "I'll give you his laptop, if you want. He bought his bus ticket from there and found whatever he knew about Demetrius Heart on it, might have saved it. The police didn't bother to take anything when he first went missing." She folded her arms. "I'll give you whatever you want, but I don't want to hear from Amanda if you find her. She's no longer a part of this family."

Gatz and Billman exchanged a glance, but said nothing. Ms. Ramirez directed them to Anthony's bedroom and the detectives gathered their evidence and left silently as the woman sat in her living room, sipping gin and staring out the window with a hollow gaze.

Chapter 30

"Don't fidget now. You've been doing so well."

"Sorry, Sir," Twenty-One whispered. She flexed her feet and her fists to keep her circulation going. She had been standing in the slave quarters for the past twenty minutes while Gabe dabbed her with a sponge coated in thick gold paint that itched and cracked with the slightest movement. The basement was far more frantic than it had been when Twenty-One had been brought down for Konri's inspection. Attendants ran to and from their posts, painting and bejeweling their slaves in a fervor. The slaves were still and obedient as always, but they were stunning caked in gold paint, their hair threaded with ribbon like Greek statues. Some of them had little gems on their foreheads, and Twenty-One noticed those with piercings had had them replaced with jewelry brighter and more garish than before. Seventeen sat on the bed while Gabe worked on Twenty-One, exquisite in gold, with snake-shaped bangles on her upper arms and red gems trailing down her midline. Gabe wore dress slacks and an undershirt. His white button-down, tie, and suit jacket hanging on the edge of the bed, safe from the paint. Twenty-One noticed a bulge in his pocket that wasn't normally there. The unmistakable curve of a gun handle poked out from his waistband and made

Twenty-One's stomach lurch. The attendants had never worn firearms before. She wanted to ask Gabe about it, but she was certain he would not explain it to her.

The dinner party would start in less than an hour. Twenty-One had tried to keep calm when Gabe had woken her for preparation, but he had sensed her nervousness right away. He reassured her while he painted, giving her the rundown of the night in between swearing at the "cheap ass shit" he had to work with.

"The dinner party kicks off the best part of the season," he'd explained. "Abigail comes down with her ten slaves, we all dress you up to some theme she's picked out, and we all eat and play games while the buyers get their first look at you and make requests and things like that. The slaves always like it because you guys get some real food if you're good. Last year, it was really classy, all black and white with the slaves dressed like ponies. You know, leather harnesses and tails and that shit. This year it's Ancient Greece. Food's going to be great, like an ancient feast."

Twenty-One's mind raced. Food? Games? More slaves? It all sounded so elaborate. The word *buyers* made her heart skip, but she knew that her Master wouldn't sell her for another year. She was safe for now. She wondered who Abigail was, and why she needed to bring more slaves. The slave quarters seemed ready to burst as it was with Twenty-One of them down there. The beds were far too small to share.

The idea of food, *real* food, also set her imagination drifting. She had had nothing but vegetable soup and fruit for so long, she could hardly picture anything more complex. Gabe had used the word *feast*. What did a slave eat at a feast?

The intercom system beeped, startling Twenty-One from her thoughts.

"Attendants, please line up your slaves in the training area," came the voice of Faith or Charity.

Gabe patted Twenty-One's head, careful not to muss her moussed hair. "We've got to get going, ladies."

Twenty-One filed into line as she did every morning. She tried to quiet her mind, as always, with her mantra. *I am Twenty-One. I am a slave. I will obey. I will be used.* But her mental chant gave way to her nervousness as Gabe and the attendants led them to stand beside one another in the training are of the basement.

"Kneel!" one attendant called.

Twenty-One knelt, surrounded by beautiful gilded women, their attendants in suits behind them. She heard the sound of the statue door opening and the prickling anxiety began anew. She took a deep breath. Her questions and curiosities about the dinner party did not matter. She would eat if her Master wanted her to. She would play whatever games they had constructed if he ordered it. Her mind drifted back to her game with the twins. She dreaded the thought of performing such humiliating acts in front of so many. If it pleased Demetrius, she would endure it.

She heard the breathy laughter of the twins, a sound that now tightened things low in her body. The heavier footfalls of her Master's boots, too, reached her ears, hitching her breath in her chest.

"Slaves," Demetrius ordered. "Look at me."

The slaves obeyed, lifting their heads.

The floor wobbled beneath Twenty-One's bare feet. Demetrius stood before his slaves in a sleek black suit, immaculately tailored to his lean, muscled frame. She had never seen him in anything but his eerie Oryx-style clothing, and seeing him in less exotic attire made him seem all the more otherworldly. He wore a skinny tie the deep yellow of goldenrod flowers. Twenty-One would never have guessed he would be interested in that shade that shone so brightly in the blackness. Likewise, his skin seemed paler against the suit, his hair blending into the jacket so perfectly that it seemed to disappear past his shoulders when he stood still. His mask looked to be made of the same material as his suit, with the same subtle gleam. The slave was so struck by her Master's appearance that she did not realize he had been speaking while she'd been staring.

"…here in twenty minutes," he continued. "And the buyers will be logging on at 9. The buyers are your future Masters, and you will serve them as you serve me and your Mistresses."

He slid his arms around Faith and Charity's tiny waists. They, too, were dressed up, wearing surprisingly conservative column gowns, their short hair decorated with small white flowers. Twenty-One studied them, but she could not linger long from the man who stood between them.

"Slaves," he said again. "What are you?"

The slaves spoke in unison. The mantra rose in a choir of soft murmurs.

"I am a slave. I will obey. I will be used. I will not question. I will please my Master."

Demetrius nodded, satisfied. "Good. Attendants, Faith and Charity will look over your charge's costume, and then you can take them upstairs and get them in position." He looked over Twenty-One's head. "Bring me the Model Slave."

Twenty-One had begun to rise before Gabe commanded her to. An error, she knew, but Gabe just smiled and shook his head as he led her to her Master. Her legs were weak as she walked and they nearly became useless the moment he hooked a finger into the D-ring of her bejeweled collar. He fished a slender golden chain from his pocket and fastened it to the D-ring. His face was placid as he looked over her body, studying the paint. But when his eyes met Twenty-One's, she felt the air around him charge in that indescribable way, his manner changing completely without his face even moving. He moved closer to her, tilting her chin up. She was close enough to kiss his mask. He gently turned her head from side to side, studying her face.

"Mon Dieu," he whispered so faintly that Twenty-One herself could scarcely hear it.

Twenty-One's heart nearly burst. He kept her gaze, drinking her in, and she did not bother hiding behind a blank face. She let him see all the need he had awakened in her, and with a subtle flex of his fingers, she knew that had they been in a different situation, up in the suite, she would be pinned between the wall and his hard body at this moment.

"Gabe," he said finally.

"Yes?"

Twenty-One had forgotten her attendant, standing so closely nearby.

"Nice job with the eyeliner."

With that, Demetrius broke away, turned his back to Twenty-One, and jerked the golden chain to jolt her into motion behind him.

Twenty-One expected everyone to head for the statue door, but the attendants led their charges in another direction, toward a hall with a row of heavy, intimidating doors. Twenty-One had never been down this hallway. For a moment, she had the urge to flee back to the slave quarters and somehow strap herself into her bed, where she felt safe. She wasn't ready for the dinner party, for a new experience. She longed for her daily routine.

Demetrius led her up the stairs and through the study without a word. Twenty-One, daring to look up with her Master's back turned, snatched glimpses of some of the books on the disorganized shelves. Some were in English, but she caught a few titles that were in French—*Paradis Perdu, Ou Le Prométhée Moderne*. Many of them were classic literature. She also saw books of history, psychology, classical music. The titles she passed made the slave realize just how little she knew about the man who had become her world. Perhaps, in the upcoming year as she served him before the new slaves arrived, she would discover more, but she doubted it. She was a possession with a specific purpose in his life, like the books in his study. She would never know the whole man.

She and her Master entered the pillared room with the table where the Attendants had their meals. The first thing she noticed were cameras, countless cameras on tripods, mounted to the massive marble pillars, pointing at the large oak table. The table was set with china and crystal on a long gold table runner. Sprinkles of loose crystals lay scattered between the plates and mounted cameras, glittering like glass. Low-hanging chandeliers strung all the way from the high ceiling. The marble pillars were laced with gold ribbon, framing the platform that she only now understood the purpose for. Someone had set two Saint Andrew's crosses no it, like the one she had seen Seventeen tied to, and a training table from downstairs, it shackles dangling from the edges. Her mouth went dry at the sight of a tall rack displaying an array of whips, crops, and other tools that made her shiver. Behind the platform, gold curtains shielded the bay windows, creating a barrier to the outside world.

Demetrius was still, studying the décor, perhaps. Twenty-One only just noticed the silence. Where had everyone else gone? She hadn't expected to be alone with her Master on this night. He tugged her leash and she scrambled to follow him to the head of the table, where a cushioned stool waited for her beside a single high-backed chair.

"Sit," said Demetrius.

Twenty-One obeyed.

"Sit straighter," he instructed. "Legs apart. Hands in your lap. Lift your chest. Good. Hold your chin high." Demetrius took her chin and lifted it where he wanted it to be. "Look at me. You will stay in this pose until I tell you otherwise. Do you understand?"

Twenty-One flexed her throat to get more comfortable. "Yes, Master."

His eyes looked so light against the black of his suit. He released her chin and ran a knuckle down her arm, testing the paint. He cupped her left breast and she couldn't suppress a soft sigh.

"Exquisite," Demetrius murmured. "Body paint suits you, *ma chère*."

He lingered, rolling her nipple in slow, teasing circles. Twenty-One felt her sex awaken immediately. But his hand was gone as suddenly as it had come. He set the leash in her lap and turned his back to her.

Konri had appeared in the dining room without Twenty-One noticing, wearing a crisp black suit with a white shirt and a goldenrod tie to match Demetrius'.

"Is Abigail here?" Demetrius asked him.

Konri nodded, adjusting his shirt cuff. Twenty-One felt his dun-colored eyes on her, and once more she felt the foreign urge to cover herself, to close her legs and cross her arms over her breasts. She stayed in her position, her back straight, her chin high. She would not disobey Demetrius because the doctor made her uncomfortable.

The twins came from the far corridor, hand in hand.

"Everything's ready to go," said Charity, pulling out a chair near the head of the table for her sister. Konri joined them. The three looked to Demetrius.

"All right." Her Master pulled a small remote from his suit jacket and pointed it at the air. "Logging in."

Music seeped into the room, a slow tempo kept by low strings. Twenty-One recognized it as Beethoven, but couldn't place its title.

"Can everyone hear me?" asked Demetrius. He brought his hand to his right ear beneath his hair, an unconscious gesture. Twenty-One guessed he wore some sort of ear piece, because he said, "Excellent," though no one in the room had replied. She glanced at Konri and the twins and noticed small white pieces in their ears.

Demetrius looked at the cameras. "Welcome to the dinner party for the 2011 slave season. For those of you who are new buyers, I am Demetrius Heart. We have a wonderful stock this year, quite a variety of glass and leather. We also have a few steel slaves for those of you who prefer a challenge or extreme punishment. With me as always are my assistants, Faith and Charity, and our house physician, Dr. Konri Boukman. My other partner, Abigail Marinette, will be joining us with her slaves as well."

Twenty-One sat with her hands in her lap, trying not to fidget.

"We are also introducing a new category this year." He gestured to Twenty-One without looking at her. "Some of you have already noticed the slave next to my chair. She is Twenty-One, our new Model Slave. A Model Slave is designed to speed up the breaking process of slaves of the new season, serving as a model for ideal protocol and obedience. Unfortunately, she is not available for purchase this season. She will be sold with next year's stock. The price for a Model Slave will be significantly higher, as she will have spent a year in my care."

Twenty-One didn't know where to look, whether or not she should look at the cameras or treat them as Masters, like Demetrius had instructed. It was disconcerting to see no faces, hear no voices. Yet she felt the cameras on her like blinking red eyes. She kept her chin high, her eyes down, and tried not to think of the gooseflesh prickling beneath her body paint, of her nipples growing hard.

"Yes, Professor, I plan on having a Model Slave for each upcoming season," said Demetrius, responding to a question Twenty-One couldn't hear. "All training currently available will be expanded upon; domestic duties and etiquette, positions and pain response, pleasure and endurance…yes." He gave the low chuckle that always made the hair rise on Twenty-One's skin. "Oh, yes, I will enjoy myself."

The twins laughed as well. Again Twenty-One was struck by the sensation of phantom eyes on her. She fought not to squirm. Demetrius spoke over the increasing volume of the melodic strings. He opened his arms wide, like a circus ringleader.

"Let's start the party."

The music reached a crescendo and the hallway the twins had come from burst into movement. Slaves and attendants and a dozen strangers in chef attire flooded the dining room. Twenty-One couldn't have kept her eyes lowered if she tried. A herd of chefs, complete strangers to Twenty-One, carried platters of food and the steel slaves, who were slung over their shoulders. They set the gilded women down on their backs along the table runner. As they were set down, their attendants came to their side, dipped a brush into a jar of honey, and drizzled the nectar down the length of their bodies.

Chefs set a slave on the table within arm's reach of Twenty-One. Twenty-One recognized her from the basement: Seven, a beautiful, heavily-tattooed steel slave with short red hair. Seven's attendant decorated her with honey and layered the sweet streaks on her body with various fruits; scoops of honeydew, strawberries, pomegranate seeds, and plump blackberries.

The kitchen staff set dishes of bread and fine cheeses between the slaves on the table runner and retreated to the kitchen. Twenty-One saw Demetrius on the platform, waving a row of nude women forward. The five glass slaves approached in perfect posture, their gait as delicate as any dancer's. They held trays of champagne flutes, identical to those Twenty-One had held the night before, but the glasses didn't shake above their steady hands. They glided over to Demetrius in unison and did a slow coordinated spin, showing off their balance skill and their elegance. Twenty-One saw Three in the middle, painted gold with her choppy white hair tied back with ribbon.

"Twenty, Three, Fourteen, Ten, and One are the glass slaves of this season," said Demetrius. "I am particularly proud of this season's glass crop. Each are delicate and very eager to please. Their skin is so easy to break that we had to punish them with water alone."

Water. Twenty-One thought back to Three's punishment, submerged in the tub until she ran out of air.

"You can see the steel slaves on the table, three of them this year. They've each been challenges in their own way." He paused. "Yes, of course. They're all obedient and desperate to serve. We have increased their pain tolerance and they will beg for the harshest punishments. They are more prone to outburst, but again, each have their own ways of being tamed. It's all in the catalogue you received."

He introduced the rest of the slaves, all with leather collars, too quickly for Twenty-One to keep up with. The attendants all came to sit, their slaves standing beside their chairs with their arms behind their backs. Demetrius, too, went to his seat and stood beside Twenty-One. It was only then that she realized she was shaking and that her skin had gone cold. The music, the swarm of activity, the stench of the food in the chef's arms, ready to serve; it was so much, so fast. She had grown accustomed to her unwavering routine. The dinner party was so controlled, yet to her it was chaos. Her hands curled into fists in her lap. She had to keep it together. She strained to recall her mantra to calm herself, but the words she had burned into her brain seemed to break up like a cobweb blown apart by a strong breeze.

Twenty-One did not notice the French doors open until the icy air hit her back. She turned around, breaking form. If her Master noticed, he gave no indication. He, too, had turned toward the French doors.

The first thing Twenty-One noticed, oddly enough, were the curling horns decorating the heads of ten men, nude and gilded just as she was. Like the female slaves, the men were uniquely beautiful and had thick leather collars around their necks. Each slave was erect and at the ready.

Two of the male slaves were a few steps behind the others, surrounded by ten men in suits; attendants, Twenty-

One assumed. A woman sat on the slaves' shoulders, supported by their strength. Twenty-One supposed she was Abigail, the partner Demetrius had mentioned. She looked like a Roman goddess, a statue come to life in a long white gown with an open front, baring plump, pale cleavage. Her dark golden hair fell in careful ringlets, pulled halfway back with ribbon similar to the slaves. She wore a slow, easy smile, as if this entire spectacle was just so amusing, and outstretched her arms. One of the slaves in front of her fell onto all fours. The two holding her lifted her up and she stepped onto the kneeling man's back to the floor.

"Oh, Demetrius," she said, her voice sweet and melodic. "You never dress for the theme! I guess you're always our Hades, though, aren't you?" She kissed Demetrius' cheeks.

Twenty-One couldn't keep her eyes off Abigail. She seemed to glow in her white gown against Demetrius' monochromatic figure as she traced his lapel with her fingertips. Twenty-One didn't understand the feeling that came over her as she watched a woman behave with such familiarity toward Demetrius, as if he were an everyday person. It burned like jealousy, but there was an edge of pain as well, an ache akin to heartbreak. Yet she was mesmerized by this woman, by every casual smile and languid gesture. She flicked her wrist and her ten slaves sprung into motion, aligning themselves behind Twenty-One and Demetrius' chair. Demetrius led Abigail to her seat, beside Twenty-One near the head of the table. Twenty-One kept her gaze on the empty plate in front of her.

"Please tell me the chefs are ready to serve," Abigail's voice rang clear over the din. "I am *famished.*"

Demetrius sat down in his chair and again addressed the cameras. "Ladies and gentlemen, we have games planned for your entertainment while we eat, though feel free to make a request should you wish to see any slave perform a task. Their attendants will be happy to oblige using any of the tools you see on the rack."

The chefs set platters of food on the table. Twenty-One saw roast pig, poultry, and lamb, heaps of roasted red potatoes, pots of stew, platters of foods she couldn't name. Between the food and the three steel slaves, there was hardly any room to move, but no one seemed to mind.

Abigail beckoned and one of her slaves appeared at her side, a trim and muscular young man with short, light brown hair, who knelt at her feet immediately.

"Ash," Abigail lifted his chin and handed him her plate. "Make my plate, darling, and you can sit next to me and this sweet little creature here."

Twenty-One felt Abigail's eyes on her.

"Look up, slave," the woman ordered. "Let me have a look at you."

Twenty-One looked at the Mistress. Abigail studied her. Her dark blue eyes seemed harder than Twenty-One would have anticipated from her warm and casual demeanor.

"So this is the Model Slave," she said with a slow, sharp smile. A coldness crept across Twenty-One's skin. "Well, she is very pretty, Demetrius, but she's certainly not stellar. Why is she the *perfect model* for future slaves?"

The air seemed to grow colder where her Master sat.

"Twenty-One has only been with me since October," he said, his voice flat and steady, "and she is better trained than most slaves are in three months. She learns and retains lessons better than any slave I have had. She is a perfect prototype for this new classification."

Twenty-One felt color rise to her cheeks. She'd had no idea how she stacked up to the other slaves. Her Master's words from long ago echoed in her head. *You were born for this.*

Ash, the handsome slave, returned, setting a plate of food down before his Mistress. Abigail smiled at him, picked up a scrap of pork from her plate, and held it out on her palm. Ash took the meat between his shapely lips without hesitation or shame. The smell of the meat was overpowering. Twenty-One's stomach had never felt so empty. When was the last time she had eaten anything but broth, water, and fruit?

Abigail plucked a second morsel of meat from her plate.

"I think our little Model Slave deserves a treat," she purred. "Ash, why don't you share this with her?"

Abigail popped the pork into Ash's mouth and the young slave approached Twenty-One. She glanced at her Master, whose eyes held a dangerous edge, but Ash's hand appeared at the back of her neck and forced her attention back to him. Ash's mouth was on hers as soon as she turned her head, his lips soft and insistent, pushing hers open as he slid the meat into her mouth.

Twenty-One's body became fire, sparked and fed by Ash's lips. The pork was more delicious than she could have imagined. When she swallowed it, the warm, succulent taste remained in Ash's mouth. She lapped at his tongue, clinging to the taste, to the tenderness of his kiss. He pulled away, licking his lips, and she met his eyes for a moment, a bluer grey than her Master's. Something was wrong. There was an urgency behind his Hollywood smile, a frantic spark in his gaze that she didn't understand. Tears threatened to swell in her eyes. She didn't know why she wanted to cry.

Ash drew back and Abigail pulled out a stool beside her for him. Twenty-One's gaze trailed down the strong chest, the hard cut of his muscular stomach, to find him hard and inviting. Her pulse jumped. She turned away. She had been surrounded by nude women, but other than her Master, she had not seen a fully naked man in this place, let alone one as model-perfect as Ash. Twenty-One stole a glimpse of Demetrius and immediately wished she hadn't. Her Master was still as stone, as still as he had been when she had struck him in the face the first night she had awoken in the cage. He stared at Ash, Abigail, and finally looked at her. She looked at her plate and wished she could make herself invisible.

Abigail shook her head at Demetrius with a bright laugh. Twenty-One tensed even more. How could Abigail not feel the dangerous static in the air?

"Oh, D," she said, shaking her head and smiling as she pushed the food around her plate with her fork. "Are you ever going to eat with us? Must you sit at the head of the table with an empty plate like a vampire year after year?"

Demetrius cut his eyes to Abigail, an icy glare that again made Twenty-One wish she could disappear. Abigail merely tossed her slender shoulders and took a sip of wine from her glass.

Demetrius turned his attention to the cameras overhead. "Ladies and gentlemen, Faith and Charity will be directing our first game. We will need two female slaves and a male slave. Whom would you like to see perform?"

Abigail laughed suddenly, making Twenty-One jump. "Willow," she beckoned one of her slaves, a towering young man with long frost-blonde hair and sharp runway features. "More than a few buyers called your name immediately. You're a lucky one."

"Four and Eight, to the platform," Demetrius ordered.

Twenty-One tried to stare at her plate, but she couldn't ignore the spectacle. Faith and Charity led Four, a pale and curvaceous girl with ginger red hair, and Eight, tall and graceful as any of the glass slaves, to the platform.

Faith came back from the tool rack with two blue and green taper candles. Twenty-One knew what was going to happen immediately. The twins bound Four and Eight's hands behind their backs and placed the candles in their mouths.

"On the table," Charity ordered.

Willow, the beautiful male slave, sprung onto the training table and extended his arms overhead, waiting to be bound. Four and Eight hovered over him, and though the candles weren't yet lit, Twenty-One's skin burned with the memory of hot wax searing on her chest and belly. It had hurt so badly. She didn't want to watch another slave suffer so, yet she couldn't look away from the long-limbed man shackled to the table.

"Slaves," said Faith to the two women, "why don't you draw a pretty tree on your canvas?"

Four and Eight set to work the moment Charity lit the candles in their mouths. They leaned forward, dribbling wax, and the attendants at the table burst into cheers and chants, as if they were watching a boxing match. The slaves tilted their heads, doing their best to direct the hot wax into shapes. Twenty-One shivered. Bright bursts of blue and green dripped onto Willow's milky skin. He threw his head back, his mouth open. If he made any sound, it was swallowed by the attendants' shouts. His sex moved with every new spot of wax, bouncing against his pelvis as his muscles tensed from the heat.

Twenty-One felt warm all over, and it wasn't from fear. The game was such a spectacle. The female slaves hovered over Willow, their breasts cast in candlelight, and Willow all but writhing on his back, thrusting his hips in the air in spite of himself, his hard sex begging for contact. He enjoyed the wax. Twenty-One wondered if she would ever be able to reach the point where she enjoyed that pain. She would have to in order to embody the title of Model Slave, wouldn't she? She already enjoyed Demetrius' nails and crop strikes while he gave her pleasure, but she could only hope that he would be able to train her to enjoy pain alone. She knew he would be able to. Demetrius was Master, after all. She only hoped she could be strong enough to learn at a pace that pleased him.

The dinner party was a flood of activity. The glass slaves fluttered about the table, serving champagne and pouring wine. The attendants gave them affectionate strokes, squeezed their breasts, patted their buttocks as they worked. Their slaves, standing beside them, were given morsels of their feast as Abigail had fed Ash. Some attendants made a game of tossing bits of food in the air and making their slaves catch them in their mouths. They even tossed food at the steel slaves, who could only open their mouths and move their heads slightly or risk spilling the honeyed fruits on their bodies and be punished. Twenty-One felt as if she were in a different world.

Something warm and almost rough brushed Twenty-One's shin, startling her. Ash caught her eye, his head bowed, looking at her. He smiled, so handsome it almost hurt to look at him, and again brushed her shin with his foot. Twenty-One swallowed, her heart in her throat, and tried to remain still. She wasn't allowed to interact with any of the other female slaves without express orders to do so. She was certain this interaction was also forbidden. Abigail was distracted, chatting with Konri across the table as she ate. Ash was little more than a decoration at her side. Twenty-One dared not look at Demetrius, lest she signal to him that something was wrong. She would not risk Demetrius' anger for a flirtatious slave.

Ash would not relent, though she kept her eyes on her plate, the food, the steel slave on the table in front of her. She felt him looking at her, felt those lovely blue-grey eyes fight for her attention. She tried not to think of the way he fed her with his mouth, of the press of his lips, but her sex bloomed, and Twenty-One was ashamed of the warmth between her legs. She sat in silence as the twins declared Four the winner of the game, unbound Willow, and threw Four onto the table in his place. Willow wrapped Four's seashell-white legs around his waist and plunged inside of her, his thrusts hard and urgent, while the dinner table erupted into cheers. Faith and Charity flitted about the coupling, occasionally striking Willow's legs or Four's breasts with a leather crop from the tool rack. The *smack* of each strike echoed over the din, sending jolts through Twenty-One. She stared at Willow, at the frost blonde hair clinging to his face. His torso was still decorated with dots of wax. Twenty-One couldn't see a tree pattern in the wax, but she was not the judge in this game. The male slave's thighs quivered with each thrust and every slap from the crop. Though he looked frantic, there was something utterly controlled about the way he took Four, a method in the chaos. She had never seen a male slave. She wondered what training entailed for them, what methods they learned for pleasing their Masters and Mistresses.

"Twenty-One."

Her Master's voice startled her. She tore her attention from the game and looked at her empty plate.

"Yes, Master?"

She wanted to look at him so badly, to see him in his black suit again.

"You must be hungry," he said. She couldn't read his tone. He was cold and even.

"Only if it pleases you, Master," she murmured. The wax game had allowed her temporary reprieve from her hunger, but now it was back in full force. Remembering the rich pork made her stomach cramp with need.

"You may eat what you can get from Seven," he said, "using your mouth."

On the table in front of Twenty-One, Seven did not react to her name. She remained on her back, her gaze on the ceiling, still as a sculpture. Abigail, Konri, and a few attendants had plucked fruit from her, but much of it remained, streaked in honey.

"Go on," Abigail said. Twenty-One had forgotten she was there. "Let's see you use that pretty mouth."

Twenty-One felt her face flush. However, the food was too tempting for her to be embarrassed for long. She leaned forward, hovering over Seven's hip, and reached for a strawberry. She was thankful her hair was styled out of her face, or it would have come down into the honey on Seven's skin. She closed her mouth around the strawberry and the moment the honey struck her tongue, her knees weakened. It was so sweet, almost cloying, but she wanted it. She sank her teeth into the fruit and the juice burst onto her tongue, so sweet, so delicious. She nearly moaned.

Twenty-One heard Abigail laugh and clap her hands, which only encouraged the slave. She dipped down again and captured a mouthful ofskiny pomegranate seeds. She ate them so frantically that a few dribbled out of her mouth and onto the table runner. But she didn't care. The honeyed fruit was ambrosial. She ate every piece she could reach, lapping at the honeyed streaks on Seven's skin. Seven stirred from Twenty-One's tongue, moaning through closed lips, but Twenty-One only wanted the fruit and honey.

Finally, she could reach no more. The honey she licked at was gone. She could only taste Seven's smooth and salty skin.

"Enough," Demetrius ordered. Twenty-One sat back down, licking the remaining juices from her lips.

Abigail clapped again. "That was beautiful! She has quite the oral talent, doesn't she, to make the little steel slave moan like that!" She ran a hand through Twenty-One's hair. "Oh, she must suck marvelous cock, D."

"She is very skilled." Again her Master's voice was cold and clipped. He did not seem to be enjoying himself. Twenty-One's heart stung. Was it something she had done?

"I'd like to see her in action, actually," Abigail rose from her seat, tossing her hair to the side, and raised her hands to get everyone's attention. "Let's have a new game. My boys have worked hard for me this season, and they need to be rewarded. Let's have a head race tonight!"

The attendants cheered, but Twenty-One felt Demetrius tense.

Abigail's hand appeared on Twenty-One's shoulder. "And let's get our little Model Slave in on the game this time!"

"No," Demetrius' voice was so harsh that Twenty-One had to look at him. He sat rigid, his fist clenched around a fork, staring at Abigail with the most dangerous gaze Twenty-One had ever seen. But Abigail only laughed, and Twenty-One could only gape at her in awe.

"Oh, come now, D, we're all curious to see what makes her so special," said Abigail with a little bite in her words.

"After all, didn't you tell me that she's better trained than most slaves are after months in your care?"

Demetrius began to speak, but fell silent, as if interrupted. Abigail laughed again.

"Exactly, Dr. Lane," she said, smiling at a nearby camera on the table. "We want to see the Model Slave in action."

Demetrius' silence was agony. Twenty-One cringed, waiting for some violent explosion, but nothing came.

"Very well," his storm-grey eyes were glowing when they found Twenty-One. "Go with Abigail to the podium."

"Yes, Master." Twenty-One's heart slammed against her ribcage, but Abigail took her hand and dragged her away from her Master. They circled the table as Abigail selected seven slaves to come up with them as the invisible buyers requested them, plucking them from the floor as if she were shopping for ripe fruit.

"This one, absolutely, how cute…and yes, you, dear, go on up, yes…oh, and of course we need this one…attendants, bring my slaves to the podium, please."

Before Twenty-One knew it, she was on the podium in a line of eight female and eight male slaves, awaiting orders. Abigail fluttered between the stock, flirting with the cameras.

"For you newcomers," she said to the cameras, "a head race is exactly as it sounds. Demetrius' lovely girls will service my slaves with their mouths until one comes. The winner will be given to Ash, my star pupil, so we can see a demonstration of his skills."

Abigail and the twins paired up the slaves as she spoke. Faith ushered Twenty-One toward a tall, lean slave.

"On your knees," she said. "You get to play with Hemlock."

Twenty-One obeyed. She glanced at her Master, so far away at the end of the room, but she didn't need to see him to sense his anger. She didn't know what to do. Would he be angry if she lost? He had said she was a quick student. Did she really stack up against the slaves who had had so much more time for training?

Hemlock, the slave she was paired with, stood with his hands behind his back. Abigail had twirled some of his long dreadlocks around the curling horns on the sides of his head, making them look almost natural. His sex was rigid and sloped slightly to the left. The gold paint covered most of his ebon skin, but his sex was not gilded. Twenty-One met his eyes. They were as blank and doll-like as the best trained female slaves.

"All right, ladies, hands behind your backs," Abigail said. Twenty-One clasped her hands together at the small of her back, ready. "And…go!"

Twenty-One leaned forward. Hemlock was very tall, so she had to stand on her knees in order to get all of him inside of her mouth. The male slave shivered when the tip of him hit the back of her throat. She wanted to savor the moment, to experience the sensation of a new person in her mouth, but she was in a race. She closed her lips tightly around his shaft and slid down the length of him, then slid forward and took him into her throat. Hemlock threw his head back, his legs quivering. He grew inside of her, stiffer and thicker along her tongue. She tasted him, exploring along every nook and ridge as she sucked up and down, rolling her tongue along the tip of him. Hemlock moaned, a piteous sound barely audible over the jeers and whistles that echoed through the room.

The slaves around Twenty-One were silent, though she could see their heads bobbing up and down out of the corner of her eye. She waited to hear Abigail or the twins call the end of the game, but nothing came but cheering. She continued, teasing Hemlock with tongue and teeth, wishing she could hear his breath or that he would begin to thrust into her mouth so she could gauge his arousal. His stillness told her nothing.

Twenty-One nearly jerked back when Hemlock gave a single involuntary thrust and spilled his seed into her mouth. She struggled to swallow and breathe at the same time, certain she would be punished if a single seed spilled from her lips. She drew back and wiped her mouth clean, finally able to catch her breath. Hemlock had given no indication that he was anywhere near orgasm. Was that what buyers wanted in a male slave?

She had no time to dwell on it. The twins encircled their slender arms around her and pulled her to her feet. The attendants were deafening, banging on the table with their fists, shouting, some of their arms in the air. Abigail's gold heels appeared in Twenty-One's eyeline. She tilted the slave's chin up. There was an edge to her smile that made Twenty-One's spine tingle.

"Well, well," Abigail purred. "Look who won?" She tossed a glance back at Demetrius, who remained at the table, unmoving. "I'm sorry I ever doubted you, D. What a mouth!"

"Thank you, Mistress," Twenty-One whispered, uncertain if she should speak.

Abigail reached up and patted Twenty-One's cheek with the tips of her fingers, "Such a good girl. I hope you enjoy Ash while you have him, baby girl. He is quite a treat."

Twenty-One followed Abigail's pointed finger as she beckoned for her favorite slave. Her chest tightened. The rest of the slaves melted away. Abigail and the twins, too, retreated. Ash approached her, growing hard as she watched, his smile wide and white and somehow terrifying.

"Give her a kiss before you fuck her, Ash!" Abigail called out. "Be a gentleman!"

Demetrius rose from his seat a little too quickly. Twenty-One took a step back even though her Master was across the room. Abigail smiled and shook her head, her lips moving. Demetrius walked off, disappearing through the gold curtains that hid the French doors. Twenty-One suddenly couldn't find her breath. Her Master was gone. She was alone in a sea of attendants and slaves and strangers with a naked man bearing down on her.

No sooner had Ash hopped onto the platform than he slipped an arm around her waist and pulled her against him for a kiss. It was a short, sweet kiss, almost polite, but the erection which pressed against her stomach was anything but cordial. Twenty-One grew wet immediately, a kneejerk reaction despite her racing heart. She wanted to break free, to run away, to find her Master, but that was not what a good slave would do. That was not Model Slave behavior.

But Ash's lips moved to her neck and she surprised herself by moaning softly, shocked by her own desire. Demetrius had trained her well. She was ready for Ash even when her mind was elsewhere.

Ash nibbled her earlobe, his hands roaming her body as if it had always been his to use. He cupped her breasts and the attendants gave a fresh roar. The hall was nearly deafening with chatter and cheers.

"What's your name?" Ash whispered in her ear. His tone was not the low growl of a man enthralled. It held an urgency, but not the urgency of desire.

"What?" Twenty-One dared reply.

Ash's fingers found her nipples, squeezing them, distracting her. His hands were quick and rough and all over the place. Something felt wrong about his touch.

"Tell me your name," he whispered. He slid a finger into her sex so suddenly that she cried out and tried to spring back, but he took her cry into his mouth with a quick, hard kiss, and his muscular arms kept her captive. Twenty-One smothered a burst of anger inappropriate in a slave. She would be used, even by another slave, if her Master or Mistress ordered it. What she could not understand was how this rough and awkward creature was Abigail's favorite. Demetrius had not trained her to be so mechanical. She was certain Abigail would not train a male slave to be an awkward lover.

Ash slid another finger into her sex, finding her wet but too tight. His fingers were almost painful, too soon inside of her.

"I'm Twenty-One," she murmured into his ear. Were they allowed to speak? No one stopped them, but Twenty-One wasn't certain anyone had noticed their exchange with Ash's busy hands to distract them.

"No," Ash whispered, lifting her chin and leaning into her for another kiss. His expression was completely different from the movie-star grin she had seen plastered on his face before. There was an intelligence in his expression, careful and concealed.

"You're not Twenty-One," he said. "And I'm not Ash. My name is Jason. *What's your name?*"

Twenty-One tried to break away again, but he held her firm against his chest.

"Don't," he warned, nodding his head toward the crowd. "Keep touching me. Don't let them know we're talking."

Twenty-One's heart leapt to her throat. Now she understood shy his hands were all over the place, why his fondling was so automatic. He was unbroken. How had he been able to fool his Mistress? Demetrius seemed to know every single thought that passed through her mind. How could Abigail have missed an unbroken slave, let alone her favorite?

"But…why?" she mumbled, forcing her hands to explore his body. She traced the grooves of his ab muscles, brushing his erect sex. If it pleased him, he gave no sign.

"What's your name?" he repeated.

"Come on, Ash, fuck her already!" one of the attendants shouted. "We've never gotten to see her in action!"

Ash responded immediately. Twenty-One found her feet off the ground in an instant. Ash scooped her into his arms as if she weighed nothing. She clung to his neck, her mind racing.

Ash slammed her against one of the crosses on the platform. She had just enough time to grab the straps on its arms before he shoved his way inside of her.

Twenty-One gasped. She was too tight and he was too big for her to accommodate him without proper foreplay. She gritted her teeth and fought not to cry out as he pulled halfway out of her and thrust back inside, fighting his way in. He moaned loudly and leaned into her, his teeth on her neck, as the crowd erupted into cheers.

"My name is Jason. I'm from Pittsburgh," he said against her skin. "I have two brothers. I moved to Los Angeles a year ago to become an actor. Who are you? Think!"

Twenty-One was too dumbstruck to think.

"I…I'm a slave," she said weakly. Ash's thrusts began to build a deep pressure within her conditioned body. She moaned, surrendering to the feeling, and gripped the straps more tightly to keep from meeting his thrusts.

"No, you're not," he said, kissing her cheek fiercely. "You're a woman with a life and a family and a name. And I need your help."

"Switch it up!" came an anonymous request. "From behind!"

Ash sighed. He grabbed Twenty-One's shoulders and flipped her around, pressing her chest against the wooden cross.

"Twenty-One, spread your legs!"

She obeyed automatically, parting her legs so they were in line with the bottom of the cross. Ash, being taller than she was, had to bend his knees in order to enter her again. He took her by the hips, lifted her up slightly, adjusting her like an item of clothing. He entered her again, and the pressure began to build immediately. Tears filled her eyes. Her mind was so far from their escapades, but her body reacted regardless. She hadn't truly understood how well she had been trained until this moment.

You were born for this…

Ash's hard chest brushed her back.

"Abigail has a cell phone," he whispered. "I'm going to make a distraction and steal it."

Twenty-One went cold. The crowd faded away into nothing. She hardly felt the leather straps to which she clung.

"You can't," she hissed. "She's your Mistress."

Ash thrust so deeply into her that she screamed, the lower part of her body burning with painful pressure. He covered her mouth.

"She's the psycho who drugged me and kept me locked up naked in a warehouse," he growled, his pace increasing. His voice rose over the sound of theirskin colliding. "She's not my *Mistress*, and Demetrius isn't your Master. We were abducted. *All of us* were abducted. I'm going to get that phone, and I need to know you're able to help me. Tell me something so I know you're still in there somewhere." His thrusts were rapid, frantic. "Tell me your name."

Twenty-One gripped the leather straps so hard they cut into her palms.

"Chloe," she whispered on the edge of her breath.

Ash gave one last thrust and drew himself out of her. He gave another theatrical moan and turned his back toward the crowd. Twenty-One felt no seed spatter her back, though everyone cheered. Ash turned her around with the same runway smile she had seen on his face earlier in the night. She knew what it hid now.

"Save us, Chloe."

Chapter 31

The sterile stench of the Ochsner Baptist Medical Center summoned unwanted memories to torment Demetrius. In the present, he saw Dede lying in the bed, her waxy skin stretched over her bones. When he closed his eyes, he saw himself from years ago, awakening confused and panicked in a Toledo hospital. Only Dia anchored him to reality. She clung to him, her face buried in his chest. She had been sobbing ever since the nurse had called Demetrius to tell him it was time to say goodbye. He didn't think they had anticipated Dede holding on this long. Nurses came and went, checking the heart monitor, but for the most part, the three were left alone while the nurses gossiped about an impending storm Demetrius knew nothing about.

"They don't know," Dia murmured into his chest. "They don't know."

"Sh, sh, sh," Demetrius stroked her hair.

He knew what she meant. The nurses didn't know who lay dying in this bed. They didn't know her as the pillar of an underground community of people from prostitutes to socialites who relied on her for spiritual guidance. They didn't know her strength, her mystery. All they saw was an old woman with terminal cancer about to draw her last breath.

Dia moved to Dede's bedside, kneeling beside her as if she were about to take Communion.

"Demetrius," Dia's voice was strained through tears.

Demetrius came to kneel beside her. He barely saw movement in Dede's chest. Her hand in Dia's was limp and nonresponsive. Demetrius did not dare look away. He stared at the body of the strange and wonderful woman who had taken him in, shielded him, and given him a name. Her breath slowed to a stop. The heart monitor flat-lined. Demetrius waited for a feeling, a sound, or maybe some sort of spiritual rush. There was nothing.

Dia collapsed into tears, clutching a corpse's hand, looking as young and as lost as she ever had. She did not notice two nurses come in to shut off the heart monitor.

"...supposed to be huge," one of the nurses whispered.

The other nurse nodded, glancing at Demetrius, staring at his attire, but saying nothing. The other nurse continued under her breath as if he and Dia weren't even there.

"Do you think we're going to have to evacuate?" she asked the silent nurse, who shook her head, looking again at Demetrius. Her oblivious companion continued whispering. She covered the shell that Dede had left behind with a sheet. "If Katrina makes it to-"

Dia uttered an alien scream and sprung from Dede's bedside, startling the nurses and Demetrius himself.

"Get out!" she screamed as the nurses backed away. "Get the fuck out!"

Demetrius got to his feet, but Dia seized the heart monitor and hurled it to the floor before he caught her. Its cord ripped from the wall and writhed in the air before the monitor crashed to the floor.

"Fuck you!" Dia screamed at the nurses. She broke in his arms, crumbling like an ash log.

Demetrius scooped her legs over his arm and held her like an infant. Demetrius looked at the two nurses, giving the chatty one a long glare.

"Move," he said.

They scattered from the door, heading toward the bed out of habit, as if their patient's corpse were in some sort of danger. Demetrius carried Dia out of the room. The incident had frozen nurses in their tracks. They gaped at the masked man carrying the sobbing girl out of a patient's room as if he were some sort of classic movie monster abducting an innocent. He didn't care. He stepped into the elevator and shifted Dia to punch the number for the bottom floor.

"Let's go home, *ma chère*," he said into her hair, holding her tightly. He was grateful for the hollowness inside of him. It was the quietest his mind had been in a long time, and the first time he had been able to hold Dia so close without that sickening flame of desire threatening to torment him. She was simply his sweet girl, his broken girl in his arms tonight.

"No," Dia whispered into his chest, her broken heart in her voice. "She's gone. I can't go there. I can't see her rocking chair and know she won't ever sit in it again."

Demetrius' chest stung, envisioning the empty rocking chair on the porch.

"Where can we go?" he asked.

Dia sniffled so sweetly against him. "My mom's house?"

Demetrius nodded. The Garden District wasn't too far from here. Though he wondered whether or not it was wise for Dia to interact with her pathetic excuse for a mother right now, he would not question her. He hailed a cab and held Dia like a porcelain doll. Dede was gone. What would become of them, her lost children, without her?

Chapter 32

Demetrius hadn't returned. Twenty-One felt strange without him or Gabe or the twins telling her what to do. She had followed Ash back to the table and sat on her stool, returning to the posture Demetrius had placed her in at the start of the night. No one had corrected her or even acknowledged her. Once she stepped off the podium, she was invisible.

Her conversation with Ash played in her head over and over again. It had been at least an hour and he had done nothing but sit obediently at Abigail's side while she chatted and answered questions and interacted with buyers. Now and then her cell phone, a small but sleek smart phone in a little blue sleeve, would emerge from a hidden pocket in her gown, and Twenty-One's heart would stop, but nothing would happen. Games came and went on the podium, slaves had been brought up and examined, and Ash had made no move for the phone. Twenty-One felt more relieved with each moment that passed. She couldn't imagine the punishment Ash would suffer if he were to act on his impulse to take the phone. Her mind wandered to more important matters. Where was her Master? She hadn't seen any sign of him and it didn't seem anyone else had left the party. Was he upset with her for winning the head race?

She knew he hadn't been happy about her playing, but he had ordered her to do so. Twenty-One felt the same way she had when she had played the retrieval game with the twins up in the suite. He was angry, yet she had to obey his orders. What could she possibly do to stay in his good graces?

"All right, everyone!" Abigail announced, rising and setting her phone aside. "I had hoped our host would be back from his…errands…before this, but it's time for dessert. As usual, my slaves will start things off by clearing the table. Boys, it's time to eat."

The male slaves sprung from their still positions behind Twenty-One and Demetrius' chairs, crawled onto the table, and descended upon Seven, who still lay prone and covered in scraps of fruit. They took the remaining fruit in their mouths and lapped at the streaks of honey on her and the other steel slaves' bodies. Seven moaned, her back arching off the table and thrusting her body into the swarm of hungry hands and mouths all over her.

Twenty-One was so mesmerized by the sight that she hadn't noticed Ash get up with the others, practically knocking over his stool. Abigail uttered a small shriek and sprang from her chair.

"The wine, you idiot!" she screeched, her cry shrill and very unlike the luscious purr Twenty-One had gotten used to hearing in her voice. Dark red wine spattered her white column gown.

The attendants burst into laughter, shouting. "Spill! Spill! Spill!"

Ash scrambled off the table and nearly backed into Twenty-One, his head bowed. Something small and solid dropped into Twenty-One's lap. She saw a little blue phone on her thighs and panicked. She opened her legs and it drop into the crevice of her lap. She clenched her thighs together. Blood roared in her ears. Had anyone seen it?

Abigail seemed like a different person, her eyes wide and sharp, her face as red as the wine staining her dress. She struck Ash across the face, jerking his head to the side, and he dropped to his knees.

"I'm sorry, Mistress!" he cried over the chants of *Spill! Spill! Spill!* "I'm sorry!"

Twenty-One stared awestruck as Abigail loomed over him, her hair like golden fire. She composed herself almost as well as Twenty-One had seen Demetrius do. She smiled slowly.

"First spill of the night," she hissed, gesturing toward her ruined dress. "Faith, Charity, if you wouldn't mind? I'm going to see if someone can get this out in the kitchen. Konri, if you would be so kind as to join me, I have something to discuss with you."

The twins scooped up Ash by the arms as Konri and Abigail departed for the kitchen. Ash rose and dared to glance over his shoulder at Twenty-One before the twins dragged him to the podium across the room. Faith strapped his wrists and ankles to the same cross that Ash and Twenty-One had used. The male slave stood almost spread-eagled against it, his back and buttocks exposed to the table.

"Clumsy boy," Charity crooned, patting his ass. "What should we punish him with?"

Attendants shouted out suggestions. The twins ignored them and looked to the cameras. Charity finally grabbed two long, slender bamboo canes and handed one to her sister. They tapped at Ash's calves, which didn't seem terribly harsh to Twenty-One, but the slave's skin reddened and he began to fidget. Twenty-One looked down when he started to shout.

She retrieved the cell phone from the stool. She hadn't seen one since before she came here, when she lived in her own apartment and…no, she couldn't think about it. The person she was before coming here meant nothing. She was a slave. She belonged to her Master. But even as those thoughts ran through her mind, her fingers crept onto the keypad and dialed numbers they knew even when she refused to acknowledge it. She stared at the number on the screen, a number from another life. She glanced up. All eyes were on the sobbing, writhing slave on the podium, who had thrust her own fate into her hands.

Save us, Chloe.

Twenty-One slid as slowly as she could off the stool and beneath the table. She pressed *send.*

She couldn't hear the dial tone over the sound of her own ragged breath. She wanted to hang up, to drop the phone, to pretend she'd never had it to begin with. She was a slave. She was meant for her Master. She deserved nothing more than what he desired of her.

"This is Dr. Leroux."

The world shattered. She was five years old, buried in her father's chest as he hummed songs to her and played games in the park. She was lost in the lilac bush, and his arms broke through the blossoms, reaching for her.

"Hello?"

Twenty-One's voice was thick with tears she hadn't known she was still capable of.

"…Daddy?"

"Chloe? Chloe! *Mon Dieu!*"

The stool behind Chloe tumbled over with a clatter and a pair of iron hands wrenched her from under the table.

Demetrius snatched the phone from her hand and threw it against a pillar, shattering it, but Chloe only noticed the crushing grip he had on her hair. He clutched the sides of her head, bringing her a millimeter from his face, his eyes as wild and terrifying as she had ever seen them.

"Where did you get it?" he bellowed, his voice loud enough to crack the Earth. "*Where?*"

The attendants were silent. Chloe fought not to speak. He dug his fingers into her face and she screamed for him. His crushing fingers did not relent. Her skull would crack if he kept going. She just knew it. Every nerve in her head ignited, maddening her.

"Ash."

She despised herself the moment the name left her lips. She wished Demetrius had crushed her skull. She looked over at the bound slave covered in red cane marks and straining to look at the scene behind him.

"Chloe!" Ash shouted, startling the entire room.

Chloe watched Demetrius' face snap from rage into complete stillness. He dropped Chloe like an afterthought. She collapsed and prepared to scramble away from further violence, but he was gone, walking over to the podium with cold, determined steps.

"D…" came a weak protest from an attendant as Demetrius passed him. He grabbed the attendant, pulled something from the young man's waistband, and strode up to Ash on the podium. Only when he outstretched his arm and revealed a handgun did Ash start screaming.

"NO-!"

Chloe didn't know what was more deafening; the gunshot or the chaos that followed. Slaves screamed. Attendants scrambled to get them to the floor and maintain control. Ash's head slumped to the side. Chloe didn't look away from the hole in his temple or the blood that flowed down his slack face. She was numb, as if she were watching the scene through a window in the distance. The attendants shoved their slaves on the floor and the slaves obeyed despite their panic, adhering to the system that had been drilled into their heads. A system designed by Demetrius to keep them under his control. Chloe almost smiled. The system worked even when the Master himself lost control.

The dinner party dissolved into silence, the slaves flat on their bellies. Faith and Charity were just in front of the podium on their knees, clutching one another tightly. All eyes were on Demetrius, frozen beside Ash's corpse. Chloe stared at him, at the man she called Master, the man who had snatched her from her life, starved her, brainwashed her. She stared at the slaves, all stolen, all conditioned into tools for pleasure, like her. She stared at the attendants; twenty young man fully capable of resisting, of saving these women, who instead aided in their torture. Gabe was crouched over Seventeen, the self-proclaimed *teddy bear* of attendants. Chloe's numbness twisted into shame. She clutched the aching sides of her head and fought not to scream. She looked at Ash…Jason…the one person who had tried to stop this, who had trusted *her* to save them all. She forced herself to stare at his corpse, at his misshapen skull where the bullet had left it. She had done this. She had failed.

Demetrius lowered his arm. He studied the room as if it were his first time seeing it. He stared at the cameras, unblinking.

"Ladies and gentlemen," his voice was flat and dull, "we apologize for the incident. We will release a statement tomorrow. Have a good evening."

He reached into his pocket with his free hand, pulled out the remote, and shut off the cameras. No one else dared move. Again, Demetrius swept the room, and Chloe felt his eyes on her, stinging her like a winter wind. She didn't look away. The gun still hung in his hand, a finger on the trigger.

"Faith, Charity," said Demetrius. "Take Twenty-One to the suite and chain her. I will deal with her shortly."

The twins struggled to their feet, pale and wide-eyed. Chloe lowered her head. She gave them no trouble as they lifted her up and held her wrists behind her back. She had lost herself completely and become a mindless slave. She had blown her only chance for escape, everyone's only chance, and she had gotten someone killed. She didn't deserve to live.

A shrill scream severed the silence as the twins led Chloe away. She turned back and saw Abigail, in a fresh dress, sinking to her knees in front of the table, screaming over and over as Konri held her by the shoulders.

X X I

The twins bound Chloe's wrists with steel cuffs and strung her on a chain from a hook on the ceiling. She sat on her knees, her arms stretched high overhead. She didn't resist the twins, but she refused to act like a well-mannered slave. She watched them as they did their work in anxious silence, daring to look them full in the face. She was surprised when they avoided her gaze. There was no sharp order to look down, no teasing about her body or crooning over her, no reprimand. They would not look at her and barely exchanged glances with each other as they fastened her to the ceiling as if she were a hanging plant. Chloe understood their detachment. They had seen Demetrius truly snap, just as she had. She wasn't their boss's pet project any more. She wasn't the little mystery in the suite or the new slave who had come so far. She was just someone who was about to die, and Faith and Charity didn't want to get caught in the crossfire. Chloe had the urge to tell them it was all right, that she wanted this after what she had caused, but she knew that was ridiculous. Even at her best, she was just another slave to these bizarre and mesmerizing women. They couldn't have cared less about her. Disgust seeped into her mouth. Last night, she had been desperate to please these women. Loved these women. She had performed humiliating acts for them. And now…now nothing mattered. She retreated within herself and focused on the memory of her father's voice on the stolen cell phone. Tears welled.

The twins were already on their way out when the door beeped and burst open. Demetrius charged in, just missing the twins as they scurried out of the room, his eyes trained on Chloe. Chloe balked, losing all resolve, scrambling to get to her feet and break free of the chain.

A strike to the face knocked her right back onto her knees. She was so preoccupied with its vicious sting that she did not notice the blood pour from a fresh cut on her eyebrow. Another hit came, across the side of the head. Her ears rang. She yanked at the chain, her vision swimming red, but Demetrius kneed her in the stomach and struck the air from her lungs.

Chloe's mind was empty, her body flailing and struggling of its own volition. She kicked her legs out in any direction she could, and she felt one kick make contact, but nothing slowed him. He grabbed her by the throat and lifted her up to her toes. Chloe stared at him through bloodstained vision as he squeezed her windpipe shut.

His eyes were ablaze, the grey of a torrential downpour that had the power to obliterate everything in its wake. Chloe tried to breathe but found she couldn't even complete the motion. Her chest spasmed over and over again, desperate to take in air. She kicked at him, fought as best she could. He remained a statue, his eyes locked on her face.

This was it. She was going to die. Somehow the most frightening part of it all was that Demetrius said nothing.

He was enraged, unlike the cold, calculated snap she had witnessed when he murdered Jason, but he was just as silent. She read the message in his face. There was no enigma anymore. It wasn't that she had caused such trouble in front of the buyers. She had been his, wholly and completely his, and now she wasn't. At least she would die with that small satisfaction.

Demetrius dropped her as her vision began to go black. She fell hard on her knees, but she didn't feel anything. She gasped in air, but Chloe thought nothing, felt nothing as Demetrius unchained her and dragged her limp body into the cage. The last thing she saw before the blackness swallowed her was the man who had been her Master walking away.

Chapter 33

NOVEMBER 30, 2011

Mr. Zachary Rhoades showed all the signs of agitation: sweating, fidgeting, and from the observation room behind the double mirrors, Detective Gatz could see his feet hooked onto the legs of his chair.

"You got him, Paul" she whispered. "Bring it home."

On the other side of the glass, in the interrogation room, Detective Billman stopped his restless pacing and sat down in front of Zachary.

"It was four o'clock in the morning," he said. "Do you actually expect us to believe you were doing yard work? You were there to pick up the girls Mr. Heart had brought to the club. We know these girls are being held against their will."

Zachary opened his mouth to argue and Billman shot him down with a stern look.

"These women were stolen from their homes," he said. He sat down and rubbed his eyes, the perfect portrait of exasperation. "From their *families*. Help us bring them back."

Gatz bit her lip. Sympathy might not have been the best route to take with Zachary. During questioning he'd been combative and defensive, like Mariane McCandal, but harder to trip up. He'd only responded to what her partner called the "angry daddy" routine, wherein Billman took on an angry but protective persona. Zachary seemed only concerned for himself. Making him appear to be the "hero" aiding in "rescuing" these women seemed an inappropriate route to take.

Zachary wiped his palms on his pant leg. He was still on the fence, but he appeared to be teetering.

"Can prostitutes *be* held against their will?"

Gatz held her breath.

"Got him!" a local officer whispered behind her.

Gatz tried not to laugh under her breath. The Oak County police had been less than charitable when Chloe Leroux had first gone missing. Now faced with possible charges of corruption, they had become a bit too eager to accommodate them in the case.

"I mean, they're all just whores, man," Zachary continued. "They don't *have* families or anything."

He was distancing himself from the situation, staving off guilt, another sign he was about to crack. Billman seemed to sense it, too.

"Look," Billman said, folding his arms over his chest. "Zach, you've got two felonies on your record. If you go down for this, it's over. I don't even want to think about how long you'd be in prison."

Back to angry daddy mode. He let his words sink in before continuing. This was why, despite the chain smoking and the occasional impulsive outburst, Gatz was happy to have Billman as a partner. His instincts in the interrogation room were unparalleled.

"There are a lot of people involved in this. Someone could pin something you didn't do on you and you'll end up getting a worse sentence, even if you're the tiniest cog in the machine. The best thing you can do for yourself is tell us as much as you can."

Gatz thanked God that Billman was able to lie so easily. Their information from Mariane was little more than hearsay, and even with the information on Anthony Ramirez's laptop, it was practically useless without a body. Rafe Raynal's participation had yielded no confessions or crimes, but he had identified Zachary and a few others they planned on bringing in for questioning. If Zachary gave no information, they had absolutely no case against Demetrius Heart; for murder, for kidnapping, for the disappearance of Chloe Leroux, nothing. Both Gatz and Billman knew they had the pieces of a huge puzzle. They needed more than a gut feeling to solve this.

"I didn't kidnap anyone," Zachary finally muttered. "All I had to do is help train *one* girl. That's all any of us do. Demetrius is the one who finds the girls, he's the one who breaks them or whatever. We just come in and help manage them."

"Oh, shit," Gatz whispered. She sat down in the office chair behind her, ignoring the officers behind her cheering as quietly as they could. Just like that, they had a case.

Chapter 34

Abigail appeared to have calmed down by the next afternoon when Demetrius came to his partners with his statement for the buyers about the incident at the dinner party. She was no longer crying, but her eyes were red-rimmed and raw, the skin around them puffed up and irritated. Her eyes narrowed the moment he walked into Konri's room. Demetrius ignored her, though her straight posture as she sat on the bed begged his attention.

"I have the statement for the buyers," he said, handing a copy to Konri. Abigail waited, then rose with a sigh to receive hers. She took it from his hand too abruptly to be consistent with her calm exterior. Demetrius watched her read it, watched her fingers tighten around the sheet of paper the further down she read.

"The execution of a dangerous slave, while regrettable, is necessary, as it only takes one bad seed to spoil the crop." Her eyes were hard as marbles when she looked up again. *"Ash* was the dangerous slave? Are you serious? Who stole my phone, Demetrius? Ash was tied to a cross, completely helpless, and that little *bitch* was under the table with my cell phone. How could you possibly call *Ash* dangerous when-"

"Ash was the true danger in this incident," said Demetrius, nearly quoting the statement. "He has been dealt with."

Abigail's eyes went wide. "Your little *favorite* was right next to me when Ash spilled the wine," she snapped. "*She* took advantage of the situation. *She* took my phone and tried to make a call while everyone watched Ash's punishment. How can you say Ash was a part of it?"

Demetrius almost sighed. "Come on, Abigail. You're smarter than that. Do you think Ash's wine spill was a coincidence?"

Abigail opened her mouth to speak again, but he shut her down.

"I saw Ash preparing you for your fetish ball in Detroit," he said. "He was rude when I first saw him, but he wasn't clumsy. Did you ever know him to make such an error as throwing an entire glass of wine into the lap of his Mistress?"

Abigail's grip on the statement was so tight that she nearly crushed it.

"So what are you saying, exactly?" she sneered. "Are you saying that Ash spilled wine on me, stole my phone, and gave it to her? Even if he *had* done that, if your slave was so well broken, she wouldn't have used the phone, but there she was, under the table."

"She didn't make a call," said Demetrius. "I know my slave. Twenty-One is fully broken. When I discovered her, Ash shouted her birth name. He had to have coaxed it out of her somehow, and manipulated her into taking the phone."

Demetrius could tell Abigail was about to lose control of herself. He was too tired for an outburst of hers, his nerves too ragged. He looked to Konri, whom he knew he could count on to diffuse her.

"They might have spoken while they performed for the buyers on the podium," Konri said softly. "After the head race. Even if that isn't the case, Ash was executed in front of the buyers. Demetrius is right to make him appear to have been a threat to the entire season."

Abigail shook her head, tossing her blonde curls to the side. She thrust the paper back into Demetrius' hand.

"So why isn't she being punished? If you want to make Ash the dangerous one, fine, he's already dead." Demetrius noted a thickening in her voice, the tremble of unshed tears. "But if any other slave was found with a cell phone, you would put them down." She squared her stance in front of him, folding her arms. "You'd never risk keeping a slave like that alive. But she's your *favorite*, isn't she? So she lives, doesn't she?"

Demetrius clenched his jaw to stave off the rush of rage that flared in his chest. He wanted nothing more than to strike the smug smirk off Abigail's face. He knew that he had snapped in front of his entire staff, the slaves, and the buyers. If he struck out again, she and Konri would decide he wasn't fit enough to run their operation, and eventually something would happen. Demetrius took a mental breath, forming the cold exterior he needed to survive.

"Twenty-One is a fully broken slave who was manipulated by a dangerous rebel," he said, taking a step toward Abigail so he was a hair too close for her comfort.

"She has been beaten and isolated for holding onto the phone, but the true danger has passed with Ash's death. Your failure to recognize that Ash was in a state of false compliance, however, is unacceptable, Abigail."

Abigail's mouth hung open, but she could find no words to fling at him.

"As for Twenty-One's punishment," he continued, "the most effective punishment for Twenty-One's transgressions is to punish others in front of her. I have done so in the past with a slave she favors. Twenty-One is a slave who drives herself mad with guilt. Ash's death is more than enough punishment for her."

Konri, as always, said nothing. He merely nodded, quietly assessing Abigail, who stood with her mouth still gaping, silent and dumbstruck.

"I will release this statement to the buyers," said Demetrius.

He turned his back on his partners. Twenty-One's bruised and broken body loomed large in his mind, beaten in rage rather than as some form of punishment. He would not lose control again. The threat had been extinguished. Now it was time to salvage Twenty-One's reputation in the buyers' eyes, and therefore their confidence in him. But first, he had to make sure he hadn't caused any permanent damage to the little disaster.

Chapter 35

DECEMBER 3, 2011

"Quand il me prend dans ses bras, il me parle tout bas, je vois la vie en rose."

Chloe jumped at the sound of tapping on the cage and her body rebelled against the sudden motion, bruised and sore. The left side of her face felt swollen, and her stomach ached as if Demetrius' knee were still there, bearing down on her solar plexus until breathing was impossible.

Three's heart-shaped face was a welcome sight.

"Hi, there," Chloe whispered. Her voice was hoarse. She didn't know how long she had been in the cage, but she was weak with thirst. Three held up a bottle of water as if she could read her thoughts.

"Thank you," said Chloe.

Three unlocked the cage and helped Chloe climb out. Every inch of her body ached. The glass slave had to help her stand, untwist the cap for her, and hand her the bottle. Chloe drank, and the moment the water hit her tongue, she knew she had been in the cage for a very long time. Flashes of memory, of being fed bottled water through the bars of the cage, came and faded. She pulled herself back from the water. If she drank too much too fast she would vomit, and something told her she wouldn't be given more.

Chloe slipped her arms around Three. She was so happy to see someone, to feel skin against hers. She had been certain that Demetrius was going to kill her. Three hugged her but pulled away quickly, pointing at the wall to indicate the hidden cameras they both knew were there. She started moving, inching Chloe forward as if she were teaching an infant to walk.

"How long have I been up here?" Chloe asked.

Three held up three fingers. Chloe sucked in a breath. Three days. She was surprised she could walk at all, even with Three's help. It took them time to get down the stairs. Chloe thought of asking where they were going, but Three wouldn't have answered her, and it didn't matter anyway. She had ruined her only chance for escape. Now all she could hope for was to slip into the warm comfort of forgetfulness, to become Twenty-One again. But her father's voice echoed in her ears, and she knew she didn't want to forget again. She would behave. She would be Demetrius' slave and serve him as best she could, but she would never again allow herself to forget her father's voice or the name he had given her. For her captor, she was Twenty-One, but in her own thoughts, she never would be again. She didn't care whether or not he would sense it in her. That one sliver of herself he could not have. Maybe he would allow it of her if she again became a Model Slave in every other way.

Three led Chloe out of the study and into the great dining room. The table remained, cleared of the food. The podium was empty. A hollow pit grew in Chloe's heart. Her legs buckled. For a moment all she could see was Jason, limp on the giant cross, his light hair matted with blood. Three held her up, patted her hand. Chloe met her eyes. She was *so* young. She couldn't have been older than sixteen and she had been snatched from her home, stripped naked, and collared. Had Chloe acted differently at the dinner party, she could have saved this girl.

"I'm so sorry," Chloe whispered, blinking through tears. "I'm so sorry."

Three's eyes mirrored Chloe's sorrow. She shook her head, took Chloe's chin, and kissed her. Chloe returned the kiss, no longer appalled by a stranger's lips. Three's mouth was soft and sweet and unlike any kiss she'd had since she came to this place. It comforted her as much as it broke her heart.

Three led her through a short hallway to a tall white door. Chloe had never been down this way. She felt as though she should be anxious, but she was too weak to summon any fear. Three knocked before ushering Chloe into a large bedroom with navy blue walls and hardwood floors. It was simple but refined with a four poster bed in the corner, a nightstand, dresser, and a large leather chaise. Konri stood at the dresser, organizing the contents of a medical bag on top of it.

"Sit on the chaise," he said without turning around. Chloe complied, settling onto the chaise, clutching Three's hand.

Konri approached her. Chloe fought not to back away from him. He poked at the cut on her eye and she flinched at the sting. Three gave her a reassuring squeeze.

Konri examined her in unnerving silence, fingering every bruise. His touch was almost unbearable, so detached yet so invasive at the same time. Again she thought of her father, also a doctor, with his inviting smile and warm, comforting personality. Was Konri as cold and mechanical with his patients as he was with the slaves? He was the sort of doctor children had nightmares about.

She endured his prodding and held onto Three's hand like a lifeline. He poked her left side below her breast and she gasped, jerking away from him, which only made the pain worse. Konri grabbed her arm and pulled her back into place, his fingers rolling along the sore spot. Chloe clenched her jaw, fighting not to pull away again. Konri shook his head, the age lines in his face deepening into a pensive frown.

"Getting sloppy," he muttered to himself. Chloe swallowed back a lump that had formed in her throat. What did that mean? Was she badly injured?

Konri's bedroom door opened and a different sense of dread washed over Chloe. Abigail entered the room, looking more casual than she had at the dinner party in tight dark jeans, a thin lace camisole, and blazer. Even in everyday clothing, she mesmerized Chloe. She strutted toward Chloe, Three, and Konri with an air about her that demanded attention. Chloe looked down immediately. Her hands began to shake. All she could think of was Abigail on her knees, screaming in Konri's arms.

"Well, look who it is," Abigail purred, her tone low and dangerous like the distant hum of a swarm of wasps. "Our little Model Slave, our paragon of perfect behavior."

She stepped in front of Chloe, too close for Chloe's comfort.

"Leave, slave," Abigail ordered Three. "I think we can handle her."

Chloe clutched Three's hand when she tried to back away. The idea of being alone with the silent Konri and this woman terrified her.

"Go," Abigail said more firmly. The edge in her tone made Chloe drop Three's hand immediately. She wouldn't be the cause for harm to another slave again. Three retreated. Chloe's heart sank as the door closed.

"How is she?" Abigail asked.

"Bruised ribs," said Konri, again poking at her left side. "Everything else will heal in a week or so."

"Poor little thing," Abigail sneered. She tipped Chloe's chin up with her manicured nails. "Demetrius can be such a monster when he's angry, can't he?" Chloe looked at Abigail and found eyes of ice. "Well, I guess bruised ribs are better than a bullet in the brain, aren't they?"

Chloe swallowed, fighting tears. Abigail tightened her grip on her chin.

"Answer me."

"Yes, Mistress," Chloe whispered. She opened her mouth to say she was sorry and stopped mid-word. One look at Abigail's face told her that sorry would do her no good. A spark of pure rage flashed in the Mistress's eyes, as if she would strike Chloe, but it slipped into a smile as quickly as it had appeared. She patted the wounded side of Chloe's face and let her hand drop.

"He marked her face," she said, folding her arms over her breasts. Chloe tried not to look at the curve of her cleavage, barely concealed by the thin camisole.

"Yes," said Konri.

He retreated to the dresser and took something out of his medical bag. Abigail shook her head. She wouldn't look away from Chloe, and Chloe didn't know what to do. She knew staring a Mistress full in the face was forbidden. She focused on Abigail's jeans, a focal point that was a safe distance between her face and the floor. Abigail did not seem to notice her struggle.

"We're losing him," Abigail muttered, almost to herself, "aren't we?"

Konri returned with a few pills in his hand.

"Hard to say," he said. "She isn't being sold this year. He didn't do any permanent damage. We already saw him lose control. This isn't that."

He pried Chloe's mouth open and popped the pills inside. She jerked back from his fingers, surprised.

"Drink," he ordered.

Chloe hesitated with the pills on her tongue. She had no idea what they were. Konri and Abigail frightened her. She reasoned with herself. Why would they kill her now, when Demetrius undoubtedly knew where she was and who was taking care of her? And what choice did she have anyway? Even if the pills were cyanide, the doctor and the Mistress would have her take them. She took a slow sip of water, her shaking hand betraying her fear.

Konri fingered her mouth open again and checked to see if she had swallowed the pills.

"The bruised ribs will prevent any harsh punishment for a few weeks at least," he said.

Chloe shivered, trying to calm herself. If he had just killed her, he wouldn't speak about her future. She was going to be okay. *I'm all right,* became her new mantra, *I'm all right. I'm all right.*

"Punishment?" Abigail said with a bitter laugh. "Oh, but Konri, didn't you hear what D said? Little Twenty-One's heart is *so very* delicate that her causing the death of another slave is punishment enough."

Chloe's chest grew heavy. Demetrius knew her very well. Jason's death ate her alive. She saw his face every time she closed her eyes. But even if what he had said was the truth, Abigail would never see it as an equal punishment. And it wasn't. Chloe should have died with Ash…Jason…that night, and she knew Abigail would never let her forget it.

Chloe found herself trying to escape within like she had when she had first begun training. She tried to find that dark corner of her mind where thoughts never found her. But Abigail approached her again, running a hand through her hair. Her nails brushed Chloe's scalp a little harder than they should have.

"Demetrius is so *distracted* this season," she said. "I find it hard to believe it's all because of you." She traced the contours of Chloe's face as if she were a sculpture. Chloe flinched despite her best efforts to keep still. The tone of Abigail's voice was dangerous. "Pretty lips," she said. "Great tits, but nothing I'd look twice at with his slaves this season.

If it weren't for this special collar, I wouldn't even notice you in the crowd."

Chloe took a risk and met Abigail's gaze. Those cold eyes were red-rimmed, her face a little puffy. She had been crying for a long time. Chloe couldn't grasp the emotions swelling in her breast. A part of it was anger. How dare this woman mourn a young man she had stolen away, broken down, and planned to sell to the highest bidder? But Chloe still felt the crushing shame of having disobeyed, having rebelled against her Master and Mistress, and as much as she despised the desire to please that had been beaten into her, it was still there. She let her face fill with her regret so Abigail could see it. Abigail smiled and shook her head.

"Not enough, my dear," she whispered. "It's not enough."

The bedroom door opened and Chloe did not have to look over to know who had entered. Abigail dropped her hand and took a step back from her too quickly. Something within her triggered a sick sense of panic. Her entire body tensed so suddenly that her ribs became fire. She gasped before she could stop herself.

"What are you doing in here, Abigail?"

Master. For an instant she was Twenty-One again. She dropped her gaze to the ground, lifting her arms to her neck, At Attention despite the pain in her side. Demetrius came to her, his boots appearing beside Abigail's heels. Chloe began to tremble, but her sex bloomed to life at the same time. She struggled against tears, but they came. She felt the same way she had when she had first come here, torn between fear and desire.

"Relax, D," said Abigail, her voice returning to the melodic purr it had been earlier at the dinner party. "I was just having a look at the damage."

Demetrius was silent. Chloe remained frozen. She wanted to look up, to try to catch a glimpse of Demetrius' face, but she didn't dare risk his anger.

"There's no disfiguring damage," said Konri. "Everything visible will fade in a week or so. But some ribs on her left side are bruised. She'll need to be handled gently for a few weeks."

Demetrius shifted and suddenly he was touching her, his waist between her knees. Chloe was overcome with the urge to fall into him, to rest her head against his chest as she had after he had branded her. Yet his long fingers on her ribs made her jump and jerk away, as if her ribs remembered who had bruised them. She whimpered despite her desperate attempt to keep silent. She couldn't handle these conflicting urges. She would go mad all over again.

Demetrius caught her and cupped the side of her face. "Sh, sh, sh."

He pressed her sore ribs, testing them. She sucked in a breath through clenched teeth. She wanted to look at him and see if he was enjoying her pain. Her stomach turned at the thought, at the memory of actually being *content* when he had enjoyed her pain. *Dieu,* had she truly felt that way? Yet despite her disgust, a part of her wished she were still Twenty-One, that she was a possession with no past, no shame, no resistance, and that she lived for the simple expectation of pleasing her Master and nothing more. God, she despised herself.

"I want her to run in the Hunt," he said.

Chloe frowned at the floor. The Hunt? Run? She remembered the games she had played with the twins and the contest with Hemlock. With her ribs, games like those would be agony.

"Are you serious?" Abigail laughed. "She stole my phone, and now you want to turn her loose in the woods?"

"Look at me," Demetrius murmured. Chloe complied. He held her gaze, searching, studying. Chloe opened herself to him as easily as she had before the ill-fated dinner party. Giving herself to him, obeying him, had become as involuntary as breath.

God, this is wrong. This is so wrong.

"This slave is broken," said Demetrius, still staring into her. "Oh, yes, she's been broken for quite some time now. What happened at the dinner party was the rebellion of *your* slave, Abigail, and that has been dealt with. Twenty-One will be in the Hunt to regain buyer confidence in our product."

Konri's face was stoic behind Demetrius.

"Her ribs are bruised. Running would be very painful. Being caught would be as well."

Chloe tried not to piece together a picture of whatever he was saying. Demetrius took a step back from her.

"Then that will be her punishment."

Abigail started to speak but something stopped her. Chloe didn't look up to find out what.

"Let's go," said Demetrius.

Chloe rose and struggled to stand on her own, her legs still weak. She followed Demetrius out of the room as best she could without aid. Konri and Abigail remained where they were, even when she stumbled.

"She looks like she's in great shape, D," Abigail called behind them. "Hopefully she won't break to pieces when she's caught."

Chloe tried not to let fear take over her. She didn't need much of an imagination to guess what the Hunt was; some sick catching game. She could barely shuffle along the hallway right now, let alone run or hide. Every breath hurt. She imagined someone catching her, wrapping their arms around her, lifting her. She couldn't imagine bearing the pain.

She was so lost in her thoughts that she nearly bumped into Demetrius. He had stopped and turned around without her noticing. She took a few frantic steps back too quickly. The room wobbled.

Without a word, Demetrius scooped her off her feet. The feeling of his arms around her brought her back to the suite, bound and beaten. She shrieked, struggling in his arms.

"Sh, sh, sh," he shushed again. "*Je sais. Je sais.* You're all right."

Chloe's panic faded into despair. She cried, not bothering to hide her tears, and buried her face in his black undershirt. French, why did he speak French? Of all the languages in the world, why did the man who stole her life speak the language she grew up hearing? His words from that first terrible night came to her. *You were meant for me.* Her tears became broken sobs.

Demetrius allowed her to cry uninhibited all the way back to the suite, and into the bathroom. The bathtub was full and foaming, the room thick with the scent of lilacs. Demetrius dipped her into the hot water and settled along the edge of the tub, wringing a sponge in his hands.

"No…" she found herself sobbing. "No more, no more…"

No more kindness from her abductor. No more tenderness from the man who had beaten her and locked her in a cage. She couldn't take it anymore. She would go mad.

Demetrius lifted her chin with his fingertips and squeezed the sponge over her head, showering her with warm water and lilac soap. She felt the water seep through her hair, run along her scalp and down her back. Her sore limbs responded, relaxing. Demetrius took her arms one at a time, running the sponge along her skin in slow, deliberate circles. Chloe leaned into the touch, defeated. Demetrius' kindness and cruelty were enough to break her, but she craved his fleeting tenderness more than she could resist it.

"How are your ribs?" Demetrius' voice was soft but authoritative as it had been the night he had branded her. Chloe took a deep breath. Her ribs still hurt, but the pain abated in the bath.

"Better," she whispered. "…Master."

The word sounded unnatural on her tongue now, almost comical. She tensed. He had to have sensed the insecurity in her voice. Demetrius sighed. He dipped the sponge in the water and dragged it along her clavicle just under her collar.

"You've suffered a setback, *ma chère*," he said, sponging water over her breasts. "And you've disappointed me."

The words stung like a fresh wound and she didn't want them to. She didn't want her heart to ache. She looked at the man she once called Master, at the finely sculpted face beneath the leather mask, at the scars on his arms and peeking around the edges of his undershirt. Would he still have this power over her if he weren't so otherworldly? She thought back, far back, to the night she had first seen him. She had been surrounded by equally exotic sights at the Oryx, but even that night he had mesmerized her, called to something inside of her that she didn't know or understand. Something inside of her had screamed *yes* when he held her against the bleeding wall, which she echoed out loud at his request.

"Say yes."

She fought not to physically shake the thought from her head. No. She didn't ask for this. Had she only known what the masked stranger at the Oryx had had in store for her, had she only known that night…strange attraction or no, she would have fled and never looked back.

"You'll come back, Twenty-One," said Demetrius. He dropped the sponge and cupped her face in his hands, smoothing back her wet hair. "Many slaves have a backslide. Some never come back and have to be disposed of, but you'll come back." His hands slipped over her breasts, waking her nipples with a single stroke of his finger. "Oh, yes. You've been mine since the beginning."

Chloe closed her eyes. The feeling of his hands on her breasts, of his words thundering in her ears, was too much to bear.

"Yes, Master," she murmured. Images of Jason and her father and lilac bushes lingered even as she whispered, "I'm yours."

Chapter 36

Dia Belaire lay in her bed, snuggled against Demetrius, her tears finally dry. He sat resting against the headboard, exhaustion threatening to overtake him. They had been in the Belaire family's gigantic plantation-style home in the Garden District for three days mourning Mama Dede in Dia's room. Demetrius had gone out to the kitchen to get them meals, but Dia had not left the bedroom since he had carried her home from the hospital. She stayed in the bed most of the time, crying until her eyes were so red that Demetrius had to wet a cloth with cool water from her bathroom to soothe the irritation. They held each other day and night, sleeping only a few hours at a time before their sorrow dragged them back to consciousness. Dia occasionally watched television, but every program was eventually interrupted by news bulletins about Hurricane Katrina's approach. Eventually she gave up and switched off the television, curling into Demetrius for a nap.

Now, however, their sparse sleeping pattern had caught up with Demetrius. He was exhausted, from sorrow, from tears, from the end of his world. Dede's face burned in his brain, ever present, haunting him. He clung to Dia like a life raft and held her as fiercely as she held him. The wind picked up outside, an ominous howl. He wondered if the storm would be as bad as the news had predicted. Most media tended to exaggerate the severity of natural disasters. He wanted to get up and pull the shades to get a look at the sky, but Dia had settled into the crook of his arm, and he wouldn't move her for the world.

A knock on the door startled them both. Demetrius coiled his arm around Dia. Her biological mother who came into the room, uninvited. Nancy Belaire was thin and frail, with too much plastic surgery for a woman in her thirties. She looked at Dia and Demetrius lying in bed with the same apathy he had seen when he had carried Dia into the house. Nancy hadn't even asked his name, or why her daughter was crying. She had simply let a masked man in black carry Dia up to her bedroom and left them alone for days. She rarely moved from the living room, Demetrius noticed from his trips to the kitchen. She lounged in front of the television with a small bottle of pills in front of her, staring at the screen with glassy eyes that looked so much like her daughter's.

"They're evacuating the city," she said to Dia as if Demetrius weren't there. "I'm leaving now. The driver should be here in a few minutes."

Demetrius frowned. Evacuating the city was a drastic step. He looked at the girl in his arms. Dia's normally sweet face contorted with a darkness Demetrius had never seen in her.

"I'm staying." she declared. "I don't want to go anywhere with you." She wrapped her arms around Demetrius' neck, stopping his heart. "I'm staying in my home with the only family I have left."

Demetrius felt his eyes fill with tears he thought had long dried. In that moment, he felt the strange sense of peace that had overtaken him the first time he had met Dia, years ago in Mama's parlor. All that he had suppressed to protect her came flooding into his veins like a drug.

If Dia's words had stung her, Nancy Belaire gave no indication. She blinked slowly, looked away from her only child, and headed for the door.

"Stay away from the windows," she said before the door closed behind her.

Dia looked up at Demetrius and his heart felt as though it would burst. *Mon Dieu.* There was nothing to hold his feelings back anymore. Every defense had been washed away by three days of tears. Oh, he loved her, loved her as he had the moment he had first seen her. Was it possible to love a person so much? The feeling was so strong that it hurt, like thorns sprouting inside of his chest. He swallowed and struggled to find his voice. He tried to think logically through the haze of her large liquid eyes.

"We should go," he could only muster a whisper.

Dia shook her head so hard her waves tossed around her.

"I won't go," she said with the stubbornness of an only child. "If we can't get back here for Mama's funeral…" her fragile voice broke. "The house has storm windows. We're safe here." She snuggled into Demetrius' chest, clutching his shirt as if letting go would destroy her. "I won't let her go into the ground alone."

Demetrius kissed the top of her head through his light muslin mask. "*Allez, allez. Tout ira bien,*" he whispered. "Everything will be all right."

Demetrius fought exhaustion as Dia's breath slowed to a sleeper's pace, but soon he began to drift. He knew it was unwise to stay in a city being evacuated, but Dia's home was secure compared to other areas of the city. The storm windows would keep them safe from the wind, and even if a little flooding did occur, it would never reach the Garden District. He could fight no longer, and he drifted into a doze, his arms around his sweet girl.

X X I

It was dusk but Demetrius could hardly see. A silver basin rested on a track of two intersecting railroads just in front of him, and he tread lightly to approach it, dodging stray nails and splintered wood from the aging tracks. Fire bloomed in the basin, though he could see nothing within it to ignite, a cool orange flame that pooled like water. Demetrius studied the basin, crouching down, afraid to touch it. The pale flames flickered in an unfelt wind. A strange sound caught his ear, a low, guttural hiss among the soft roar of the flame. He leaned in closer. Yes, there was a soft, slithering whisper coming from the flames themselves. He would be able to decipher its message if he could hear it better. He leaned in closer.

Tendrils of fire lashed out and coiled into a great white snake before Demetrius could spring back. The serpent struck, wrapping its powerful body around him and stealing the breath from his body. His ribs crushed against his spine. He struggled, opening his mouth, but no air came to his aid. He screamed silently as the white snake crushed his bones.

Demetrius woke to the sound of old wood straining against wind. The storm wailed outside, bulleting rain against the windows like the strike of a thousand snare drums. HIs clothes were soaked in sweat, his mask slipped down around his neck. He sucked in a breath of air. His ribs ached as if the serpent had followed him from his nightmare to crush him in reality.

He looked around and remembered that he was Dia's bedroom. She lay undisturbed, curled against his chest. She moaned softly, as if experiencing a nightmare of her own. Outside, the storm battled the city, battered the Belaire house. Demetrius shifted as gently as he could, trying to slide out from underneath Dia without waking her. He had to assess the severity of the storm. If it was as dangerous as it sounded, they had to go into the basement.

As Demetrius gently lifted Dia, she stirred in her sleep, whispered his name, and pressed her lips to his.

The storm ceased to be. Demetrius ceased to be. There was only Dia, Dia and the smell of jasmine and her succulent mouth against his. She was food and drink and air, and if her kiss ended, he would die.

But it did end. Dia was asleep. She slumped, her head fell back onto Demetrius' arm, her eyelids flickering, in the midst of a dream from which she hadn't woken.

"I love you," she whispered.

Demetrius lay with his heart crumbling inside of him. He knew those words were meant for him. She loved him, as he loved her. Dia and Dede's Vodou conversations flooded back to him, Dia's dreams of sleeping curled in the coils of a great white serpent, the loa Damballah.

"You're loved by Damballah, girl."

It was ridiculous. He knew that. Dede and Dia's countless conversations about the girl's Damballah dreams had simply crept into his own dreams. There was no ancient spirit protecting Dia. But Demetrius looked at the sweet girl asleep beside him and instead of love, the sickening flame of his "demons" came, awakened from their temporary dormancy after Mama's death. His head flooded with terrible images; Dia in tears, naked beneath him and screaming, pleading for mercy, bleeding and pale with terror. He cried out, tried to fight his mind, tried to fight his own arousal. It was disgusting. Not her. No. Not her.

"You'll destroy that poor child."

Demetrius sobbed like a child, his cries swallowed by Hurricane Katrina. Whether the dream was prophetic or superstitious, its meaning was clear. It was over. Dia was not safe.

He had to leave.

Chapter 37

Demetrius was far too weary for this part of the season. He had tried to calm his fraying nerves by mixing music, something he didn't really have to do this time of year. November and December were the slowest months for the Oryx, affectionately known as the Post-Halloween Recession among regulars. His DJ duties were on autopilot until mid-January. But mixing soothed him, so he spent the last hour before the Hunt doing it. Now, though, it was time. He slipped on a long leather coat trimmed in black fur, an old gift from a buyer years ago. He wore gloves also, though he suspected he wouldn't need them. Today was surprisingly warm for December in Ohio, which was lucky for the slaves, who would be running around the forest half nude. Demetrius checked the bud in his ear. It was online.

Everyone was already in the backyard when he pushed open the French doors and stepped outside. They applauded as he headed toward the lawn chairs where Abigail, Konri, and the twins stood waiting for him. Abigail always pushed him to make a grand entrance, like she did at the dinner party, and he always refused. Abigail never understood that his subtlety was a perfect foil to her drama. Too many theatrics and the buyers would wonder why they needed all of the smoke and mirrors and begin to distrust the product.

Abigail kissed his covered cheeks. She shivered despite the cream fur coat wrapped around her voluptuous frame. In cold weather, he was almost grateful for the mask. He took his seat and his party followed. Ten slaves sat on their knees a few hundred feet in front of him and Abigail. They wore white fur boleros and matching fur boots that crawled up to their thighs, secured by leather straps. The rest of their bodies were nude, shivering in the thin layer of wet snow under their knees. Their attendants stood beside them, holding them secure on long leather leashes. Nine of the ten had been selected by the buyers for the Hunt, and they were the cream of his crop. One was there, of course, and Seventeen, though Gabe held two leashes as Twenty-One's unofficial attendant. Demetrius allowed himself a brief moment to drink Twenty-One in. She was breathtaking as she knelt in the snow, framed by white fur, her pink nipples diamond hard. He ignored the slow burn rising in him.

"Ladies and gentlemen," Demetrius addressed the cameras he knew were in his eyeline. Many were scattered in the woods so the buyers would be able to view some of the takedowns. "Welcome to the Winter Hunt. You have selected ten slaves to be let loose on the property and hunted down by Abigail's stock."

"Is that girl on the end the Model Slave?" came a voice from his ear piece. American, a new buyer whose voice he did not yet recognize. He felt Abigail's eyes on him.

"Yes, Twenty-One is running in the Hunt this season," said Demetrius.

"Mr. Heart," a soft Irish brogue that could only belong to Dr. Cillian Lane, his client for three years. "Do you think it wise to let loose the girl who caused such trouble at the dinner party?"

Demetrius clenched his jaw behind his mask. "The slave who rebelled was dealt with, as you all witnessed. As I said in my statement, I have evaluated Twenty-One and deemed her a perfectly broken slave. Ash stole Abigail's phone and put it in Twenty-One's hands, but she did nothing with it."

He felt Abigail's gaze burning a hole in his cheek. He had not been there to see Ash's transgression, but he knew his slave. She would never have gone for the phone on her own. She was just as awestruck with Abigail as she was with the twins, and with him. He had seen her slide beneath the table and he had gotten there before any call could possibly have been made. Of that, he was certain.

"Twenty-One is a Model Slave," he said slowly, deliberately. "She is obedient, well-mannered, and desperate to please. You will witness it today."

He gestured toward Abigail. She did not move for a moment, a subtle defiance, but she crumbled the moment he met her eyes. She stood with exaggerated grace and pulled a whistle from the confines of her fur coat.

"Without further ado," she said with a laugh Marilyn Monroe would have been proud of. "Ladies and gentlemen, let the Winter Hunt begin!"

X X I

Abigail blew a piercing whistle and the slaves around Chloe sprung to their feet. Chloe froze for just a moment. She looked at Demetrius. Gabe had only given her the vaguest of instructions as he had prepared her for the mysterious Hunt: When the whistle blows, run like hell. She flashed back to her escape attempt, the last time she had been in the backyard. The Hunt felt strangely similar. Demetrius caught her gaze. He nodded at her. Chloe swallowed and got to her feet.

"Run, girl!" Gabe urged. "Into the woods!"

He slapped her on the buttocks. Chloe yelped and the shock threw her into motion. She ran past Gabe, past the crowd of cheering attendants, and into the woods. Her ribs ached with every breath. The pills Konri had been giving her all week helped dull the pain.

The other slaves were ahead of her, scattering in all directions like startled deer. Her mind raced as quickly as her heart. She gathered from Abigail and Demetrius' conversation that Abigail's slaves would come after them at some point. Did the other slaves know that, or did they receive the same instructions Gabe had given her? Were they teased with the possibility of escape?

Chloe veered right, uncertain of where to go. Her toes were numb against the frosted leaves and sticks carpeting the ground. She wished she could pull her fur bolero over her breasts. Having fur lining her shoulders and legs but leaving the rest of her exposed was torment. It made her feel all the more naked in the bitter air. For a moment, she wondered what month it was. She had lost track of time so long ago. The snow suggested winter, but she could guess no further than that.

She wandered aimlessly, trying and failing to come up with some sort of strategy. She looked up into the trees and spotted mounted cameras high on the branches. Someone had climbed up into the trees to set them there. Maybe climbing was a good way to hide. She saw a tree with a low, thick branch. She wrapped her arms around the branch and crippling pain in her side stopped her mid-motion. She whimpered through gritted teeth. Her ribs were too hurt to allow her to climb.

In the distance, another whistle blew. Chloe's stomach dropped. That could only mean the male slaves had been released. Chloe ran again, stumbling over twigs.

"Hey! Hey, over here!"

Chloe stopped. She spotted Rodney, crouched behind a fallen tree, beckoning her. He glanced up somewhere into the trees and crouched a little lower.

"Come here, baby," he said. "Hide over here. Hurry!"

Chloe hesitated. Rodney was the only attendant she saw in the woods. The rest were with Demetrius and Abigail in the backyard. What was he doing there?

"Get over here," Rodney ordered, his face turning red beneath his shaved blonde hair. He glanced up once more. "You need to hide or the game will end too fast."

Chloe hugged herself and complied. Rodney was an attendant, her superior. The last thing she wanted to do was disobey an order and end up in trouble again. She knew

Demetrius and Abigail were watching her closely after the dinner party. She did not want to give them any reason to doubt her again. She knew she would not be given another chance.

She approached Rodney. He grabbed her wrist and pulled her back away from the tree. Her ribs protested the sudden movement with a stab in her side. She cried out.

"Shh!" Rodney hissed. "Follow me. Quick!"

Chloe followed, trying not to trip. In the distance, she heard a sharp scream that jumpstarted her heart. Someone must have been caught.

Rodney stopped at a patch of leaves. He bent down and lifted up the edge of a brown tarp, which had been covered in the foliage like a hunter's trap.

"Hide here," he said. "Don't come out til I come get you."

He glanced behind Chloe, then grabbed her arm and dragged her under the tarp. Chloe shouted again, her ribs throbbing.

"Shut the fuck up," Rodney snarled. He piled leaves over the tarp and disappeared as quickly as he had shown up.

Chloe sat, her pulse heavy in her ears. She peeked out through the tarp and found she was too far away from the others to see anything but small figures in white fur. Something felt wrong as she sat there. Perhaps it was simply the fact that Rodney made her skin crawl, but it felt deeper than that. She wasn't sure if any other attendants were out there helping other slaves draw out the game, and Rodney's behavior had been strange. Why had he been crouched and hiding? Why had he looked up into the trees?

Chloe heard another squeal, and the distant sound of cheering. She strained to see past the tarp. She spotted a figure in black and one in white, entangled in some fashion, but she couldn't see clearly enough. One by one, she heard cries, cheers, saw figures in the distance heading back toward the yard, and again she felt that something was off. She felt too far away. She wondered if the cameras could still see her.

Chloe gasped. The cameras. Rodney had been hiding from cameras in the woods. He could have been hiding so the buyers wouldn't know that the game was so controlled. But why choose *her* to hide? Demetrius said he had wanted her in the Hunt to demonstrate her obedience to dubious buyers. Chloe swallowed hard. She could either stay here or listen to her gut and reemerge, but that would mean disobeying an attendant's order.

The screams and cheers had diminished. Chloe finally rose from the tarp and headed back the way she had come. She trembled with fear from having disobeyed, but the gnawing feeling in her gut would not allow her to remain.

It was not long before Chloe spotted movement. A male slave stood a few yards from her, scanning the woods. He wore nothing but an open black fur coat that barely brushed his waist. Chloe took a deep breath and waited for him to notice her.

She lost her nerve the moment his wide brown eyes locked onto her. He charged and she turned and ran without thinking to. He was an animal chasing her, and she took on the role of prey instinctively. She screamed when his arms locked around her waist and they fell to the ground. Adrenaline kept the pain in her ribs at bay. She struggled in his arms, but his weight against her was solid and strong. He flipped her onto her back. There was no mistaking his intention. He entered her, claimed her, and she writhed, her back digging into the frozen ground. He had Cupid's bow lips, so feminine on the body of a young man with a blonde mohawk and tattoo sleeves all the way down his arms. She met those lips with teeth and tongue, dragged her nails down his lean torso. A vicious heat sparked in her at the sight of the marks she'd made on his pale skin. Was this how Demetrius felt when he marked her? The thought inflamed her. She sank her teeth into his lower lip until he growled for her, a primal sound that maddened her. She shoved his chest with all her might. The slave teetered off balance. With a snarl of her own, Chloe shoved him onto his back and took him inside of her again. She rode him, biting his neck, his chest, anyskin she could, while he moaned beneath her and dug his fingers into her hips.

Control. It was an ecstasy, so exotic after so long in submission. She rode that feeling over the brink, screaming her orgasm to the grey winter sky, as the slave beneath her bucked and groaned. She didn't give a damn how many buyers were watching, or even if Demetrius was. Damn the buyers. Damn Demetrius. This was hers, and they couldn't take it from her.

When the warmth faded, the male slave slipped out from under her, hoisted her over his shoulder, and carried her back to the yard. She put up no fight. She did not blush when the attendants cheered.

Abigail's voice cut through the glow of satisfaction like an ice blade.

"Well, Rowan, we thought you'd never find her."

"I told you a search wouldn't be necessary, Rodney," came Demetrius' voice.

Chloe glanced up. Rodney stood in front of Demetrius. Abigail's glare cut her down before she could see anything more. Her stomach turned. If she had stayed where she was, Rodney may have convinced Demetrius to search for her. Something told her that wasn't how the game was supposed to go. She slid off Rowan's shoulder and they both knelt in line with the other slaves, who seemed to have been waiting for them. Chloe caught them shivering out of the corner of her eye.

"Slaves," said Demetrius.

The slaves looked up at him. Chloe couldn't read him from this distance. She remembered the rage she had felt from him after Ash had taken her against the cross. Would he behave that way again? After all, he had wanted her in the Hunt. He was stone-faced with his mask.

"Excellent Hunt," he said, his voice as unreadable as his eyes. "The captured slaves will be mounted for the night, and we will continue the party with our remaining slaves. Take your trophies to the dining room."

Not a glance her way. Chloe despised the ache in her chest. Rowan rose and swept her into his tattooed arms again, and as she and the other female slaves were carried to the dining room, she tried very hard not to look back at

Demetrius sitting there with Abigail like some twisted King and Queen of frost and fur.

Chapter 38

"I am Twenty-One. I am a slave. I will obey. I will be used. I will not question. I will please my Master. I am Twenty-One. I am a slave."

Chloe whispered the words over and over, focusing on them, trying desperately to believe in them as she once had. This was not a place for Chloe. This was a place for Twenty-One. She and the other "trophies" of the Hunt were in the dining room, attached to the most humiliating device Chloe had ever experienced in this place. Her arms were suspended over her head by a bar, her splayed legs shackled. She had been mounted from behind onto a polished wooden phallus, raised at an angle so Chloe had to stand on her toes. She had been blindfolded and gagged, a nasty little strap with a small rubber phallus on the inside. Chloe and the other slaves stood that way for what felt like hours, impaled by sex and by mouth, their legs numb and trembling.

She could hear the other slaves close behind her, shifting and moaning, but she could not see them. She was thankful for the blindfold, in all honesty. The darkness helped her keep calm. But she felt the phallus filling her sex with every small movement, and without being aroused, it was painful. It was harder than any human organ. It reminded her of the horrid little golden ball the twins had slipped inside of her.

Chloe tensed at the sound of heavy footfalls. She hadn't heard anyone pass by after she and the other slaves had been displayed.

"There you are," Gabe's voice startled her. "Twenty-One, Seventeen, Demetrius wants both of you with him tonight."

Chloe was too relieved to be afraid at the moment. All she could think about was the ache in her limbs when Gabe unbound her wrists and ankles and hoisted her off the phallus. She took a deep breath through her mouth when he removed the gag. Her jaw hurt from accommodating the phallus for so long. Gabe removed her blindfold. Night had fallen; the dining room was in total darkness, save for the lights in the backyard which seeped through the French doors. Seventeen stood beside her, her long black hair rumpled from the blindfold. Gabe stripped them of the fur boots and boleros. Chloe was once again fully nude. She welcomed the air that chilled her freshly exposed skin.

"Let's go."

Gabe led Chloe and Seventeen through the study in silence and knocked on the door Chloe had nearly opened when she had tried to escape. At Gabe's urging, she followed Seventeen into a cavernous room with navy walls so dark they were nearly black. Chloe first noticed the flat screen on the far wall, so large she had first taken it for a window. Then she realized there were no windows in this room, though two thin black curtains hung from the ceiling over the king size bed. She saw Demetrius standing on the other side of the bed, nude and gleaming in all the darkness. Chloe's breath caught in her throat. She tried to keep her eyes down, tried not to trace every scar and curve of muscle on his body. She failed. She had never seen him nude without distraction, without being entwined with him.

"Thank you, Gabe," he said.

Gabe left with a nod, and Chloe and Seventeen were left standing At Attention across from Demetrius. Chloe fought to keep her breath slow. Demetrius looked at her, his grey eyes sending a jolt down her spine.

"You put on quite a show in the woods, didn't you, *ma chère?*"

Chloe knew she was in trouble the moment the words seeped through his mask. His voice was low and dangerous. Every muscle in her body was tense in an instant. There was no exit but the door behind them. She knew she would never be able to escape, even if she turned and ran that very moment.

"Oh, yes," Demetrius growled. "It was very entertaining for the buyers, but not the behavior of a Model Slave, now, was it?"

Chloe's voice failed her for an eternal moment.

"Was it?" Demetrius repeated in a snarl.

"No, Master," she replied as steadily as she could.

"No, no," Demetrius echoed, tossing his long black hair from his shoulder. He still wore the mask from the Hunt, black leather with a line of fur down the center. "No, a Model Slave would never be dominant, now, would she? She would never wrestle a man to the ground and mount him like a broken horse. Oh, no, *cheri*, you weren't my slave

387

in that moment, were you? That was all for you, now, wasn't it?"

Chloe bowed her head. "I…I'm s-sorry-"

Demetrius rounded the corner of the bed and came at her so quickly that she shrieked and broke form, curling into herself to stave off a blow. Demetrius caught her in his arms, crushing her against his naked waist, growing hard against her thigh. Chloe's ribs throbbed with pain, but her cries fell on deaf ears. He twisted her head up by her hair. His face was an inch from hers. Seventeen remained where she was, motionless, At Attention, her eyes on the bed.

"Have you completely forgotten yourself?" he hissed. "Have you forgotten to whom you belong?" He stroked her face with hard fingers, wiping away tears she couldn't keep from falling. "You dominated that slave like you were some sort of Mistress. Is that what you are now, *Twenty-One*? Is that what you want to be?"

"No, Master!" Chloe cried. His grip tightened on her hair and she screamed for him. He grew harder against her, digging into her thigh. "I'm your slave!"

"Oh, I think you're lying, *ma chère*, I really think you are." Demetrius' fingers became talons against her throbbing ribs. She gasped, but his grip was far too strong to wriggle out of. "I think you need to know what it feels like to be a Mistress. You only had a little taste, didn't you? You must want more."

"No, Master," Chloe didn't know what he had in mind, but she didn't want to find out. "I'm sorry! I'm so sorry! I didn't mean-"

"Oh, but I think you did." Demetrius' voice fell calm in a flash. "I think you meant every moment of that...*performance*."

He stopped squeezing her but did not let go, trapping her in his arms. Chloe drew deep shivering breaths, terrified of the sudden stillness. She found his gaze on her, waiting for her to look at him. His eyes burned with a sickening fire, storm clouds caught in lightning.

"Let's see what you can stomach, my little Mistress."

He released her so fast that she stumbled. It hurt to breathe. She resisted the urge to hold her side. Demetrius reached beneath the bed and pulled out a studded leather belt and a small grey object Chloe couldn't see very clearly in his hand. Her heart jolted.

"Seventeen," said Demetrius. "Get on the bed and kneel At Attention."

Seventeen obeyed. She knelt on the bed, facing the headboard, her hands at her neck, elbows spread wide. Demetrius approached her and moved her long olive black hair from her back.

"Come here," Demetrius beckoned Chloe.

Chloe didn't want to approach the bed. She didn't want to play whatever game was coming. Demetrius snatched her hand the moment she got close enough. Chloe fought not to jerk back. He looped the studded belt around her right hand and held up the grey object. It was shaped like an electric razor, but a long plastic wand protruded from the top. Demetrius pressed a button and a high-pitched electric whine emanated from it. Chloe's blood ran cold.

"Strike her," Demetrius ordered. "Her shoulders, her back, her ass, her legs. Avoid the kidneys. Strike her until you draw blood, little Mistress," he wriggled the wand in his hand, "or I hit her with this."

Chloe's stomach dropped. She saw the muscles in Seventeen's back tense. Other than that, the slave remained still.

"Electricity is the one roadblock Seventeen has yet to overcome." There was a purr to Demetrius' voice that made Chloe feel ill. "You don't like shocks, do you, Seventeen?"

"If it pleases you, Master." Seventeen's rich voice was tight with fear. Chloe had heard her voice calm and hollow, or roaring with rage. She had never heard fear come from the steel slave. The dark bedroom grew fuzzy for a nauseating moment.

"Master," Chloe's own voice was weak. "Master, I can't. Please…please punish me. Seventeen has done nothing."

Demetrius stared at her in a silence infinitely more frightening than anything he could have said. He pointed the wand at Seventeen and tapped it against her right hip.

A nasty static *zap* and a tiny burst of light sent Seventeen's voice to the sky. She shrieked, curling in on herself, breaking form before Chloe for the first time.

"No!" Chloe cried, reaching for the slave. Demetrius held up a warning finger, the wand looming close to Seventeen as she recovered, whimpering, and came back to attention.

"Tell me how to treat my slave again, Twenty-One." Demetrius' voice held venom. "Tell me again."

Chloe sobbed so hard she nearly fell to her knees. She felt sick. The belt in her hand turned her stomach.

"Master…"

"Strike her," Demetrius said calmly. "This is what you wanted, Little Mistress."

Chloe nearly choked on her own tears. Seventeen's entire body trembled. Her skin was raw pink where the wand had hit her.

"Now," Demetrius ordered.

Chloe clutched the studded belt and, with a cry, struck Seventeen.

The steel slave's back bowed. Chloe had caught her just beneath the shoulder blade. A mark formed immediately, angry and red, but no blood came.

"Pity," said Demetrius. "You're quite the cruel Mistress, aren't you, to strike so softly and hurt her again?"

Chloe shrieked along with Seventeen as the wand came again, striking her thigh with a flash of lightning. Seventeen's cries were agonizing. Chloe couldn't take it. She screamed and struck Seventeen again, hitting her square across the back. Again, no blood. Demetrius shook his head and hit Seventeen in the buttocks. The steel slave's cries only grew louder.

"Please, Mistress!" she screamed. "Please strike me!"

Chloe's world shook on its axis. She felt Demetrius' eyes on her, but she couldn't look away from Seventeen's body, at the bright pink firework patterns the wand caused, and the two red marks she had made with the belt. Chloe shoved back all thoughts of shame and pain. Beneath them, a rage bloomed, a rage she fanned until it consumed her.

She struck Seventeen again, hard enough to lurch the slave forward, but it was not enough to break skin. Chloe used the inevitable wand strike as fuel for her anger. She drew her arm back and belted Seventeen across the buttocks, drawing a cry from the steel slave's throat, but before Demetrius could use the wand, she struck again. And again. And again. Chloe screamed over the vicious *slap* of the studded belt, using her full arm, striking with abandon. Demetrius faded away. Seventeen's screams became nothing. There was only the slap of leather againstskin, the raised red streaks blooming brighter and brighter, as bright as the hatred inside of Chloe.

It seemed an eternity before Demetrius' cool hand wrapped around her wrist, stopping her blows. Chloe slowly came to. Seventeen had collapsed onto her hands and knees, her back marred by swollen streaks. A thin stream of blood trickled from a brutal strike near her back ribs.

Chloe's rage evaporated.

"Oh, God…" she whispered, staring at the sweat-drenched and whimpering woman before her. "Oh, God."

"Good girl." Demetrius' voice was rough and strained. Chloe looked at him. He was staring at Seventeen, his chest heaving as if he had been the one striking her. He was fully erect. He seemed to be drinking in the image of the bloodied slave. Chloe let the belt drop from her hand. Her body felt numb. She remembered when she craved Demetrius' attention, the feeling of accomplishment she experienced when her own pain brought him pleasure. Now she just felt sick.

Demetrius reached out and brushed Seventeen's back. The steel slave screamed as if he had struck her, collapsing onto the sheets, writhing in pain. A low growl permeated Demetrius' mask. He looked at Chloe, and the hunger in his eyes wasn't for her.

"Twenty-One," he said. "Sit at the corner of the bed, and hold the bedposts."

Chloe stumbled over her numb feet to crawl into the bed. The sheets were damp with Seventeen's sweat. Demetrius reached beneath the bed again and came up with rope. Chloe knew what was coming. She bowed her head and let silent tears fall as Demetrius bound her wrists to the wooden bedposts, her arms spread just shy of uncomfortably wide. Demetrius bound her hastily, his eyes cutting to Seventeen's panting form every chance he got. Something burned in Chloe, some shadow of the rage she had felt as she struck Seventeen.

Demetrius finally looked at her. His hair had fallen over one eye.

"What are you?" he asked.

Chloe stared at him for a long moment, trying to understand the feeling growing inside of her. "I am a slave."

"Again."

"I am a slave."

"Yes." Demetrius patted her hair in an idle, distracted manner. "And you will never forget it again, will you?"

Chloe shook her head, unable to speak. Demetrius seemed to accept a weak reply for once.

"You will sleep like this tonight, to remind you of what you are."

He had barely finished speaking before he turned to Seventeen.

"Slave," he said to her. "Spread your legs."

Seventeen had barely obeyed before Demetrius fell onto her. He gripped her hair in one hand and entered her from behind. Seventeen moaned, a pleasure sound Chloe was not expecting. Demetrius rode her, running his fingers along every streak Chloe had made on Seventeen's back. The feeling burned brighter in Chloe's chest and prickled up through her temples. Demetrius did not look her way a single time. She expected him to, to stare at her, to mock her, punish her by showing her this…but why would that be a punishment? He was not hurting Seventeen. Chloe herself had done that. No, he was fucking her, running a hand through her hair, dragging his nails along her wounds to make her cry out. Chloe was invisible to him. Seventeen was everything.

Chloe finally understood the feeling that pestered her. It was envy. And it grew every moment Demetrius failed to look her way, burned when he spent himself across Seventeen's streaked back, and finally consumed her when he shackled the steel slave to the headboard and stroked her breasts affectionately, whispering, "good girl" into Seventeen's ear. Demetrius slipped out of the room without another word. Chloe was alone with her own thoughts for far too long. She wrestled with envy and self-loathing for an eternity. She was his, even though her hatred for him returned with her name, even though she knew she shouldn't want to be. She had no choice but to be his. But Demetrius was not hers. She had known that before this encounter, but never before had it stung her so badly. She drifted off, finally, bound to the bed posts, staring at the bruised and battered slave across from her until her eyelids sunk.

Chapter 39

Demetrius had just finished posting the last of the dolls for their final night at the Oryx when he heard Rafe's footfalls echo across the empty dance floor.

"Rafe," he greeted, stepping away from Five. The dolls had been decorated with silver garlands and tinsel for the holiday. Much like Abigail's theatrics, he found this particular theme for the dolls ridiculous, but each year the crowd loved it.

"Got a phone call, Boss," said Rafe, running a hand over his bald head, an uncharacteristically nervous gesture. "Some detective."

Demetrius frowned. A detective? Of course Rafe was nervous. They dealt with police regularly, like any bar, but a detective was an unusual caller. He thought back through the month. Bobby was sitting in jail at this very moment, up on charges after the tire slashing incident. There was no need for a detective in a case like that. The Oryx had been quiet otherwise, save for one thing.

"Has Mariane been around lately?" asked Demetrius.

Rafe gave him a blank face.

"The little blonde *piece* who gave Bobby a hard time a while back."

Rafe folded his arms. "Oh. Not that I've seen. Don't remember seeing her since then."

That clever little bitch.

"Is the detective on hold?"

"Yeah. In the office."

Demetrius headed toward the office, thinking fast. If Mariane had gone to the police, he would have heard from his contacts at the station by now. But he couldn't think of any other reason for a detective to be calling him. He closed the office door behind him and picked up the phone.

"This is Demetrius."

"Mr. Heart, hello," came a monotone female voice. Demetrius sighed internally. He had long ago come to terms the ridiculous surname, but still damned Mama Dede for it. "This is Detective Jamie Gatz of the FBI. We're investigating a missing person's case, and the name of the Oryx came up as the last place they were seen."

Detective Gatz paused, as if waiting for him to speak. Demetrius flexed his fingers.

"Doug Dorn is the owner of the bar, Detective," he said. "I'm only an employee. I can put you in contact with him for this sort of business."

"Well, actually, Mr. Heart, he was coming to talk to *you*."

He was coming to talk. So Mariane *was* the reason for this. Demetrius almost smiled. She'd known she had no evidence to implicate him in Chloe's disappearance, so she dredged up her one card against him, that one night years ago, when the idiotic brother of one of his slaves had turned up at the bar. He felt the urge to touch the bullet scar near his collarbone.

"I was wondering if you could come down to the Oak County Precinct and answer a few questions for us?"

Demetrius mulled this over. Legally, he didn't have to. Detective Gatz had chosen her words very, very carefully. They were vague, and she paused at deliberate points, as if waiting for him to speak. She was fishing for information, hoping he would fill in blanks and possibly bring suspicion upon himself. If they had any sort of solid evidence against him, she wouldn't be searching for a lead like that. Mariane was their only connection to him, and she was more than easy to discredit. It would be best for him to go in and endure an hour or so of Detective Gatz trying to trip him up with her leading questions. Once he discredited Mariane, the incident would resolve itself.

"I'd be happy to, Detective," he said. "Though I have to tell you, I meet new people every night. You're going to have to refresh my memory."

"Of course, Mr. Heart," said Detective Gatz. "We'll be happy to."

Chapter 40

The attendants were just as excited as they had been before the dinner party. Chloe and the rest of the slaves stood in the dining room on a long tarp as their attendants brushed them with sharp smelling paint. Chloe was tense, standing At Attention as Gabe coated Seventeen's legs in dull pastel streaks that became bright metallic green when they dried. He painted her to look like some sort of mermaid. Other slaves were painted with tiger and zebra stripes, and a multitude of other animal pelts. Abigail flitted about the basement in a skin tight blue gown, directing the twins as they decorated the walls with streamers. Chloe tried her best to avoid drawing attention to herself, but every now and then she felt Abigail's gaze boring into her. She tried to focus on the décor around her. It was easy to pick up on the circus theme. There was even a large tank full of water set up in the center of the podium for Seventeen and the other "mermaids." The shackled table and the rack full of nasty little tools were still there from the dinner party. Chloe was relieved to see that the crosses had been removed.

Gabe stepped back and studied Seventeen. Chloe followed suit. Her legs were green with a black scallop pattern from her thighs to her ankles. He had painted stripes on her feet to simulate a fin. Her nipples were coated in the strange green paint as well. They glittered like gems set in her lush breasts. Her hair fell long and glossy over her shoulder, half concealing her kohl-rimmed eyes and shimmering green lips.

"All right, you, go sit by the tank while I finish up here," he beckoned to Chloe. "Hurry up, sweetie, we're already behind."

As Chloe and Seventeen crossed paths, Seventeen caught Chloe's hand for a breath, squeezing and letting go before Gabe could notice. Chloe frowned. She watched Seventeen walk by as Gabe posed her. The beautiful slave looked over her shoulder at her, and her eyes held the same terrible sorrow Chloe had seen before they had had the photo shoot. Chloe's heart constricted. Gabe had covered up the bruises Chloe had left on Seventeen's back the night Demetrius had forced her to be a Mistress, but Seventeen's eyes held every ounce of pain she had endured. Chloe remembered the feeling of being sucked into those large dark eyes, and for a moment, she liked the idea of being trapped in Seventeen's sorrow, of losing herself in that inviting blackness.

Gabe lifted Chloe's chin and painted along her jawline to the edge of her collar. The paint smelled terrible, sharp and acrid like ammonia. She tried to breathe through her mouth and looked at the jar in Gabe's hand. The paint inside looked grey and milky. She wished she could see the color it became as it dried. She could feel it on her neck, tightening and becoming more resistant. Chloe lifted her chin to stretch the front of her throat. The paint fought her, urging her neck to spring back to its original position. It tensed like a rubber band.

"It's weird, isn't it?" said Gabe with a smile. He went to work coating her chest just beneath her collar. "You'll get used to it. But you need to hold still 'til it dries, or you'll tear holes in it. That's the problem with liquid-"

A deafening crash brought startled cries from the crowd of slaves and attendants. Chloe looked up to find that Seventeen had overturned the training table on the podium. The attendants moved at once, dropping the slaves to the floor. Gabe, however, headed right for Seventeen, leaving Chloe standing frozen in shock. She had seen one of Seventeen's outbursts before, in the baths, but she had assumed the attendant Seventeen had bitten had provoked her somehow. This tantrum was unprompted.

Abigail and the twins dropped their decorations and rushed at Seventeen.

"Slave!" Abigail shouted, catching Seventeen's attention away from Gabe. "On your knees. Now!"

Seventeen grabbed a jar of paint beside a nearby slave and hurled it in Abigail's direction. Abigail shrieked and dodged the projectile. Gabe advanced on his charge, but the wild slave ran behind the rack of tools and shoved it with all her might. The rack hit the podium wall with a crack, scattering whips and floggers on the marble floor. Seventeen snatched up the nearest tool, the bamboo cane that the twins had used on Ash during the dinner party. She swung it in Gabe's direction, making a threatening *whoosh* sound. She swung it at Abigail and the twins to keep them a safe distance away as well.

Chloe was astonished. In a split second, this slave had gained the upper hand against a room full of attendants. She knew it would not last long. Seventeen had cornered herself on the podium. She had nowhere to go, and eventually someone would brave a blow from the cane and capture her. But for now, Seventeen was in control. Chloe felt hot all over. The back of her throat tingled, and she could feel her heart picking up speed. She wanted to cough, to clear her throat, but she didn't dare break the silence. Finally, Seventeen opened her mouth and spoke.

"I am Elena Andolini," she said. Her voice was lush and smooth, a low alto burning with conviction. "I am not a slave."

For a moment, the world stood still. Then Gabe and the twins charged at her.

Seventeen swung wildly, nearly catching Charity's hand as they advanced.

"I am Elena Andolini!" she cried. "I am not a slave! I am Elena Andolini! I am not-"

She continued to scream, over and over, a chant to shatter the mantra that had become the prayer of twenty women. She swung at the twins and Gabe caught her around the waist while they disarmed her. Chloe and the crowd of slaves and attendants watched in awe. Seventeen's eyes were bright and wild, as savage and beautiful as Chloe had remembered upon seeing them for the first time, and she fought in Gabe's arms with a ferocity to rival the rebellion in the baths. Even Gabe, twice her size, seemed to struggle to keep ahold of her. He kicked her legs out from beneath her and dragged her up the steps of the tank on the podium.

Chloe's throat went dry. She remembered when Gabe had dunked her again and again in the baths. She did not want to witness such a brutal act again, but she couldn't look away. Her chest was tight, as if her ribcage were slowly turning to lead.

"I am Elena Andolini!" Seventeen screamed at the top of her lungs. "I am not a slave!"

Gabe threw her into the tank and held her under the water, dodging her flailing limbs. Chloe watched her writhe in the tank, twisting and kicking her painted green legs. Holes formed in the bizarre paint where she moved, tearing like cloth. Her gasp was audible when Gabe finally lifted her up for air.

"I am not a slave!" she screamed again, thrashing against Gabe's grip. "I am not a slave!"

Gabe dunked her again, shouting unintelligible words over the struggle. He held her under again and again, but Seventeen did not slow or tire like she had in the baths. With each breath, she screamed, "I am not a slave!"

The words and the sound of splashing water bounced off the walls like a drum calling to arms. Chloe's knees felt weak. Watching Seventeen submerged over and over again made her own breath short, as if she were the one drowning. The room began to blur, and all Chloe could see was Seventeen's lithe body in motion under water, fighting, flailing, weakening. Chloe did not realize she was walking toward the tank until she tripped over a slave on the ground and nearly lost her footing. Not a single attendant moved to stop her. Even Abigail and the twins were distracted, watching Gabe dunk Seventeen, hold her, lift her, dunk her again, as she finally began to slow.

Chloe was close enough to see Seventeen's face behind the glass. She watched the slave open her mouth and gasp as if water were air. Chloe's own breath felt as if she were inhaling water, thick and labored. By the time Chloe had stumbled to the tank and pressed her hand against the glass, Seventeen had stopped struggling, and those big dark eyes had gone dim and glassy, unblinking as her long hair veiled her face. Chloe felt as if she herself were floating. She was in the water with Seventeen, weightless and still. They were free.

Chloe collapsed just as Gabe pulled Seventeen too late out of the water. Chloe's skin was on fire, her throat felt too thick, a wall of flesh slowly closing. She opened her mouth and fought for air, and stupidly she thought, *Put her back in the water! Put her back! We belong there!*

The dining room erupted into movement, but Chloe was nearly deaf from the sound of her frantic pulse in her ears. Konri appeared in her blurred vision, shouting, louder than she had ever heard him speak.

"…under control. Now!"

He shoved a few attendants who had gathered around Chloe aside. "Move! Move!"

Chloe scratched at her throat as if she meant to make a new airway, but her fingers came back with sticky, stretchy white paint. She stared at the paint, and it was as if she were back in the dentist's chair of her childhood, choking on her own tongue from the dentist's latex gloves. Konri scooped her into his arms. The twins appeared at her side, their black eyes wide with panic.

"I'll take care of this," Konri said to them. "Move."

Chloe flopped like a fish in Konri's arms as he barreled through the dining room. Her lungs felt like they were growing bigger and thicker, resisting air as much as they craved it. She tried to speak, tried to tell Konri about the latex, but her lips were heavy and useless. He had to know. She had told him about her allergy. He had to know what was in the paint.

She came down hard on a hardwood floor, knocking precious air from her lungs. She tried to sit up. She was in the study, surrounded by Demetrius' shelves of books. Konri stood in the doorway, his hand on the door. He was silent as ever, staring at her. His dun-colored eyes were wide and raking up and down her body as if he hoped to memorize every cough and convulsion. Chloe tried to scream, to beg for help. She reached for the doctor and he brushed her arm aside with his foot as if it were a pebble in his path. In the distance, she heard the cries of attendants. No one was coming for her. Someone called Konri's name. With one last lingering glance, Konri stepped back and slammed the door. Chloe stared at the door as the air got thinner and thinner.

Chapter 41

DECEMBER 13, 2011

"Rafe. There's been an incident at home. I won't be in tonight. Sarah should be able to handle things."

Rafe slipped his cell phone back in his pocket and looked at the girl standing at the bar a few feet away from him. She looked woefully out of place, and not because it was 7 at night and the bar had not yet opened. She was a fully grown, stylish woman, leaning against the bar in a double breasted white coat and designer jeans tucked into black boots, but the way she carried herself made Rafe think of her as very young, or at least vulnerable. Maybe it was how tightly her arms were folded, almost as if she were hugging herself, or the way she looked up at him with her head slightly bowed, her face veiled by the curtain of dark wavy hair. She looked like the doe-eyed freshmen who occasionally wandered in from the nearby campus, in awe of the Oryx. She was not the kind of girl he would expect Demetrius to be affiliated with, but he was the man she had come to the Oryx looking for, begging to be let in to wait for him.

Now that Rafe had received a voicemail that Demetrius wouldn't be coming in, he wasn't sure what to do with the girl. He sighed. Truth be told, he was anxious about letting her see Demetrius. Maybe he planned to do to her what he'd been doing to One…but he had been trying very hard not to think about that. The detectives who had given him the bug told him they would keep him abreast of any new developments…

"Miss?" Rafe approached the girl, and she looked up at him with that strange expression, as if she were in some sort of trouble and he was the only person who could help her. Her large, liquid brown eyes were red-rimmed, her small nose an adorable shade of pink. He just didn't know what to make of her.

"Demetrius isn't coming in tonight," he said. "He has to stay home for something."

The girl's lower lip trembled a little.

"I have to see him," she said in that urgent, tremulous voice that had caught Rafe off guard at the door earlier. "Do you know where he lives?" she leaned forward and gripped his arm with surprisingly strong fingers.

Rafe wanted to back away. The look on her face was so raw with grief, or desperation, or something…had he known her even a little, he couldn't have resisted the urge to wrap his arms around her, to hold her as if he were consoling a child. How could this delicate little piece be related to Demetrius? She was as open as Demetrius was unreadable.

"I don't think that's a good idea," he said. "Boss prefers privacy. He doesn't like visitors."

"Please," she murmured again. She seemed on the verge of tears. "Please, sir. Demetrius is my only family. I need to see him."

Rafe ran a hand over his bald head. He didn't want this girl to go up to Demetrius' place alone, but there was no way he could leave the bar. He didn't particularly want to find out what "incident" had kept Demetrius at home, anyway. But he had never heard someone call Demetrius family before.

"Please. I know how he seems," the girl said softly. "But he'd never hurt me."

That startled Rafe. He sighed. He didn't know anything about her, but she seemed to know Demetrius pretty well. "All right...all right. I don't know the address, but I can tell you how to get there."

The girl uttered a small cry and wrapped her arms around him. Rafe was too surprised to move for a moment.

"Thank you," she whispered. "Thank you so much. Thank you."

Rafe found himself putting his arms around the stranger, even stroking her hair.

"Just be careful," he said. "All right? Don't make me regret this."

Chapter 42

Demetrius leapt out of his car, already at a run up the driveway. He had been about halfway to the Oryx when Charity had sent him an urgent text about Seventeen. At first, he didn't plan on turning around. Charity had simply texted *417*, *4* being their code for a slave lashing out followed by their number. At this point, Gabe could easily handle Seventeen's outbursts on his own, even if she hadn't had one in quite some time. But a minute later he received another text, a single word: *Break*. It meant that a slave broke from their submissive state completely. It often happened early on, when a slave was particularly convincing with false compliance, and then would attempt escape in some way. But it never happened this late in the season, and never with a slave as well trained as Seventeen.

The dining room was secure. The attendants held their charges on the floor, flat on their stomachs, as was protocol. He saw Abigail, Gabe, and the twins standing on the podium. Faith and Charity were holding hands, a typical sign of distress in the two, and Abigail stood beside him with her arms shielding her torso, one hand at the base of her throat. Gabe was drenched in water, atypically pale for his Samoan skin. Something had gone wrong. Konri knelt a few feet away, his hand at the neck of a limp slave sprawled on the floor, coated in ripped green latex, her wet black hair fanned out around her on the marble.

Demetrius blew past the attendants and their slaves and dropped to his knees beside Seventeen. He pushed Konri's hand out of the way and pressed his fingers against the side of her neck, confirming what her glassy eyes had already told him. Rage ignited, a burst of flame just under the skin. He cut his eyes to Gabe. Abigail and the twins took a step away from the attendant. Gabe's face was horror-stricken. He stared at the corpse of his charge, oblivious to the danger everyone else sensed. Gabe was a careful and patient attendant, yes, one of Demetrius' best. He had a way of calming the fiercest slaves, which was why Demetrius had assigned him to Seventeen. It was very unlikely that Gabe had lost his temper and accidentally drowned the girl.

"Gabe," Demetrius muttered, biting back his anger.

"I don't even know what happened." Gabe's voice was barely a whisper. "I did the same thing I do every time. She didn't even slow down. She was just fighting and screaming, and then…"

Demetrius looked over the body. She hadn't lost much of her color yet, but those lovely lips of hers would soon be blue beneath the green paint. He noted burst blood vessels in her eyes.

"Did she speak?" he asked.

A heavy silence followed his words. Glances shifted back and forth. Finally Faith looked at him, a nervous hand buried in her hair.

"She said…her birth name," she said. "And that she wasn't a slave."

Demetrius bowed his head, his hair falling over his face. He had seen this type of rebellion before, but never so late in the season from a slave long broken. Six months of breaking, of training, of discipline, wasted. Six months and probably a profit of millions lost to suicide. How could this have happened this close to the auction, this far into the training process? There had to have been signs, there always were. He had given Seventeen a great deal of one-on-one attention, far more than the other slaves, at least until he'd found Twenty-One.

Demetrius' head snapped up. A hollow pit formed in his stomach, a gnawing sense of dread. He scanned the room. Nineteen slaves were on the floor, their attendants beside them, watching him. Abigail's nine slaves lay in a line as well. Demetrius rose.

"Abigail, where is Twenty-One?"

Abigail looked at him, her eyes unfocussed, uncomprehending. She looked around the room.

"I-"

"Did you put her somewhere?" Demetrius' heart jolted, but he smothered the frantic feeling in his chest with anger. Abigail took a step back, her hand returning to the base of her throat, a sure sign of stress.

"No, D," she said, glancing at Konri, still on his knees next to Seventeen. "I thought Konri-"

"-I saw her standing while the others went down," said Konri, standing and brushing off his slacks, "but I don't remember seeing her since. She may have taken the opportunity to run again."

Demetrius turned to the twins, who had huddled closer together.

"Find her," he ordered. "Everyone search the grounds."

He turned on his heel and headed back toward the front door. In his rush, he'd left his car keys in the ignition. If she had escaped through the front, she could feasibly get in the car and drive off. If he lost her…

A soft scratching noise stopped him from passing the study door. He cracked it open, and there she was, on the ground, and something was wrong. She lay limp on her side, her chest convulsing, her arm outstretched toward the door. Her face looked terrible, red and strained, the whites of her eyes flashing between fluttering eyelids. Liquid latex coated her neck and chest, ripped as if she had tried to peel it off. The skin beneath the paint was red and swollen. She opened her mouth to breathe, and the sound was labored, frantic, as if she were choking on air.

Mon Dieu, no.

Demetrius gathered her into his arms. Her limbs were limp and heavy.

"Konri!" he bellowed.

He pushed through the study and into his bedroom, setting the barely conscious girl on the bed. He brushed her sweat-drenched hair from her face and ran his hands over her neck and chest and ribs, feeling for some sort of clue.

"Chloe," he urged, gripping her shoulders. "Chloe, tell me what's happening. Look at me."

Her eyes fluttered and for a moment he caught a flash of hazel. She brought her hand to her throat, trying to curl her fingers around the shreds of latex, but she was too weak. She opened her mouth and the tiny wheeze of breath she took in made his stomach knot. At once, it clicked. Konri appeared at his door.

"It's anaphylaxis," Demetrius said to him. "Get me an epi pen. *Now.*"

But the girl on the bed had stopped struggling. She went limp, her eyelids growing still, her mouth open in a silent gasp. Demetrius straddled her waist, ripping latex paint off her skin with experienced fingers. Her airway was closing. If he didn't do something soon, she'd suffocate. He tilted her chin back, shoved his mask aside, and blew into her mouth. Her chest lifted, just barely. He blew into her again. *Breathe, Chloe.* he thought, as if she could hear his mind screaming. *Breathe!*

Konri came into the room with an epi pen and a bottle of antihistamines. Demetrius held out his hand, throwing his hair over his right side to shield his unmasked face. Konri only hesitated a moment before handing him the drugs.

"Out," was all Demetrius said.

Konri went, shutting the door behind him. Demetrius sat up, fumbling with the epi pen. He couldn't remember the last time he was this frantic. Chloe's chest stopped moving. Demetrius ripped off the cap and jammed the epinephrine into her thigh.

X X I

Chloe was floating, drifting in fog. The pain in her lungs, the terror of being unable to take a breath, was gone now. In fact, she felt nothing; no fear, but no sense of peace that allegedly came with death. She simply *was*, and distantly she knew that she would not *be* for much longer. She was lost in the darkness of Seventeen's eyes, and it pulled her down deeper and deeper into itself, into numbness.

Then air came, and with it came light and pain.

Chloe gasped, gulping in air. She was hot, so very hot, as if her skin was molten, hissing and bubbling over her bones. But air, oh, God, it filled her aching lungs until she feared they would burst. The light and blurred shapes, a face looming over hers, shrouded by black hair. Fingers pressed into her mouth, depositing several small oblong things into it. Water filled her and she panicked, but the fingers sealed her mouth shut until she swallowed. Slowly she became aware of a low, urgent voice murmuring her name.

"That's it, Chloe. You're okay, little one."

Focus returned. It was Demetrius in front of her, his grey eyes wide. Chloe blinked, trying to clear her vision. Something was different. Something was missing, but he wrenched her against his chest, clutching her to him, rocking back and forth. His breath was hot on her neck.

"Oh, Chloe, Chloe…"

His voice was clear, as clear as the night he had blindfolded her. She pulled back from his arms and found out why. His ever-present mask was gone, and for the first time, Chloe saw her Master's face.

His cheekbones were sharper than she would have thought, the lower half of his face more angular than the mask allowed to show. His lips were full and perfect and only a shade darker than his pale skin, with two stud piercings below his lower lip on one side. That side of his face was beautiful, so beautiful that her heart ached to look at it. But the other side of his face tore her newfound breath from her lungs. The first thing she noticed, oddly enough, was the unnatural sheen of the scar tissue, almost glimmering in the low bedroom light. The word *mangled* lodged itself in her mind. The right corner of his mouth was split with a lattice-like scar crawling to his cheekbone, a permanent and grotesque grin. This was the longest and the deepest wound, but other deep, dark, chaotic grooves gored his cheeks, along his strong jawline, some nearly to the beginning of his earlobe. His skin didn't seem to sit right on that side of his face, as if it had been stretched too tightly.

Demetrius' eyes studied hers, reading her shock. He began to recoil, but Chloe leaned forward without making the decision to, as if she were meant to, and pressed her lips to his.

She expected Demetrius to stiffen, to hesitate, but all he did was whisper, *"Oh, God"* into her mouth before he melted into her, delivering that devouring kiss, as insatiable as it had been when a storm had whirled around them in the backyard. He split her lips with his tongue and claimed her mouth, his hands snaking up her spine. Chloe matched his kiss, feeding off his ruined mouth, running her tongue along the pad of scar tissue at its corner. Desire roiled inside of her as it never had, an all-consuming need that threatened madness. He uttered a sound she had never heard before and he came to his feet, lifting her by the waist and pressing her into the wall above the headboard. He ground himself into her, hard behind his black jeans, tearing a moan from her. He held her pinned against the wall with his body, kissing down her neck and back up to her lips as he pulled his sex from his jeans. Chloe was swallowed by the need to have his mouth on hers, filling her with fire. Yes. Yes, the only word her mind understood as he tasted every inch of her neck, her chest, starved for herskin. His mouth closed around her nipple and he thrust inside of her. She became light and heat, ignited by the rough brush of scars against her breasts, the flex of his strong fingers in her hair, the length of him inside of her, pressing her against the wall until her skin bruised. She wrapped her legs around his hips, pulling him in deeper, sinking her teeth into the soft saltiness of his neck, gripping his hair. There was nothing but this, nothing but his body melded to hers. Their mouths found each other again, as they were meant to, collidingskin and scar and metal, and the world vanished.

Chapter 43

"Look, I already told you, I don't know their names," Zachary Rhoades insisted. "Demetrius gives them numbers instead, like Three and Eight and Nineteen."

"And why does he do that?" Detective Gatz asked as she sifted through the Leroux file in her hands.

"He said it helps break them," said Zachary, taking a deep drag from a cigarette he had bummed off Billman. "It makes them forget they're people."

Billman had called her in when he had finally convinced Zachary to make a statement. The more detail he went into about what went on in Demetrius Heart's home, the more agitated he became, his round face dewy with sweat. Gatz allowed him to smoke but drew the line at chewing. Her stomach had become a mass of knots while Zachary had described the horrific goings on at the manor, and watching Zachary spit tobacco juice into a cup might tip her into full nausea. She couldn't believe the story he told. Starving, beaten, naked women, collared and categorized like dog breeds, assaulted and brainwashed over a period of months. She'd heard similar stories of starvation and mental manipulation in other cases of human trafficking, but not to this extent. Zachary described Mr. Heart's "methods" as if it were part of a business plan, meticulous and painstakingly structured. If everything he said was true, when this story broke, Gatz suspected psychiatrists would spend a very long time analyzing this twisted system of poses and mantras and depersonalization. Had this really been going on for six years, as Zachary claimed?

"So you don't know names," said Billman, who had been pacing for the last hour and a half. "Do you know anything about them? Like where they come from?"

Zachary shrugged, fiddling with the little silver horseshoe pierced through his septum.

"We're not supposed to talk about it. D said some of them are hookers, escorts, whatever, from all around. But we don't, like, *ask* them or anything. They're not allowed to say anything except *yes, Sir,* and stuff like that."

"Would you be able to identify any of them if we showed you pictures of missing persons?" asked Gatz.

Zachary shrugged. "I guess. But wouldn't that take forever? I figured you'd want to get to them before they're sold."

Sold. Like cattle at the county fair. Gatz clenched her jaw.

"Walk us through that," she said, trying to keep her voice even. "How are the women…sold?"

Zachary hesitated.

"You can give me immunity, right?"

"We can't promise immunity," Billman corrected him, "unless you tell us everything."

"D's going to kill me, man," Zachary muttered, his fingers shaking as he put out his cigarette. "He's got people all over this fucking town."

"Mr. Rhoades," said Gatz, leaning forward and taking his hand. Just as Billman played the protective father, it was her turn to play mom. "Zachary. We'll make sure you're safe until we can get him off the streets."

Zachary rubbed his eyes furiously, like a child with shampoo on his face.

"There's an auction," he said finally, resting on his elbows and covering his face with his hands. "This year's is…on the 18th."

Gatz swallowed. That was this Sunday. She met eyes with Billman, but did not interrupt.

"They get sold to the highest bidder," he said. "Then around Christmas they get shipped off. We go with our girl, like, make sure they get to the buyers. We go wherever they go and spend a week there so it doesn't look suspicious. It's like Christmas vacation for us. Some of the guys even bring their families."

"Where are the girls shipped?" Gatz asked. "Where do you depart from?"

"Some of us use the Toledo airport. Others go to Detroit or Cleveland. It depends on where they're going. Last year I went to Mexico. Year before that was just California. But I've been to France, too. Other guys' charges get sent to China and Brazil and shit. They go everywhere."

"How the hell do they manage that?" Billman's voice was edged in anger. Gatz almost smiled a little. It was good to know she wasn't the only one hit hard by this story.

Zachary shrugged again, flipping the little horseshoe in and out of his nose. Gatz wanted to reach over and slap his hand from his face.

"I dunno, man. D handles all that shit. We just have to make sure our passports are up to date. He gives us IDs for the girls, and we just…go."

"Are the women shipped right after the auction?" asked Gatz. She opened the file in her lap and looked down at a picture of Chloe Leroux. She was the reason they had been brought into this investigation, yet they had no evidence that she was even a part of this whole mess. Mariane's insistence wasn't enough to hold up in court. But if they could catch Heart before the women were shipped out, maybe…maybe she would be among them.

"Some go out right after," said Zachary. "Some go a few days later. It's all spread out. Probably because it's less suspicious, I guess."

Gatz met Billman's gaze again. They'd have to move quickly. Their appointment with Mr. Heart was the day after the auction allegedly took place. With this information and everything else they'd gathered, she was hopeful that they'd be able to secure a search warrant in time, but it was a huge risk. Perhaps if they could identify at least one woman in the house, put a face to the case to urge a judge along, they could get there in time.

"Zachary," she said, slipping a photo over to him. "Is this woman in the house?"

Zachary leaned over and studied the picture, a casual shot of Chloe Leroux smiling. Then, much to Gatz and Billman's surprise, he burst out laughing.

"Oh, shit," he laughed. "*She's* why you guys are here? Oh, shit!"

Gatz didn't know how to react, so Billman spoke. "Is she in the house, Zach?"

Zach flashed them a tobacco-stained grin.

"*Oh*, yeah," he said, shaking his head. "She's in there. She's the one who fucked *everything* up."

Chapter 44

Demetrius didn't know how to handle this current situation. He lay against the headboard, his heart a frantic drum in his chest. The adrenaline and ecstasy of reviving and embracing Chloe had worn off, and he only now fully realized what he had just done. For the first time in years, he was exposed in front of another human being. His mask lay somewhere on the floor when a mask had always been within arm's reach. He was torn between two urges: to hide his face or to kiss Chloe again, kiss her until her lips were bruised, until the sweet taste of her skin buried itself in his tongue and he would never lose it. He licked his lips, playing with his piercings, a nervous habit now revealed to the world.

Chloe twisted in his arms, turning to look at him, and his heart jumpstarted.

"No," he growled, gripping her shoulders and pressing her back into his chest. "Don't."

He was not accustomed to hearing weakness in his own voice. He was not accustomed to this…fear. He wrapped his arms around Chloe, holding her against him, and turned his head so she had to rest against his left shoulder, see the left side of his face. He bowed his head, letting his hair slide over the marred skin, shielding it just enough to calm him.

He felt Chloe's eyes on him and he nearly ordered her to look down out of habit. He let her take him in. He was no Master right now, not in his mind and not to this girl who seemed destined to ruin him.

He looked at her, little Chloe, his biggest mistake in six years. She was paler than she should have been, her eyelids a little heavy. Her neck and chest were red where the latex had been. It would take her a few hours to fully recover from the anaphylactic shock. He could not believe he had almost lost her to something so mundane as an allergy, something so avoidable. It was sloppy, stupid, and unlike him to make such an oversight. He met her hazel eyes and again, he felt truly bare. She looked at him the way she always did, as if he were an otherworldly thing she could neither comprehend nor resist. Her fingers twitched, hesitating, before she brought up her hand and touched the left side of his face. He almost stopped her, but the feeling of another person's touch on his cheek was so foreign that it overrode him. She traced his cheekbone, the edge of his lower lip, his jaw, and each line she drew with her finger sent chills across his skin. He closed his eyes, reveling in the sensation, but her fingers strayed to the right side of his lips and pleasure snapped to panic. He caught her wrist so quickly it startled them both.

"Stop."

He hadn't meant to whisper the word, hadn't meant to look away from her. He let go of her hand and sighed, coiling his arms around her slender frame, squeezing her just shy of too tightly, and let his forehead rest against her head.

"It's over," he muttered into her hair, and he didn't know what he meant, or what was over. All he knew is that he felt walls crumbling in his mind, walls that had held fast for so long that they had become a part of him, like his mask. He nuzzled into her neck, hiding his face. It was a placating urge, a childish urge, and he despised it. Oh, everything was slipping away, everything he had built. At this moment, Chloe was his only anchor to sanity.

Chloe made a small sound, as if she meant to speak but stopped herself.

"*Parle, ma chère*," he said into her neck. "This won't last forever."

Another small sound from that tantalizing little throat. He kissed her neck, tasted her. The sensation thrilled him. Oh, he was lost.

"Why do you hide your face," she whispered slowly, choosing her words carefully, "but not…everything else?"

She touched one of the many smooth scars on his forearm to illustrate her point.

"Ah," Demetrius murmured, catching her fingertips and tracing them along the scars. "These scars that are smooth and straight, I made myself."

Another hesitation. She fingered the scars. "Why?" she asked finally.

"To hide the ones I didn't make."

He nearly laughed. He had never said it aloud, his motivation for years of cutting hisskin with a scalpel and decorating his body with symmetrical lines. It had never been a matter of catharsis, nor a matter of release through pain. He hardly felt the pain when he had done them.

Sometimes he treated them as punishments for when his "demons" longed for Dia, but in truth they were distractions, adornments, like the tattoos that adorned the skin of normal people. He had so many scars on his body, but people only noticed the ones he had created himself. They did not ask about the others.

Chloe turned and this time he let her face him. Oh, she was lovely, so cautious and curious and conflicted. A part of her didn't trust this lack of structure, this strange vulnerability in him, no, and why should she? He didn't understand it himself. He didn't know when it would release him. She reached for the right side of his face again, and again he stopped her hand, automatically, as if she came at his eye with a needle. He sighed, let go of her, and brushed his hair aside. Knowing that she was looking at his scars, his greatest kept secret, stirred a maddening feeling in him somewhere between anger, fear, and agitation. He fought it. She seemed to sense his struggle enough to refrain from touching his face.

Her voice was hardly a whisper, as if she feared he might snap. "What happened?"

Demetrius opened his mouth to speak but found himself voiceless. Unprovoked rage burned in his chest. He snatched her chin, startling her. She tried to pull back but she was trapped between his fingers. She showed him wide eyes, which soothed the rage with satisfaction. He growled in frustration and pulled her toward him, taking her lips, tasting her mouth. This was all a struggle for control, a defense mechanism, and a weak one. He released her. There was no point in fighting right now, as there was no point in hiding. He forced himself to answer her.

"A gang," he said, his jaw tight, "from somewhere in Toledo, found me in New Orleans. They tied me to a chair and made a small incision at the corner of my mouth." He touched the pad of scar tissue. "And they tortured me." He licked his lips and resisted the urge to bow his head. "The more I screamed, the bigger the incision got. Until…" he traced the thickest of the scars, running from his mouth nearly to his ear. A Glasgow smile. He'd learned the term later, years afterward, from Mama Dede, the only other person to have seen his face.

"But…why?"

Demetrius looked at Chloe. There was pity in her eyes, pity that he despised, that made him want to close his fingers around her throat, to make her scream until she called him Master again. He looked away.

"I don't know," he muttered. "I'd done something to them, something to make them look for me for years, but I didn't remember what it was. I didn't remember anything." He sighed again, embracing Chloe so she was forced to face forward, holding her tight against him. "My first memory is waking up in a hospital bed in Toledo nine years ago. They told me I'd thrown myself off the roof of the Valentine Theatre."

In came the flood of memories he rarely allowed himself to think of; waking in panic, choking on a breathing tube, a herd of nurses restraining him so they could remove it. The doctor offhandedly informing him why he was there, that he had been in a coma for three weeks, that a social worker would be in to see him shortly.

He had ripped the IV out of his arm and fled, fled without direction, desperate to escape, driven by a terror he didn't understand…the older woman he had seen in the waiting room, with tears in her eyes she was too tired to shed. He didn't remember her, didn't remember anything, but he knew, somehow, that she was there to see him, that she knew him. He had dodged her, slipping into a stairwell that led outside. Getting to the Greyhound bus stop was still a blur. How he had traveled in a hospital gown with no one stopping him, he never understood. The bus driver had either pitied him, sensed his desperation, or both, because he let him on without a single question and gave him a spare uniform to wear. The bus's destination was New Orleans, though he hadn't cared at the time. It could have been going anywhere, so long as it had been going *away*. He didn't want to know what had caused him to leap off the Valentine Theatre; the thought of even learning his name terrified him. So he went to New Orleans, and there he remained, wandering, waiting for fate to direct him.

"I don't remember what I did to earn this," he brushed the scars on his face. "I don't remember who I was before New Orleans. Not even my name."

Chloe was silent in his arms, but she stirred. He ran his hands along her, tracing her shoulders, her neck. Now that he had begun, he couldn't stop words from spilling out of him. He leaned into her hair. It smelled like the lilac shampoo he always used on the slaves.

"How did you find out your name?" Chloe whispered.

Demetrius shook his head. "The name *Demetrius* was an accident," he murmured. He traced her earlobe with his lower lip, savoring the softness. A few months had passed, and it had been late summer in New Orleans. He had been watching a Shakespeare performance in the New Orleans City Park. After the show, a woman looking for the actor who played a character named Demetrius called out the character name near him. He had looked up instinctively. Demetrius must have been close to whatever his true name had been. He knew he would need a name eventually, rather than just using the names of the drunk men whose IDs he stole in bars to get by. Demetrius was as good a name as any to adopt.

Chloe stopped his idly stroking hands, interrupting his thoughts. She turned and he allowed her to face him. He expected her gaze to roam his face, his scars, all of the new skin exposed to her. She remained locked on his eyes, as if she could read his mind through them, see his thoughts as easily as he could see hers while he trained her. Was this how it felt, to be laid bare in body and mind to another person?

"Demetrius." His name was strange on her tongue, uncomfortable for her, but hearing it sparked the flame of need in him once more. His heart constricted. "Before…this…ends, please tell me this…why did you-"

The high-pitched wail of the security alarm ripped through her words and shattered the strange peace like a rock through a window.

Chapter 45

Dia Belaire hadn't expected to pull up to a mansion at the end of the big bouncer's directions. A small cabin or a private apartment complex, perhaps, but not a mansion. She would never have pictured Demetrius living in something so grandiose no matter how successful his business was. Her heart began to pound again as soon as she stopped the rental car in her driveway beside a Dodge Magnum. For the hundredth time, she asked herself what the hell she had done. Somewhere in the French Quarter of New Orleans, her fiancée's heart was breaking. She had written him a note, of course; it seemed the right thing to do; but a note alone wouldn't undo the pain. She had left him at the altar. He would never forgive her.

Dia wiped at her dark eyes. She procrastinated, pacing around the rental car, the Magnum. Yesterday should have been her wedding day. Right now she should have been in Daniel's arms, dozing on a plane as they headed to their European honeymoon. Instead she was somewhere in Ohio, looking for the man she hadn't seen face-to-face in six years. He was her only family, her best friend. And, before Daniel came along, she'd thought Demetrius was…or could be, one day…

She told herself that wasn't why she couldn't go through with the wedding. She told herself that she was worried. She and Demetrius had kept in constant contact since the month he abruptly left New Orleans, and all letters from him had stopped when she told him about the wedding. Why? She had to know. She couldn't get married without an answer. She *had* to know.

She peeked into the Magnum. The door was cracked, the keys in the ignition. Through the crack in the door she caught the sharp, sweet scent that transported her back to every moment she had touched Demetrius, every lingering hug, every late night walk down Bourbon Street. Her entire body tingled. The body remembers such strange things. She would never forget the smell of his skin, so pleasant and distinct without any cologne. This was his car. She pulled the keys out of the ignition. There were house keys dangling from the keychain. If Demetrius did not open the door, she would let herself in. She would not let him ignore her anymore.

Dia made it to the front door of the gigantic house and hesitated, her breath hitched in her chest. Was her sweetest friend truly behind this door? Would she recognize him after six years? Maybe he had given up his masks and his makeup and wore suits now. Maybe his hair was short and back to its natural brown. She thought back to the nights when she had helped him dye his long bizarre hairstyle in Dede's bathroom. Each time had taken two bottles of dye and Dia always came away from it stained from her fingertips to her elbows. Those nights had always been fun, full of laughter and bourbon and Mama's good-natured digs. *You're higher maintenance than a drag queen, boy.*

Dia's smile faded before it fully bloomed. Years changed a person. Demetrius might be completely different now. Maybe he had become as arrogant as any other rich man she had ever dealt with, as money seemed to do that to good people. She couldn't imagine it. She couldn't imagine Demetrius being anyone but the man who stayed out with her all night, who listened to every story and every thought that passed through her head, who held her close on sticky summer nights while Mama Dede told them stories about the loa of Vodou. Dia's shrine to Damballah in her apartment was a sight to behold. She had a photograph of Dede just beside Damballah's crystal egg.

He didn't seem to have changed much from his letters. He never talked about his business in detail. She knew he was a DJ at that scary club, so he still probably "dressed like the devil," as Mama used to tease. He still went on about his classic literature and music. He'd helped her choose an aria when she wanted to take voice lessons a few years back. He still quoted Paradise Lost. And he always had advice for what was happening in her life, always said exactly what she'd needed to hear to solve a problem. No, he was still her Demetrius. But he had stopped writing to her, and she deserved to know why.

Why was she so afraid? What did she expect to happen when she finally saw her sweet friend in the flesh and told him that she had skipped out on her wedding because she couldn't get married without…what? Without seeing him again? She didn't even know what to say.

Dia rang the doorbell. A silence stretched. Each passing minute twisted her stomach. She rang again. Still nothing. The bouncer had said Demetrius would be home, that he was staying in tonight. She glanced up and noticed a security camera in the upper right corner of the doorway. Did he see her face on some screen in the house? Was he ignoring her like he had her letters? The sorrow of the thought soured to anger. They were family. Demetrius had said it often enough as he snarled at leering drunks who eyed her in crowded bars, as he whispered in her ear while she dozed in his lap. How dare he ignore her? How dare he cut off contact from her, from family, when she needed him most? She had abandoned her wedding for this, for him. She wouldn't be cast aside as if she were one of the countless scantily clad conquests he had tried to hide from her. No, she deserved answers. She would not be ignored. Dia took the keys she had found in the Magnum, the car that smelled so much like him, and slid the house key into the lock.

She stepped into a grand marble entryway that bled into a dining room crowded with people. A party. Demetrius had skipped out on that club to host a party? That didn't sound like him. She approached the crowd, waving her arm.

"Excuse me!" she said. "I'm sorry to just walk in, but I'm looking…"

Her voice trailed off as she got a better look at the crowd. There were naked women everywhere, covered in paint with collars around their necks. There were men there, too, some of them also naked, some in black jeans and shirts, painting the women. She caught sight of a raised area, a stage of some kind in front of a large table, where a blonde woman and an older man were talking. A figure lay on the table, covered by a sheet. A hand peeked out from underneath the sheet, limp and lifeless.

Dia backed away, her heart sinking. She couldn't process what she was seeing. What was going on? All eyes fell onto her. Everyone looked startled, panicked. She knew from the hair standing up on her neck that she had made a grave mistake.

"I-I….sorry," she stuttered, stumbling back to the door. "I'll just…I-"

The room burst into motion. The naked women flopped down onto their stomachs, and the entire group of men broke into a run, running for *her.* Dia sprinted for the door.

"Stop her!" someone shouted. "Stop!"

Someone caught Dia around the waist and she screamed, trying to wriggle from their grasp, but it was no use. More hands appeared, clawing at her arms, her legs, dragging her screaming and struggling toward the dining room.

"Help!" she shrieked, digging her nails into whatever skin she was able to catch. "Let me go!"

"Sound the alarm!" the blonde woman at the table shouted. "Find Demetrius!"

Chapter 46

Demetrius sprung up from the bed, scrambling for his mask on the floor. The alarm hadn't gone off in four years, with the exception of Chloe's attempted escape early on. Tripping it meant a true emergency. He retrieved his jeans and rifled through the nightstand for his Beretta.

Chloe sat on the bed, hugging herself, her eyes wide with terror.

"Stay here," Demetrius ordered, and he was out the door and through the study, gun raised, ready for anything.

He first noticed that the front door was cracked open, letting in the winter air. In the dining room, the slaves were once again on their stomachs, left alone. Their attendants had all gathered in a group, clutching a struggling, screaming figure in white. Abigail and Konri stood a safe distance away with the twins, staring at the commotion in disbelief. Seventeen's corpse lay on the table. Whomever had come into the house had seen everything.

Demetrius approached the attendants and their captor, his finger on the trigger. This was a disaster. The person's screams were female, a vaguely familiar voice. If she was the detective he was supposed to interview with, he was in for trouble. Killing a detective would be the biggest disaster he had ever tried to conceal.

"Put her down," he ordered, raising the gun. Detective or Jehovah's Witness, she had seen everything, and therefore everything was jeopardized. The attendants dropped the woman on her knees and tried to restrain her while keeping out of Demetrius' way.

The woman looked up just as Demetrius pointed the gun at her head. Large liquid brown eyes, skin flushed with terror, her pouting lips open as she gasped for breath.

Demetrius dropped the gun.

No. No. No.

He took a step back. The world tilted.

"Let her go."

The attendants did not respond.

"Let her go!" he snarled. He lunged, wrenching their hands away from her. He shoved them back hard enough to knock a few of them down. Only then did the crowd retreat to a safe distance.

Dia Belaire sat shaking on the marble floor. Six years had changed her. She was a woman now, her features less girlish. The photos she had sent him with letters did her no justice. She had grown more beautiful than he could have ever imagined. Dia, his sweet girl, in this place. He reached for her instinctively, folding her into his arms, and the scent of jasmine permeated his mask for one brief ecstatic moment. Dia screamed again, shoved her little hands against his chest until he dropped her.

"Get away!" she screamed. "Get away from me!"

She scrambled for the door. Demetrius followed her, unable to speak, unable to think. The attendants moved to stop her and he could only utter a dangerous, unintelligible growl to keep them at bay. He caught her outside by the arm.

"Dia," his voice was raw. "Dia, stop. Please-"

Tears cut the roses in her cheeks. She ripped her arm away from him and stared at him full in the face. Her rage and terror cut him to the core.

"Stay away from me!" He hadn't seen her so distraught since Dede's death. "What is this? What *are* you?"

She stumbled toward a blue Honda parked beside his car, and he knew if she got into that car…he couldn't even finish the thought. He caught her again, held her against his chest, squeezed her when she struggled to get away from him. Dia shrieked again, slapping and scratching at him. For a moment she weakened, collapsing against his chest and melting into his arms, and he held her as she sobbed, kissing her forehead through his mask, her hair. He held onto the moment as long as he could before she tore herself from him and backed away.

"What have you become?" she cried. She drew further and further away. Demetrius couldn't follow. He couldn't move. She opened her mouth to speak again, her sweet lips trembling, but she turned and ran in the other direction. As her car sped away with squealing tires, Demetrius stood where he had held her, clinging to the vanishing scent of jasmine.

Chapter 47

Demetrius couldn't stand the sight of Abigail's face, that sardonic smile she used to mask her discomfort. She didn't want to be alone with him, and he didn't blame her. He wanted nothing more than to throw her into the bedroom wall. She called herself a Mistress and though he could not deny her skills no matter how much she irritated him, she was not as talented as she believed herself to be. If she weren't his business partner…oh, to give her the smallest taste of what he did to his slaves. She would break in a week, he guaranteed it.

The thought of Dia came again and his rage gave way to sharp, incomprehensible pain.

"What have you become?"

Oh, my sweet girl. I've always been this. You just didn't know. I made sure you didn't know.

The way she looked at him…the expression he'd seen on countless faces of slaves, prostitutes, women foolish enough to take him home, on *her* face…what little shreds he had left of humanity died in that moment. He had died in that moment.

Farewell, happy fields, where joy forever dwells…

Abigail was talking again. He couldn't have cared less. To hell with business. To hell with the name he had built for himself. Nothing mattered. He had been numb to it before and he was numb to it now. He had enough money to live three comfortable lifetimes. He had no need to continue this. But what else was there for him, especially now?

"We need to decide what to do with Seventeen's body," said Abigail. "It's been on ice in the kitchen since you let that…well, since you locked yourself away."

She reached over the electric piano that stood between them and touched his hand. He didn't realize he had stopped playing idle melodies in a feeble attempt to quiet his mind. Her hand on his disgusted him. He pulled away.

"Burn it," he muttered. "Like always."

Abigail came around to stand beside the piano bench, but he cut her a look that sent her a step back. He barely tolerated her incessant pawing in front of the buyers' cameras, her kisses and caresses, as if he were one of her lovers. He would not tolerate it at all now, alone and away from those for whom he pretended to enjoy her company. She sighed, masking her nerves with folded arms and an impatient toss of her hair. Her clenched fingers betrayed her. But Demetrius didn't care. He wanted her gone. He wanted them all gone.

"D," Abigail purred, her voice saccharine and sickening as if she were charming a buyer. "We've lost two slaves this season, and they were our highest predicted sellers. But Konri and I know we can salvage the season. Konri is ready to ship the body to a contact of his in a mortuary. He can embalm her-"

"What's the *point* of that, Abigail?" Demetrius snapped. He pressed his fingers into the keys, straying into a melody somewhere in the middle of Beethoven's *Ghost*, an old favorite. Abigail was obviously uncomfortable, but she always recovered quickly from his aggression, since he couldn't harm a business partner. Once more he felt the savage urge to break her sense of security, to show her that the only thing keeping her from the very worst of him was their partnership.

"Dr. Ghede is very interested in her," she said. "I know you refuse to do business with him, but D, he's willing to pay quite a bit for the body. I think I can talk him up to maybe-"

"Fine," Demetrius muttered. "Do it."

Abigail didn't move. He didn't have to look at her to read her shock. She had expected some argument. Dr. Ghede was blacklisted because he killed the slaves he purchased. It was a waste of time to seize, break, and train a slave that ended up strangled a couple of weeks after the auction.

"Seventeen is already dead," he said. "So do it."

Abigail smiled. "We'll get it done. We'll ship her out around auction time."

She circled behind him, and he felt her eyes on him like the pressure of a mosquito buzzing by his ear. She leaned against him, brushing her breasts against his bare back. The stench of her too-sweet perfume permeated his mask.

"Come back to us, Demetrius," she murmured, putting a forced purr in her words. Her lips grazed his ear. "We need you. You haven't been yourself. Ever since you took that gir-"

Demetrius shot up from the piano bench and whirled around to face Abigail. She sprung back as if expecting a blow. Her so carefully constructed image crumbled for a moment. His grin behind the mask was a fierce baring of teeth.

"Get out."

Abigail stood straighter, rebuilding that lush, sensual persona as he watched. She turned, deliberately showing her back to him, but that compensation was pointless. He had already seen her fear.

"See you at the auction, darling," she said over her shoulder.

Demetrius turned back to the piano, burning with savage satisfaction. He held on to it for as long as he could, until the image of Dia's terror eclipsed Abigail's fleeting moment of insecurity, and he sank into darkness once more.

Chapter 48

Chloe was surprised to see Gabe come through the door of the suite. In the past few days, only Three had come up at her scheduled times to bathe, groom, and feed her. In the past, isolations like this had been maddening, but this time she had not been bound or thrown in the cage. The twins had seen her peeking through the study at the commotion, watching Demetrius with the woman who had broken into the Manor, and had taken her upstairs. Konri had come up to examine her. She had been terrified to be alone with the man who had tried to kill her. But he had given her more antihistamines and a few dark words, *Tell him and you die.* Chloe had seen the look in his eyes as he had watched her struggle to breathe. There was no doubt in her mind that he would keep his word. He left and she was alone, filling the time sleeping, doing yoga, and waiting for Three's silent but welcome company.

Where was Demetrius? She obsessed over their last encounter. His mutilated face haunted her whether she was asleep or awake. His words echoed in her head as if they played over the loudspeakers hidden around the suite. Did he really remember nothing of his past? How had he survived without a memory, without an identity? How could he live without knowing who he was? What had he done in New Orleans? His story raised so many questions, but she knew she would never again have a chance to learn their answers. That strange, frail period of vulnerability had vanished the moment the alarm had sounded. The mask went on and he left the room as guarded and volatile as he had ever been. However, he had become a different person the moment he recognized the woman in the attendants' clutches. Whomever she was, she meant more to Demetrius than anyone in the world. Chloe knew that. Anyone who had witnessed him holding the girl knew that, she suspected.

Gabe shuffled in with a bowl of soup in his hands. Chloe dropped to her knees, spreading them wide, her hands at the back of her neck.

"Abigail told me to keep you in the suite for the auction," he said, "and since I don't have a slave to sell, I figured we could watch it together from up here."

Chloe frowned at the floor. The auction was happening? Right now?

Gabe patted her head. "Come on, sweetie, I have your dinner. Sit up on the bed so you can eat while we watch."

Chloe rose, letting Gabe lead her to the edge of the bed. Gabe was the first person to address her with a sense of the old formality, but it was still not where it should have been. She felt oddly uncomfortable without the structure to which she had become so accustomed, the dichotomy of superiority and subservience. She looked up at Gabe to see if he would order her to look down. He had shadows beneath his eyes and his normally cheerful round face seemed worn and weary. He smiled and gave her a gentle chaff under the chin.

"Don't forget your manners," he chided, leading her into a sitting position. "Just because it's been crazy here lately doesn't mean the rules don't matter. Things will get back to normal with you, and then you're going to be alone with the boss 'til next year, remember. So don't slip up now."

Chloe pondered his words as he propped his phone up on the pillows. All of the other slaves would be gone after this auction, off to who knows where. She supposed the attendants would leave, too. She couldn't imagine the Manor being empty. Her heart constricted with the thought of being alone with Demetrius. The part of her that was still broken ached to see him again, though she had no idea how he would behave toward her. Perhaps Gabe was right. Things would settle down and he would be her Master again, as if she had never nearly died. As if she had never seen his face.

Gabe sat back beside her on the bed. "All right, we're logged on."

He picked up the soup and gave it to her by the spoonful. Chloe ate, her eyes on the little screen. The dining room podium was the center of the auction, surrounded by chairs of attendants. Abigail, Konri, and the twins sat along the edge of the podium on raised chairs. Demetrius stood in the center, wearing a suit similar to the one he had worn at the Dinner party. Chloe's breath caught in her throat at the sight of him. He was masked, of course, addressing the cameras with a long black crop hanging idle in his hand.

"Next we have Three, the youngest of our glass slaves this season, at sixteen years old," he announced.

"See? There's your little friend," said Gabe, pausing her feeding so she could watch. Three approached Demetrius on the podium, led by her Rodney on a long leash glimmering with crystals. Her eyes looked even larger with makeup around them, though they were wide with fear.

"Three is an exceptional glass slave. Rodney, if you would," Demetrius said as Rodney took her in a circle around the podium as if he were showing a dog in a tournament. "She is physically delicate…quick to tears, as you can see…and she is by far our best slave of the season in domestic services. She also has quite the oral talent."

Three bent into a series of rehearsed slave positions as Demetrius spoke, much like the series Chloe had gone through whenever she could. She was very flexible, touching her toes with ease, dropping to her knees with a dancer's grace. She rolled onto her back and thrust her pelvis into the air, her legs parted. Demetrius came forward and spread the outer lips of her little pink sex with his free hand.

"Another highlight of this slave is that she is virtually untouched," he said. "So the bidding will start on the high end at thirty million."

He released Three's sex. The girl came to her knees, At Attention, eyes down, while Abigail and the twins raised their arms, bidding for buyers.

"Forty five from Dr. Lane," said Abigail, smiling at the cameras. Demetrius pointed at her.

"We're at forty five."

Faith raised her hand. "Professor Touissant for sixty."

Chloe's eyes filled with tears as faceless Masters and Mistresses bid on a young girl like a calf at the county fair. It had never been clearer that her fate was out of her hands. She and the slaves were livestock to be herded and sold and shipped off.

The bidding lasted only a few minutes. Demetrius tapped the crop against his boot, waiting, listening. Chloe saw no sign of the man she had seen without the mask. She knew she should not have been surprised. Whatever he had gone through to get here, whatever humanity occasionally peeked through the cracks in his walls, Demetrius remained a monster.

"Sold for sixty million. Congratulations, Doctor."

Gabe grinned and patted Chloe's head. "Ooh, that's lucky. She's going to Ireland," he fed her a spoonful of soup. "Professor Touissant's in Dubai. Not the best place for Rodney to spend Christmas."

Chloe's chest hurt. Three had been the closest thing she'd call a friend in this twisted place. What would become of her in Ireland? What would become of all of them?

Gabe and Chloe watched the auction, with Gabe chiming in as if he were watching a football game as the slaves she had come to know went on and off the auction block, prancing, posing, their faces tense, their eyes empty. Chloe tried to keep numb. She didn't want to think about the other slaves. She had already failed to save them. It was too late now. They were already gone; gone the moment Demetrius had dragged them into his world. And so was she.

The suite door began to beep just as Gabe picked up the soup bowl to depart. Abigail sauntered in, tall and beautiful in a black dress that was somewhere between an evening gown and a nightgown, her blonde hair thick and loose over her shoulders. The moment she locked eyes with Chloe, a pit of dread formed in Chloe's stomach. Abigail seemed very pleased, almost smug. Chloe slid off the bed and into position, eyes to the floor.

"Hey, Abigail," Gabe greeted. "We were just watching the auction."

Abigail's tone was sweet and pleasant. "It was quite a success, all things considered. I do have some good news for you, though, Gabe. It looks like you get a vacation after all."

The satin hem of Abigail's dress appeared in front of Chloe. She tried not to tense.

"What's happening?" asked Gabe.

Chloe felt Abigail's hand in her hair, her nails gliding delicately across her scalp. She did not dare breathe.

"Due to the issues we've had this season," said Abigail, "we've decided that it's best to abandon this Model Slave experiment."

Chloe's heart stopped.

"We might try it next year," Abigail continued, idly stroking Chloe's hair. "But I doubt it. It seems a bit...unnecessary, don't you think?"

Chloe tried to keep her face as blank as possible while the world spun around her. Panic pumped through her limbs. It was all she could do not to spring up and run. But she had nowhere to run. Her frail sense of security in this place had disintegrated. What would become of her? Gabe's voice was a blurred hum beneath the barrage of her thoughts. Abigail's reply cut through the din.

"We sold Seventeen's body to Dr. Ghede in St. Croix," said Abigail, "and we decided to sell him Twenty-One as a token of good faith. With all the trouble we've had with her, we could only ask for so much, but he was gracious enough to take her off our hands for sixty thousand. That gives you a six grand bonus in addition to your cut from Seventeen."

Chloe looked up at Gabe. His dark eyebrows were raised. He looked from Chloe to Abigail.

"Well, I thought you'd be happy, Gabe," said Abigail with a theatrical pout. "You get a tropical vacation and two bonuses."

Gabe nodded, flashing a tight grin. "Oh, no, that's awesome, trust me, I'm on cloud nine right now. I'm just confused. Or surprised, really. Demetrius seems pretty attached to-"

"Yes, well, you know D," Abigail interrupted with a toss of her hair. "He may have his little preoccupations once in a while, but in the end, he's a businessman."

Chloe didn't even feel the tears rise. They simply appeared in rivulets on her cheeks. All questions stilled in her mind, eclipsed by a pain that turned her body to stone. Gabe and Abigail conversed. Nothing they said mattered anymore. She thought of her last encounter with Demetrius, of his mangled lips on her skin, of what he told her about himself. Maybe that was why he changed his mind about keeping her. He knew she could never truly be his slave again. She belonged to someone else now, someone who also bought Seventeen's corpse. Why would someone want a corpse? What sort of life could she expect in St. Croix?

Abigail met Chloe's eyes. "I guess this is goodbye, little girl." Her words held a sting to them, a sting that summoned Ash's face to Chloe's memory. "You be good for your new Master." She gave Chloe a kiss with those small, well-formed lips, the coldest kiss Chloe had ever received. Then she retreated, addressing Gabe over her shoulder.

"I'll have her passport ready in a few hours," she said. "And some clothes. And Gabe, it'd be best if you kept her out of D's sight. He's still being moody, and she's been a thorn in his side for quite a while now."

Chloe was too numb for her words to hurt.

Gabe opened the door for Abigail. "I'll just keep her up here. Will he be around when we leave?"

"No, he'll be out. Some interview or something."

Abigail was gone. Chloe let her hands drop from her neck. She had no will to keep her manners. A cloud had come over Gabe's face. He looked at her and forced a weak smile.

"Looks like we leave in the morning, sweetie," he said. "You'd better get some rest."

Chapter 49

Detective Paul Billman was too tense to even light a cigarette. He and five uniformed police officers stood in the backyard of Demetrius Heart's mansion, waiting for word from the SWAT team that had just entered the basement from the back entry way Zachary Rhoades had informed them of. Every second that passed was agonizing. This case had gone on for too long. Securing a warrant had been a miracle and they only had a miniscule window of time in which to strike. If the SWAT team messed anything up now, the whole case might be blown.

"Sir," came an officer on the SWAT team over the radio, "the scene is secure."

Billman practically sprinted down the stone stairs, mentally bracing himself. He'd dealt with cases of human trafficking before, and though Rhoades didn't describe it as such, Billman found himself expecting a scene similar to his past cases: half-starved women lying on mounds of old sheets and ratty blankets with the stench of sweat and human waste thick in the air.

He entered the basement. The SWAT team stood over a crowd of thirty of forty people, lying on their stomachs, their hands behind their backs. Most of the men were clothed in black, and the women were half-clad or completely nude. The basement itself was neat, almost immaculate, a large cement space with rows of strange shackled tables and doors the SWAT team had left open.

"Everyone was in a room with a bunch of beds," Officer Hayden, in full SWAT gear, informed Billman. "They were putting clothes on the ones with collars."

Billman nodded. "Cuff everyone. We'll question whomever we can. Separate the men from the ones with collars. Trafficking victims are hard to get answers out of when their captors are around."

"Trafficking? Are you serious?" came a voice by Billman's feet. He looked down at a tall man in black sprawled on the floor. He smiled at the officers. His face was tomato red all the way up to his blonde crew cut.

"Keep your head down," Hayden ordered, planting his boot between the man's shoulder blades. The man complied, but he laughed into the cement floor.

"Officers," he said, "this isn't trafficking. It's just Master slave shit. BDSM. Nobody's forced to be here. We're just a fet community."

"Fet?" Hayden looked at Billman. Billman shrugged.

"Fetish community," another man on the floor said into the floor.

The man with the crew cut dared to roll his face up at the officers. "We're a kink group. Doms and subs. We do a retreat here every year, man. These girls sign up for this. We all do. We do our BDSM shit and then we go home." He grinned up at Billman. "Does this *look* like human trafficking?"

Again Billman swept the room. The women seemed in perfectly good shape, unlike the starved and beaten waifs he had encountered in other trafficking cases. He noticed handcuffs and small floggers on the belts of some of the men, two tools more affiliated with BDSM than anything criminal. The SWAT team made no mention of drug paraphernalia, which was so often seen in tandem with trafficking. He remembered his interview with Zachary Rhoades. There was no way the young man had been talking about a BDSM retreat.

"This is all just kink." The man with the crew cut turned his head toward a nude woman beside him. "Tell them, One. You may speak. See, guys, we don't even use names here. It's an anonymous BDSM retreat, that's all."

Billman knelt down beside the woman. She remained frozen, her head pressed into the cement. She was small and mocha-skinned with braided hair and a small glass collar around her neck. Her breath was shivering.

"Miss?" Billman said carefully. He reached out and touched her elbow. "…One?"

The woman turned her head, flashing him bright green eyes.

"Is Rafe safe?" she whispered, her voice as fierce as her gaze.

Billman frowned. "What? Rafe, the bouncer at the Oryx?"

"One…" the man with the crew cut warned, but Hayden silenced him with a shout.

The young woman's gaze tore through Billman. He was speechless for a moment.

"Is he?" she demanded.

"I…yes, so far as I know, he's fine. Why?"

The woman closed her eyes and took a deep breath. A thin stream of tears seeped from the crease in her eyelids.

"My name is Adrienne Danto," she whispered. "I'm here against my will."

Chapter 50

DECEMBER 19, 2011

Demetrius sat back in the chair of Detective Gatz's makeshift office, a local detective's office she had borrowed for the time being. While Demetrius was surprised that the FBI had been called in on a three-year-old missing person's case, he easily gleaned that Gatz had next to no evidence tying him to the disappearance of Anthony Ramirez. They had found information about the Oryx on the missing man's laptop, and from the way Gatz led the questioning (*Do you remember a time around three years ago where someone was lingering around your truck?*), Demetrius was certain they had spoken to Mariane. He answered her questions calmly, careful not to let his impatience invade his tone. Detective Gatz had tried multiple times to trip him up, to catch him being inconsistent. It was transparent and tiresome. Still, he kept his demeanor pleasant, bordering on helpful.

"It's just been years since he might have come to the Oryx," he said, injecting an apologetic lilt into his voice, "and I meet new people every night I work there. I might have met him, but I just…don't remember."

He looked at the photograph of the man who had shot him through the shoulder and gave Gatz a blank expression. The ball was in her court. She had very few directions left to go with his interview without revealing that Mariane had

453

spoken with her. He wished she would mention Mariane already so he could discredit the little bitch and go home. The attendants were clothing the slaves today and having clothes on led to momentary back slides in some slaves. He needed to be there to reinforce the depersonalization, though truthfully, he didn't want to deal with that either. He wanted this disastrous season to be over, for his home to be clear of naked slaves and chatty attendants. He wanted to be alone. Or rather, he wanted to be alone with Chloe. He had no idea how he would react to seeing her after that bizarre encounter in his bedroom. After Dia. But if he thought about that again, he would snap.

Someone knocked a quiet but frantic pattern on the office door. Gatz practically leapt from her chair, yet she didn't seem startled. Rather than drawing in to herself in some way, she sprung up right for the door. She wasn't startled. She was eager. Demetrius watched her closely as she cracked open the door and a young officer muttered to her.

"Sorry to interrupt, but Paul is on the line out here."

Gatz nodded. She then closed the door, an odd thing to do if she was going to step back out in a moment.

"I have to take this," she said. "If you don't mind staying just a little longer, Mr. Heart, I only have a couple more questions for you and this will all be cleared up."

Nothing in her words or her tone indicated deception. In that department, she was well trained. But as she spoke, her entire body shifted to face Demetrius, blocking the door with her frame. Blocking his exit. She wanted him to stay here, badly. He knew then that he had to leave as quickly as he could. He stood up, stretching his arms, as if sitting for an hour had been a draining activity.

"I'd be happy to, Detective," he said, smiling, though she couldn't see it through the cotton mask. "I just need a quick smoke break."

Detective Gatz tensed around her mouth. She didn't like that idea, no, no, but she had no way of keeping him inside. Oh, yes, he had to get out of here. Something was going on. Something was terribly wrong.

He approached Detective Gatz and opened the door for her.

"Your phone call won't take too long, right?" he asked. "I won't keep you waiting if I smoke, will I?"

"No," Gatz's word was clipped. "No, it'll be quick."

Demetrius almost smiled to himself. Gatz was a good detective, but she needed to work on her mannerisms. She was still a bit too readable.

"Meet back here in five, then?" he asked, stopping just short of winking at her.

The detective nodded. She forced herself out the door, her legs stiff. She watched him walk down the hall toward the front door. Demetrius fished around his pockets for an imaginary cigarette, nodding at her as he went. He picked up the pace the moment he was out of her eye line. Gatz was inexperienced, but she wasn't stupid. She would probably send an officer out to pretend to smoke and keep an eye on him. He had precious moments to get out.

He pushed his way through the doors, waving to a couple of incoming police officers, both patrolmen with whom he dealt regularly at the Oryx. Their smiles were too tight and they waved from the hip. Demetrius' heart began to pound. Something was terribly, terribly wrong. He leaned against his car, making a show of taking out his lighter, until the officers had gone inside. When the coast was clear, he slid into his car and waited until he was a safe distance away from the precinct before dialing Abigail's number, his heart pounding faster with every passing moment.

Chapter 51

Chloe had been wearing clothes for twenty-three hours and they still felt foreign to her. The jeans felt too tight, the light cotton shirt scratchy and confining. The bra was completely unbearable, reminding her of its presence around her every time she breathed.

The past day had been terrifying. She hadn't been out of Demetrius' house in months, with only Demetrius and company interacting with her. She and Gabe boarded a private jet provided by Dr. Ghede, her soon-to-be Master, at the Toledo airport. Though the jet was located on the other side of the airport than the commercial airlines, Chloe felt trapped. The world outside the Manor was a massive and terrifying place with hoards of strangers swarming around like bees in a hive. She clung to Gabe every moment she could, staring at the shoes on her feet as they walked through the airport.

Gabe was devoid of his usual cheer. He held her close to him, a supportive lover or spouse to the casual onlooker, but his tight grip on her arm reminded her of what she was and why she was on this trip. They spent the plane ride in silence, Chloe longing for sleep but too frightened to doze. She hadn't been on a plane in years, and a private jet was a new experience entirely. It was strange to be the only two people on the plane with a pilot. It felt simultaneously intimate and isolating.

Gabe fastened Chloe's seatbelt for the final descent. They were landing in St. Croix. Chloe's terror bloomed afresh. She looked over at Gabe, at his weary face, as she checked messages on his cell.

"Oh, my God," he murmured under his breath. He met Chloe's eyes for the first time during their trip. "It's a girl," he whispered. "I'm having a girl."

Chloe actually smiled. She couldn't help it. It was a kneejerk reaction to such news, to the expression of awe on his face.

"Congratulations," she whispered.

Gabe grinned, staring at his phone, and Chloe thought about how strange it was to share such a joyous moment with the man who was there to ensure her delivery to her new captor.

"Wow," he muttered. "A daughter." It was as if the melancholy that had hung over him for the entire trip had evaporated. He laughed. "I can't believe it. We're going to spend the next four months arguing over names. I don't even know what to name a little girl." He patted Chloe's knee, his first tender gesture since he'd clothed her.

"What's your name, sweetie?" he asked. He seemed as surprised by the question as she was. He swallowed, but kept his gaze on her, expecting her to speak, though she could only muster a murmur.

"Chloe."

Gabe's eyes darkened. The joy faded from his smile.

"Chloe," he repeated. "That's beautiful."

He looked away from her, patting her knee absently, as if she were a table to drum his fingers against.

"I…can't do this anymore."

Chloe was too stunned to reply, too afraid to break the moment. Gabe stared at the screen on his phone.

"I'm about to be a father," he said, his voice thickening with tears. "To a little girl. And *this* is my job. I…I help steal…" he buried his face in his hands. Chloe wanted to pat his shoulder, but she didn't dare move.

"I mean, what am I going to do?" he asked. "Every year, just drop a woman off at some rich sadist's warehouse and go meet my wife and daughter on the beach for a little family vacation? What the *fuck*?"

Chloe began to cry. The plane had landed but Gabe didn't seem to have noticed. He gripped her knee almost painfully.

"I drowned a girl for saying her name."

Chloe thought of Seventeen, drifting weightless in the swim tank.

Gabe shook his head as if he could dislodge the memories. He clutched Chloe's hand.

"I'm sorry," he whispered.

If Chloe spoke, she would choke on tears. She nodded. Gabe unbuckled his seatbelt and rose, shoving his hands in his pockets, searching.

"Here," he said, releasing Chloe from her seatbelt. He stuffed a fistful of bills into her hands. "When you get into the airport, run. Just run. Get security." He seized Chloe's shoulders as she stood numb and dumbfounded. "You don't understand. This guy, Dr. Ghede, he's a necrophiliac.

He only wants dead bodies. The rumor is Demetrius stopped selling him slaves because he just killed them."

Chloe was frozen. Demetrius had sold her to her death? The pilot opened the door for them to exit, stopping her thoughts. Chloe saw a gun at his hip. Gabe's grip on her shoulders tightened. She met his gaze. His dark eyes were wide, his arms tense.

"Chloe," he hissed. "Run!"

He shoved her aside, charged at the pilot and tackled the unsuspecting man.

Chloe jolted into action, spurned by the cries of the struggling men. She sprinted toward the door, dodging Gabe and the pilot entangled on the floor. She didn't have time to thank him, to question, to think. She just ran down the staircase. A popping sound ripped through the air the moment she hit the pavement, a pop that transported her back to the dinner party, with Demetrius'a wild-eyed face hover over Ash, who was slumped over, bleeding from his ear.

Chloe came to a dead stop. She turned around and looked up at the jet. The pilot was on his knees over Gabe, who was too silent, too still, sprawled onto the first step. The pilot rose, clutching the gun, his eyes trained on her. Chloe spun around and slammed against a solid brick wall of a man. She screamed, trying to back away, but he had a grip on her arm that could crush her bones. He smiled at her, a great gap-toothed grin, and then a blow come from nowhere, and everything went dark.

Chapter 52

Detroit was usually a place of comfort and ease for Abigail, where she and her slaves were legend and their performances at the annual fetish ball were never missed. Tonight the city held no comfort for her. The tequila that Konri had fished out of the mini bar for her had done little to dull her nerves. A raid. She couldn't believe it. Demetrius had every precinct in Northwest Ohio paid off to leave him alone. How the hell did this happen?

She glared at Konri, who sat on the hotel bed reading a book as if he were on vacation. He seemed to be having no trouble with his nerves. He hadn't even seemed frightened when they had heard the alarm sound in the basement, when he had dragged her out of the house and to his car in the back lot behind the house.

"Honestly, Konri," she snapped. "Don't you feel *anything?*"

Konri looked up over the ridges of his spectacles and looked back down again without a word.

Abigail sighed and paced around the hotel room, checking her phone every other step for word from Demetrius.

"He's gone," she said, twisting her hair around her fingers. "They got him. I know they did."

"He'll be here," said Konri, turning a page in his book. "It takes time to drive here from Hollington, Abigail."

Abigail tossed the empty mini bottle at the door.

"A whole season, Konri," she said, hiding her face in her hands. "A *whole season*. God, what are we going to do?"

Konri glanced at her. "I hope you realize it's not just the season we've lost, here."

A knock at the door froze Abigail before she could process his words.

"Open the fucking door," came Demetrius' unmistakable growl.

He blew past Abigail the moment she let him in, peering through the blinds in the window.

"What happened?"

Abigail threw up her hands. "What happened? A *raid*, Demetrius. A SWAT team broke into the basement and hauled everyone away. The twins, the attendants, everyone. *Everyone*. How did this happen?"

Demetrius turned to her. "The FBI questioned me this morning about a missing person. It was a diversion. If they were able to conduct a raid, they have evidence." He tossed his hair over his shoulder. "My best guess is they got ahold of one of the attendants. But I don't know why."

Abigail thought back to the faces of the attendants. She knew hers, but Demetrius' were worthless strangers. She hadn't bothered memorizing their faces well enough to notice one of them missing that day.

"They'll have our names soon," said Konri from the bed, finally closing his damned book. "It would be best for us to separate."

"Yes," Abigail muttered. "Yes. Separate. In a year or two, when this blows over, we can start-"

Konri uttered a dark, humorless laugh. It was the first time Abigail had heard him laugh in the six years she had known him.

"Really, Abigail, be serious," he said, standing up and brushing off his slacks. "Once this story hits the news…I think it's safe to say that our little enterprise is over."

Abigail clenched her fists until her manicured fingers bit into her skin. Her world, the empire she had built with these two men, had been destroyed in the blink of an eye. The room shook beneath her feet. She felt sick.

"No," she said, her fury returning like a burst of flame from a torch. "No, no, we can just move it. We sell slaves all around the world, Konri. I don't see why we can't-"

"Did the SWAT team call out any names?"

Abigail paused, turning to look at Demetrius. His eyes were distant.

"What?"

"Did they call for Chloe Leroux?" he asked.

Abigail couldn't think of what to say for a moment. "We were upstairs," she said finally. "We didn't hear them. The alarm went off."

Demetrius nodded, frowning in thought. Something about his demeanor fanned the flame of Abigail's temper.

"Who is Chloe Leroux?" she demanded. "And what does she have to do with anything?"

Demetrius fixed her with a cold stare. "Twenty-One."

Konri furrowed his brow. "Twenty-One is Dr. Leroux's missing daughter?"

Demetrius didn't reply, but the look he and Konri exchanged set off an alarm in Abigail's head.

"Konri," she said slowly, "what is going on? Who is Dr. Leroux and what the hell does this have to do with the raid?"

Konri looked from Demetrius to Abigail in that calculating manner he always had, as if assessing the risk of speaking.

"*Konri,*" Abigail demanded, not caring that her voice had taken an unflattering snarl. Demetrius remained silent, though the air seemed to get thicker around him.

"Dr. Leroux is a colleague of mine in Cleveland," said Konri, his frown continuous. "His daughter went missing from the university. I don't know much about it. She went missing long after the slaves were collected. I didn't even guess…"

He trailed off, looking at Demetrius, who stared back at him, his expression unchanged. Abigail was silent for a long time, struggling to find words through the anger. She was as surprised as the men were when she laughed.

"Demetrius," she said, grinning so hard it hurt. "You stole a doctor's daughter? From the *university*? *That's* what you call *low risk*? No wonder the police came!" She dissolved into laughter. She laughed until her ribs ached, until tears of rage flooded her cheeks. "Oh, D, you finally have gone crazy."

Konri had stepped away from them, closer to the wall. Abigail shook her head, wiping tears from her eyes, her laughter fading. She stared at Demetrius, her so-careful business partner, who only chose *low risk* girls to steal away;

prostitutes, runaways, drug addicts with no families; who constantly chided her for her self-indulgence and favoritism. He had ruined their entire enterprise for an unexceptional bitch with hazel eyes.

"I hope she sucked one hell of a cock, Demetrius," she hissed, staring right into that dangerous glare. "I hope she was worth it."

Konri stepped in. "They took everyone in the basement away," he said to Demetrius. "I'm sure they've found her upstairs by now."

Abigail laughed again. "Oh, Konri, don't bullshit him. What's the point?"

Konri looked at her, screaming a silent warning she ignored. Nothing mattered now. Their partnership was over. She had no reason to speak to either of them again. She walked up to Demetrius, sneering at his angry eyes, at the ominous energy that always seemed to surround him. She'd never feared him, not truly. She knew he only lashed out at subordinates and slaves. He never dared turn his temper on anyone who mattered.

"*Chloe* isn't even on the continent anymore," she said, coming close enough to spit on that idiotic mask he always wore. "She went with Seventeen's body to Dr. Ghede. For sixty grand. It was a little thank you from Demetrius Heart for his patronage."

Demetrius didn't speak. She brushed a lock of hair from his face. "We did it for you," she said. "She made you sloppy, Demetrius. We'd never seen you so distracted. You *killed* a slave in front of the buyers because of her. You disappeared when we needed your help handling

Seventeen's accident, to save her from an allergy." She smiled. "It was nothing personal, darling. We just wanted our partner back."

Demetrius' eyes had gone blank, all that anger had disappeared with no slaves to take it out on. He looked like a shell, a sad, defeated shell behind the theatrical and spooky exterior Abigail had never understood. She sighed, shook her head, and turned her back on him.

"I'm going to freshen up," she said, "and then I'm getting the hell out of here. I suggest you two do-"

The impact that brought Abigail to the ground was so hard that she first thought Demetrius had thrown the desk at her. As she twisted onto her back, she realized it had been Demetrius himself, that he was on top of her, that his hands had closed around her throat. She fought as her windpipe constricted, fought with fists and nails, but Demetrius was stone, his eyes a cold inferno. Breath stopped and she fought harder, but she fought a statue. Abigail reached for Demetrius' face, for that mask, but her arms went limp. His fingers tightened and tightened until darkness descended, and Abigail Marinette felt nothing.

X X I

Demetrius lifted himself off Abigail's limp body. He took his stiletto knife from his pocket, clicked it open, and turned his attention to his other partner.

Konri had not moved from beside the bed, though he had pressed himself against the wall. It took Demetrius a moment to realize that the doctor had a pistol in his hand, pointed in his direction. He froze. For a moment, Demetrius thought, this was it. To hell with the gun. To hell with everything. This was his time to die.

But then he thought about Chloe, on a private jet to St. Croix, heading to her death.

Konri met his gaze, as blank eyed as ever, as if they were holding a regular conversation instead of pointing weapons at one another. Ever the silent partner, Demetrius should have known that his silence held deception. He should have known better than to put his trust in him.

"I'll find you," Demetrius swore. He closed his knife and put it back in his pocket. Konri did not lower his gun, but he did not fire it. Demetrius could only guess why. Konri had his own reasons for everything, and he rarely elaborated.

"Goodbye, Demetrius," said Konri.

Demetrius nodded. He turned his back on Konri, stepped over Abigail's body, and left the hotel.

Chapter 53

Chloe no longer knew the difference between being asleep or awake. She drifted in and out of consciousness in a dark bedroom, tied to a bed with rough rope when alone and forced to perform her "skills" when roused by the gigantic gap-toothed man who had knocked her unconscious on the runway. She could no longer tell when his crushing weight was actually on top of her or when she was having a nightmare. He had given her no food in days, precious little water when it came to his mind. She assumed the man was her new Master until Dr. Ghede had actually shown up, coming in from the main house Chloe had never seen, and she learned through their conversation that the gap-toothed man was Dr. Ghede's bodyguard and personal assistant. The doctor himself was a tall, wiry man with coarse grey hair and small eyes. His skin was rough and leathery when he examined Chloe. She had no idea why he examined her. She had never seen someone less interested in another person. She remembered when she had considered Gabe's treatment of her to be like an animal or the coldness she experienced in Konri's hands. Dr. Ghede was far worse. It was as if he had never touched a human body before, unable to intuit what hurt. She had cried out the first time he had examined her sex and tried to cram all of his fingers in at once. He had sprung back, horrified by the sound of her scream.

"Make her quiet," he told his bodyguard before leaving that day. The man had taken his boss's words to mean, make her scream until she had no voice left when the doctor returned.

The doctor had not been around for the past few days, though the bodyguard assured her that he would be back for her "when the other one rots." Until then, she was the bodyguard's plaything, and play with her he did. His favorite game involved pressing the end of a hilted switchblade against her breast while he took her mouth, warning her that if he came too hard, his hand might *slip*.

Chloe welcomed the perpetual blackness of the bedroom, the inability to discern dream from reality. She lay in the sticky tropical heat of St Croix and watched the tiniest pinpoints of light pass through the boarded window. She saw her father's face, Demetrius, Three, Gabe, even Mariane, drifting in and out of the corner of her eye like shadows. Seventeen occasionally drifted by, her hair flowing around her as if she were still underwater. She had even begun to see another figure, an old woman with faded brown skin, clothed in a loose cotton dress that hung over her too-slender frame. Sometimes she looked different, as dark as the room itself, clothed in a denim dress. Sometimes she even had Chloe's own mother's face. As Chloe's hold on reality grew weaker, the woman grew more and more prevalent, leaning in and wiping the sweat from Chloe's brow, sitting beside her like a nursemaid. No matter what her form, she had deep scratches on the right side of her face. Chloe had never thought to question them. Of course she had scratches on her face. Mama always had scratches on her face. Occasionally the woman would hum softly, would whisper in her ear words Chloe would never remember afterward, and Chloe would hear her own voice, raw and dry, whispering, "Yes, Mama. Thank you, Mama."

Tonight, though Chloe was not certain it was night, Mama was there, and she was whispering without words, but Chloe understood her message perfectly. Get up, child. Time to get up now.

"Yes, Mama."

Chloe sat up in bed, her head heavy. No ropes scratched at her wrists. She was unbound. She probably had been for some time, when the bodyguard believed she was too weak to escape. Mama stood by the side of the bed, smiling a strangely fierce smile. Her face switched from dark to light and back again. Her teeth were small in her mouth, filed down from years of grinding. She pointed at the side of the bed and Chloe knew where to go, what to do. She dug her fingers into the space between the mattress and the box spring and came back with a splinter of wood the width of her fist, ripped from the dilapidated bedframe. She had picked away at it until the end came to a point. Mama put a finger to her lips and patted Chloe's head. Chloe nodded again, almost feeling a cool kiss on her forehead.

"Thank you, Mama. Yes, I will wait, Mama."

Chloe tried to remain calm. Mama's soundless voice rang like a bell in her mind. Someone was coming soon, and it would be her or them. She sat, waiting, reacquainting herself with her limbs, gathering all the strength she had left in her starved body. She thought of Three and Seventeen, of all the nameless slaves she had seen in the basement. They were gone now, shipped off to every corner of the map, trapped and tormented, like her. Three's big blue eyes loomed large in Chloe's mind. She had only been sixteen when her life had been ripped away from her. Chloe had failed her at the dinner party, and now she was in a foreign country with a foreign Master, probably subjecting her to all that Chloe had experienced at the hands of Dr. Ghede's bodyguard. Chloe gripped the knife. It had to end. She had to do something. She may not have been able to free herself and the other women, but she would at least deliver *some* sort of justice to a small fraction of this terrible business, even if she died doing it.

Footsteps came from a part of the house Chloe had never seen. She knew the pattern well. The door would open and the bodyguard would amble in, lean over her to see if she was breathing, and rouse her for whatever terrible games he had planned for her that day. But today, she had her weapon. She buried it in the filthy sheets on which she lay, clutching the handle as if it would slip away from her.

The door opened and closed. Chloe squinted her eyes open, catching sight of a figure coming toward her. She felt the weight of a hand on the bed as the figure leaned over her, coming close to her face, checking her breathing. Mama's voice rang in her bones. *Now. Now.*

With a raw, guttural cry, Chloe ripped the wooden shard from the sheets and jammed it into the figure's neck.

The man stumbled back, squealing like a wounded pig, and Chloe went with him as if her hand were glued to her weapon. Her cry became a scream as she ripped out the shard and embedded it again, clinging to the sweaty, solid body as he pushed at her, struggled with her. Blood spattered her face, hotter than she would have expected, and the man fell to the floor, screaming his swine-like scream. Blinded by blood, Chloe slashed and stabbed wildly, hitting air and flesh and the floor. The hands clutching at her grew steadily weaker, and she finally found a cavern of solid body and stabbed again and again, until her own arms gave out and she collapsed, falling onto her back, her ragged breath in tune with the wet, sputtering gasps of the man beside her. Eventually all she heard was her own breath, her own heart, her own unintelligible cries.

Are you proud of me, Mama?

More footsteps, heavier and more frantic. The door opened, casting light into the room, and Chloe found herself staring into Dr. Ghede's lifeless eyes, his blood-spattered face slack and still. She had little time to dwell on it before the bodyguard's cries deafened her.

"What have you done?" he screamed.

He wrenched her body from the floor and she had no strength left to struggle, no strength to catch herself when he threw her against the blinding white wall. She hit the floor hard, landing on her right arm with a snap. Pain hissed through her body like hot oil in a pan, but it didn't matter. The bodyguard would soon realize that trying to revive his boss was useless, and he would turn his fury on her. She was ready.

The bodyguard turned to her, his eyes wide, his mouth open. The muscles in his neck bulged as if they would burst and he would bleed out like the doctor on the floor. He took a step toward her. Chloe saw a gun in his hand, drawn and ready. She began to close her eyes in order to find some image to hold onto until she had breathed her last, but a blur of black and white stopped her. The bodyguard was on the floor before she blinked, the gun skittering across the hardwood near her, and it took Chloe a moment to realize that Demetrius was truly there, truly struggling with him. Chloe picked herself up, sitting with her back against the wall, cradling her wounded arm. She grabbed the bodyguard's gun before he could retrieve it in the struggle. She hid it behind her back. This was real. Demetrius was really there, the wild-eyed madman dressed in black in the tropical heat, slamming the bodyguard's head into the floor over and over again.

Chloe's heart felt like it would burst; from terror, from relief, from exhaustion. The sight of her old Master brought her back to herself completely. There was no mysterious face-changing woman in the room anymore, no voice in her head. There was just the pale man rising from the limp bodyguard, his hands coated in blood, panting heavily. He pulled a handgun from the waistband of his jeans and Chloe heard that dreaded sound for a third time, that dreaded *pop* that sounded like a firecracker. Like Ash, like Gabe, the bodyguard would not rise again.

Demetrius turned to her and she met the cold grey eyes she never thought she would see again. He dropped the gun on the floor, crossed the room in three strides, and she was in his arms. The pain in her arm meant nothing. There was only his heat, his arms around her, his murmuring her name over and over in her ear.

"Chloe, Chloe…"

Chloe cried tears she didn't know she had left in her and collapsed in his arms, burying her head into his scarred chest, clutching him as hard as she could with a wounded arm and a gun in the other hand. She took him in, the sharp scent of him marred by gun powder, the strength of him. He pulled away from her enough to look into her eyes.

"You certainly made a mess of the doctor," he said, erupting into a burst of wild laughter. He clutched her to him again, his hand in her hair. "Oh, Chloe. *Tu m'as manquée, ma chère.*"

Chloe pressed herself against him, her tears staining his shirt. She wanted nothing more than to be in his arms until the adrenaline faded and she collapsed, weak and starved. But her resolve from before, when she had resolved to kill her tormentor, returned to haunt her. The faces of Three and Seventeen, of Ash, of Gabe, would not let her lose herself in the comfort of his embrace. She had killed the man who had bought her, the man who had planned to kill her. But he had not stolen her from her life. He had not stolen women from their lives for six years, imprisoned them, broke them and molded them into subservient slaves to be sold. He was not the reason for all of this suffering. Demetrius was. The man whose touch she craved, whose body seemed made to meld with hers, was the root of it all. Chloe shook her head, sobbing, mouthing the word *no* over and over again, though she no longer had a voice with which to speak.

She raised her wounded arm to Demetrius' face, so close to hers. It took all her strength to take the black mask between her fingers and pull it down from his face. Demetrius tensed, as if he meant to jerk back, but he looked at her and pulled the mask away. Once more, Chloe beheld his face, so beautiful and so ruined, and tears rose again. She kissed him. The rush of lips on hers returned, *his* lips, the firm press of muscle mixed with the brush of metal and mangled scars, the heat of his energy melting into her body, penetrating her, owning her. She fell into the embrace, fell into him, allowed herself to be lost completely. Yes, she was his. She would always be his.

Chloe pressed the gun against him and fired.

They both jerked back. The recoil of the gun rocked Chloe's weak frame. Demetrius stumbled, frowning, his eyes unfocused. He looked down at the fresh wound in his upper thigh. Blood bloomed on his jeans. He took several steps back, nearly out the door. Chloe sobbed, choking on tears. She raised the gun, though her hand trembled. He was now several feet from her, and she had never fired a gun before, let alone with her left hand. Demetrius only stared at her. He read her expression in that penetrating way to which she had become so accustomed. His mangled face fell, a perfect expression of sorrow without the mask to hide behind. He bowed his head, his hair falling over his scars, and for a moment, he was perfect, heartbreakingly beautiful, and Chloe wanted to run to him, to fall into his arms again, to kiss him until her lips were bruised. But she held the shaking gun where it was, her vision blurred with bitter tears.

Demetrius looked at her, his eyes as tormented as she had ever seen them.

"Do it," he whispered. He opened his arms.

Chloe screamed, squeezed her eyes shut, and fired.

She did not open her eyes when she heard the heavy thud of a body hitting the floor, nor the *clank* of her gun as it hit the ground beside her. She clutched her head, curled her knees into her chest, and screamed. She screamed until her throat was raw, screamed for madness to take her. She sobbed until she had no more tears. Only then did she open her eyes and get to her feet.

Demetrius lay crumpled on his stomach just outside the doorway, his hair veiling his face. A small pool of blood formed on the floorboards beneath him. Chloe nearly collapsed again. She looked at the room beyond him, and moved toward the exit, closing her eyes to pass him. She couldn't look again. She wouldn't. It was time to go home.

Epilogue

FEBRUARY 21, 2012

There are SO many people here! Literally everything's green and purple!
I'm so jealous! Take pictures. I want to hear everything when you get back!

Chloe slipped her cell back into her coat pocket with a smile. Of all the things these past few months had brought her, she was most thankful for having kept in contact with Hailey Wood, though it still felt odd not to call her Three. It had been an adjustment to spend time with her out in the real world, fully clothed, but now it felt strange to be without her, so far away.

Chloe's father put an arm around her, his scruffy beard brushing her forehead as he planted a kiss there. Chloe hugged him closely. He hadn't let her out of his sight for more than a few hours at a time since the police had handed her over to him at the airport. He had insisted upon coming with her on her trip, despite her asking him otherwise. But right now, in the massive crowd of cheering, jostling parade-goers, she was happy for the company. He was a good anchor to root her to reality, keeping her from losing herself in dark memories.

She pulled her coat open. It was 50 degrees in New Orleans, a sharp contrast to the bitter cold up in Ohio in February, and the presence of so many moving bodies seemed to make it even warmer. She kept her eyes on the parade even as her mind drifted. The writhing merriment, the swarm of bright colors, all of it reminded her of the lush theatrics of the dinner party, the Hunt, the circus night that had ended before it had begun. In every bright, elaborate mask that passed by, she saw *his* half-covered face.

Chloe gripped her father's hand to stave off a wave of nausea. She didn't need to have a panic attack now, on the street during Mardis Gras. They invaded her life far too often, triggered by the most innocuous things, like a bunch of grapes or the sound of running bathwater. Maybe when she returned from this morbid pilgrimage, she would finally go to therapy.

Dreams of New Orleans haunted her every single night since she returned from St Croix; dreams with the same surreal clarity she had experienced during her hallucinations of the woman whose face changed in the dark, the figure in denim she had called Mama. Most of the time the dreams involved her simply walking down a street full of wealthy houses in the early moments before sunrise, searching for someone, though she didn't know whom. A strange whispering sound led her in her dream, a low and unintelligible hiss. She followed until she awoke, every night, consumed by memories of Demetrius' touch, his breath, his face.

A man in a black and white domino mask brushed past Chloe and her father. A jolt of panic jumpstarted her heart.

She took a deep breath, whispering what had become her new mantra over the past two months, *It's not him. It's not him. He's gone.* Demetrius was gone. She knew it with every breath. Her Master was dead.

Cameras flashed, reminding her of the crowds of reporters she'd had to fend off for weeks after her rescue. She was happy to be free of them down here. She watched a float drift by, a truck disguised as a white dragon or snake of some sort with big blue eyes that glowed. Chloe followed it down the line until the distance swallowed it, and a young woman in the crowd made her heart jump. She was beautiful, with long dark hair spilling over a white wool coat, holding hands with a tall man with smooth mocha-colored skin. It took Chloe a moment to realize that she had seen the woman before, in that very coat. She was the one who had gotten into the house when Chloe lay in Demetrius' arms, during his most vulnerable moment. She was the woman Demetrius had run after and tried so desperately to embrace. The woman whose fear and disgust had destroyed him.

Chloe took a deep breath. She knew that this woman was why she was in New Orleans, the person she had been searching for in her dreams. She knew it like she knew Demetrius was dead, like an ache in her bones. She squeezed her father's hand.

"Daddy, *je reviens*," she told him.

Her father frowned a moment, troubled, but he nodded.

"I'll be here, *ma bichette*."

Ma *bichette*. Chloe's chest burned.

The young couple stood right at the Bourbon Street sign post, watching the parade. They were huddled in close to one another, as if they couldn't get enough physical contact. Every few moments they smiled at each other, kissed, embraced. Chloe wanted to smile just looking at them.

"Excuse me."

The young woman turned to her, and the joy in her face became shock.

"Hi," Chloe felt awkward, strange. "My name is Chloe Leroux. I know this sounds-"

"I know who you are," said the woman. She took Chloe's hand and the moment their skin touched, Chloe felt a feeling of peace wash over her, a peace she had forgotten how to feel. The woman's liquid brown eyes gleamed with unshed tears. "I've seen you on the news. My name is Dia…Blanc." She bit her lower lip. "I had a dream about you the other night."

Chloe nodded. Her words did not seem odd, nor was it odd that Chloe knew the tears in Dia's eyes were for the man who tied the two women together.

"Dia," Chloe whispered. She hesitated, then reached forward and wiped a tear from the woman's cheek. "We need to speak."

A Rather Unprofessional Author's Note

Twenty-One means a hell of a lot to me.

This story has followed me, in some form or another, through over a decade of self-discovery, cross-state moves, name changes, loves, heartbreaks, triumphs, breakdowns, and all the passions and poisons that life doles out to us. Through it all, Demetrius and Chloe have walked with me; ghosts that always seemed to re-materialize just when I thought they had finally been laid to rest.

As the years pass, as the world changes—as *I* change—and parts of this story age less-than-gracefully, as all stories are wont to do, I will still love *Twenty-One*. I love this novel with all my little black heart because it is a piece of me that refused to lay buried in a pile of half-formed ideas; the story that insisted I see it through to the end—and then some.

Thank you for reading.

Alice

www.ingramcontent.com/pod-product-compliance
Lightning Source LLC
Chambersburg PA
CBHW031107160726
47991CB00004B/1261